THE DEVIL'S LIBRARY

TOM PUGH

CRUX
PUBLISHING

For Katia

AUTHOR NOTE

There is a legend that claims the first men left paradise of their own free will, pursuing the knowledge that would allow them to return as God's equals. Humanity multiplied, and the sacred task was entrusted to a priestly caste, unbound by ties to any land or king, free to follow the shifting currents of power. Traces of the library they created have been found among the ruins of Babylon, in Cairo and on the island of Samos. Variously described over the centuries as the *Hall of Records*, the *Satyr's Library* and the *Oracle of the Dead*, it appears in these pages only by its most common name, the *Devil's Library*.

CHAPTER 1

Rome, April 23rd, 1558

Rome. City of God on Earth.

Mathern Schoff shook his head in wonder. Until his father's death five weeks earlier, he'd never travelled more than fifty miles from Lübeck.

Schoff had lost weight on the journey south and looked like a boy in his lawyer's robes. He was just twenty-one years old, but he'd braved the lonely road and the brutish behaviour of the sailors with barely a thought. For the last twelve years he'd lived a lie, breaking bread with neighbours, hiding his fear that one of them would see through the exhausting facade. Now, for the first time in his life, he was among men of the same mind and faith.

Schoff hurried through the crowded streets, averting his eyes from the shacks and lean-tos. Rome was a city of ruins, ancient squares colonised by scavenger pigs, beggars sleeping on beds of cracked marble. Schoff ignored them, hardly looking left or right until he reached St. Peter's.

The great square rang to the sound of stonemasons' hammers. Not yet finished, the new basilica was already more of a wonder than Schoff had dreamed. A smile lit his pale face, as he stared at men from every part of the known world. Theologians, priests and pilgrims, notaries, clerks and secretaries, all hurrying towards the Vatican. A detachment of the Pope's Swiss Guard in orange and blue. The immense dome towering over them all.

Schoff's heart soared as he thought of the men he'd left behind in Lübeck. Pope Leo X had invited them to contribute to this glorious church. The merchants should have fallen on their knees in gratitude. Instead, the tight-fisted fools had listened to Luther the Apostate, condemning their souls to eternal damnation for the sake of a few pennies.

The great church continued to soar into the heavens, while Martin Luther was bones in a box, his soul consigned to the flames of Hell these last twelve years. Schoff shuddered; he'd been a child of ten when his father forced him through the crowds in Lübeck's main square, taken a grip of his collar and forced him to watch men suffer the same terrible fate.

Small fires are the cruelest. The flames rise reluctantly, licking toes and ankles.

"Anabaptists," his father had hissed as he pointed at the writhing heretics, holding the back of Schoff's head so he couldn't look away. "Worse than animals."

Memories of fear were supposed to be fleeting, but Schoff still saw the flames rising from the meagre pyre, caressing calves and thighs, hands and torso. The dreadful stench of it. Only one of them had spoken; a young man, wild hair dancing in the waves of heat, screaming at the crowd until his vitals cooked.

"Remember," his father had ordered that evening. "They burned Anabaptists today, but it could have been us." He towered over his trembling son. "That young man's fate will be yours if you breathe a word of what I'm about to say."

When the city converted to Luther's new confession, Schoff's father had remained true to the old faith. He was a secret Catholic, raising his son to smile at Lutherans but despise them in his heart. There was no greater cause, Schoff had learned, than the destruction of the new heresies, and the ultimate triumph of the one true Church.

Mathern Schoff crossed the River Tiber, walking east along a street lined with tenements cobbled together from blocks of ruined stone. Only once did the vista open out, granting a view of the fabled Pantheon in one direction and the high gates of the Rione Sant'Angelo in the other.

The crowds grew thicker around a group of men lifting the cracked flagstones, attacking the hard-packed earth with pickaxes. Schoff paused to ask a well-dressed merchant for directions to the Angelus. He spoke in Latin and received a courteous reply in the same language.

The university was an austere building. Schoff arranged his features into an appropriately solemn expression. He read the motto carved into the massive stone doorway – *To Contemplate and To Bear the Fruits of Contemplation to Others* – before knocking.

The door swung open.

"Mathern Schoff to see the Master of the Sacred Palace."

A young monk led him through a beautiful garden. Schoff looked around in wonder. "What trees are these?"

"Orange and lemon," the monk smiled. "Pistachio, olive, fig, palm and laurel." He pointed to a crumbling fountain in the centre of the garden. "You saw the men digging in the road? Rebuilding an old aqueduct from the time of the Caesars. Another year and we'll see this tumble of stone brought back to life."

The monk led him to a bench. "The Master is busy. He's unlikely to see you today."

"Of course not." The stone bench was cool after his walk through the city. Schoff leaned back and closed his eyes. Gregorio Spina was one of the most important men in

Rome; of course he wouldn't have time today. Schoff smiled, remembering the way his neighbours in Lübeck whispered when they mentioned Spina's name. *"The Master of the Sacred Palace has spies in every city in Europe. Ceaselessly, he urges the Pope to burn more heretics, condemn evangelicals in ever stronger terms."*

Never before had anyone risen so rapidly through the ranks of the Dominican Order to become Master of the Sacred Palace. Spina was the Pope's private theologian and Chief Censor in charge of the Vatican's List of Forbidden Books, known in Latin as the *Indices Librorum Prohibitorum.*

Another monk arrived, silently gesturing for Schoff to follow him into a large scriptorium. The young lawyer had never seen so many books in one place, bound in different colours but strangely uniform in size; stacked waist-high in the centre of the room and all the way to the ceiling in the corners. Schoff followed his guide through the maze, past a score of seated prelates. Each held a quill in one hand, poised above pots of red ink.

"In here," the man's tone was abrupt. "The Master will see you now."

The Master? Schoff blinked; he'd been expecting a clerk, perhaps a secretary. A simple desk stood in the centre of the room, chairs to either side. A wheeled stepladder climbed to a series of high shelves, piled with papers. Tall windows, hung with gossamer silk, opened onto a private courtyard.

A man sat behind the desk, regarding Schoff with unwavering eyes. He was about fifty, slim and tanned, with glossy black hair surrounding a neat tonsure. He gestured to the empty chair, a diamond on his forefinger catching light from the windows and cutting a line through the gloom.

"Mathern Schoff of Lübeck."

The young man bowed: "Master, my father is dead." Spina's face remained expressionless. Schoff drew a deep breath: "I am here to put my life in your hands."

"To what purpose?"

Schoff hesitated. Spina's eyes were the colour of mahogany. "It was my father's last wish."

The Master of the Sacred Palace smiled. The effect was chilling. "Your father told you nothing of his work for me?"

Schoff shook his head, lacing his fingers to keep them still.

"He never talked to you of Epicurus?"

The peddler of pleasure? Schoff frowned. "My father insisted I read Dante. He would often test me in the evenings. The Epicureans occupy the sixth circle of Hell. They are the first heretics to appear, because they represent the ultimate heresy."

"*In this part we shall find the burial place of Epicurus and all his followers,*" quoted Spina, nodding. "*For whom the soul dies when the body dies.* Your father was preparing you to carry on his work."

The Master of the Sacred Palace rose to his feet. Schoff followed him through cloisters decorated with huge frescoes of the world: ships bobbed artfully between Europe and Africa, monsters guarded the Indies, but there was no sign of the Americas.

Spina took a seat beside the silent fountain. "Epicurus wrote three hundred discrete works during his life; the Church burned every last one, but the Devil is cunning. A poet named Lucretius wrote an account of his hero's philosophy. A single copy survived, hidden in a German monastery. When it was discovered, early in the last century, it unleashed *such* a plague."

Spina's mouth tightened. "I would rather face a dozen Luthers, ten thousand Mohamedans. Did your father explain Epicurus' Four-Part Cure?" He didn't wait for an answer.

"*Do not fear God. Do not worry about death. What is good is easy to get. What is terrible is easy to endure.* People are terrified – you will have noticed as you travelled south – the talk of witches, strange objects in the night sky, complaints of a new disease that destroys its victims' flesh. Some claim it comes from the New World; others that it's a punishment sent by God. Most see no point in trying to make such distinctions – they only wonder whether this world is still a place they can trust."

There was only the sound of Spina's voice, which never rose in volume, but seemed to fill with passion. The hairs rose on the back of Schoff's neck. He did not understand everything Spina said; he could not ask for fear of breaking the spell.

"People are scared," continued the Master of the Sacred Palace. "Easy prey for men like Luther, who sense the quickening of history, but lack the ability to understand. Petty prophets, with small-minded visions of pestilence and blood. The time of the final battle draws near – but these men are bakers, cobblers, coiners; ignoramuses whose scaremongering plays into the hands of the Antichrist."

In the sunshine, Schoff saw lines around Spina's dark eyes and ached to reassure him. "But the reforms agreed at the Council of Trent. The creation of the *Indices Librorum Prohibitorum*," he felt his heart beat faster. "The expansion of the Tribunals of the Inquisition..."

"Steps in the right direction," agreed Spina, standing and looking down at his visitor. "It was no accident that Lucretius' poem was re-discovered. St. Paul warned that the Antichrist would come at a time of great upheaval, flooding the world with novelty – ideas, objects, knowledge, even a new continent – blinding the faithful with the low physical pleasures of life on earth. Epicurus was also a pleasure-monger, who denied the immortality of the soul."

Schoff forced himself to meet Spina's eyes. "Why are you telling me this?"

"Publicly, your father was an implacable enemy of Rome, a stance which brought him to the attention of a group of heretics. They will approach you too, soon after you return to Lübeck, and ask you to carry on his work."

Schoff flinched. "My father was no spy."

"Your father put aside personal honour for a higher cause." Spina turned on his heel and strode through the cloisters. Schoff hurried to keep up, almost crashing into him as he stopped in front of a closed door.

"You can keep a secret, I trust?"

Schoff felt the colour rise in his cheeks. "I've spent my life surrounded by heretics and never revealed my true feelings, by word or deed."

Spina's eyes bored into his. "The Antichrist sows doubt among the faithful. Do not misunderstand me, my friend, or underestimate my commitment to God's cause, but the fires of the Inquisition are a poor defence against his tricks. To defeat the Devil, we must study the ways of his servants." Spina opened the heavy wooden door and ushered the lawyer inside.

Men in black robes sat at long tables, among a vast tangle of alchemical tools. Alembics – finely wrought stills to separate active ingredients from inert matter – and aludels to reduce them to ash and dust. Hessian crucibles, retorts and heating mantles. The walls were lined with vitrines displaying exotic plants and nautilus shells, bones and fossils, all neatly labelled. Everything was exquisitely crafted, from the copper pipes to the glass bowls and hardwood display cases. None of the men looked up from their work, and few wore monk's tonsures.

Spina read Schoff's thoughts. "They have a special dispensation to wear their hair as laymen do. Sometimes it is necessary for them to move among their fellow men discreetly."

He led Schoff further into the room. At one long table – its surface scarred and pitted from a thousand experiments – a monk filled a large, earthenware vessel with sawdust, while another polished a thin sheet of copper.

"An experiment based on ancient Indian texts," explained Spina. "And here," he led Schoff on, "the Toys of Dionysus; a golden serpent, a phallus, an egg and spinning top. We also collect and investigate the knowledge of the ancients." Spina's voice was a painting, full of light and colour. "We are at war. It is our duty to fight the enemy with every available weapon."

Schoff could hear the beating of his own heart as he followed Spina into a small, private courtyard. He did not want to return to his grey city on the Baltic Sea.

"Let me stay, Master. Let me join you."

"Your place is in Lübeck, collecting intelligence on the Otiosi."

Schoff recoiled. The group of heretics Spina had mentioned? Even the name was repellent.

"They spread Epicurus' doctrine," continued Spina. "Their leader passes himself off as a harmless scholar, but make no mistake – Giacomo Vescosi is just as much a prophet of the Apocalypse as Luther."

"Of course," Schoff's voice rose. "Vescosi must be destroyed."

"And make a martyr of him?" Spina shook his head.

"The Lord is good, Schoff; *wherever the greatest danger lies, there you will find the path to Man's salvation.* Unwittingly, Vescosi and the Otiosi serve our purpose, sending mercenaries in pursuit of ancient manuscripts, studying them for references to the Devil's Library. Like us, they mean to discover the secret of its location."

Spina's stare seemed to penetrate Schoff's soul. "Thousands upon thousands of heretical texts; a swamp of lies and error. Scrolls that belong in the Vatican Library to be studied by men trained against their seductions; if that proves impossible, they must be destroyed.

"But among the filth, like a diamond at the centre of the Devil's black heart, God has placed a treasure, a weapon to defeat the Antichrist and pitch his hordes back into Hell. There is a book among the countless volumes of the Devil's Library that will teach us to unchain soul from body, to move freely among the angels who flow around us like a hidden river. This world is an illusion Schoff, conjured by Satan to stop us reaching Paradise. The book I speak of will lay waste to his lies. It will give us the power to remake this world as God intended and no man need ever doubt again!"

Spina kissed Schoff on both cheeks. His dark eyes shone in the afternoon light. "Return home, Mathern Schoff of Lübeck. Denounce the true Church. Spit on the Eucharist if they make you, and pray each night for tidings of the Devil's Library."

CHAPTER 2

Amsterdam, August 21st, 1561

Matthew Longstaff heard footsteps on the stairs, approaching his room in the eaves of a modest inn. He remained at the window, clear blue eyes tracing the squat towers of Amsterdam in the evening light. He was thirty-five years old and powerfully built from a decade's soldiering in the south – brutal work, but there were few honest trades open to a man without land or country.

His visitor knocked; three quick taps. From habit, Longstaff was armed – stiletto in his left boot, short blade strapped to the inside of his forearm, and a dagger taped beneath his short-waisted jerkin – but he wasn't expecting trouble.

"Come in."

The door was unlocked. The man who entered was in his fifties, out of breath from climbing so many flights of stairs. He wore a black tunic and fanned himself with a wide-brimmed hat. Longstaff smiled. He'd known the Dutch merchant Quist for three years and liked him.

"Good to see you again, Meneer."

Quist smoothed the tails of his long black coat and sat heavily on Longstaff's bed. The ropes were loose and the mattress sagged beneath his weight.

"Great Lord," he shouted, falling backwards.

Longstaff reached out a hand, laughing as he helped Quist regain his balance.

"You have a commission for me?"

"Another book, my friend. Greek this time, written on middling parchment, neatly bound in red leather and inlaid with metal. You do know Greek?"

"I know the characters."

"Good." Quist's face was lined, but the eyes sparkled as he searched his robe for a piece of paper. "The book we want is a thirteenth century copy of a manuscript by Aristarchus; *On The Planets, Their Characteristics and The Orbits They Describe Around The Sun.*"

Longstaff remained silent. A book of astronomy, from the title – perhaps they were hoping to find support for the theories of the Polish stargazer, Copernicus.

"Where is it?"

Quist spread his paper on the bed to reveal the floor plan of a large building. Longstaff counted at least two dozen rooms.

"You're looking at the upper storey," said Quist, placing his fingertip on a pair of windowless rooms in the centre. "The book is here."

It wasn't like Quist to play games. As far as Longstaff knew, the merchant was a member of a loose-knit group of antiquarians, well-funded amateurs with an eccentric desire to preserve the last remaining scraps of the past.

"What is this building?"

"Before Constantinople fell to the Turks – more than a hundred years ago now – the library there was the finest in the world… "

"Constantinople?"

The Dutchman shook his head. "Emperor Paleologus put up a brave fight. Before he was killed at the end of a seven-week siege, he made it possible for many of his subjects to flee. His niece escaped with several hundred books."

"Several hundred? She must have been a courageous woman."

"Sophia Paleologina was an extraordinary woman," replied Quist. "Her reward was marriage to Ivan III, brokered by Pope Paul III in an attempt to unify the Catholic and Orthodox Churches. She took her books with her when she went to Moscow. Today, they form the heart of her grandson's library."

Longstaff let out a short bark of laughter. "Moscow? You're out of your mind."

"We're offering a substantial reward."

Longstaff gestured at the hand-drawn map. "What building?"

"The Terem Palace, where the royal family have their apartments. We know the exact location of the book…"

"Suicide," Longstaff traced a line around the sketch. "The Terem Palace stands within a citadel. The Russians have been building the walls for the last three hundred years."

"You've shown great resourcefulness in the past."

"I'm not negotiating, Quist. I won't do it."

The Dutchman walked to the window. "Give me one last chance to change your mind?"

"You're wasting your time."

Quist raised his hand. "You never talk about your past, Meneer Longstaff, but it wasn't difficult to discover a few facts. You made quite a name for yourself, fighting with Il Medeghino in the south."

"I am no longer a soldier." There was a hard edge to Longstaff's voice. He did not want to be reminded of his years in Italy.

"No longer much of anything."

Footsteps sounded on the stairs. Longstaff drew a dagger from his sleeve. "What is this?"

The door swung open. Two men stood in the entrance. The first moved like a soldier. Longstaff raised the dagger.

"No need for that." The second man was richly dressed in a bottle-blue doublet. He wasn't handsome – the eyes were too small, nose too flat, the mouth too wide – but he carried himself with unmistakable authority.

"Matthew Longstaff," said Quist. "Allow me to introduce Sir Nicholas Bacon."

The newcomer turned to his bodyguard. "Wait outside. Come at my call." He looked hard at Longstaff before gesturing at the window. "Faces the docks. Deliberate on your part, or chance?"

An Englishman? Longstaff lowered the knife. Had they truly discovered so much of his past?

"Terrible waste," continued Sir Nicholas. "A man of your talents working as a thief."

Longstaff took a step forward. People were usually more circumspect in his company. "How I make my living is no business of yours."

"Must have been a wrench for you, exiled from England at such a young age and abandoned at the home of a Lübeck herring trader."

It wasn't possible. Longstaff turned to stare at Quist.

"Don't look at him, sir. Look at me. I've come a long way to make you an offer," Sir Nicholas stood with hands on his hips. "What would you risk for the chance to wear your father's name once more – walk his lands as their master?"

His father's name? Sir William Longstaff had owned an estate at Martlesham in Suffolk. Longstaff hadn't seen it since the age of nine. Memories were all that remained

of the only place he'd ever called home – green lawns
and the small parlour where his father used to sit in the
evenings. Sir William had been a great traveller, coming
into contact with Luther's creed on the continent.
Longstaff still remembered men arriving at Martlesham
to construct a printing press. Four of them, shouting and
joking in a language he couldn't understand. Soon after,
pamphlets began to appear on the streets of Ipswich,
Bury St. Edmunds, Cambridge, and finally London, which
was when they came to the attention of the King. Henry
VIII ordered Sir William to the scaffold, confiscated his
property and banished his son from the country.

Longstaff spat: "There's no way back for me."

Sir Nicholas laughed. "I'm Lord Keeper of the Great
Seal of England, Longstaff. Give me a year of your life and
I'll make it possible for you to return home with Elizabeth's
blessing, and lay your father's ghost to rest."

Longstaff stared at Quist. "A small group of scholars
and clerks?"

"We seek a mighty prize, my friend. The kind which
brings powerful friends."

Longstaff missed the slight hesitation in the Dutchman's
voice – when he might have added, "… and enemies." He
was too busy remembering his final hours at the house in
Suffolk. His father had gone to Cambridge for the day, and
Longstaff had felt nothing but excitement when a score of
the King's men arrived.

One of his father's oldest friends had ridden at their
head; a well-built man named Jarrel, with a neat beard and
crooked teeth. Longstaff had run forward, expecting to be
grabbed beneath the arms and thrown into the air. A soldier
seized him instead, and held him still while Jarrel directed

the rest to the stacks of pamphlets in the cellars and the printing press in the stables. Minutes later, Longstaff and the servants were up against a wall in the great hall, Jarrel pacing back and forth in front of them.

"By the King's command, this estate is now mine. I hope you will find me a merciful master. There is no reason why unknowing service to a traitor should ruin your prospects of a secure future… "

Only Longstaff had fought, hands hooked like claws, aiming for the eyes. Jarrel had knocked him aside with ease. "As big a fool as your father."

Quist's map of the Terem Palace lay on the rumpled bed. Longstaff stared at the neat sketch without seeing it, his mind's eye focused on another time and place; his father crashing through the heavy doors at Martlesham, sword drawn, his face a mask of fear and anger.

Longstaff had stared at him from the far side of the room, held fast in Jarrel's arms, head yanked painfully to one side, knife at his throat. Sir William faltered in mid-stride – and his old friend laughed. Jarrel spoke, and Longstaff felt the knife-edge graze his soft flesh.

"A signed confession, or the boy dies."

Quist perched at the end of the bed. Sir Nicholas shifted impatiently at the window. Longstaff could still refuse their offer. *And then what?* England would remain closed to him. He would lose Quist's patronage. He could return to soldiering or become a thief in earnest, find a post as fencing master to an inbred princeling – each option worse than the last. Longstaff shook his head, and Quist's drawing of the Terem Palace swam slowly into focus. The Dutch merchant had pointed at two adjoining chambers.

"What are these rooms?"

Quist smiled. "Ivan's wardrobe and his library, but the Tzar rarely visits either. They're nearly always empty."

CHAPTER 3

Moscow, January 24th, 1562

Moscow seethed and festered in the winter months. The Square of the Conflagration at the heart of the city was a daily melée of fear and folly. Hawkers roared the virtues of hot bliny and home-made kvas, acrobats turned cartwheels and minstrels recited ballads, but nothing could lift the shadow cast by the high walls of Ivan IV's citadel.

Longstaff made his way through the press of people, snow crunching beneath his boots. Sparrow walked beside him; the dog was a cross – mastiff and greyhound, black as night against the dirty snow. Longstaff rested his hand on the hilt of his old *katzbalger* as he stepped over a drunk. The sword was nothing special, a straight, double-edged blade the length of his arm, but he'd grown accustomed to its weight and balance over the years.

The journey east had been almost pleasant. Travelling by boat and road through an unseasonably mild October, Longstaff had passed the time polishing his few remaining memories of Martlesham, excitement building at the thought of home. He had no desire to resurrect his father's trading empire, but with tentative, growing hope he remembered the fields around the old house, stretching as far as the eye could see.

He paused beside the extraordinary new church, eight unequal cupolas in all the colours of the rainbow, a splash of joy in a city of snow and fear. He'd been busy since arriving in Moscow ten weeks earlier. He'd found lodgings, picked up a few words of the language and made contact with a group of Saamid wintering nearby. For a price, one was willing to harness his team of twelve dogs and drive Longstaff west. He wasn't trapped in the city until spring arrived, only for as long as it took him to acquire the book.

Longstaff turned his back on the church, hardly glancing at the citadel as he made for his lodgings. He pinched the inside of his forearm: *patience*. Ivan had been in residence throughout the winter, but was due to leave the city soon, leaving only a skeleton guard at the citadel.

Longstaff had found a place to stay, and an ostensible reason for being in Moscow, with a German merchant in a neighbourhood of small traders and artisans. The house was cramped – two small rooms on the first floor with a single open space for stock below.

He followed Sparrow up the narrow stairs and opened the door.

Herr Fischer was in his mid-fifties, narrow shoulders sloping to a round belly. Beneath the grey hair, his normally sour face was wreathed in smiles.

"Are you alright?" asked Longstaff.

"Never better. A messenger came today. The new Tzarina has invited Moscow's leading merchants to display their wares."

Longstaff looked up. *Was this the chance he'd been waiting for?* "When?"

"Tomorrow. In front of the Terem Palace," Herr Fischer threw open a chest, producing a bottle of spirits and two glasses. Longstaff had never seen him so animated.

"You'll take me with you, of course."

Fischer froze: "Out of the question."

Longstaff reached for his purse. "Would one of Moscow's leading merchants appear without someone to do his fetching and carrying?"

"I have a boy. Our arrangement is for board and lodging."

"Arrangements change," Longstaff made an effort to soften his tone. Ten years ago, Herr Fischer had been one of the city's wealthiest merchants, before the English had forced a new route to Muscovy and smashed the German monopolies. "Your boy is a slack-jawed imbecile. Imagine the impression he'll make on the Tzarina and her court." Longstaff weighed the purse on his palm.

Fischer licked dry lips: "You'll do exactly as I say?"

"You have my word," said Longstaff.

*

The heavy cart rumbled over the ditch, which separated the Square of the Conflagration from the citadel. Herr Fischer turned on his seat, catching Longstaff's eye. "Don't speak," he whispered. "Don't look at anyone. Give them a single reason to think ill, and they'll murder you. Then me, then your mutt."

Guards stopped them at the gates. The merchant produced his invitation. Even after so many years in the city, he still spoke Russian with a heavy accent.

Longstaff looked up as the guards waved them on, narrowing his blue eyes against the pale winter sun. The high walls bristled with cannon; soldiers stared down from the gate tower.

The citadel was a city within a city. A long wooden barracks led away from the gates, warehouses to the left, then a cluster of towers and spires beyond an expanse of open land. Longstaff sat beside the merchant, hoping he cut a believable figure in the servant's smock he wore over his leather jerkin – a bodyguard pressed into menial service by his tight-fisted master.

Fischer shifted on the hard seat. "Be calm," said Longstaff softly. "Nothing is going to happen."

The wagon rumbled past a tall stake set in the frozen earth. A pale woman, in a thin white dress, traced stumbling circles round a rigid corpse. She was talking to herself, arms wrapped around her body for warmth. A shudder ran through the merchant's soft frame.

"Prince Yuri," he muttered. "That woman is his wife. If she can protect her husband's body from scavengers for twelve days, the Tzar will let her have it for burial. As a child, they say Ivan tore the feathers from living birds and dropped puppies from the citadel walls. Before her death, the first Tzarina was able to curb his grosser depredations. The new wife's an illiterate fifteen-year old from Kabarda. She does nothing but encourage him."

Longstaff forced his weather-beaten features into a smile, masking his disgust. The Russians were tough bastards – previous rulers had hardly showered them with the milk of human kindness – and even they'd taken to calling this one 'the Terrible'.

Flanked on three sides by stone churches, the great square was crowded with servants, guards and at least two-dozen of Ivan's boyars – his men-at-arms. Fischer steered towards a group of fellow merchants, arranging their wares in the shadow of the Terem Palace. Longstaff breathed a sigh of relief; from the outside, at least, it matched the sketch

Quist had given him. A two-storey wooden building, with a narrow gallery running round three sides and a wide staircase leading to the main entrance. If the Dutchman was right, Ivan's windowless library was at the centre of the first floor.

Fischer reined to a halt. "We have work to do."

Longstaff touched a finger to his brow, lowering one side of the cart and helping transform it into a make-shift stall. Fischer handed him a bowl of water. "Wash your hands before unpacking the merchandise."

Some of the traders sold fabrics from the East; others dealt in delicacies from the South. Herr Fischer had been a wholesaler once, Longstaff knew, until the arrival of the English forced him to part with Flemish linens at a loss and pay more for Russian furs and metals than they fetched in Bruges. Now he specialised in finished clothes from Italy and France, clocks and musical instruments from Germany, and curiosities from the new world.

It was noon when the Tzarina appeared, muffled in fur, at the top of the staircase. Twenty men and women accompanied her out of the Terem Palace, while dozens more rushed to join them from the square. The women were dressed to imitate their Empress, the men wearing layers of brightly coloured shirts to keep out the cold. Each had a dagger in his belt and a thick beard cut square to the chest.

The company moved quickly. The merchant pulled his fine robe across his round belly and pinched his cheeks until they glowed. He was everywhere at once, complimenting clients, laughing at their jokes. He sold three clocks, a dozen gowns and an emerald necklace without losing sight of the Tzarina. Fischer might be a coward and a cheat, but the German was a consummate salesman.

The Tzarina was a silent presence at the centre of the storm – a child with a thin, bird-like face. She pointed to a large beauty case on Fischer's stall and he bowed so deeply his fingers brushed the snow. The Tzarina turned away, drawing the crowd to the next wagon.

The merchant smiled at Longstaff. "She'll never pay, but her patronage is worth a fortune!"

Longstaff looked away. In the distance, Prince Yuri's wife ploughed her circles in the snow. With Fischer distracted by the Tzarina's Treasurer, Longstaff retrieved the beauty case and joined the line of merchants' seconds carrying bolts of cloth, tapestries, clocks and sweetmeats into the Terem Palace. He dropped his shoulders, trying to make himself as small as possible. A guard barked. Longstaff lowered his eyes, following the seconds into a vast storeroom.

It was dark inside, the winter sun barely penetrating high, mica-filled windows.

A volley of commands sounded outside. Alarmed, a young merchant's assistant dropped a packing case. Longstaff kept walking, past chests and rough-woven sacks, waiting for someone to stop him.

A boyar climbed the wide staircase, boots clattering on the wooden boards. "Prince Vorotynsky is resisting arrest!"

There was a stunned silence in the room, everyone knew of the famous conqueror of Kazan. It seemed another of Ivan's closest advisers had fallen from favour. Longstaff heard the distant clash of steel on steel. He crouched, to set the beauty case down in a corner.

"All of you out!" roared the Captain of the Guard. The seconds dropped their burdens and fled. Longstaff didn't move. He counted to five, heard the storeroom door slam shut and the sound of fighting fade into silence.

He held his breath. Had he seized an opportunity sent by heaven, or embarked on a path to suicide? Longstaff drew his dagger, certain the storeroom door was about fly open. They would try to take him alive, save him for torture and execution. It would only take a misplaced word from Fischer, a headcount at the citadel gates. And Sparrow? Longstaff shook his head; he could rely on the dog at least. He willed Fischer to pack up and leave, return to his cramped home in the city and pray – if he valued his life.

The door remained shut. Hardly two hours past noon, the room was already beginning to melt into darkness. Longstaff kept low, flinching every time the floorboards creaked above him. He looked up, thinking of the path he would have to take in the dead of night.

CHAPTER 4

The Terem Palace was silent. With luck, the guards would be dozing against their pikes. Longstaff used dirt to darken his face and removed his white shirt. The short-waisted jerkin he wore beneath was padded and lined with silk. Over the years, he'd sewn half a dozen small medallions into the lining; campaign medals from Metz and Marciano, as well as tokens of friendship and remembrance from fallen comrades.

Would he join them now? Fear threatened in the darkness. If the Tzar's men caught him, it wouldn't be a clean death. Gossips in the city claimed Ivan spent hours in the citadel dungeons each night, personally extracting confessions from men he suspected of treason.

Longstaff opened the storeroom door and peered into the corridor. Empty. Moonlight filtered through the gallery windows on the first floor. Thick carpets swallowed his footsteps up a wide flight of stairs. He tested each tread, praying the next wouldn't betray him.

He moved through the palace like a ghost, following the directions Quist had given him. A lone soldier leaned against the wall at the end of a corridor, grey cloak over his chain mail coat, whip curled at his belt.

Longstaff approached in shadow, listening to the even rhythm of the guard's breathing. The man was asleep on his feet, cap pulled low over his eyes, a key hanging from a hook on his belt. Was the door locked or unlocked? Longstaff held his knife a fingers-breadth from the guard's throat and reached for the handle with his free hand. Unlocked. He pushed it open an inch, terrified it would creak, expecting to see the guard's eyes flicker open. The door swung open on silent hinges. Longstaff slipped inside and closed the door.

Figures loomed from the shadows.

He stabbed, wildly. Felt the knife-point strike cloth and hair.

Dummies. Lit by a single, flickering candle and clothed in Ivan's ceremonial habits; the lesser and the greater, both lavishly ornamented with gold and jewels. Longstaff breathed a silent sigh of relief, sweat cooling on his neck as he looked around. The walls were lined with rows of clothing: furs, tunics, boots and half a dozen crowns. An open door on the far side of the room led to a second chamber.

Longstaff crept across the dressing room. He put his cheek to the doorframe and listened for signs of life.

Nothing. He peered inside, at a strange mixture of armoury and library. Two of the walls were covered with weapons: straight and curved swords, a lance, a poleaxe, a dozen knives and daggers, several pistols. On the third, a huge icon of Christ hung above a heavy wooden chest. And, just as Sir Nicholas had promised, the fourth wall was covered in books and scrolls.

A cat lay asleep among furs on a divan in the centre of the room. A glass stood beside a stoppered decanter of wine on a low table. Longstaff picked it up – a film of dusty sediment suggested no one had been here in days. There was a book on the table, bound in poor-quality leather. He flipped it open. The frontispiece was familiar; he'd seen copies in Germany and the Low Countries; a chronicle of the atrocities committed a century ago by Vlad Tepes Dracul of Wallachia. The new printing presses were fuelling a thirst for sensation and horror.

Longstaff moved to Ivan's collection of scrolls and books. He forced himself to work methodically, look at each in turn. An ancient timber groaned and the breath caught in his throat. *A small book, neatly bound in red leather and inlaid with metal.* He scanned the shelves, feeling panic uncoil in his gut. There, tucked away at the end of one high shelf – haltingly, he made out the Greek characters: *On The Planets, Their Characteristics and The Orbits They Describe Around The Sun.*

Footsteps, the soft murmur of a man's voice. There was no time to hide, only to throw himself down behind the heavy chest.

A painfully thin man, stoop-shouldered and hollow-chested, walked unsteadily through the door. He held a staff in one hand, tipped with an iron point. The callus on his forehead was well known in the city – the result of hours prostrated in front of icons. Ivan the Terrible. He looked nearer fifty than thirty; hooded eyes lost in his lined face. What in God's name was he doing here, alone, in the middle of the night? The Tzar poured wine into the dirty glass, drained it at a single swallow and lay back on the divan. From the way he moved, it wasn't his first of the night. A shudder ran across the sharp features as the cat licked his fingers.

Minutes crawled past like hours as Longstaff waited for the gentle rasp of snoring. He rose silently, shoulders cramping, the book in one hand and his knife in the other.

Ivan turned in his sleep. Longstaff froze, staring at the Tzar's lank hair, the mottled skin, a thin ribbon of spittle running into his sparse beard.

Please God, let him go on sleeping. Longstaff stole across the room, his eyes fixed on the Tzar. He reached the outer chamber, ears cocked for danger, waiting in the darkness until his heart was calm. He hid Aristarchus' book in his jerkin and opened the door to the corridor.

The guard jumped smartly to attention, eyes widening in horror as he realised his mistake. Longstaff buried his knife in the man's throat, wrapped an arm around his neck to stop the blood, forced him silently to his knees and held him there until the body went limp.

Ivan's snores reached him from the adjacent chamber. He dragged the body inside and bundled it behind a tapestry. Longstaff's sleeve was now drenched in blood, his hands were shaking. He pinched the inside of his forearm. *Be patient; find a way out of the Terem Palace, reach the citadel gates before dawn.* He stepped into the silent corridor.

Sentries would be guarding the entrance below. *The gallery?* Longstaff locked Ivan's rooms with the guard's key and crept towards a door at the far end of the corridor, secured with a simple iron bolt. He eased it back and slipped outside.

The freezing night air was like glass in Longstaff's throat. Guards stood round a brazier in the centre of the square, torches burned at the entrance to the church and at regular intervals on the walls beyond. The country was at peace, Longstaff reminded himself. No one was looking for him. The Tzar was safe – feared and loved in equal measure, worshipped as the father of his people. Aside from the few bright spots of torchlight, the citadel was dark and silent.

Longstaff dropped ten feet into shadow. He stayed close to the palace, trailing fingertips along the wooden wall, then along the rough stone walls of the Church of the Twelve Apostles. Now the ground was open, nearly fifty yards to the complex of barracks and warehouses beside the gates. Dawn approached. Longstaff put his head down and ran.

He dropped into a crouch beside the barracks, panting, waiting for the rush of guards. Minutes passed, people stirred on the other side of the wooden wall. Longstaff's fingers cramped on the knife-hilt and still no one came. The barracks offered cover until he was twenty yards from the gates, beside a train of covered wagons. Beyond them, grim-faced guards roused carters from their blankets.

Another minute and the rising sun would strip Longstaff of his last remaining hope. He crawled to the nearest cart, rolled silently on the unpaved ground and pulled himself up, limbs crossed around the heavy axle. He heard a shout and several answering cries, before the wagon rumbled slowly through the gates.

The city was the Tzar's first line of defence, a maze where attackers could be cut down at will. In a dark alleyway, Longstaff rolled clear of the cart – sprawling like a drunk in the gutter. No one gave him a second glance. The wagon train was still in earshot when he picked himself up and hurried to the merchant's house.

He found Sparrow curled beside the door. Herr Fischer was inside, still wearing yesterday's clothes. He turned when he heard Longstaff, looking past him with bloodshot eyes.

"You're alone."

Longstaff nodded. "No one noticed I was missing?"

"What in God's name were you thinking? I nearly had a heart-attack when you didn't reappear."

Cannon–fire. Both men flinched. Church bells rang as Fischer turned to the window and scanned the street. "What have you done?"

"Nothing." *Ivan must have found the dead guard.* "Calm down, Herr Fischer. We're safe." He poured a glass of spirits for the merchant. "Everything is arranged. I've paid a Saamid

huntsman to drive me west. Take me to their camp beyond
the city walls. An hour's work and you'll never hear from me
again."

Longstaff produced three gold coins from his jerkin.
"It'll be like I never existed."

The merchant shook his head. Longstaff slapped him.
"Think. What will happen if they find me here?" He
withdrew a fourth coin. "You have no choice, Herr Fischer."

Longstaff lay beneath a sheet of canvas, wrapped in his
heavy cavalryman's coat, pack and weapons beside him on
the flat bed of Fischer's cart. Were they heading for the
Saamid camp, as he'd instructed? He pulled back a corner
of the cover. There was Fischer, Sparrow beside him on the
hard wooden bench. They were moving north, away from
the citadel. The cart jolted to a stop as they reached the
outer wall. *Remember what I told you, Fischer. Ivan has a long list
of enemies; it will never occur to him to suspect a humble merchant's
second.* He braced himself, expecting to see the canvas pulled
back, a guard's face sneer down at him. Tethers snapped
against the ox's hide. The cart moved again, passing through
the gates of Moscow.

CHAPTER 5
Lübeck, January 31st, 1562

Mathern Schoff sat in shadow at a chipped wooden table, dark robe pulled close around his body. The Golden Cow had a reputation in Lübeck as a place where the sons of good families went to be fleeced by card-sharps and swindlers. Not at all the kind of establishment he would have chosen.

Four years had passed since his meeting with Gregorio Spina; four years of living among these heretics, accepting their invitations to dinner, settling their disputes. The Otiosi had made contact six months after his return from Rome, in the form of a visiting Bremen merchant. As Spina had predicted, the man came armed with letters, indisputable proof of his father's involvement in this cabal of blasphemy. Forewarned, Schoff had performed the part of a proud son, face shining as the merchant talked.

Slowly, he'd earned their trust. Each autumn he sent Gregorio Spina an encrypted report of his activities. In all other respects, he was a loyal servant of the Otiosi. He took their oaths, served as a postbox, and provided money or lodgings. The members were dull and trusting. He found an odd pleasure in repeating their heretical notions, seeing the faces glow with enthusiasm, but hated dealing with the mercenaries they hired to find their books; unpredictable, violent men.

Gaetan Durant, it appeared, was an exception to this rule. The Frenchman occupied a table ten paces away. Schoff had

recognised him easily from the description he'd been sent
– tall and slim, invariably dressed in black, with dark hair
combed straight back from a pale face.

Durant also carried himself like a gentleman; he'd
swept into the tavern as if it belonged to him, barely
tasting a glass of wine before getting drawn into a game of
cards – hardly appropriate for someone about to attend a
confidential meeting. He looked more a like a man in need
of distraction, as he lounged at the table and baited the
young dandy opposite.

Schoff sat quietly at his corner table, observing the man
he'd come to meet. Unusually for a bookfinder, Durant had
sought out the Otiosi, initiating contact through a Bruges
bookseller and proving his worth on several occasions since.
He'd accept a fee, or course – what mercenary wouldn't? –
but claimed his true goal was enlisting the aid of the Otiosi
in the search for his missing daughter.

Durant and the dandy played Landsknecht with a pack
of block-printed cards. A simple game, named after the
German pikemen who'd invented it. Schoff could hear
their conversation clearly, even amidst the press of men
and whores.

"You're bluffing," the young man's cheeks were pink
with alcohol. A gentleman of fashion from a wealthy family,
Schoff judged, who didn't object to losing, but expected
flattery in return.

"Perhaps," the Frenchman's voice dripped with contempt.
"Tell me, did it take you long to dress this morning? It's
admirable, the way you've judged the exact point at which
breeches become too brash… "

"Enough!" A note of triumph in his voice, the young
man placed his cards face-up on the table.

Schoff caught the Frenchman's scent – a cloying perfume. Durant looked bored as he flicked over his cards.

The dandy stared in disbelief. Schoff could hear him breathe, great indignant snorts of air.

"It's not possible."

The Frenchman raised an eyebrow. "What are you suggesting?"

The young man lurched to his feet. "I'm not suggesting a damn thing. I'm calling you a cheat." He stumbled over his stool and bumped the neighbouring table. Dice fell from a gambler's hand. An ominous silence descended on the room, broken by the sound of ivory on flagstones.

Schoff held his breath. The Frenchman merely laughed. "It'll be the Devil's own task for these gentlemen to discover which dice were loaded with quicksilver and which with lead, sponges, chaff and coal."

Mutters rose in the dark tavern.

Durant looked around. "You see. No one likes being called a cheat."

The dandy drew his sword. A fencing blade, hardly more than a toy.

Pressed against the rough wall, Schoff watched in horrified fascination as the Frenchman placed both hands on the tabletop. He rose with intimidating precision, not stopping until the point of the sword pressed against his chest.

The boy's eyes sought support from the tavern's patrons. Some stared at him, some studied their shoes. Two men made discreetly for the door.

"When you threaten a man," said Durant, "have the courtesy to look at him."

The boy lost his nerve. "I apologise. I spoke without

thinking." Stiffly, he walked between the tables and pushed through the thick velvet curtain.

Durant threw back his head and laughed. Every other man in the room was silent. The Frenchman had called them cheats and chased away an easy mark. Schoff waited to see them stand and issue challenges. Wasn't that how these things were done? He watched in near disbelief as the card-sharps and gamblers returned to their games. Durant resumed his seat, idly toying with his winnings.

Schoff stared at his glass. Should he leave? What could the Otiosi want with a man like this?

Durant was staring right at him. Despite his efforts to remain anonymous, it seemed the Frenchman had recognised him at once. Schoff took a deep breath and nodded at the chair opposite. Loudly, Durant scraped the coins into his purse and approached with a swagger.

"Herr Schoff?"

"Sit."

"Don't mind if I do." He hooked an elbow around the back of the chair.

Schoff leaned forward, keeping his voice low. "I've never seen such irresponsible behaviour. The Church in Rome, a dozen princes here in the north – they want us dead. The new humanist philosophy is a direct threat to their own authority."

"I know, I know. A group of scholars and clerks, whose only protection is anonymity," the Frenchman waved a hand. "It was *me* who sought out the Otiosi. Not the other way round."

Schoff inclined his head. "To offer your services in return for help finding your daughter. I believe her name is Laure?"

Durant's expression hardened. "Is there word?"

Schoff drew out the moment before shaking his head. "The message I was given is that you should not give up hope."

The Frenchman replied with a smile of such bitterness he was forced to look away.

"What is it this time," asked Durant. "Another book?"

The lawyer folded his arms, suddenly determined to make the Frenchman pay for his arrogance. "Perhaps it's time we found someone more reliable."

Durant sighed. "Just tell me, Schoff. Your superiors know my worth, even if you don't."

CHAPTER 6
Livonia, February 1st, 1562

Longstaff kept low by day, listening to the hiss of runners as they cut channels in the snow and the low panting of the sled-dogs. Sparrow ran alongside for an hour each morning, a black burr on the white blanket of snow, before conceding defeat to her distant cousins.

At night, Longstaff fetched wood from the sled to build a fire, while the Saamid driver saw to the dogs. The Englishman wanted to talk, but he and the driver, Gosha, had no common language beyond a few words of Russian.

Rolling onto his front, Longstaff stared at the silent country as the dogs ate away the miles beneath a slate grey sky. In the far distance, he saw the silhouette of a castle. They had passed burnt out villages in Livonia's eastern marches – courtesy of Ivan's raiding parties – but this castle was the first sign of life in nearly four days. Longstaff breathed a sigh of relief. With luck they would reach Riga tomorrow. The timing was perfect. It was February 1st, final day of the winter embargo. The Hansa captains were free to sail again and it would be a simple task to secure passage to Lübeck, where Quist and Sir Nicholas had told him to deliver the book.

Longstaff sensed movement in the empty landscape and sat up, scanning the horizon. Nothing. The cold wind tore through his heavy jerkin and long cavalryman's coat.

He pulled a fur around his shoulders and strained his eyes. There. A smudge of dirt in the snow. They had been climbing steadily for most of the afternoon, he estimated the distance at five miles.

It might be coincidence, though few men were foolhardy enough to travel this route in winter.

The smudge disappeared. It took Longstaff a moment to realize that they were no longer climbing, the contours of the buried land almost invisible in the flat, white light. He crawled along the sled, hauling himself up beside Gosha. "Men behind."

From deep within his furred hood, the Saamid stared at him expressionlessly. Longstaff looked up at the dull sky. "Probably nothing." He nodded. Even if those distant figures were the Tzar's men, they wouldn't travel by night. Tomorrow, he would be safe behind the high stone walls of Riga. The townsfolk hated Ivan, and would side with any man against his soldiers.

Gosha lifted his eyes to the sky. "Losing the light." How long ago had they stopped climbing? How far to the edge of the plateau? "Another mile," said Longstaff, looking back.

The Saamid slept beside his dogs. Longstaff made himself comfortable beside the low fire, warming his hands in Sparrow's thick coat. Above, a few stars were visible through lowering clouds. Behind, there was only darkness. Longstaff shivered, hearing the thin, dismal cries of wolves in the distance. He collected more wood from the sled and threw it on the fire.

Torches.

Six bright flames had appeared by the time Longstaff pounded Gosha awake. The Saamid required no explanation.

He whistled his dogs together and buckled them into harness. Longstaff watched impatiently, but knew his clumsy fingers would only slow the huntsman. Already the torches seemed to have halved the distance. He scrambled aboard the sled as Gosha jerked the dogs into life.

Behind, six orbs of smokey light. Ahead, Gosha's stocky silhouette. Everywhere else, nothing but the great, swallowing darkness. Could they hide? Longstaff thought of ordering Gosha to swerve to one side, but even a child could follow sled tracks in the snow.

He jettisoned the last of their firewood as the six flames grew gradually brighter. Snow emerged from the darkness, a yawning expanse of grey. Longstaff looked up. Heavy clouds still hung in great curtains above. It wasn't the moon lending a dull light to the snowfields, but the first glimmers of dawn.

Two sleds emerged from the gloom, three horses to each, another four men on horseback. Longstaff heard a distant shout. They'd seen him and the sleds surged ahead of the horsemen. The downward weight of the riders was enough to break the hard crust of snow, the softer stuff balling in the hooves of the horses and slowing them.

But the sleds were gaining fast. The drivers lashed their beasts, less than a mile behind now.

"How much further?" yelled Longstaff. Gosha pointed at a wide strip of forest. The trees would provide cover. Beyond them, Longstaff made out the tall spires of Riga. He felt a surge of hope.

Boyars, two on each sled. No doubt that these were Ivan's men, his bloodhounds – Longstaff recognized them by the tall hats and thick beards. Their long, fur coats lay open to reveal curved sabres. Longstaff retrieved his musket from beneath the furs. It was already primed and loaded. He made sure the powder was dry, lit a match from his tinderbox, aimed at the nearest driver and touched the firing pan. There was a bang, a flash of smoke. Six men ducked low on the onrushing sleds. They all straightened, unharmed. The range was too great. The Russians raised their own muskets and returned fire.

Longstaff steadied himself, poured powder and ball into the musket-barrel, tamped it down. A few more grains in the pan. The trees were close now – less than half a mile – the boyars a hundred and fifty yards behind. It was going to be desperately close.

Lead shot bit into the sled's left hand runner, sending splinters of wood flying through the air. Longstaff flinched. *To have come so far.* He closed one eye, cheek against the hard wooden stock and looked down the long barrel. He drew a bead on one of the horses, took a deep breath before firing.

The horse screamed as the musket ball tore a streak of pain along its flank, rearing, dragging its companions sideways.

Then they were plunging into the forest, the second sled only yards behind. Ivan's men threw down their muskets and drew sabres, grinning behind the heavy beards. Gosha swerved left. The horse-drawn sled went right, picking up speed on a track beaten in the snow. Longstaff dropped his gun, drew his own *katzbalger* sword. The snow was so deep he could see the boyars' tall hats above the trees, overtaking, about to jump down and butcher him.

Longstaff took three rapid steps, leapt and landed on the horse-sled's nearside runner. He slipped, lunged for the rail and swung his sword in a hard, flat arc. The Tzar's men stumbled away from the whistling blade as Longstaff hauled himself over the side. The driver swerved left, attempting to trample the dogs. Gosha snapped the reins; stripped of Longstaff's weight, the dog-sled shot forwards.

The two boyars lurched sideways, surprised by the sudden change of direction. Longstaff stepped inside a clumsy swipe and drove his sword through the nearest man's stomach. The Russian flopped against him, trapping the weapon as the second assassin closed. Longstaff dug the toes of his boots into the thick furs, lifted the dying boyar off the rocking sled and barrelled forwards, knocking the second man aside.

He wrenched his sword free, let the corpse fall against the driver. The man yanked at the reins. The near-side horse began to rear, his running-mates pulling in different directions. The sled bucked wildly, threw the driver clear, cannoned through the trees and toppled over.

Longstaff landed in the soft snow. The boyar had been less fortunate. He lay motionless at the foot of a tree, bleeding from a shallow head wound. The first sled was coming again. Longstaff caught a glimpse of it through the trees. He'd only winged the horse and it was running gamely now.

Longstaff crawled across the snow, praying he wouldn't sink through the thin crust. He reached the horses, hacked at the tethers, severed the thick leather on the third pass. Men shouted. The sled hurtled towards him.

Longstaff helped a horse to its feet, mounted in the same movement and spurred the animal forward. Muskets fired. He bent low, arms thrown around the broad neck.

The trees thinned. He emerged into a wide ring of cleared land, with Riga less than half a mile away. People filled the open ground. Some skated on the frozen ponds, while others hauled fodder towards the thick walls. They looked up in surprise, staring at the dog-sled, the bareback rider one hundred yards behind and the horse-sled emerging from the trees. When they saw the tall hats and curved swords, fishermen seized their ice-knives, woodmen their axes and ran to intercept the hated invaders. A soldier on the city walls raised his musket and fired a warning shot.

Longstaff turned his stolen horse. The horse-sled had stopped one hundred yards behind. The boyars stood at the rail, arms folded on their chests.

Matthew Longstaff laughed with relief as their driver turned the sled, retreating into the trees. He had half a mind to roar insults at these men who'd been sent to kill him. Instead, he lifted an arm in mock salute, wheeled his saddleless horse and cantered the last few hundred yards to safety.

Longstaff's arrival attracted attention. The Captain of the Guard cleared a path through curious townsfolk, waiting impatiently while Longstaff settled with Gosha. He gave the huntsman double the agreed sum. Gosha nodded, his face as impassive as ever. Three Saamid appeared, unharnessed the dogs in silence and led them away. Gosha followed, taking his leave without a word.

Four well-dressed young men cantered into view while Longstaff wrapped his musket in greaseproof paper. They wore swords at their sides and muskets strapped across the saddles. The Captain stifled a curse, barking a command to his men.

"No one leaves. Keep these idiots here until I get back." He nodded for Longstaff to follow, striding through the narrow streets to the main square. A hurried conversation took place on the steps of the Town Hall. The Captain marched away without a backward glance, while a young clerk in a woollen robe tugged at Longstaff's sleeve, escorting him to an empty chamber. "Someone will be with you shortly."

A warm decanter of wine stood on the mantelpiece. Longstaff helped himself to a glass before taking a seat with a view of the door. All sense of triumph had vanished. How had the boyars found him? He and Gosha had left the Saamid camp before dawn. It had been snowing, thick flakes covering the wide tracks of the sled. Was it simple bad luck? Had Ivan sent search parties in every direction, skimming across the buried roads to Kazan, Minsk and Veliky Novgorod? Or had the merchant talked? The Tzar was well known as a friend to informers.

Longstaff didn't want to consider the alternative – that he'd been recognised, a connection made between Herr Fischer and the thief in the Terem Palace.

An older man walked into the room, pulled a cloth cap from his head and threw it to one side. He stopped when he saw Sparrow.

"Bitch looks minded to take my arm off."

Longstaff pinched his forearm. *Patience.* "She's as gentle as a mother. She'll give you no trouble."

The man rubbed a callused hand across his jaw. "Unlike her master."

Longstaff raised his hands. "I'm passing through, seeking passage to Lübeck."

"It brings me no pleasure, seeing Ivan's men this far west. And I have no sympathy with spies."

"My disagreement with the boyars is a private matter," replied Longstaff. "I've committed no crime."

"Nor have those Muscovites, as far as I'm aware. The fools in this city were ready to go after them just the same, those who haven't already taken the Tzar's gold. It's precisely the sort of incident Ivan can use as an excuse for war."

Longstaff drained his glass, trying to close his ears to the appeal in the man's voice. "Ivan will come when he's ready. Divine right is all the excuse he needs."

"And what will Lübeck do when he comes? Stand idly by?"

The old man was clearly desperate, willing to let him go in return for a morsel of hope. Longstaff felt sick, though he showed no trace of it. He knew Lübeck. It was the city his father had sent him to, before mounting the scaffold and dying for his faith. Longstaff dropped his voice, giving his words a significance they did not possess. "The city fathers are gathering information. They won't do anything until they have all the facts."

The man stared at him: "Not everyone wants to ally with Poland; tell them that. There's still time to revive the old alliances – Lübeck, Hamburg, Bremen, Cologne."

Too late, thought Longstaff, rising to his feet. He could have wept for the old man; the League of German cities was exhausted, dominated by merchant princes too rich and well fed to go to war, but he would let the old man go on hoping if it meant safe passage out of Riga. He offered his hand: "I'll do what I can."

Longstaff made one detour on his way to the port, turning aside when he saw the wooden steeple of a nearby church. He knocked the snow off his boots, still angry with himself for deceiving the old man, and stepped inside.

He thought of Herr Fischer – had the merchant fallen into Ivan's clutches? – and the boyar he'd killed just hours earlier. Lies, fear, and violence: for the sake of a book.

Longstaff dropped to his knees on the stone floor, staring blankly at a painted screen in front of the altar, the only splash of colour in the dour interior. The wooden boards were crowded with naked figures. Some marched triumphantly into Heaven, others suffered the torments of Hell. It was a large, confusing image – and incomplete. Three human-shaped outlines stood ominously blank against the painted boards. The city had declared for Luther and the holy family had been condemned as idols, leaving only images of pain and cruelty.

Longstaff closed his eyes. His mother had died in childbirth and he'd spent his early years with the servants at Martlesham. His father would appear every few months, always smiling, with a bag full of presents slung across one shoulder – until Luther's doctrine wormed its way into his heart. Longstaff remembered sitting on his father's broad knee – he couldn't have been more than seven. Sir William had opened a slim folio, caressing the soft leather as he pointed to a page of ugly script, the sketch of a man with heavy jowls and sloping forehead.

His father had been executed two years later, but not before King Henry permitted him to make arrangements for his exiled son. Longstaff had arrived in Lübeck soon after, to begin a new life in the home of his father's friend, Paul Lammermeier, staunch Lutheran and wealthy merchant. Longstaff still remembered his first night in the city, lying awake in the unfamiliar bed, stiff sheets against cold skin, staring at the high ceilings and intricate tapestries of his new home. Nine years old, half wild with fury; he'd blamed Lammermeier, Luther and the King.

Longstaff's father had died by his own hand; Henry's lawyers had given him the chance to recant, but he'd chosen a point of doctrine over life and family.

Longstaff sighed. Once again, he was bound for Lübeck; once again he was blaming the wrong people. He couldn't hold the Otiosi responsible for the boyar's death. In the cold church, Longstaff bowed his head and prayed. *Forgive me, Lord, for what I have done. Forgive me for what I must still do.*

He rose to his feet. Sir Nicholas Bacon had demanded a year of his life. Nearly seven months of their contract remained, before Longstaff could return to the country he had not seen in twenty-six years and finally lay his father's ghost to rest.

CHAPTER 7

Tosterup Castle, Denmark, February 1ˢᵗ, 1562

Gaetan Durant tried to adopt the servant's gait. He pulled the cloth cap low over his dark hair and shortened his long stride. It didn't come naturally; he had been educated as a gentleman and raised in a beautiful house near Bordeaux – soft hills studded with vineyards and wide tracts of old forest. His grandfather had bought the estate after making his fortune in fish, wine and the precious blue dye known as woad. Durant had married young and settled down to a life of country pursuits and domestic bliss. He would have been there still, if plague hadn't devastated the region in 1549.

The corridors on the first floor of Tosterup Castle were long, monotonous and deserted. A fresco covered the ceiling. Durant stared at the poorly executed figure of a woman, eyes hidden behind a blindfold, two fat cherubs buzzing like flies around her head. *Justice is blind.* He sneered. *Justice is a bulky woman decorating the corridors of a Danish castle.*

Durant's step faltered. Unbidden, an image of his wife rose in his mind. Body wreathed in plague sores. Light dying in her desperate eyes, ice-cold limbs bathed in sweat. He remembered lifting a cup to her lips and watching the wine trace a bloody path along her sunken cheek. That was God's justice, for any artist with the courage to look.

The servant glanced nervously up and down the corridor before pointing to a closed door. "Tycho's chamber."

Durant nodded, "Wait here. Knock if anyone comes." He slipped inside, turning the key behind him.

The floor was covered with thick carpets, any one of which might conceal a loose floorboard. The oak-panelled walls and modest stone fireplace were obvious hiding places, but the Frenchman guessed he would be wasting his time. The Otiosi, in the form of that tedious lawyer, Mathern Schoff, had sent him to find a palimpsest; Danish script on the surface, Latin text beneath. Parchment was expensive and people often scraped the pages clean to reuse them. Sometimes, over a period of months and years, traces of the original reappeared.

He took a long, slow breath. The carpets had been liberally sprinkled with herbs; he identified marjoram, camomile, germander and lavender. Durant looked past the fireplace and heavy oak bed. It was the bookcase and secretaire which stood out with greatest clarity, and the duelling blades mounted on the wall – fine pieces of modern workmanship, at odds with the rest of the room. The lawyer in Lübeck had told him that Tycho was sixteen. The castle belonged to his uncle, one of Denmark's leading statesmen, who'd forcibly removed the boy from his brother's care as a baby. No one in the family had ever explained why.

Durant opened the glass doors of the bookcase and stepped back, tapping fingertips against his bottom lip. At chest height, where the eye fell naturally, he saw an ornate collection of letters patent and a beautifully bound family history. These were a feint – the thick layer of dust proved as much – positioned to distract casual viewers from seeing what really mattered.

A large empty space lay in the centre of the second shelf. Durant looked at the collection on the right, stacked with their spines upward to protect the pages from dust. These books were beautifully illustrated, each written in a subtly different hand, whereas the books on the left were printed, and seemed to lurk with menacing uniformity. Durant read the titles. Treatises describing the various errors of the Roman Catholic Church; books of poetry, including Boccaccio's *Decameron* and Dante's *Inferno*; tomes concerning science and philosophy.

He looked for further clues to Tycho's character in the order of the volumes. They hadn't been arranged alphabetically, nor, it seemed, thematically. He stared at the gap between the two rows. It wasn't a question of old and new. At least half the printed books had been written centuries earlier. It was their ubiquity that made them indestructible, whereas each of the painted books was a work of art in its own right. Durant thought of the scribes who'd spent their lives in draughty scriptoriums, copying information from crumbling manuscripts, hoping to preserve these fragile links to a half-forgotten world. Humble men, they'd known that no two copies would ever be the same and believed that every error they made was one new flaw in the fabric of God's world.

The gap in the centre of the shelf was a battlefield, where a war was being fought between those who believed in the inevitability of decay and those who believed in the inevitability of perfection. Tycho had ensured that the two sides were evenly matched, allotting equal space to past and future.

He had been less discriminating on the bottom shelf of his bookcase, where old and new were jumbled together as if they meant nothing to their owner. Taken together, they amounted to a small collection of Apocalyptica. Durant saw the *Apocalypsis Nova* and the *Malleus Maleficarum,* the Hammer of Witches. He rolled his eyes at man's enduring obsession with the end of the world.

With quick, practised fingers, he shook each book gently, before putting it back on the shelves. Nothing fell from between the pages.

It was getting dark. A tinderbox and tapers lay on the mantelpiece. Durant lit one of the thick, beeswax candles and leaned against the wall, contemplating the desk.

There was a knock. Durant crossed the room in three strides, pressing his ear to the door.

"Anders?" he called softly.

"Yes."

"Alone?"

"Yes."

Durant set his weight against the door and turned the key. No blade whistled through the thin gap and he risked a look.

The servant stood in the empty corridor, pulling at the collar of his liveried tunic. "How much longer?" he asked. "If I'm caught, they'll have my..."

Durant took hold of the man's round cheek, twisting the soft flesh between long fingers.

"I have paid you generously and by God, you'll earn your money," Durant twisted again. "No more interruptions."

He locked the door, closed his grey eyes and took a deep breath, not wanting to be infected by the servant's impatience. He walked across the scented carpets to Tycho's desk. The drop-down cover was sealed. Durant picked the lock with a bent nail and flicked through the drawers. There was nothing of interest – a few letters from Tycho's mother, bills from the tailor.

Durant took a step back, tapping his lips. Tycho was young. His secrets were essentially a child's secrets. Had he tried to lend them dignity by concealing them in a hidden compartment?

Durant removed the lower drawer. Nothing seemed suspicious, but he measured the depth with a ruler he found among Tycho's collection of stationary and found a discrepancy. He discovered a slight depression, no bigger than his fingertip, pressed firmly and heard wooden springs give way. Durant slid the central section towards him, revealing a good-sized document box. Sitting cross-legged on the floor, he arranged the contents on the carpet.

There were several small pieces of jewellery and a number of religious medallions. Some were made of gold, some set with precious stones, but most were worthless. The lawyer had told him Tycho was a magpie. The household was careful with its possessions when he was around.

Pushing the trinkets aside, Durant turned his attention to a series of luridly coloured prints. There were four in all, each showing a scene from the life of Saint Agnes. In the first, Agnes – naked, high-breasted, bleeding from a dozen cuts – was being dragged through the streets of Rome. Durant knew the story. The girl had spurned an offer of marriage. The old laws forbade the execution of virgins and the young suitor's father, a Roman Prefect, had ordered her taken to a city brothel. The second print showed Agnes among prostitutes in various states of undress, looking on in horror as a young man clutched his eyes, struck blind for trying to deflower the virgin. In the third, a naked Agnes was tied to a stake, tall flames refusing to consume her perfect body as she gazed to heaven. She wore the same ethereal expression in the final print, indifferent to the soldier stabbing her in the throat. Durant stared at the images. There was something compelling in the mixture of piety, pain and eroticism.

"Tycho," he murmured, "I believe I'm beginning to like you."

There was only one item left on the carpet. Durant unrolled a long sheet of parchment. *Dear Tycho*, he read, *your mother and I are both well.*

A letter between father and son on the surface, the Lübeck lawyer had said, with Latin text beneath. Secrets bequeathed from one generation to the next.

Durant pinched the material between his fingertips. The parchment was brilliantly white, without bump or imperfection, uterine vellum from the skin of an aborted calf. It was a fantastically expensive material for such mundane correspondence. He held it up to the window and saw the shadow of a second text. *Memmiadae Lucretius salutem...*

Lucretius sends greetings to Memmius. Durant's breath grew short. He knew true Latin when he saw it, unlike the Church's bastard version, but it wasn't only the vintage that made his hands tremble with excitement; it was the flavour. Durant recognised the diction, knew the odd, rhetorical flourishes.

Sixteen hundred years ago, Memmius had been Lucretius's patron. This letter wasn't the original, of course. Almost nothing from that period survived, except in copies made by semi-literate monks. Durant's fingers went to his chest, touching the small book he wore like a guardian angel beneath his doublet – Lucretius' famous poem, *On the Nature of Things* – rediscovered during the last century and immediately condemned by the Pope's censors as "a lascivious and wicked work". Durant had chanced upon a copy printed illegally by the Otiosi. The Church claimed just reading it would see his soul condemned to damnation, but

the poem had provided solace when his wife and parents
were taken from him by plague. It had provided arguments
in his battles with the doctrinaire professors at the medical
faculty in Montpellier, and a reason to go on living when his
daughter disappeared.

Tycho's letter transported Durant from Tosterup Castle
to the Roman countryside. He could almost see Lucretius,
sitting comfortably in the sunshine, writing to thank his
patron for a recent weekend party. As the poet's letter
moved from compliment, to insight, to the conclusion of
a story, Durant had the sense of eavesdropping on a more
civilized world; a company of friends, seeking answers to
life's questions in observation and reason. So different from
today, when people believed the Devil lurked behind every
misfortune and plotted a course through life according to
the flight of birds or the turn of a card.

*As I told you, the man who approached me in Rome was nondescript,
almost deliberately so, and demanded I provide him with the complete
works of Epicurus for inclusion in something he described, with
admirable seriousness, as The Devil's Library.*

Durant stopped reading. Lucretius' great poem, along with the
rediscovery of Plato, had inspired the intellectual daring of
Cosimo de Medici and Copernicus, of Vesalius and Columbus.
But Lucretius was the disciple, his poem only a hymn of
praise. Not a single work by Epicurus had ever been found.
Durant thought of what had already been achieved – advances
in science and medicine, voyages of discovery. What further
marvels might occur if the Master's works were rediscovered?

A sharp tap at the door. Durant had already stayed too
long. He rolled the parchment, tucking it deep in the folds

of his doublet, took one last look around the austere room, and hesitated. He had the measure of this young man; the apocalyptic texts, stolen keepsakes, the hidden compartment. Tycho was lonely and secretive, too clever for his own good, waiting for life to begin, and Durant was about to deprive him of his most treasured possession. He sat down at the desk and found a sheet of paper. What would console this boy for the loss of his palimpsest? Durant had to hurry. He scribbled furiously, penning a short letter which he left in Tycho's secret drawer.

My Dear Tycho,

Prayer cannot alter destiny. Good works cannot alter a fate determined even before the act of creation.

My Son, God has spoken, and named you as a fellow member of the Elect. Listen for me, for I shall come to you on the wind and together we will do God's work, and lay waste the high and mighty and scour the earth of hypocrites, so that the calf and the lion cub may feed together.

And when our work is done, those of us who remain will live on God's Holy Mountain, and know neither harm nor hurt. For we shall be filled with the knowledge of God, as water fills the sea.

Until that day, rest assured that I will guard your letter with my life,

Your friend in God,

G

*

Return to Lübeck and deliver the palimpsest at once. Durant had no difficulty following the first of the lawyer's instructions, boarding a trading cog to make the short crossing from Malmo. He read the palimpsest a dozen times, sheltered behind the crates on deck. Then the light went and nothing remained on the paper but Tycho's letter from his father.

Durant lay on the hard boards and stared up at the stars. He still remembered the first time he'd opened his own modest copy of Lucretius's epic poem, reeling from the death of his wife, subject to daily attacks of sweating and breathlessness. The priests had been worse than useless with their stories of punishment and retribution, urging him to cherish his grief as evidence of what he'd be spared in the life to come.

Lucretius' poem had warmed Durant like the dawn of a new day. Beautiful words, surpassed only by the beauty of the ideas.

And I insist on the testimony of the senses, against all other claims of authority. And I will work by the light of this testimony towards an understanding of the hidden structure of things.

Durant could think of no better description for the wave of new thought breaking across the continent. How, then, to account for Lucretius' sudden descent into the sort of slippery riddles beloved of charlatans and doomsayers? What did the poet mean, when he declared in his letter to Memmius that *"the shining sun does never look upon them, but the moon shows them the way, and we, by Jupiter's leave and damning Ptolemy's eyes, journey with them into Hell"*?

Durant shook his head. The verses were clumsy, sensationalist; a far cry from the unrhymed, six-beat lines in which Lucretius cast his poetry. And what was the meaning of the word, VITRIOL, repeated three times, and always in capitals?

And what was the meaning of the short anecdote – the stranger who'd approached Lucretius in Rome. *To my own surprise, I agreed to provide him with the complete works of Epicurus for his library*. And then the story finished. Elsewhere, Lucretius described the glories of his patron's table, the warmth of the sun on his back, the changes wrought by illness on the face of a mutual friend. He was a poet, a storyteller. Where were his descriptions of the mysterious librarian who wanted the works of Epicurus for something he called – *with admirable seriousness* – the Devil's Library?

A Riddle? The more Durant thought about it, the more convinced he became – Lucretius had encoded the location of this secret library in the text of his letter to Memmius. He couldn't begin to guess at the true meaning – couldn't even conceive of which questions to ask – but if anyone could, then surely the man who sought it...

Durant shook his head. Could such a Library possibly still exist; the complete works of Epicurus, and God alone knew what else?

It was late afternoon when the cog bumped gently against the quay. Durant said farewell to the captain and marched down the gangplank. The guards at the dock asked him to recite the Freeman's Oath. He rattled it off absentmindedly, so lost in thought that the crowds in Breite Strasse came as a surprise. He turned smartly aside, narrowly avoiding an over-burdened servant. Mathern Schoff's fine townhouse lay nearby. Durant had not liked the lawyer, and found he couldn't yet bring himself to place such a priceless document in his hands.

He returned to his rooms in Lübeck's third best inn, by the landlady's own reckoning, to wash and eat, putting off the moment when he would have to part with the palimpsest.

He untied the drawstrings of his heavy pack, looking for fresh clothes among the various boxes and bags. The strips of silk on his Coat of Seven Colours caught the light. Durant sank into an armchair. The young doctor who'd treated his wife had worn it as protection against the plague, and stayed with his patient long after the priests and servants had fled, pulling at the damp collar in fear and helplessness, but doing everything he could to alleviate her pain.

Durant had been a different man in those days, still believing it might be possible to fashion meaning from tragedy. Inspired by the doctor's courage and infuriated by his ignorance, he had taken his young daughter to Montpellier and enrolled as a student in the Faculty of Medicine. For seven years, he'd listened to the learned professors in their high pulpits, read everything in the university library, and paid precious little attention to Laure. Until the day she disappeared.

Restlessly, Durant rose to his feet and pulled on a clean black doublet. It was dark outside – too late to visit Mathern Schoff – but he knew he wouldn't sleep and had no desire to spend the night tossing and turning on the ill-slung mattress. He crept downstairs and let himself out through the back door. It was already past the hour of curfew, but he lit no torch to show he was abroad on legitimate business. Instead, he closed his black doublet to hide the white shirt and took his chances with the watch.

The tramp of heavy feet sounded in the distance. Constables pursuing some criminal or troublemaker, moving with the ease of men born to Lübeck's ways. Durant paused to listen for the rumble of chains. In a moment, the guardsmen would wind them from the drums on every corner, to block the streets and trap their prey. *There.*

Durant smiled; pleased to think he had the measure of this place. Once, Lübeck had been the centre of a mighty League of German trading cities. Now, they couldn't even keep Livonia safe or stop the English from trading directly with Muscovy. Profits were down, wages were falling and confidence was low.

The chains shook the townsfolk from their beds. Windows swung open and men leaned out, dutifully lighting the torches mounted on the sides of their homes. Durant stepped into deep shadow and waited for Lübeck to grow quiet.

His daughter had been twelve when she disappeared. Coming home from the university one evening, Durant had walked into her room to say goodnight. An empty bed, nothing missing from the wardrobe, no sign of a struggle. He'd scoured Montpellier for weeks, interrogating her friends and hounding strangers. Then he'd expanded the search. For months, he'd accused innocent villagers of unnatural crimes, and paid the landless men who lived in the hills for scraps of information. Eventually, rumour and desperation took him to Marseille. He'd been drifting from city to city ever since, asking questions, practising medicine, deliberately risking his life for the Otiosi and spending too many of his nights in gambling dens.

For the first time in years, Durant closed his eyes and pictured his daughter. She'd had her mother's eyes, his pale complexion and high cheekbones. The girl in his imagination smiled. Durant thought of the secret library, filled with the promise of a better life for others. He thought of the sour-faced lawyer who'd sent him to Denmark, and knew he couldn't simply hand over the palimpsest.

CHAPTER 8

Florence, February 7th, 1562

Giacomo Vescosi was tall with a narrow frame and soft paunch. Past fifty, his shoulders were bowed from long hours spent poring over manuscripts and the once fine head of hair had receded to a pair of grey tufts, poking up behind each ear.

As a young man, he'd inherited a fine house overlooking the Piazza della Signoria, and enough capital to save him from the necessity of earning a living. The people of Florence knew him as an eccentric scholar, lucky enough to live from the achievements of his forebears, while most members of the once proud family were forced to work as small traders and clerks.

The door of the scriptorium banged open. Vescosi looked up from his work. Aurélie's cheeks were flushed with suppressed rage, blue eyes ablaze with indignation.

Vescosi set down his quill. "I see you've heard."

The Church had passed an edict, threatening booksellers with excommunication if they failed to provide lists of their customers' purchases. Written in the Pope's name, it was no secret this was Gregorio Spina's work. The Master of the Sacred Palace had made it clear that sufficient resources would be made available to ensure compliance.

Aurélie pushed a lock of blond hair out of her eyes. "I know you're trying to protect me, Giacomo, but enough is enough. Why go to the trouble of educating me, only to shut me out of the most important part of your life?"

"What do you think you know?"

She stepped into the room, eyes roaming over the bookshelves and glass-fronted vitrines. "Twenty years ago you founded a society known as the Otiosi, dedicated to printing and distributing books banned by the Pope's censors," she grinned; it was clear she'd waited a long time to deliver this speech. "You acquire these works via a network of clerks and scribes, and distribute them through sympathetic merchants. The Otiosi's main printing press is in Strasbourg, but I suspect there are others; in locations where high-ranking noblemen are able to provide discreet protection."

Vescosi rocked on his heels. *How in God's name…* It was like witchcraft. "Twenty years?" he snapped. "How do you arrive at that figure?"

She had the cheek to laugh. "It would have taken something powerful to tear you away from your books."

He scowled, to mask his curiosity. "Well?"

"The *Indices Librorum Prohibitorum*. Lists of banned books appearing in cities throughout Europe; that was the catalyst."

She smiled in triumph. Vescosi's expression must have betrayed him. He attempted to scoff. "And you claim I founded this cabal of do-gooders? How do you suppose I built this continent-wide network of clerks, scribes, merchant and noblemen?" He ticked them off on his fingers.

Aurélie's blue eyes turned hard and flat. "Don't treat me like a delusional girl," she took a deep breath. "Ten years ago you saved my life, when you rescued me from marriage. Now I'm asking you to give it meaning."

Vescosi could only admire the art in her appeal. No one would have her for a wife, not anymore. He'd seen to that when he agreed to take her in, perhaps even earlier when he'd taught her to read. Aurélie's father was a distant cousin, driven to distraction by the girl's endless questions. Vescosi still remembered how the man had framed his proposal. *She'll make a good match one day, if you'll only cure the cleverness. And she'll be company for you, all alone in this big house.*

Vescosi would have refused, but he felt guilty at how much he disliked the man. In the following months, Aurélie became the daughter he'd never had, and he found he couldn't refuse her when she begged sanctuary from the marriage her father had brokered.

He looked at her fondly now, saw the passion written in every line of her body, and remembered his own youthful indignation at the creation of the *Indices Librorum Prohibitorum.* He'd hoped to put this moment off, indefinitely if impossible, but she was a grown woman and a good deal abler than most men he'd met. He glanced at the pamphlet he was writing, denouncing Gregorio Spina's new edict.

"Come here and read."

He stood in the window, staring down at the busy piazza below.

"Giacomo," her voice broke with excitement. "When people read this… "

"… they'll demand my head on a stake," he turned to face her. "The Egyptian God, Horus; how was his birth heralded?"

"A star in the east."

"When was Mithras born?"

"Twenty-fifth of December."

It was their familiar routine of question and answer. Aurélie hardly paused to consider her replies.

"Who were Krishna's parents?"

"A carpenter and a virgin."

Vescosi watched her eyes grow wide as she began to see the connections.

"How did Adonis die?"

"Crucified..."

Vescosi shrugged. There was no need to point out the obvious. "And Buddha fed five thousand people from a small basket. The information is out there, though people would rather see us dead than acknowledge it. We'll know we've started making a difference when they light the fires beneath our feet," he stared at her. "Are you sure you want to be a part of this?"

She didn't hesitate, "Of course."

"Then fetch the horses. There's something you have to see."

Vescosi tried to make himself comfortable in the saddle. Winter lingered in the air and he fastened the collar of his thick robe, envying Aurélie's youth. She'd shaken out her long blond hair and rode with her head up, blue eyes shining with excitement.

A fortified villa came into view. Vescosi gestured, the sweep of his arm taking in the wild fields around the deserted building. "The Villa Medici," he announced, "where it all began."

She stared at the overgrown gardens and crumbling galleries. "I don't understand."

"The middle years of the last century saw a great flowering in art and natural philosophy. Cosimo de Medici was at the heart of it, commissioning strange new works from Fra Angelico, driving poor Brunelleschi half mad with his demands for the Cathedral dome. Cosimo was an extraordinary man, fortunate enough to live in extraordinary times. The discovery of Lucretius' poem had already encouraged a few brave souls to look at the world with fresh eyes. Then strangers arrived from the east, chased out of Constantinople by the Turks.

"My great-uncle, Niccolò Vescosi, was a young clerk in Cosimo's service at the time. He went to hear one of these newcomers speak, a philosopher named Gemistus Plethon, and left in a daze, unsure of whether he'd been listening to God or the Devil. He begged Cosimo to come back with him the following day, into that heady swamp of ideas, which stretched both brain and nerve to breaking point.

"It was a turning point; Cosimo had been a simple banker before Gemistus arrived, albeit one of the most powerful in Europe. Now he was a man possessed."

An old man challenged them at the villa gates, employed to prevent vagrants from moving into the abandoned rooms. Vescosi gave him a few coins. "A relative of mine lived here once."

He led Aurélie through the dusty courtyard, up a flight of stairs to an open gallery. The distant hills were still draped in the reds and browns of winter.

"This villa was at the heart of everything Cosimo tried to achieve," continued Vescosi. "Gemistus presented him with a complete edition of the works of Plato – the first seen in western Europe in a thousand years – a dozen volumes which Cosimo used to attract the greatest minds of the age. He set them a beautifully simple, utterly blasphemous challenge; study man on his own terms and not as a reflection of God; raise him from his knees, shake him free of the terrible weight of the supernatural."

Aurélie looked round. Creepers lay heavy on the walls. A few scraps of silk still hung in the open windows. "What happened?"

"Gemistus disappeared, Cosimo grew old. As death approached, he fell prey to the priests' tales of hellfire and damnation. His confidence had been shaken; successful in so many of his endeavours, he'd failed completely when it mattered most."

Vescosi turned to face his young ward. "It wasn't chance which brought Gemistus here. The volumes he gave Cosimo were a symbol of good faith, and an invitation to help him find the greatest treasure on earth."

Vescosi shook his head helplessly, aware that he was moving too fast, drawing her in when he should have been pushing her away. "This is a tale of dreams, Aurélie, and the glue which binds the Otiosi together. A form of madness that infected me when I was still young; it will consume you, too, if I continue."

Aurélie hadn't blinked when he'd talked of being burned at the stake. Now she hesitated. A wrinkle appeared between the clear blue eyes. "You're trying to scare me."

"You should be scared."

She squared her shoulders, planting her feet on the dusty flagstones. "Go on."

"Cosimo de Medici sent men to scour castles and monasteries for old manuscripts. My great-uncle was given the task of cataloguing the fruits of this labour. Cosimo knew the value of information, but this wasn't idle curiosity; he was looking for something specific.

"I was still a young man when I inherited my great uncle's home. Stumbling across his journal, I learned about his work for Cosimo, his accidental discovery that

Gemistus had come to Italy in search of something called the Devil's Library. The philosopher stayed in Florence for several years, before disappearing as mysteriously as he'd arrived. Soon after, Cosimo de Medici came to see Niccolò at his home – our home. My great uncle had never seen his master so agitated. Cosimo left a small, rosewood case in Niccolò's care, ordering him to keep it safe, sealed and secret. His final act before leaving was to strip Niccolò of his most cherished pleasure, when he forbade him from ever returning to the Academy he'd founded here at this villa."

"What was in the box?"

"My uncle was a man of his word. He never opened it."

"But you know."

Vescosi looked down at the empty courtyard, slowly withdrawing a slim volume from his robe. "My uncle's journal. Twenty years passed before Niccolò heard from Cosimo de Medici again." Vescosi ran his fingertips across the worn binding before handing it to Aurélie. "Read the entry for July 31, 1464."

Impatiently, she flicked through the pages. "I'd heard Cosimo was gravely ill, but his summons, after twenty years, still took me by surprise." She looked at Vescosi.

"Continue."

The meadows around the Villa Medici had been fields once; I'd worked the soil myself in happier times, enjoying the hard labour after hours poring over old manuscripts.

I dismounted in the silent courtyard and followed an old retainer to Cosimo's chamber. The curtains hung open, but the thick walls permitted no more than a single slab of sunlight to fall across Cosimo's narrow bed, leaving the rest of the chamber in darkness.

My former master appeared to be sleeping. I was shocked at the change in him; his ears seemed too big for the shrunken head, the full lips pierced by sickness and his skin the colour of bleached bone.

He stirred, staring up at me with tired eyes. "Have you brought it?"

The rosewood case barely made an impression on the smooth sheets. Cosimo's fingertips brushed the flawless lock. "All those years and yet you never dared open it?"

I felt colour rise in my cheeks. After all the sacrifices I'd made, Cosimo had no right to insult me. He produced a key, fitting it to the lock and opening the lid with a hand grown claw-like with age.

The book was slim, nestled in velvet. Shame gave me courage; I reached forward to open the frontispiece and read the title of the book I'd kept for so many years – Confessions of Benedict of Nursia.

A tonsured man emerged from a dark corner of the room. He stepped forward and bent low over Cosimo, whispering.

I cleared my throat. "I had not realised his condition was so serious."

The Dominican monk straightened and fixed me with unwavering eyes. "Cosimo de Medici is a man like any other. His sins are no less mortal than ours."

I stared at Cosimo, hoping to see him strike the Dominican for his impertinence. The Master of Florence managed no more than a sigh. "Brother Jerome is right. My sins are grievous." His eyes rested on the rosewood case. "I was led astray. I gave in to temptation."

The monk locked the case and pocketed the key. "You were fortunate, my son," his voice was soft. "Had you found what you were looking for, it would have corrupted you beyond redemption."

"No." I thought of that unparalleled store of human knowledge, waiting to be discovered. Why had I never forced the lock on the case? Simple cowardice or unquestioning faith in Cosimo de Medici? I fell on my knees, imploring him. "The case will disappear. It will be locked away and forgotten." I gestured angrily at the monk. "He probably won't even open it."

*Cosimo would not meet my eyes. "The Church is life... not death,"
he whispered. "They will know what to do with it."*

*I task myself with cowardice so often I fear there must be truth in
the accusation. I turned my back on the greatest man I'd ever known
and left him at the monk's mercy. Turned my back on the book I'd
guarded with such loyalty for so many years and returned to Florence, to
my books and antiquities and to the compliments of fools.*

Aurélie looked up. Vescosi saw her blink, returning to the
present time. "Benedict of Nursia?"

"St. Benedict," he nodded. "The sixth century miracle-
worker whose Rule is still followed in monasteries throughout
Christendom. I imagine I know more about his life than
any other man alive. After reading my uncle's journal, I
became obsessed, contacting scholars and collectors across
the continent. The Otiosi grew from this network of like-
minded men; when the Pope created his lists of banned
books, we realised we were in a position to act. Many of
the merchants and clerks who assist us do so from a simple
sense of outrage. But for the original members, the true aim
has always been the Library."

She almost stamped her foot in frustration. "What
library? What was Cosimo looking for?"

Vescosi grinned. He felt almost young again.

CHAPTER 9
Lübeck, February 9th, 1562

Mathern Schoff stood at the study window of his fine, gabled townhouse in Lübeck, hiding his excitement from the Frenchman. The window overlooked Lübeck's main square and Schoff felt his father's hand on the back of his neck as he stared down. Servants ran back and forth in the morning sunshine, wealthy burghers discussed business and hökers called their wares. Small-minded fools, all of them, convinced the world revolved around their tiny ambitions.

For more than four years, Schoff had smiled and nodded as Otiosi members claimed that observation was a more certain guide to God's creation than scripture, hiding his true feelings, waiting and praying for this moment. His visitor had just uttered the words he longed to hear more than any others, in passing, as if the Devil's Library were the least interesting part of his story.

The sun disappeared behind cloud, and Schoff caught sight of his reflection in the thick glass. A young man in a lawyer's robe, two spots of colour high in his pale cheeks.

The Frenchman was still talking, lounged across an armchair, his expensive black doublet bunched at the shoulders. "A complete set of the works of Epicurus, Herr Schoff. Imagine what a blessing that might prove for mankind."

Schoff forced a smile, remembering how Spina had described Epicurus. *The ultimate heretic, for whom the soul dies when the body dies. I would rather face a dozen Luthers, ten thousand Mohamedans.*

"Of course, Herr Durant. A blessing," he turned and held out a hand for the palimpsest.

Durant frowned. "Weren't you listening, Herr Schoff? I don't have the letter with me."

"You don't?" Schoff nodded uncertainly. *What had he missed, standing at the window like a fool?*

"The palimpsest is too important. I won't hand it over until I know what's to become of it."

Schoff felt the stirrings of alarm. "Your letter will be studied by the finest minds in Europe. Rest assured, Herr Durant, if the Otiosi discover the lost works of Epicurus, they will seek to distribute them as widely as possible."

"They?"

"We, Herr Durant," Schoff heard impatience in his own voice. He squared his shoulders. "Your instructions are quite clear."

"To deliver the palimpsest to the Otiosi. How will you pass it to your leader, Schoff? Why entrust it to a messenger service when I'm willing to take it myself?"

"There are protocols, Herr Durant."

The Frenchman lowered his voice, "I fear I must insist."

"And jeopardise the search for your daughter?"

"You've never found so much as a trace of her. She would approve of what I'm doing now."

They were interrupted by a soft tap at the study door. A face appeared.

"What is it?" snapped Schoff.

The servant reddened. "Another gentleman to see you, sir."

"He shared his name, I suppose?"

"Longstaff."

Another of these cursed book-finders, but Schoff knew all about Matthew Longstaff; above all that he was pledged to serve the Otiosi for another seven months. Perhaps he could enlist the Englishman's aid. "Send him up."

"Very good, sir."

Durant frowned. "Hardly an appropriate moment to receive visitors." He turned at a sound behind him, dropping a hand to his rapier.

The Englishman paused in the doorway. He removed his long, cavalryman's coat and draped it over one arm; a casual gesture, but the thick leather would make an effective shield. He raised his free hand; a gesture of peace, with the handle of a knife visible in his palm.

Schoff attempted to regain control. "Come in, please."

Longstaff glanced in his direction. "I'm interrupting."

"On the contrary. You could not have timed your arrival more agreeably. My name is Mathern Schoff. This gentleman is Gaetan Durant."

Longstaff remained in the doorway.

"Herr Durant has brought me a manuscript," the lawyer tried to keep his voice even. "As have you, Herr Longstaff."

Durant stood. "Longstaff?" His grey eyes were hard. "I've heard of you."

Longstaff looked him up and down. "Then you have me at a disadvantage."

"It's not a compliment," Durant sneered. "Not in our line of work."

A black dog – broad across the chest with a heavy, square head – emerged from the shadows on the landing, pushed past her master and settled in front of the open fire. Schoff watched Durant retreat to the far side of the armchair.

"Come in, Herr Longstaff," he repeated. "Were you successful in Muscovy?"

The Englishman gave Durant a wide berth, staying close to the ranks of ledgers on the far wall. He wiped fingers on his trousers, then reached inside his jerkin for a small book, neatly bound in red leather.

Schoff smiled at him. *Be polite. Remain still. These men will not be impressed by exaggerated legal gestures.* "On the desk, if you'd be so kind."

A second shadow fell across the table. Durant, standing disagreeably close – scent of rich fabric and expensive wine – peering down at the slim volume. "*On the Planets, their Characteristics and the Orbits they describe around the Sun.*"

The Englishman ignored him, joining his dog beside the fire.

Schoff stared at Durant. "What could be easier? Give me the palimpsest and it will be as if our conversation had never taken place."

The Frenchman shook his head.

"Herr Durant is being difficult," Schoff looked at Longstaff. "Perhaps you can make him see sense?"

The Englishman pretended not to hear. Schoff struggled to control his temper. He was younger; he knew he must appear soft and pampered to these two men.

Pointedly, the Frenchman turned his back on Longstaff, his accent making a song of the hard German consonants. "Tell me where to find your master. He will be able to unravel the code, if anyone can."

Schoff shook his head. Why couldn't the stubborn fool simply hand over the palimpsest? "You think the Otiosi are playing a game, Herr Durant, that our leader risks his life on a whim? The Church would kill him if they discovered his identity. Your childishness places us all in jeopardy."

"I'm sure you can show me how to find him without compromising his safety."

"Give me the letter," the lawyer kept his voice even. "I will see it reaches him, along with a note of your concerns."

"A note of my concerns?" Durant raised his eyebrows. "Not a word by Epicurus has survived. We know nothing of the man beyond a few lines of poetry written three hundred years after his death. But think of the difference that poem has already made. Fifty years ago the world was still flat, an unmoving object at the centre of the universe. The Roman Church had it all worked out – not a flaw in the vast edifice of lies. Until Lucretius was rediscovered and struck a spark of curiosity in Erasmus and Columbus; Luther, Copernicus, Leonardo, Gutenberg; a host of other restless minds."

Longstaff cleared his throat. "Perhaps, Herr Schoff, you and I might conclude our business now. You can continue your discussion with this gentleman later."

Durant didn't bother to turn. "Of course, a man like you wouldn't understand."

Schoff's eyes slid towards the Englishman, hoping he would take offence.

"A man like me?"

The dog rose to his feet, but there was no sign of anger on Longstaff's face.

"Herr Durant acts against the interests of the Otiosi," interjected Schoff. "An organisation you have agreed to serve for one year of your life."

Longstaff shook his head, blue eyes creased in weariness. "I agreed to find your books, not settle your arguments."

They both despised him. Schoff could feel their contempt. "Rest assured, Herr Longstaff, I have a book for you to find." He spoke without thinking, rash words prompting an idea. He was a lawyer, trained in finding elegant solutions to intractable problems. It didn't matter what they thought of him. What mattered was ensuring the palimpsest reached Gregorio Spina as quickly as possible.

"Sit down. Both of you. I need to think."

Longstaff sighed before taking a seat beside the fire. Durant took the opposite armchair, provocatively tapping fingertips against his pursed lips.

Schoff stared at them. The Frenchman was unpredictable, but Longstaff seemed steady. A man able to survive in Muscovy would certainly ensure that the palimpsest arrived safely in Italy. The lawyer's thoughts raced on; there *was* another book, hidden in a fortress above Lake Como. Not a huge detour, but it would give him the time he needed.

Schoff removed a sheet of paper from his desk and began tracing an audible line across the page. He kept them waiting longer than necessary, to remind them of his authority and give himself time to think. Where could he send them? A smile lit Schoff's bland features as Spina's words returned to give him strength. *Among the filth, like a diamond at the centre of the Devil's black heart, God has placed a treasure, a weapon to defeat the Antichrist and pitch his hordes back into Hell.* Assuming the palimpsest did reveal the location of the Devil's Library – and surely, that was a risk worth taking – the Otiosi had outlived its usefulness.

He looked up. "Herr Durant has a document in his possession, which he is bound to place in my keeping. He refuses to do so, however, insisting he will only deliver it to my ultimate superior. I do not approve of blackmail. It galls me deeply to yield, but it seems I have no alternative."

Schoff paused. "Herr Longstaff, I will provide you with an address, no more than three week's journey from here. You are to deliver Durant and the palimpsest to the man who lives there."

"Wait," interjected the Frenchman. "None of this is necessary."

"Hold your tongue," snapped the lawyer. "You have forfeited my trust, Herr Durant. You are an oath-breaker." He saw the Frenchman flinch. *Good.* It was a question of control. He turned to Longstaff. "Take Ivan's book with you, and I advise you to keep the address a secret…"

Longstaff interrupted. "I killed a man in Livonia and another in Moscow." He looked angry. "You sit here risking men's lives for the sake of paper and ink…"

"For the accumulated knowledge of centuries, if Herr Durant is correct. The complete works of Epicurus, and who knows what else." He stood. "I know you have been promised a reward by one of our members. Follow my instructions, and I will ensure that Sir Nicholas discharges his obligations to you without delay, waiving whatever remains of the seven months you owe us."

Longstaff grew still, Schoff smiled. Now he had the man's attention. "There are two addresses here. The first reveals the location of one final book. It isn't far out of your way."

"Have you lost your senses?" snapped Durant. "This is hardly the time for detours."

Schoff froze him with a look. He was in command now, lying fluently, buying time for Spina to make his preparations. "On its own, your palimpsest is worthless. It is encoded, as you say, and requires a key." He turned to Longstaff, not waiting to see Durant's reaction. "Three weeks, give or take a few days. Then home."

Longstaff approached the desk, warily glancing down at the paper. Schoff saw him flinch when he saw the name – Il Medeghino – and the location in the hills above Como.

"I understand you've been there before," Schoff's voice was light.

Longstaff stared at him. "I'd hoped never to return."

"There's no one else I can trust," Schoff slipped the paper between the pages of Ivan's book and offered it to Longstaff. "I'll send boys for your things. Take your pick of the horses from the stables at the head of the Old Salt Road."

The Englishman looked round at Durant, who shrugged.

"Do you accept the commission?" persisted Schoff, feeling certain of the answer. There was no need to point out what would happen if Longstaff refused; the web of control he'd woven about both men was secure enough.

With ill grace, the Englishman snatched the book from his hands.

Mathern Schoff could still hear the two book thieves, clattering down the stairs and into the street, when the exhilarating sense of power began to wane. His hands shook as he poured himself a glass of wine. He drank it slowly at the study window. The good burghers of Lübeck were still there, discussing business on the very spot he'd stood on as a child to watch the heretic Anabaptists burn. He still saw the dying men in his dreams, their faces etched with fear, lank hair lifting on the waves of heat.

Schoff turned in disgust, sat down at his desk and began to write.

Revered Master,

You have impressed upon me how vital it is that I do nothing to jeopardise my privileged position with the Otiosi. Only in one, exceptional circumstance am I permitted, indeed encouraged, to deviate from our agreed protocols. Today, I was visited at my home by a thief

who claims to have discovered a letter that refers to The Devil's Library.
Knowing how much importance...

Schoff felt a sudden, paralysing surge of frustration. Would
Gregorio Spina be pleased or disappointed? Should he
apologise for failing to lay hands on Lucretius' letter? Should
he write, "I could not safely insist, for fear of revealing too
much?" No; too much like an excuse. Wiser, surely, to draw
attention to his speed of thought? Durant would protect
the palimpsest and Longstaff would protect the Frenchman.
Schoff felt a twinge of doubt at having sent them after
another book, but it had been the only way to win enough
time for his letter to reach Spina in Rome. Admittedly, Il
Medeghino had a fearsome reputation, but he and Longstaff
were old comrades in arms…

Schoff's thoughts brought him full circle. What should
he write? How best to phrase it? The thought of losing
Spina's approval was unbearable. He drank a second glass
of wine, then snatched the unfinished letter from his desk
and threw it on the fire. He would travel to Rome in person
– there was no one else he could trust.

CHAPTER 10

Ivan's book weighed heavy as Longstaff strode through the streets of Lübeck, ignoring the Frenchman alongside. He didn't like the man, and he'd liked Mathern Schoff even less, but that wasn't the reason for his anger.

He'd first walked these cobbled streets as a nine year-old; too young to understand the calamity that had befallen his family or the reasons behind his sudden flight from England. Paul Lammermeier, the man his father had chosen to be his guardian, had done his best. Longstaff had repaid his kindness by repeatedly running away, determined to return to England and avenge his father's death. He never got far; not then, never had anything to show for his efforts but cuts and bruises.

There had been better times, when the grey squares of Lübeck seemed to fill with Lammermeier's passion for the place, with its vast shipyards and warehouses, the forests of steeples and towers, but Longstaff's enthusiasm for a merchant's life had always been short-lived; a poor match for dreams of fame and glory.

He hadn't set foot in Lübeck for seventeen years and Lammermeier was long since dead. Was there anyone left in the city who would know him? Longstaff turned off the wide thoroughfare and walked through the artisan's quarter, a warren of narrow streets and closely packed houses: cutlers and coopers, scythe-smiths and brass-smiths, pewterers and polishers, all hard at work in their ground-floor workshops. The noise was deafening.

Longstaff slowed as he passed three fine new houses. Crumbling walls had stood here once. There had been a gate, hidden by ivy, and a secret garden where he'd kissed his childhood sweetheart for the first time. Marie would be married with children now, he guessed, and changed beyond recognition, just as he was.

Durant cleared his throat: "Are you sure we're going the right way?"

"Why couldn't you have just given the lawyer what he wanted?"

"I've done you a favour, Longstaff. Saved you six months of your life. You should be grateful."

They had reached a patch of scrubland against the city wall. Longstaff looked around; some things hadn't changed with the passage of time. He pointed: "You'll find the stables beyond the southern gate."

"And you?"

Longstaff shrugged. The Frenchman couldn't leave without him; the lawyer had seen to that.

The trailing hem of Longstaff's coat kicked up dust as he traced the passage of an ancient fight. Six months after arriving in this city, a group of local children had cornered him on this spot, to remind him that he was an outsider, an exile, a landless orphan. The boys had poked him with grubby fingers; a blow drew blood from his nose. Longstaff had lashed out, sending one crashing to the ground. The rest attacked, beating him about the head and body. A moment earlier he'd been exhausted. Now he roared in fury, biting, scratching, tossing and tumbling to shake himself free.

Longstaff had been fighting ever since. Paul Lammermeier had offered to make him his heir. Marie had offered everything a young woman could. He'd abandoned them both for a solider's life. Drifted south, full of plans to fight the Ottoman Turks and become a great Christian hero.

Longstaff had little to show for those years except scars and Sparrow, the dog he'd adopted after deserting Italy's most feared soldier of fortune. He hunkered down and scratched her between the ears. She'd been a pup at the time, hardly bigger than the bird he'd named her after, chest fluttering in awful terror as a lad struck her with a spiked stick. It hadn't been idle fun: she was being trained for a career in the bear-pits, where roaring crowds would goad her into a frenzy of blood and slather.

Longstaff had been a boy when he'd fallen into Il Medeghino's clutches. The mercenary general's methods were more sophisticated, but their effect had been much the same.

With one hand on Sparrow's head, Longstaff swore to himself that when he got home to Martlesham he would throw away his sword and raise crops, spend his life performing acts of kindness and earn a small reputation for generosity. It was an embarrassing dream, modest and vainglorious in equal measure, and more than he deserved after the things he'd seen and done in Italy.

Was that why God was sending him back? Was it a test, to see if he was worthy of a second chance?

He arrived at the stables a few minutes later, where Durant was standing with a proprietary hand on the neck of a tall, high-stepping chestnut with a wide mouth and broad nostrils, ears pointing forward like spears. He might be an arrogant fool, but the Frenchman was clearly an excellent judge of horseflesh.

"Your friend already has the pick of them," acknowledged the stablemaster, a bandy-legged man who looked long and hard at Longstaff, before recommending a big grey with an ugly cast in one eye.

Schoff's two servants arrived minutes apart. The first of them was out of breath from running across town to collect Durant's baggage. Longstaff stared – the man was hardly more than a pair of legs beneath the enormous pack.

Durant set to work, rearranging the contents to sit more comfortably across the chestnut's rump. He spread a large cloth on the cobblestones, which quickly disappeared beneath a bone saw, half a dozen phlebotomy cups, and a set of small golden bells with the clappers carefully wrapped in cloth. Longstaff felt at liberty to stare; Durant's head was buried deep in the pack. Only his arm snaked out from time to time, adding new items to the growing pile; herbs bound with ribbon and powders in thin leather bags; writing materials; a small mahogany box; a dozen phials. Was this man thief or apothecary?

The second servant arrived from the docks. Longstaff strapped the old *katzbalger* sword around his waist and removed his musket from the greased wrapping paper. It was a beautiful weapon, made by the finest gunsmith in Suhl. He stared down the barrel, taking pleasure in the clean, straight lines.

"I suppose you have names for them, too?" Durant was laughing, hand on hip. "Devil's Bane? Thunderstick?"

Longstaff pointed at the contents of Durant's pack, strewn across the yard. "You've enough baggage to satisfy a new married girl and the nerve to insult me?" He pulled himself onto the ugly grey. "We have a long journey. It's time we started."

"A moment," Durant looked down at his scattered possessions.

Whistling for Sparrow, Longstaff rode out of the yard with a clatter of hooves.

The Frenchman drew level before he'd gone two miles. "You might have given me time to pack, or was that English humour?"

"You were the one making pleasantries, Durant."

They passed a roadside inn shortly before sunset. Without a word, Longstaff nudged his horse through the tall gates, dismounted in the courtyard and inquired after two rooms. Satisfied he and the Frenchman wouldn't have to share, he made himself comfortable in the quiet common room, where a serving girl came to take their order. She was about twenty, with pretty blue eyes and full lips. Longstaff had been on the road for weeks, and the months before in Moscow had provided little in the way of diversion. "What's your name, young lady?"

She rolled her eyes, "Francisca."

"Is it always so quiet in here, Francisca?"

"What can I bring you?"

"Meat and drink. And the pleasure of your company?"

She looked him up and down, managing to wink and look indignant at the same time, then turned on her heel and walked to the kitchen. Longstaff admired the roll of her hips.

"Do you actually want her?" sneered the Frenchman. "Or was that performance for my benefit?"

Longstaff's smile faded. "We have a long journey ahead of us, Durant. Shouldn't we try and make the best of it?" He put his elbows on the narrow table. "Tell me more about the palimpsest."

Durant aped his gesture and tone: "Tell me more about our destination."

Longstaff's hand shot forward, seizing the Frenchman's collar. "The lawyer said nothing about delivering you in one piece."

"How far would you get with a corpse strapped to your horse?"

Longstaff felt the point of a knife against his belly. He released his grip, smoothing the collar of Durant's doublet. "Expensive cloth," he smiled. "We'll see how fine you look after a week in the saddle."

The serving girl returned with a platter of meats and roasted vegetables.

Durant leaned back, passing a hand across his mouth. "I think you've overestimated our appetites."

"Perhaps," she looked at Longstaff. "What do you think?"

Longstaff heard the invitation in her voice. *To hell with Durant.* This wasn't a partnership. It was a job, his last for the Otiosi. Longstaff admired their courage, but it wasn't his fight. He would deliver the Frenchman, collect his reward and return home. He met the girl's eyes. "Rest assured, Francicsa. I have a healthy appetite."

The girl was gone by the time Longstaff woke. He stretched out a hand; the mattress was still warm. With a smile, he imagined her slipping out of bed and dressing in the pre-dawn light. He sat up; the coins he'd left beside her clothes were gone.

As he dressed, Longstaff bound Ivan's book and the lawyer's sheet of paper to his chest. He wasn't concerned about bandits on the Old Salt Road — one of the safest thoroughfares in the Holy Roman Empire — but Durant was a different matter.

The Frenchman was waiting for him in the stable yard, the two horses already saddled. "I trust you enjoyed the evening."

Longstaff mounted: "More than you, I suspect. Shall we?"

They rattled onto the road, riding at a steady, mile-eating canter until Durant's mare threw a shoe.

"Your damned pack," cursed Longstaff.

The Frenchman dismounted. "Shoddy workmanship."

Longstaff shaded his eyes. Smoke rose from the chimneys of a hamlet, about a mile from the road. He made a point of remaining in the saddle, grumbling about the delay, while Durant walked his horse alongside.

The smith was an old man with failing eyesight. Longstaff listened to the uncertain ring of the hammer, his mood darkening as clouds rolled in from the east.

"Stop pacing," snapped Durant.

"I don't suppose there's anything in your pack to keep us dry. A closed carriage perhaps?"

"The nail was bent. This horse could carry twice the weight."

The old man straightened, pronouncing himself satisfied as the heavens opened.

"About time," Longstaff swung into the saddle, kicking the big grey into a heavy canter. He was soaked to the bone by the time they finally reached the next inn, wanting nothing more than a decent meal and a warm fire.

A boy ran through the rain to take their horses. He was skinny with a running sore on one side of his head. Longstaff slid gratefully from the saddle and peered through the inn windows. A welcoming fire, a middle-aged woman in a spotless apron, tray in hand. And three heavy-set men with their feet up on iron firedogs. Longstaff stared in disbelief. They'd put away their long fur coats and tall hats, but no power on earth would persuade them to shave the long beards. Ivan had sent four boyars, but the fourth lay dead in the snows of Riga with a ragged hole in his belly.

How is God's name? Longstaff's breath came in short gasps. He'd spent the afternoon making comments about the size of the Frenchman's pack, now it turned out he was trailing assassins across the Holy Roman Empire.

The stable boy scratched his sore. "Stop it," said Durant, climbing from his horse. "You'll only make it worse."

For a moment, Longstaff thought he'd rather take his chances with the boyars. "A word," he drew the Frenchman into the stables. "We have to ride on."

"I'm tired and hungry, and in no mood for jokes. I want something to eat and a warm bed for the night."

"There are three men inside. They're here to kill me."

Longstaff watched as Durant approached the window and peered cautiously at the hard-bitten assassins.

"Who are they?"

"Boyars. In the pay of Ivan the Terrible. I never thought…" Longstaff shook his head. *How could he have been so stupid?*

The Frenchman spat on the wet stones.

"Boy," said Longstaff, "re-saddle my horse." The lad looked at him as if he were mad. "Re-saddle the horses. Now!"

The rain fell in sheets. It was so dark they had to lead the animals for two long hours until Durant finally spat in disgust. "The horses are blown. This is pointless; better to rest now and move on at first light."

Longstaff followed him away from the Old Salt Road, into

the fringes of a forest. It promised to be an uncomfortable night. He slung his cavalryman's coat between two beech trees, making a dry space beneath by raking the top layer of undergrowth. He lay on his back, chewing on a piece of the hard, twice-baked bread known as *zwieback*. They'd have to leave the road, cut away west in the morning…

"We should have taken our chances with the Russians," said Durant. "At least we'd be dry." He tapped fingertips against his lips. "The stable-boy is bound to talk."

"What would you have done? Slit his throat?" Longstaff bit his tongue; he'd no business, and no right adding insult to injury.

"I am a man of imagination," replied the Frenchman. "Reflect on that, instead of judging me by your standards."

Longstaff remained silent, disgusted by his own carelessness. The boyars had followed him across the frozen wastes of Livonia, where he'd killed one of their comrades. He'd been a fool to think they would simply give up and return to face their master's wrath. The old man in Riga had said Ivan the Terrible had spies in the city – the work of a moment for them to discover his destination, and arrange a rendezvous with a greedy ship's captain in a quiet bay close to the city. The trail would have gone cold at Lübeck's docks, but he'd been stupid again, allowing Mathern Schoff to send a boy for his pack and weapons, and bring them to the stables at the head of the Old Salt Road. The stablemaster had seen them off along the only road south. The boyars must have overtaken them while Durant's horse was being shod…

Sparrow's square head loomed in the darkness. She used her teeth to give his coat a warning tug. Longstaff took a final bite of *zwieback*, before climbing to his feet. It didn't take him long to weave several branches together into a kind of bower. Once again, he raked away the wet earth, before leading the big grey into the makeshift shelter. What was the horse's name? The stable master had told him more than once. Durant's chestnut was called Rudi – that much he could remember – but the grey? Something that sounded vaguely French, he thought. Claude? Trompette? It wasn't important. Longstaff had owned a dozen horses in his time and they'd all become Martlesham within a day or two.

"At least the rain will hide our tracks," he muttered in the darkness. Sparrow shook the water from her coat and settled down beside the horse.

CHAPTER 11

Fear wrenched Longstaff from sleep. His fingers closed around a wrist, iron grip threatening to tear ligaments and break bones.

Someone shouted at him to let go; a voice he recognised. Shaking his head to expel the fog of sleep, he released his hold.

"God's teeth," muttered Durant, "I only wanted to wake you." He flexed his wrist backwards and forwards. "Next time, I'll use a stick."

It had stopped raining, the sky a deep, dull grey, the sun still an article of faith beneath the horizon. Longstaff sat up, rubbing a hand across his face.

"Time to go," said Durant, "unless we want your Russian friends dogging us all the way to Italy."

The bastard was trying to catch him off guard. "Who said anything about Italy?" snapped Longstaff.

They hadn't gone far when Durant turned off the road and dismounted. Longstaff nudged his horse after the Frenchman. The rising run revealed a walled town, less than a mile away, surrounded by a ring of heavily worked fields. The brewers and fishermen were still in bed, the hop gardens and ponds untended. Only in the far distance could Longstaff see any sign of life, where two young women walked towards the forest, muffled against the cold, heads thrown back in laughter.

Longstaff glanced at his travelling companion. The Frenchman stood at the edge of a new cemetery and helped himself to a portion of dried meat and a flask of weak beer from his pack. He looked strangely at home among the half-dug graves, wrapped against the morning chill in a dark cloak.

Durant looked past him. "Perhaps we should have done something about the stable boy, after all."

Longstaff turned in his saddle. The three Russians were at the foot of the long, shallow slope, urging their horses into a gallop. Longstaff hesitated in the face of such grim determination; they had pursued him all the way from Muscovy. They would not stop until he was dead.

Durant had soft hands and a light sword – Longstaff couldn't trust the Frenchman when it came to close-quarter killing. What then? Meet them alone?

Durant mounted his horse, narrow face perfectly calm. "Would you like me to provide the solution? Or do you feel the need to attempt something spectacular?"

"What do you have in mind?"

Durant laughed: "A simple demonstration of the advantages of brain over brawn."

He spurred his horse across the open ring of land, making for the distant trees. Sparrow bounded after him. Longstaff cursed and kicked Martlesham in pursuit. Durant's horse was swifter; the Frenchman disappeared into the trees. Longstaff crouched low in the saddle and urged his horse across the broken ground. Sparrow entered the forest. Seconds passed like hours, then Longstaff crashed through the trees, Russians snapping at his heels.

A low branch whipped the top of his head. He reeled in the saddle, grabbed at Martlesham's mane. A narrow track ran through the dense tangle of undergrowth, the floor littered with stones and broken sticks. He broke out of the trees into a wide clearing. A woman stared at him in terror, then threw herself to the ground. Longstaff checked Martlesham's stride. The horse cleared her by inches.

"Papists!" screamed Durant. "Agents of the Antichrist. Thieves. Help us"

There were people everywhere. *What in God's name?*

The lead boyar crashed into the clearing. A man raised a hand in protest. The Russian ran him down. The labourer fell, neck twisted at an impossible angle. Longstaff heaved on his reins, twisted in the saddle and caught the boyar's curved sabre on the edge of his *katzbalger*.

"Papists!" bawled Durant.

Men and women swarmed across the clearing, furious at the death of their friend.

Spurring Martlesham, Longstaff forced his adversary back into the mob. The man kicked a steel-shod boot into a labourer's face, his eyes blazing with rage. Hands clawed at him – cramped the curved sabre, as he was dragged down into the sea of wild men.

Labourers streamed like ants from their flimsy shelters. The boyars fought bravely, but were hopelessly outnumbered, drowning in the dark wave of fury. Sparrow raised her head and howled.

One boyar cleared a path with his sabre, hauled himself up onto his horse.

"He's getting away," said Durant.

Longstaff raised the musket and took aim at his broad back. He hesitated, long enough for a labourer to grab the boyar by his boot. Another lunged at the toppling man, and raked the eyes from his face.

Longstaff lowered the musket, heard the plaintive wail of an abandoned baby. Women appeared, yelling encouragement; girls in clean skirts, who could have passed for serving girls; crones with reddened lips and exhausted eyes. Beggars hammered at the dying boyars with such ferocity it was impossible to tell which were the abrahams, who made their living by shamming madness, which the deaf and dumb dommerers, and which the palliards, who made sores on their bodies with ratsbane and spearwort. Longstaff looked away. Durant seized him roughly by the shoulder.

"Keep watching," he shouted angrily.

The inhabitants of this forest camp stripped the boyars of their possessions. Durant rose in his stirrups, as if he'd been waiting for this first sign that the frenzy was ebbing.

"Bravo, my friends," he shouted. "You have done God's work, truly." He threw several silver coins into the clearing. "Take these criminals to the Duke. He will reward you richly for your loyalty."

Durant turned and kicked his horse into a canter. Longstaff stayed a moment longer, pinching the inside of his forearm. He should have waited for Ivan to leave Moscow. These three boyars – and the fourth outside Riga – would still be alive if he'd borne the fat merchant's company for a few days more.

He pulled Martlesham round in a half circle and followed Durant deeper into the forest, away from the shrieking and chanting.

*

Gaetan Durant slowed his horse to a walk, peering up through the high canopy of leaves to get his bearings.

He closed his eyes and thought of the terrible scene he'd orchestrated. Vicious fools, so depraved they were willing to kill at a stranger's command. Not one had questioned his wild claim; it had been enough that the boyars looked different, shouted their fear and rage in a foreign tongue.

Quietly, Durant cursed these ignorant, fearful times; who'd ever heard of papists wearing beards to their waists or wielding curved swords? *But had the world been so much better in the past, the people kinder, the sun warmer?*

In his youth, Durant had mocked old men for railing against a world mired in sin and depravity. Now, old before his time, he mocked himself for the same flaw. It was impossible to know the truth of it. Had people always been willing to tear strangers limb from limb, or had they really been debased by half a century of cruel propaganda? The Roman Church blamed Martin Luther, claiming the monk's certainty that he was living in the Last Days had unlocked forbidden passions. The split in Christianity had undoubtedly caused an orgy of blood and violence. At first, the slaughter had been official, but common folk had soon learned to kill their fellows and celebrate these crimes as acts of piety.

Durant held all churchmen in contempt, but he was still looking forward to being back in Catholic lands, where it was inconceivable for a butcher or tailor to claim he knew the will of God. Priests might be corrupt in the south, but they were rarely as terrifying as these earnest northerners in their reformers caps, who seemed to find such cold joy in silencing bells and extinguishing candles, blinding their followers to the most beautiful objects man could make.

Durant shifted in the saddle and stole a glance at Longstaff. Just the sight was enough to anger him – the sensible, hard-wearing clothes, the dirty blond hair, the dog.

The incompetent fool must have left a trail a mile wide for the Russians to follow.

The Englishman was a liability and Durant wasn't prepared to devote weeks of his life to keeping him alive. The letter he carried was too important.

He didn't think it would be difficult to prize the lawyer's paper from Longstaff's possession – it might even be fun – leave the blundering fool somewhere on the road. What had Mathern Schoff said? *On its own, the palimpsest is worthless. It is encoded and requires a key.* Durant felt confident that if he acquired this key, as well as the palimpsest, then the mysterious leader of the Otiosi would overlook the Englishman's absence; the world was imperfect, after all, and men of Longstaff's temperament were prey to a great variety of dangers and distractions. Durant smiled.

"Something amuses you?" asked Longstaff.

Now that he'd decided to abandon him, Durant was prepared to treat the Englishman graciously. "I was picturing the look on Duke Wilhelm's face when a group of his least appealing subjects arrive at the palace with three mutilated corpses."

Longstaff shook his head: "Forgive me if I fail to see the joke."

"Of course," Durant dropped his voice. "I wouldn't be laughing either, if I were responsible for three dead and another thirty souls stained with the sin of murder."

The Englishman winced. Durant had struck a sore spot – as good a time as any to begin winning Longstaff's confidence. "I'm sorry. That was uncalled for."

"No," Longstaff shook his head. "How did you know?"

"That those forest-dwellers would behave as they did?"

Longstaff coloured as he pushed blunt fingers through his hair. "How did you know where to find them?"

"You remember the cemetery? Lutherans are forever digging up corpses and carting them off to the middle of nowhere. They don't like having the dead in towns. Makes it too easy for priests to gull the superstitious into paying for pardons and masses in the hope that parents and grandparents will put in a good word for them at the gates of Heaven. One consequence is an influx of landless men – grave-diggers, bringing beggars and whores in their wake. They aren't welcome in the towns, and set up camp nearby. You saw those two women walk into the trees?" Durant smiled. "A bit early for picking mushrooms. They were on their way home after a hard night's whoring. And now the Duke has three new bodies for his cemetery and peasants demanding rewards. They'll get a whipping for their impertinence, even though these cemeteries are a profitable business – the old Catholic burial grounds were always in the best locations."

"I'm impressed. That wouldn't have occurred to me."

Durant shrugged: "I told you last night, the world never lacks for options – only people with the imagination to grasp them."

"You've a talent for reasoning," acknowledged Longstaff. "And a gift for manipulation. It's a hard thing to use a man's religious feelings against him."

"*Touché*," Durant inclined his head. "I hope I wouldn't use a man's love of God against him. But I regard religious feelings as fair game."

"A fine distinction."

"Not really. You asked why I hadn't simply handed over the palimpsest? I hope it will lead to a better future," Durant gave a short, bitter laugh. He had grown used to hiding this last kernel of idealism, and was only revealing it now to gain Longstaff's trust.

"Lucretius believed God to be as different from man as we are from ants. What would you say if an ant raised its head and claimed: *All the parts of the universe have me in view; the earth serves for me to walk on, the sun to give me light and the stars to breathe their influences into me; I gain this advantage from the winds and that from the waters, for I am the darling of nature.* Lucretius rejected the idea that we win God's favour through prayer, or incur His displeasure through sin, and claimed the most telling emblem of religion was the death of a child." Durant fell silent, thinking of the priests who'd plagued him with tales of God's sacrifice after his daughter disappeared.

"And that's what you hope to find?" asked Longstaff. "Ammunition against the Church?"

Durant ignored the question. "What are you doing here, Longstaff? You seem more suited to the life of a soldier, winning fame and glory on the battlefield. I imagine war is a straightforward business."

"I was a soldier. Spent my days outside city walls, cutting supply lines, starving women and children. Fame and glory are for storytellers."

"All for the sake of religion," said Durant.

Longstaff shook his head: "The men I served didn't fight for God. They fought for wealth and power. A place in history."

"Yes, but whose history? The Church describes a downward spiral; every generation sunk deeper in sin than the last. I prefer Lucretius' version. In the beginning, men were no better than animals, communicating in grunts and whistles. But they began to feel love for one another –

pride, jealousy; call it what you will. They created language, took the first tentative steps towards civilization. The poet wants us to take pride in our accomplishments, not dwell on our sins. He wants us to ask ourselves what more we might achieve."

CHAPTER 12

Matthew Longstaff set a hard pace towards the River Rhine, insisting they avoid the towns en route. He claimed to have no patience with the bribes and paperwork, the petty officials and their endless questions. There was truth in his argument, though it did not fully explain his impatience. He was more interested in learning what he could about Durant.

The Frenchman had been talkative since their encounter with the boyars. Longstaff met his attempts at conversation with silence — the sudden change in Durant made him uneasy — and kept a careful watch. The Frenchman looked soft, with his fine clothes and pale complexion, but rode well and was unfailingly polite to the smallholders — an extended family of farmers, a garrulous beekeeper, a small community of glass-makers — on whose hospitality they imposed.

On the fourth night, they passed a large quarry where Longstaff thought they might be offered beds for the night. Durant's mood remained buoyant even when the quarrymen ran them off with picks.

"We should count ourselves lucky if these fellows are the worst of our problems." He began to list the various bandit troops supposed to infest the region. "The best are disaffected knights and burghers' sons gone bad, but there are Leapers in these lands, and Batenburgers and Swarmers."

Longstaff shook his head in irritation.

"You disagree?"

"Thirty years ago, maybe. Those days are past."

Durant smiled, as if pleased to have persuaded Longstaff to break his silence. "Imagine what it must have been like — Luther's message of a universal priesthood spreading through the countryside like wildfire. Ordinary men and women inspired, throwing down their tools, banding together to demand freedom from unfair taxes and indentured service to their lords."

"For all the good it did."

Durant burst out laughing: "They fell some way short of their aims."

Longstaff scowled: "They were hunted down and killed like dogs," he said. "Mutilated bodies set up in trees as examples to the rest."

"It's the survivors I was speaking of," Durant inclined his head, as if Longstaff had proved his point. "Driven to fanaticism by the massacres."

"A few dozen men at most, half-starved, arguing over doctrine in the depths of the forest."

"Simple men," continued Durant, as they made their own impromptu camp. "They thought they were giving up the plough and needle for a place in Christ's army. Now they live like beasts, robbing and pillaging in the name of faith. Translate the Bible, said Luther. Preach the true word and Christianity's wounds will miraculously heal. Luther couldn't even make himself clear to his own followers. He spent his life railing against the Catholic cult of saints; now *his* old home is a place of pilgrimage. People hang his picture in their homes as protection against fire!"

Martin Luther. Longstaff closed his eyes as Sparrow curled up alongside him, but sleep was slow in coming — the monk's name stirred painful memories of his father.

The small town of Gernsheim made a good living from
its position on the River Rhine. It was market day when
Longstaff and Durant arrived, the common a forest of
stalls. Crowds bunched and shifted around mountebanks
and preachers perched on high wooden boxes.

"By appointment to the Duke. Teigmann's Teeth
Whitening Powder. Results guaranteed."

Others were selling universal antidotes, tinctures for
everything from scurvy to sore eyes. Longstaff and Durant
stopped in front of a wild-eyed preacher. "The Day of
Judgement nears. The ranks of the Elect have been filled.
The door to salvation is closed. Do not weep. Repent now
and survive the coming of the Last Days."

Durant kicked the preacher's box. The doomsayer
reached out to steady himself on his assistant's shoulder. The
boy dropped his pamphlets amid a swirl of feet. Separated
from her mother, a child began to wail. Longstaff looked for
the Frenchman, but instead saw a young penitent in a grey
smock, face and hair smeared with ashes. In his wake came a
crowd of women and children, their voices raised in tuneless
song, words loud in Longstaff's ears.

First Luther tells us that we all
Inherit sin from Adam's fall,
In evil lust and foul intent
And avid pride our lives are spent;
Our hearts are black and unrefined,
Our wills to horrid sins inclined,
And God, who judges soul and mind
Has cursed and damned all human kind.

Longstaff fought his way through the crowd, drawing a skittish Martlesham in his wake. He found quieter streets, sloping down to the docks on the banks of the river. It didn't take him long to find a captain willing to make room for them on his flat-bottomed boat.

"I shove off on the evening tide," he said, "with or without your companion."

Durant rode on-board just as the captain's patience expired. Rivermen dragged the gangplank onto the boat and the swift tide pulled them out into the middle of the Rhine.

Durant led his horse forward to the wide bow, where Longstaff had tethered the grey. He stumbled as the boat fishtailed round a buoy. "Where are our berths?"

"You're looking at them."

"With the horses?"

"There's plenty of space." Longstaff lay down on the hard deck as the sun disappeared into a bed of vineyards and wheat fields. He had the soldier's knack of being able to sleep whenever opportunity presented, but the Frenchman grumbled ceaselessly, lying flat on his back, then curling up like a baby, hands clasped beneath his head, before flipping onto his front. Every night, the same endless performance.

"Lie on your back and wait for sleep," Longstaff snapped. "Use your saddle as a pillow. Shouldn't be a problem, given how much you talk out of your arse. Close your damned eyes."

The day rolled by to the beat of the river. The rivermen worked their boat around the reefs, putting in at each town they passed to pay the tolls. Church spires sliced upwards between solid houses; glowering castles commanded the heights. Longstaff wouldn't have been a trader in the Holy Roman Empire for all the money in the Emperor's treasury. He was an adventurer – some would call him a thief – never more than a wrinkle's distance from the hangman's noose, but a saint compared to the princelings in those castles.

The horses stood calmly at the rail. Longstaff sat nearby, scratching Sparrow between the ears. With the lowering sun warm on his shoulders, he dangled his feet over the boat's edge and watched the traders on the dock run expert hands over barrels, sacks and bales of goods.

Durant joined him and silently offered a wineskin. Longstaff drank; the German wine was sweet and strong. The traders finished their negotiations and rivermen began loading and unloading. A group of about twenty children played quoits on the dock, trying to land woven rings over long stakes. Longstaff watched as they grew bored of the game. A gap-toothed boy, blond hair in his eyes, grabbed one of the sticks and held it between his legs like a horse. Two more boys joined him, and a dark, dirty-kneed girl.

The four riders herded the remaining children into a group. The blond boy announced he was War. The girl was Pestilence. Longstaff took another long draft of wine and watched as the Four Horsemen of the Apocalypse organized their playmates into a line, wheeling the stick horses, trotting to the front. As the cavalcade passed, the younger children collapsed amid groans and screams.

War moved among the motionless children, poking them with his stick.

"Here," shouted Death. "David moved his hand."

"Did not."

"You'll go to Hell if you don't admit it."

David climbed to his feet and stalked away. "Stupid game, anyway," he called over his shoulder. "When the Last Days come, see if it matters whether you move or not. It's what's in here that counts." He thumped his chest.

"And when the lamb opened the seal," quoted Durant softly, "I heard the voice of the fourth living creature say, 'Come and See'. I looked, and there before me was a pale horse. Its rider's name was Death, and Hades followed close behind. They were given power over one fourth of the Earth to kill by sword, famine, plague. And by the wild beasts of the Earth." He took a long drink. "Do you think that means us?"

The rivermen poled them away from the dock. The river was calm ahead, and they planned to float with the tide through the long night. Longstaff and Durant continued to pass the wineskin back and forth.

"Poor children," said Longstaff. "Dark images to form young minds."

"Barbaric," agreed Durant. "It's a sin to speculate on the End of the World."

"According to the Roman church."

"According to Saint Augustine. Do you disagree with him?"

"No," Longstaff shook his head, offering Durant the wineskin.

"We'll be in Italy soon," said the Frenchman. "People are like iron, Longstaff. Supple when they're warm, able to hold a range of contradictory opinions, as a civilized man should. Northerners are strong in pursuit of simple goals, but brittle when it comes to thinking. They lack a sense of theatre, insist on treating everything as a matter of life and death." He paused. "I make an exception for the English, of course."

"Good of you."

"I remember your King Henry celebrated one of his weddings – I forget which – by burning three Romans and three Reformers the same day."

The wine had loosened Longstaff's tongue. "My father was executed by Henry's command," his hard, blue eyes bored into Durant's. "He was a merchant. Trade took him to Europe, and into contact with Luther's doctrine. He thought the monk pointed the way to a better future, so much so he began printing pamphlets. The King took exception."

"I am sorry," Durant spoke quietly. "I should not have spoken flippantly."

Chains splashed in the water and the riverboat came to a gentle stop. A man rowed out to collect the toll.

The land climbed steeply here, to another castle perched on the heights. Longstaff could see torches carried by watchmen on the ramparts. The boat moved on, leaving the stars masters of the sky. Longstaff was drunk; maybe that was no bad thing if he kept the sense of well-being.

"Belief's a strange beast," declared Durant. Longstaff heard the wine in his voice. "I had a patient once, an educated man. One day, he found he could no longer perform his conjugal duty. Went to the local whorehouse – same result. There was nothing wrong with him physically, so he knew he must have been cursed." Durant laughed. "I gave him a coin engraved with celestial figures. Told him to perform rituals before attempting intercourse; laying the coin on his kidneys, tying it around his waist, propping it up in the crack of his arse. It worked." He wiped away tears of laughter. "Most of my patients were too stupid to save."

"Is that why you stopped?" asked Longstaff, laughing now.

Durant took another draft. "Ever been married?"

Longstaff thought of Marie, the girl he'd deserted at seventeen. He might have settled down with her in Lübeck, worked for Herr Lammermeier and forgotten about England. He shook his head.

"Sensible man," said Durant. "Wives die. Children disappear. There's no more beautiful a life than that of a carefree man."

"It's getting better, though," urged Longstaff. "Said so yourself."

"What?" asked Durant.

"The world. Growing. Look at the printing presses. People are learning to read and write, lifting themselves out of ignorance."

"Think of those children and their games," countered Durant. "That preacher and his End of the World. There are new diseases abroad in the land. Crops fail, peasants talk of two-headed snakes, monstrous births. Christianity is at war with itself and attacked by the Ottomans. What you call progress, most people call the Devil's work."

Longstaff shook his head. "Most? A handful shout louder than the rest, trying to drown out the discoveries of men like Copernicus." He paused to wet his throat. "Think of those books we've taken, the secrets being rediscovered. Thousands of years ago it was common knowledge that the Earth was round; the centre hollow, like the drive wheel of a crane." He frowned. "I've heard pygmies run there endlessly. To spin the Earth, you understand. Make sure each region receives its share of the Sun's warmth. Well, I'm not sure about that."

"To Hell with pygmies. When the time comes, the joke's on us. We'll be no more able to defend ourselves than newborn babes." Durant held up the wineskin and shook the dregs into his mouth. "We're drunk, Matthew. Time for sleep."

It was the first time Longstaff had heard the Frenchman say his name. It sounded like he was sneezing: *Mattchew*. Longstaff lay on the deck, looking up at the stars, listening to the slap of the Rhine against the blunt nose of the riverboat. The last thing he saw, before falling asleep, was Durant lying flat on his back, using the saddle for a pillow.

CHAPTER 13

Aurélie was dressed as a serving girl, an artful smear of flour down one cheek. Her long blond hair – a rarity on the streets of Florence – was neatly bound, hidden beneath a coif. She was playing a role, puffing out her cheeks and gormlessly moving her jaw from side to side.

She walked along Via dell'Agnolo, past stalls and dyers' workshops. The street was crowded with people returning from a hanging outside the Porta alla Croce, but Aurélie wasn't going so far. She strode past the open gate of a hostelry and made a pantomime of having forgotten her errand. No one appeared to notice. She walked back and ducked inside, lingering a moment in the shadows.

A baby cried nearby, the sound drifting through an open window and Aurélie heard a woman's calming lullaby. The tune was hauntingly familiar, transporting Aurélie back to her father's house, thirteen years old, lying awake with tears streaming down her cheeks. Her sister had attempted to sooth her with the same soft melody.

The words eluded her, but other memories returned with powerful clarity. Running away from her father's house, certain she'd rather die than marry the man he had chosen for her. A mad dash through the city to Giacomo Vescosi's home.

Vescosi had tried to send her back. He'd taught her to read and she used her learning against him, anticipating his arguments and countering with quotes from Pliny and Cicero, until he was forced to concede defeat.

The woman hushed her baby. A potboy sat in one corner of the inn's courtyard, grinding a length of hellebore into fine sneezing powder. Aurélie approached him quietly, watching the slow, methodical movements. She cleared her throat and the boy jumped, scattering his careful work. Aurélie stifled a laugh.

"I'm sent to find someone. Do you have a Strasbourg merchant here by the name of Michaelis?"

The lad looked confused. Aurélie had spoken too well, her accent a poor match for her modest appearance.

"Come with me, signora."

The ground floor taproom was full of merchants, adventurers and whores. Aurélie kept her eyes on the floor as she followed the boy's mazy path between tables. He stopped at the foot of a flight of stairs.

"Stay here. I'll see if he wants you."

She saw the grin on his face before he turned and dashed up the stairs, happy he'd found a way to pay her back for her own piece of mischief.

Aurélie stood in the taproom, determined not to make eye contact with the women or their clients. She checked a feeling of compassionate superiority, reminding herself she was no better than them, just luckier. She stole a glance round the room; it was just the kind of place she might run into her father. As a child, Aurélie had pestered him with endless questions, the torrent slowing to a trickle as she saw him repeatedly snatch defeat from the jaws of victory, then blame his luck on God or the turn of a card.

Aurélie felt eyes on her body – a man in a faded green *lucco* was staring at her. He had fine features, but his hair was thin, bound at the neck with a scrap of cloth. A whore approached, he brushed her aside without looking up.

Aurélie tried to warn him off with a look, feeling relieved when the boy beckoned to her from the top of the stairs.

She paused in the doorway while her eyes adjusted to the dim light. The young merchant sat behind a desk, in a small parlour busy with over-stuffed furniture. An ugly dog lay on the floor beside him, asleep on a thick blanket.

"Who do you come from, girl?"

Aurélie curtseyed, more for the potboy's benefit than this merchant. "Signor Bartolli, but perhaps I have made a mistake."

Aurélie caught the flash of surprise on his face. "To err is human," he said.

She smiled. "To forgive divine," she completed the password.

Michaelis grunted, in command of himself once more. "I hope Signor Bartolli doesn't think I'm going to feed you," he waved the potboy away. "Come in, young lady. What can I do for you?"

Aurélie waited for the door to close behind her. Michaelis was dressed in silk, a fur-lined cape drawn casually around his shoulders. Dark eyes danced with intelligence beneath a full head of glossy brown hair.

"Giacomo sends his greetings."

"You can tell him from me: it's a coward's trick to send a woman."

Aurélie took a deep breath. Giacomo had told her what to expect, warned her that offering explanations would only make it worse.

"A coward's trick," she wondered aloud, "or inspired misdirection?" She smiled and turned her back on the merchant, hitching up her long skirt to remove a thin book and packet of letters.

"*De Re Anatomica* by Mateo Colombo," she kept her voice low. Possession of the book was enough to get them both killed. "Banned last year, condemned to the *Indices Librorum Prohibitorum*." She held up the letters. "For our friends in Strasbourg. Giacomo has written a text for their printing press, denouncing the Pope's recent decision to compel booksellers to keep records of their customers."

Michaelis walked to a heavy travelling chest, tilted it back, releasing a hidden spring. He removed a packet of papers and passed them to Aurélie. "There's a letter from Bacon. I was in England before Christmas. The rest I collected from the printer in Strasbourg. He doesn't like being used as the Otiosi's postmaster."

Aurélie flicked through the letters and frowned. "Nothing from Lübeck?"

"Not this time."

"And your journey, Signor Michaelis? Nothing out of the ordinary as you travelled south?"

"Usual irritations. Bribes and paperwork, permits, bills of lading. Nothing out of the ordinary, until you."

Aurélie ignored him. "I hope that trade has been good."

He laughed. "I have several hundredweight of wool at the port, and the best offer I've had won't even cover my expenses."

"I am sorry to hear that."

He waved a hand. "All part of the game. Trade is fine, thank you for asking. Or it would be if I could find someone who wanted two dozen wheel-lock muskets."

Aurélie blinked.

"I purchased them for Duke Cosimo. Lugged them all the way from Suhl, and now the pompous fool says he won't buy anything made north of the Alps," he shook his head.

"The first Cosimo will be turning in his grave."

"I'm sorry for your trouble," Aurélie bent to hide the packet of Strasbourg letters. "A gentleman should turn his back."

"God be praised, I'm just a humble merchant."

Aurélie's nerve was steady, but she found herself blushing.

"I'll send word before I leave the city," Michaelis was grinning at her. "Unless you'd like to renew our acquaintance?"

Aurélie smoothed the front of her dress and stared at him.

"No?" Michaelis shrugged. "You know where to find me if you change your mind."

Aurélie walked away quickly. *Bastard.* She was risking her life for the Otiosi, just as much as he was. She turned off the broad thoroughfare, thinking to take a short-cut home. Still an hour before they rang the bell for curfew, but the sky above the city was slate grey, throwing the alleyway into shadow. There was no one here, no sound but the gentle slap of her closed sandals against the cobblestones. She heard an echo and a second set of steps keeping pace with her own. Aurélie walked faster, slowing as she reached the end of the alley and looked back over her shoulder. A shape at the far end, a flash of colour. Green perhaps, but the light was poor. She blinked and it was gone.

She thought of the heretical letters hidden beneath her skirts, heart thumping against her ribs. The fish market was near. Out of her way, but she'd find people there. She almost ran along the cobblestones, heard the vendors before she saw them, packing up their wares. Aurélie turned at random between the empty stalls. Men offered her discounts on the last of their stock. She allowed them to draw her into conversation, scanning the meagre crowd while they sang the virtues of whitefish and gudgeon.

She saw no sign of the man in green, nothing to account for her fear. Nothing, she told herself, except her own imagination and Giacomo's tales of fire and pain. Still, she lingered among the fish longer than she should have done, reluctant to re-enter the warren of streets.

The Palace of the Bargello flanked one side of the marketplace, a dozen men of the nightwatch clustered in front, swapping jokes as they waited for the curfew bell.

Giacomo had told her a dozen times; behave as if you have nothing to hide. The battlements on top of the high walls were decorated with corpses. Thieves, bankrupts and sodomites reduced to torn skin, lank hair and decaying flesh. A deterrent for the townsfolk and food for crows. Aurélie fixed a bright smile on her face, before approaching the guardsmen.

"I seem to have lost track of time." A crow interrupted his meal at the sound of her voice and idly flapped its wings. "I wonder if you could escort me home. It's not far. It will only take a minute."

The men made jokes, but Aurélie had picked well. Out of sight of his fellows the young watchman dropped his swagger and led her swiftly through the narrow streets, taking his leave with the courtesies due a lady.

The gate lay open; Giacomo believed in the wisdom of hiding in plain sight. Each night, the servants simply swung it closed. Dropping the latch, Aurélie leant against the solid oak planks.

Marco appeared in the courtyard. A friendly, gap-toothed face to settle her heart. The cook's boy was nine years old.

"Where have you been? The old man's been pacing in his room for hours."

Aurélie ruffled his dark hair. "And how would you know?"

Marco realized he had no ready answer and scampered away across the courtyard.

Aurélie took a deep breath before entering the house. She'd begged Giacomo to let her play an active role in the Otiosi and didn't want him to think she'd been jumping at shadows. The scriptorium lay on the second floor, but she heard him clear his throat as she passed the reception room on the first.

He sat at the writing desk, quill nonchalantly to hand. "Is that you already, Aurélie?"

She gave her warmest smile. "Marco told me you were upstairs. He thought he heard you there, pacing up and down."

Giacomo Vescosi only used the reception room for visitors and he was enough of a fixture in the city that he didn't have to entertain more than twice a year. He set down the quill. "Would you blame me? I might have sent you to your death. A thought like that weighs heavy on an old heart."

She told him about her adventure, but omitting the man in green and her attack of nerves. She could bear Giacomo's lectures well enough, but not the fear he suffered on her behalf.

He was a natural teacher; she a gifted pupil, who never flinched when confronted with notions her upbringing had trained her to avoid. She knew how much pleasure he'd taken in teaching her, leading her gently into the world of ideas.

She placed the packet of letters on the writing table. "Still nothing from Lübeck."

He nodded to an armchair. "Our agent there knows how to contact me directly. He has no need to send anything via Strasbourg."

"We should have heard by now. How hard can it be to rob a sixteen year-old Dane?"

"Patience, Aurélie. The Frenchman doesn't know how important the palimpsest might be. He has no reason to share your sense of urgency."

"But is he trustworthy? He's bound to read it. What if he realizes the significance?"

"Then he'll redouble his efforts to see it reaches me," Giacomo smiled. "Durant isn't motivated by money. He shares our interests."

Aurélie looked through the silk drapes, into the courtyard below. "It's the waiting that's so hard."

"The Devil's Library has driven men mad. It's a dream, Aurélie," he smiled, "and will come as a dream does, in its own good time. Or not."

Aurélie grimaced. Since Giacomo had told her about the Library, she lay awake for hours each night, imagining the knowledge it contained as an explosion of light, people walking in giddy disbelief towards a better future.

"Did the merchant have any other message for me?"

Aurélie shook her head, flushing slightly as she remembered the way Michaelis had looked at her. "The printer is grumbling."

"The printer is always grumbling."

"And it seems Cosimo's taken against products from the north. Michaelis is holding two dozen muskets with no one to sell them to."

"Muskets?" Giacomo steepled his fingers beneath his chin. "Gregorio Spina's brother has a well-known weakness for modern weapons."

Aurélie smiled. Giacomo made a point of studying his enemies, but she hadn't realized his interest extended to their family members.

He examined his left palm, a habit when weighing an argument. "Michaelis has been good to us. It wouldn't hurt to put him in the way of a swift, profitable sale." He looked at his right palm. "Then again, perhaps it's wisest to leave well enough alone. We wouldn't exactly be sending him into the lion's den, but not far off."

"Michaelis can take care of himself," replied Aurélie. "If Spina hears his brother is wasting the family fortune, it might distract him from persecuting innocent men."

Giacomo cocked his head. "And the risk?"

"What risk? Unless you think Michaelis might offer them a spontaneous confession. They don't know who we are."

Giacomo frowned. "Blind luck. We might have been exposed a hundred times," he passed a hand across his eyes. "Your trip through the city has made you excited, Aurélie, and reckless."

She lowered her head. "I'm sorry."

Giacomo tapped her forearm. "When you advise the old, counsel caution. We elders would far rather ignore good advice, than follow bad." His eyes shone with sudden mischief. "Send Marco with a note for Signor Michaelis in the morning."

CHAPTER 14

Longstaff insisted they make for the Gotthard Pass, ignoring Durant's objection that it was far too early in the year. The lower passes would cost them days, even weeks, snaking pointlessly back and forth between the high peaks, and Longstaff had crossed the Gotthard before, seven years ago. Success then had given him confidence.

They set out from Lucerne, hurried along the road by a clutch of wild-eyed preachers, whose imprecations were designed to make them think again before crossing into Catholic lands.

"The time has passed for raising children to become farmers, smiths or merchants!" screamed a rake-thin old man with greasy hair. "Listen, for I speak of Satan's wiles. When he sees men of weak mind, he takes them by storm. When he finds them dauntless, he becomes as cunning as a fox. He has a thousand ways to deceive!"

"With God's permission you mean," said Durant.

The old man flushed. "Naturally, I mean with God's permission."

Durant crowed in triumph. Longstaff would have preferred the Frenchman to follow his own policy of ignoring doomsayers and the endless tales of damnation.

The Alps rose dramatically ahead of them, a forbidding white wall, bearded by a mass of pine trees. Longstaff put a hand on Durant's forearm and brought him to a halt. In one smooth movement, he drew the musket from Martlesham's saddle, lit a match from the tinderbox and touched thin flame to the firing pan. Thirty paces away, a plump rabbit collapsed onto the hard earth.

"Supper," said Longstaff. "Hopefully we'll get a couple more before nightfall. The way ahead looks unlikely to provide."

That evening, they made an uncomfortable camp beside an abandoned mine. Durant stared at the charred meat. "I was in Limoges not long ago; they do the most extraordinary things with rabbit. Stews a man might kill for."

"Eat," said Longstaff. "You'll need your strength tomorrow."

The pair were silent as they led the horses across broken terrain. The distant peaks disappeared into cloud as a freezing rain began to fall. Then the sky disappeared as the forest grew thick around them. In the evening gloom, strange rock formations loomed out at them from among the trees. The two men sheltered under overhanging rocks. Rain had soaked the bundle of firewood strapped to Martlesham's saddle and it took them an hour to build a fire. A pathetic thing, hardly worth the effort, which spat and gave off precious little warmth.

They put on heavy blankets the following morning, wrapping Sparrow and the horses against the bitter weather. The rain became snow, obscuring the shepherds' path. Longstaff took the lead, beginning to regret his foolhardiness. He'd been travelling south to north the last time he passed this way and nothing looked familiar. They left the trees behind and scrambled across loose stones, exposed to the full fury of the elements. Durant fell. He rolled onto his back and lay panting. "We have to turn back."

Longstaff shook his head. "We'll reach the pass tomorrow."

"And tonight? We'll freeze to death."

They built a crude shelter against the worst of the wind and snow, and huddled together between the animals. The darkness was absolute. Longstaff could feel the Frenchman's breath on his face, smell the fear and anger. *Please God, let me be right.* If they didn't reach the pass tomorrow, the mountain would kill them both.

They woke before dawn, chilled to the bone, stamping their feet while they waited for the morning light. Durant's face was a mask of barely controlled fury. Longstaff managed a wan smile in reply. He led the way, switch-backing up the steep slopes and squeezing between giant crags as the wind whipped snow into his face. When he lost the feeling in his cheeks, he tore two long strips from a blanket, handed one to Durant, and wrapped the other around his head, leaving only a thin slit for the eyes. The Frenchman followed his example.

Winter blizzards had turned the path into treacherous, hard-packed ice. Durant slipped twice, the second time heavily. He stared up at Longstaff. "You've killed us, you bastard, and I still don't know where we're going. What a damned stupid way to die."

"There," roared Longstaff. He seized Durant beneath the arm, half-carried him into the lee of a huge stone and pointed at a tall cross, carved deep in the surface. "They say a shepherd begged the Devil to build the first bridge here," he shouted over the wind – a great wave of relief giving him renewed strength. "As his price, Lucifer demanded the first soul to cross. The shepherd tried to trick him, driving a goat from one side to the other. The Devil grew angry and picked up this stone, intending to destroy the bridge. An old woman appeared, marked the stone with a cross and the Devil no longer had the strength to lift it." He jerked a broad thumb over his shoulder. "The Gotthard Pass. Take a look."

The Frenchman did as he asked. When he pulled his head back into the shelter of the stone, his face was white. "You've lost your reason, Longstaff."

"The shepherds promise their headman to rebuild the bridge whenever it gets too run down, and the headman promises his lord to have it rebuilt in stone, and somehow, between all the promises, nothing ever happens."

Durant looked back the way they'd come.

Longstaff grinned. "If we turn back, we die. The mountain is kinder on the far side."

Durant spat. "You first."

Longstaff shook his head. "Sparrow goes first."

The bridge was as wide as a man is long, more ice than wood. If there had once been handrails, the elements had long since sent them tumbling down into the gorge. The wind raced out of the depths, dementedly.

Longstaff and Durant put blindfolds on the horses, and watched as Sparrow dragged her belly across the frigid wood. She was a brave, sure-footed dog, but Longstaff was certain the wind would pitch her into the abyss. He turned away, unable to watch. The seconds crept past as if they, too, had been wrapped in ice. "She's made it!" shouted Durant. "She's safe on the other side."

Longstaff led Martlesham onto the bridge, holding him by the bridle. He would rather have kept his distance, but the horse needed to feel that he was near. The wind tore at them. Despite the cold, he was bathed in sweat. He edged forwards, drawing the horse in his wake. He looked down, and swayed dangerously in place, saw himself falling. Far below, the walls of the gorge were only a few feet apart.

He couldn't move, his will unchained by the image of his mangled body. He forced himself to look up. The big grey tossed his head and Longstaff pulled savagely at the bridle. It was enough to return him to himself and start them moving again. He reached the far side and sank to his knees.

Durant claimed to have no clear memory of leading his horse across the planks, only vague impressions; short, quick steps, toes probing for treachery, a wave of relief when he felt the solid earth beneath his feet.

They hurried down from the pass, the wind doing its best to slice the flesh from their bones. The descent was forgiving and they made good time, slipping beneath the snowline before sunset. They found a nook of sheltered rock beside a stream of racing snow-melt. Longstaff drank his fill of the cold water. The horses were tired and angry. Only Sparrow seemed unaffected by the day's exertions.

While Durant built a fire, Longstaff rubbed the horses down. He skinned the last rabbit and set it to cook before wrapping a blanket around his shoulders. The flames cast little heat at this altitude. He was cold, the muscles in his legs quivered with exhaustion. Without thinking, he reached for his sword, took a whetstone from his pocket and began sharpening the blade.

He was back in Italy and could no longer put off thinking about the task ahead. One more book to steal, before heading to Florence and their rendezvous with the Otiosi leader.

Longstaff looked up. By the weak light of the fire, he could only see the sharp vertical lines of Durant's face. "You do speak Italian?"

"Well enough."

Longstaff grunted. He'd been eighteen years old when he met Il Medeghino in the foothills of the Alps and spoke the language like a native. Had he been in search of adventure or a home? Italy's most notorious general had answered both needs, claiming to see echoes of his own younger self in the rootless Englishman. Longstaff had been flattered, taking vicarious pride in Il Medeghino's savage reputation.

It had taken the Battle of Marciano to break the spell. Even then, Longstaff had nearly stayed to follow the bloody path marked out for him by his mentor. Now he was going back, of his own free will, in pursuit of a book, and a house in England he hadn't seen in over twenty years.

Longstaff put the sword to one side. After what they'd been through together, Durant deserved to know what lay in wait. "The book we're seeking is written in Latin," he said abruptly, "bound in red leather with an ivory panel of St. Christopher carrying Christ across a river." He picked a stick out of the fire and scored a series of sooty lines on the flat stones; a terrified child, fingers tangled in the long beard of an old man. He used the heel of his boot to scrub the picture into a dull smudge.

Durant inclined his head. "Thank you. I appreciate trust."

Longstaff thought of the soldiers who had put their trust in him at Marciano. Simple men, caught in the rip-tide of war. He could have borne their deaths – soldiers died, after all – but Il Medeghino had stripped even those poor souls of the honour a man earns when he falls in battle.

Durant boned the rabbit, dividing the scant meat between them. Longstaff put aside a few morsels for Sparrow as the Frenchman filled a pot with snow and set it to warm on the fire.

"Where is it?"

"The book? In the high hills above Lake Como; in an old fortress at the head of a valley."

Longstaff saw it in his mind's eye; the wild mountains, the fortress crouched at the highest point of a narrow ridge. He imagined Il Medeghino on the ramparts, awaiting the return of his protégé, disdaining the stories told about him in these parts – people buried alive in heaps of manure, thrown into wells and ditches or left to die like dogs.

Durant handed him a hot drink and he took a long draft, then set the cup down for Sparrow, burying cold hands in her fur. How much of his past was he obliged to share with the Frenchman? He didn't want to talk about the daily foraging expeditions, roaming from village to village, stealing every movable object – when there was anything to steal – threshing and grinding when there wasn't.

He remembered waking in his ill-slung tent on the morning of Marciano, the drone of ten thousand men speaking with lowered voices, the ring of chain against armour. The field was a wide, bleak plain. His Italian irregulars had the centre. On the left were two companies of Landsknecht in brightly coloured doublets. To his right, an army of Castilian peasants, forged in the bitter conflict for Granada.

He had ordered his men to raise their deadly forest of pikes, feeling as if he might burst with pride. His men weren't the best in that field, but they were motivated by more than just money. "You'll see, my lord," he'd told Il Medeghino the previous night, "honour and loyalty still count. The battle for Italy's soul will not be decided by foreign mercenaries."

Adrenaline and fear; the calm before battle. Nothing like it in the world. Fifteen thousand men welded into a single, lethal force. The drummer boys and fifers, toying with their instruments to stop the shakes.

Longstaff, in bright cuirass and iron skullcap, had raised his double-handed war-sword and given the order to march. Three thousand men followed him into a hail of musket balls. They stood shoulder-to-shoulder, not a chink between them, setting the ends of their eighteen foot pikes against the hard earth to present a massive spiked wall. The enemy swept down from the hill. The long wooden shafts splintered. Men on both sides shut their eyes to avoid being blinded. Bodies fell to the ground. Survivors drew swords. The men in front fought hand to hand beneath the dipping pikes. Longstaff no longer stood on grass, but on the bodies of fallen soldiers, entrails hanging out, skulls smashed, fingers still twitching on severed arms. But his men were moving forward across the grisly carpet, gathering momentum as they went.

The enemy gave orders to reinforce the line. Longstaff had looked for a response from Il Medeghino's platform. Nothing. A regiment of veteran French came off the hill, hit the line with a mighty crash. Still, Longstaff waited for the blast of trumpets – this couldn't be a mistake – Il Medeghino was a superb tactician.

Trapped, consumed by the grunt and hack of soldiers wedged together, a tangle of limbs and steel, Longstaff remembered his boast – that his native irregulars would decide the battle for Italy's soul – and the smile on Il Medeghino's face. The press of bodies lifted him off the valley floor. He shook his shoulders furiously, jack-knifing his body, desperate to win a few inches of space.

Trumpets.

Now, the Spanish and German mercenaries began to march, shoring up the disintegrating regiment, to win the battle and collect the spoils. Later, Longstaff reckoned the cost of Il Medeghino's deliberate delay at five hundred men. They'd served their purpose; the general had no interest in feeding and quartering part-time soldiers.

Longstaff felt his concentration waver. The day must have taken more out of him than he realized. He heard Sparrow whimper. Feebly, she snapped at the air, before sinking reluctantly onto her forepaws beside the empty cup. Longstaff reached for his sword and toppled to one side, a terrible lethargy pressing him into the hard earth.

The Frenchman loomed above, holding a small phial between his thumb and forefinger. "An infusion of belladonna and mandragora. I haven't killed you, Matthew. I don't envy you the headache you'll have when you finally wake."

He opened Longstaff's jerkin and probed inside the shirt. He found the book, bound to the Englishman's chest, sliced it free with a short knife from his sleeve. Durant rifled through the pages until he found Schoff's letter explaining where to find the next book, then the Otiosi leader. The Frenchman smiled. "Comfortable?"

Longstaff's oath echoed in his head.

Durant pulled him closer to the fire, arranged his limbs beneath blankets. "Nothing personal, but you nearly got us killed today, and I can't stop thinking about our encounter with the Russians. Trailing assassins across half the world?" He shook his head. "No doubt you have your uses on the battlefield. But you're a blunt instrument and Epicurus is too important. I won't allow you to put the recovery of his work at risk."

Longstaff couldn't reply. He wanted to warn Durant that he was making a terrible mistake, but was too tired. He lost the Frenchman's outline, the glow of the fire blurring as consciousness faded away.

CHAPTER 15

Strange dreams racked Longstaff throughout the night. A parade of faces stared at him with loathing; a man he'd cut down in single combat, a farmer he'd dispossessed gathering supplies for Il Medeghino. He saw corpses strewn across a battlefield, heard dogs fighting over the spoils.

Danger! Longstaff fought the unnatural sleep. Sparrow stood at his head, teeth bared at a trio of mountain wolves. They approached together, so close they might have been a single, three-headed beast. Longstaff tore the blankets away. His sword was there – he grabbed the worn hilt and charged on unsteady legs, scattering the scrawny animals; the pickings were slim at this high altitude.

Black fury kept Longstaff running, swinging the *katzbalger* above his head like a club. He imagined his hands around the Frenchman's neck. *Stupid, stupid bastard.*

The wolves disappeared into the grey landscape. Longstaff knelt beside the stream, plunged his face in the icy water. The shock calmed him, but did nothing for the hard ball of anger in his gut, rising to his chest at the thought of Durant. Rage like he hadn't felt since he was a child, ripped from his family, powerless in a cold city on the Baltic coast.

The horses were gone. There was only his sword and bedroll, a piece of black bread wrapped in cloth. Longstaff chewed mechanically. His arms ached with the need to inflict pain. He forced himself to his feet, strapped the bedroll across his back and ran. Sparrow bounded ahead. The dog

was preternaturally sure-footed and Longstaff followed
where she led. He ran for an hour, reaching the fringes of a
forest before his strength gave out. He had to eat. The task
consumed him. He raided birds' nests – cracked the tiny eggs
directly into his mouth – scoured the forest floor for rabbit
trails, unwrapped wire from his sword hilt and fashioned a
noose, suspended a hands-length from the ground. He built
a fire several hundred yards away, then returned to find a
plump doe in the snare.

Slowly, methodically, Longstaff skinned and gutted the
animal, then set it to cook on the fire. There was nothing
to do but wait. He stared into the flames. *What now?*
Durant had the horses; there was no way of overtaking the
Frenchman before he reached Il Medeghino's bolthole.
Did it matter? An image of the house at Martlesham
appeared in his mind; oak doors guarded by the Italian
general. Anger had driven Longstaff south as a young
man, the same ungovernable anger that had seized him
again today. Il Medeghino had placed a high value on his
fury, shaping it into a weapon of devastating violence.
Had Longstaff learned anything in the years since, or had
he simply been running? He stared at the fire – he would
learn the answer soon enough.

It took him two more days to reach the fortress. He
peered up at the ramparts, narrowing his eyes against the
sun. The place was old, built when this desolate crag had
overlooked an important crossroads. Now, it was half
forgotten, a victim of shifting borders and new trade routes.

Longstaff had seen several signs of Durant's passing as
he walked – flattened grass and cold fires, the earth beneath
still holding a trace of warmth. The Frenchman was most
likely dead already, swinging at the end of a rope. Had he

talked before they strung him up? Longstaff pictured his old mentor, waiting with the palimpsest in his hands.

Il Medeghino had fed and sheltered him, taught him to fight, but any debt he owed had long been paid. Longstaff walked up the narrow ridge to the heavy, outer gates.

Faces peered down at him from the top of the wall. "New recruit?"

Longstaff raised empty hands. "Il Medeghino and I are old friends."

The men on the wall wore iron skullcaps. One of them was horribly disfigured, his face a web of puckering scars. "The General doesn't have friends."

"That's what he'd have told you."

All the men laughed, except scarface. Longstaff spat — not even through the gates and already making enemies.

Sparrow flattened herself against the ground and set up a low growl as three guards stepped out through a narrow door, cut into the huge gate. Scarface, with two others. They scanned the bleak landscape, though there wasn't a scrap of cover for a thousand yards, and cast a wary eye at Sparrow.

"Bitch shows a tooth and I'll slit her throat," Scarface held out his hand. "Sword."

Longstaff unbuckled the *katzbalger*. "I'll want it back."

Scarface stepped uncomfortably close. "Strip."

The man's breath was foul and Longstaff fought the urge to take a backward stride. He took off his cavalryman's coat and heavy jerkin, shivering in the thin air while the men searched him with expert fingers. Scarface confiscated the long stiletto from Longstaff's boot, the blade strapped to the inside of his forearm and the knife inside his shirt.

"Get dressed. The dog stays here."

One of the younger men produced a short length of rope. Longstaff let them bind his hands, followed obediently across a killing ground between the outer and inner walls. A low gate swung open; Scarface pushed him through, into a courtyard full of shouting, jeering soldiers.

A man swung a great-sword as if it were a rapier. He was taller than Longstaff by a head and clearly proud of his monstrous physique. A smaller man ducked beneath his own raised sword, using it as a shield to deflect the giant's blow.

Longstaff stared at the uneven contest. The second man was just a boy – gasping for breath, bleeding from superficial wounds, hopelessly overmatched. He should have yielded. Instead, he threw himself forward. Belatedly, Longstaff realised he'd interrupted an initiation ceremony.

The giant parried easily. From habit, Longstaff examined his technique. Did he show the young man too much of his right shoulder? Perhaps, but the weakness was barely perceptible.

When it came, the end was brutally swift. The giant stepped inside the young man's flailing sword and crashed a fist into the side of his head, disengaged and leant on the crossguard of his great-sword. His victim collapsed in a heap, blood running in a thin stream from one ear.

The crowd screamed at the young swordsman. Two hundred men, Longstaff guessed. Perhaps a few less, but it was always wise to estimate high – another lesson he'd learned from Il Medeghino – mostly young novices come to learn their trade at the hands of Italy's acknowledged master.

The beaten man tried to lever himself to his feet, but his arms gave way and he rolled onto his back, blowing bubbles of blood and saliva.

The crowd groaned. Scarface jabbed a sword in the small of Longstaff's back, pushing him into the circle of men.

"General," he shouted, adopting the tone of a man about to deliver a joke. "This person claims to be your friend."

The old man had aged; that was Longstaff's first thought, as he waited for the laughter to die down. Il Medeghino sat alone on a high platform, a blanket round his shoulders. He wore a padded jerkin and felt skull cap, but the blue eyes were just as Longstaff remembered, washed of any human quality.

"Gottlieb," he said quietly, "that person *is* a friend of mine. Matthew Longstaff, the Hero of Marciano. Cut his bonds."

Longstaff was probably the only man present who knew the title was meant to wound as well as praise. Low whispers ran among the men. Il Medeghino stood, letting the blanket fall to the ground. He'd grown thin. Even from a distance, Longstaff could detect the sharp points of his shoulders. The general wore his breeches too high, as if refusing to see how his powerful body had wasted.

Longstaff flexed stiff fingers. "It has been a long time."

"Yes, it has, Matthew," replied Il Medeghino. "Eight years since Marciano." He pointed at the young swordsman, twitching feebly on the ground. Two men jogged forwards, carrying a small brazier between them. The first had a pair of tongs in his free hand. The second held a milking pail filled to the brim with slurry and wore a short stick tucked into the waistband of patched, yellow breeches.

The young man's body was covered in sweat and blood, ugly welts already darkening into bruises. As Longstaff watched, the man in yellow breeches removed an ornate cross from the brazier, pressed it against the boy's bicep while the second man held him down. Smoke rose and the smell of burning flesh drifted on the breeze.

Il Medeghino waited for the screaming to end. "I know Roberto would count it an honour to have the Hero of Marciano complete the formalities."

He knew how much Longstaff had loathed these ceremonies. Typical of the old bastard to offer honour and insult in the same breath, and set him a test. Had he come here in friendship? Longstaff took the pail from the man in yellow breeches. He plucked the stick from his waistband, kicked the initiate in the stomach, propped his mouth open and poured the slurry down his throat.

The boy soldier rolled into a ball to defend himself against stomach cramps, before flopping onto his elbows, retching as his comrades roared their approval.

Il Medeghino invited Longstaff to walk with him on the high ramparts of the fortress. He waved his bodyguard away. Gottlieb stepped back reluctantly, one hand on an axe, suspicion irritating the scars on his face.

Longstaff peered over the parapet. It was a long way down to the valley floor. It would only take a second, a gentle pressure on the old man's back. Il Medeghino seemed to read his mind.

"I had a hand in making you, Matthew," he said, pulling the blanket around his shoulders. "Whatever you're doing here, you haven't come to kill me in cold blood."

Longstaff pretended not to hear. He craned his neck for a glimpse of the men at weapons training in the courtyard.

"Aren't you bored of all this?"

A noise emerged from deep inside the old man and it took Longstaff a moment to realize he was laughing.

"After Marciano they wanted to load me down with another hundredweight of titles. Put me in a palace in Rome. But I am *condottiero*," – he spat onto the flagstones, – "a free soldier, not a courtier. My place is here, even if my bones no longer keep out the cold." He glanced at Longstaff. "Eight years since you disappeared like a thief in the night. You might at least have said goodbye."

"Would you have let me go?"

The old man sighed. His beard was thin, heavily streaked with grey.

"Marciano was your final lesson. You could have risen high, Matthew."

Longstaff shook his head.

"I was an Englishman, fighting over an Italian town, in a battle decided by Spanish infantry. It wasn't my fight."

Il Medeghino shrugged.

"Only kings get to choose why they fight, if they're lucky. I thought you'd have worked it out by now – why you left, I mean – but I see you're as blind as ever."

He must have read the confusion on Longstaff's face. He laughed again, and his laughter became a coughing fit. Scarface hurried forwards but Il Medeghino pushed him away, filling his lungs with ragged gasps of air.

"I'll tell you why you left, Matthew Longstaff. Because you were afraid."

In the Great Hall, whole deer and wild pigs turned on giant spits. Il Medeghino stamped his feet to shake out the cold, while his men arranged themselves at two long trestle tables. The last rays of the setting sun broke against the windows, soaking the room in soft light as Longstaff looked up. A large iron cage – ten by five, half as high as a man standing

– hung from the central beam. Fingers gripped the bars. A face appeared, eyes hollow with fear.

Gottlieb gave up his place at the top table with ill grace. Longstaff sat down beside Il Medeghino. *How much did he already know?*

"Friend of yours?" Longstaff lifted his eyes to the cage, keeping his tone light. "A student behind with his studies?"

Il Medeghino shrugged.

"A foolish thief who should have known better. We found him in my private chambers, rifling through some old books."

Longstaff hid his relief in laughter. "Don't tell me you've learned to read."

Il Medeghino spat.

"The previous owner kept a small library, before he died in tragic circumstances."

Longstaff hooked an elbow around the back of his chair. "The thief managed to get as far as your chambers? Standards must have slipped in the last few years."

"He scaled the walls in the dead of night," the old man shook his head. "There are easier ways to commit suicide."

Il Medeghino said grace, his men clasping hands and lowering their eyes. Two hundred Amens rolled around the room. Novices served meat from huge platters, while pitchers of wine circulated freely.

"Are there no women?" shouted Longstaff over the conversation.

Il Medeghino nodded. It was growing warmer in the Great Hall and he allowed the blanket to fall open on his shoulders.

"My men can whore in their own time."

Once, Longstaff had thought of Il Medeghino as a second father. He noticed the wasted thighs, despite the thick breeches; the old man was rank with the scent of death and he found it hard to keep his pity in check.

"They do what I tell them." Il Medeghino watched the men paw at their plates. "Still means something to bear my mark. Guaranteed work, a chance to get rich." He removed his felt cap and scratched short, grey hair. "But you haven't come looking for work, Matthew, or to keep me up with tales of misspent youth."

Longstaff looked at the cage, high above the cooking fires. Durant would be fit to eat in a couple of days.

"I want that thief," he said. "I've been tracking him for weeks. There's a price on his head."

"I never thought you'd become a manhunter."

Longstaff flushed. "We all have to earn a living."

"We're executing him in the morning," Il Medeghino shrugged. "Take his head with my compliments."

"I need him alive. He's worth nothing dead."

Il Medeghino stared at him. "You wouldn't deny an old man the pleasure of killing a common thief."

"Name your price," said Longstaff. "I have no time to bargain."

"No time to share a meal with an old friend?" Il Medeghino pushed his plate away. "These days, I have to remind myself what it means to be young. I will not have women here and punish drunkenness. Some of the men think I act out of jealousy, though they'd never say that to my face." He looked at Longstaff. "I saw you earlier, running the rule over my men. Tell me what you think of them."

Longstaff forced a smile.

"What do I think of men careless enough to let a thief break into your private chambers?" He shook his head. "A woman of ninety could defend this place with a broomstick."

A tall warrior rose to his feet – Longstaff recognized him from the initiation ceremony – and tossed a thick slice of meat at the cage above. Durant's face appeared, pressed against the bars.

"Your last meal, Frenchman. Chew it well."

Don't react, begged Longstaff silently, imagining Durant's confusion at seeing him in the place of honour beside Il Medeghino. For a moment, the two book-finders made eye contact. *Keep silent, you stubborn bastard, or you'll get us both killed.*

"My champion, Gattuso," Il Medeghino gestured with his cup. "You saw him fight. Tell me what you thought."

"I saw him play with a novice, which is hardly the same. He seemed competent."

"Competent?" The old man chuckled. "Could you beat him?"

Longstaff spread his hands.

"I hope I never have to find out."

"Matthew," said the old man fondly. "I don't know whether to kiss you or kill you. So I'll let fate decide, and provide my men with some entertainment into the bargain."

Longstaff should have known. He imagined himself in England, mounted on a fine horse, approaching the doors of his ancestral home. He pointed at the cage.

"I need them both, the man and the book he wanted."

"Why?"

"God knows," Longstaff shook his head. "Just trying to fulfil the terms of my contract."

"What's a book to me? I'm a man of the world, Matthew, not a monk. It will be a small price to pay for the pleasure of seeing you fight again. Tomorrow morning."

Longstaff looked at Gattuso. The huge warrior was already on his second plate of meat, chewing with his mouth open, head thrown back in laughter, half a dozen men competing to pay him compliments.

Longstaff closed his eyes. "If he kills me, see that someone gives my dog a home."

CHAPTER 16

In a small chamber off the Great Hall, Longstaff commended his soul to God. No longer the young fighter he'd been eight years ago, could he claim to have gained in experience what he'd lost in speed and power? He still practised with the sword, but it had been years since he'd last fought a duel.

He wasn't risking his life for Durant's worthless skin. He climbed stiffly to his feet, thinking of the house at Martlesham, of his father's shade wandering restlessly through rooms inhabited by the man who'd denounced him to King Henry.

He stretched neck and shoulder muscles, forcing thoughts of England to one side. *Fight to win.* If he fought for any other reason, he would lose. Longstaff swung the *katzbalger* until his body was covered in a film of sweat. He was still quick, still strong.

The doors to the Great Hall opened. The tables had been cleared away and sunshine poured in through the high windows. Il Medeghino's men stood in a rough circle around the walls, carrying shields made from wood and ox hide. Longstaff was pleased that none of the spectators wore swords.

Gattuso stood in the centre of the hall, long hair caught in a twist of leather. He wore a sleeveless leather jerkin, so that Il Medeghino's cross-shaped brand was clearly visible on his bicep. He raised a great-sword above his head when he saw Longstaff, and two hundred men cheered.

Gottlieb led Il Medeghino onto a platform beneath the windows. The prospect of the fight appeared to have given the old man new energy. The platform was covered with thick carpets and, as he walked forward to address his men, motes of dust swirled into the morning light.

Longstaff glanced up at the iron cage, swinging gently on its chain. He could see Durant's fingers, the side of his face pressed against the bars.

Il Medeghino raised his arms.

"I lie awake at night thinking about what it means to be the best. A man might think he can paint, until he sees the Sistine Chapel. He might think he can sing, until he hears Maddelena Casulana," he pointed at Longstaff and Gattuso. "These two men are the best I've seen. This is the level you have to reach if you want to bear my mark and win your fortune as *condottieri*." He stared down at his men. "Longstaff fights for the Frenchman, Gattuso for the honour of our brotherhood."

A weak voice interrupted from above. Durant, fingers curled around the bars of the swaying cage.

"None of this is necessary, Il Medeghino. Let me join you; I have skills you can use, medical skills… "

Il Medeghino gestured. Gottlieb unhooked his double-headed axe, threw it in the same fluid motion so it struck the iron cage with a deafening crash. Il Medeghino let his arms fall and the men beat fists against their shields, pounding out a slow tattoo.

Gattuso attacked. Longstaff gave way under the heavy blows. The clash of steel produced roars from the crowd. Gattuso thrust at his stomach, tried to gut him left to right. Longstaff turned the longer sword aside, too slowly. The point of Gattuso's sword pierced his leather jerkin, nicked the flesh above his hip.

The men howled at the sight of blood, faces a blur of hate. Gattuso struck at Longstaff's eyes, etched a thin red line across his cheek. Longstaff barely felt the wound. He countered with a controlled stroke from right to left. Gattuso swatted the blade aside.

Longstaff stepped back. He flexed his shoulders as long dormant appetites demanded satisfaction. He swung in a wide arc − sword-arm moving with the old fluency − expected to bury the blade in Gattuso's side. The giant countered easily. Longstaff pressed him against the shield wall.

Gattuso seized an unwary novice by the hair and threw him at the Englishman.

Longstaff stumbled, grabbed at the novice, and felt the boy's hot blood across his face. Gattuso shook his sword free, neatly reversing the swing. Longstaff stepped backwards, tripped on the corpse, and fell awkwardly to the stone floor.

"Move!" Even above the din made by Il Medeghino's men, Longstaff heard Durant's yell of warning. He rolled to his right as Gattuso's great-sword struck the stone floor. It sent up a shower of sparks. For a moment the champion seemed to lose sight of his opponent.

Gattuso charged, attempting to cut a hole in the Englishman's side. He shifted his weight from right to left and carved a broad, backhand stroke in the air.

Longstaff ducked beneath the whistling blade, countered with a wild swipe, his brain working as hard as his sword arm. Gattuso always attacked on the left. Yesterday, he'd shown the young initiate too much right shoulder. Did he have a blind spot, a shadow at the edge of his vision?

Longstaff disengaged, assumed the formal *en garde* position and held his head perfectly still. Only his eyes moved, tracing a tight triangle from Gattuso's eyes, to his left and right shoulders.

As he looked right, so the tip of Gattuso's sword followed. Longstaff feinted to strike from that direction. Gattuso moved to counter a blow that never fell, overextending himself. Longstaff's lighter blade came whistling down from the other side, to tear a shallow furrow along Gattuso's bicep.

Longstaff stood in the eye of the storm. The mob cheered at Gattuso's blood. They'd forgotten he was their man, seeing nothing but a fight to the death.

Longstaff stepped forward as Gattuso lunged. It was a clumsy stroke, easily turned. He remembered something Il Medeghino had told him many years before. There is no irresistible thrust, no reason why a fight between two well-matched swordsmen cannot go on forever, except that everything must have its end. The man who lives is the one who keeps fate at bay for a fraction of a second longer than his adversary.

Finally, Longstaff's blood broke out into the old fateful song of death and violence. He retreated smoothly beneath a sequence of heavy blows, as Gattuso tried to bludgeon him into submission. The crowd jeered, but Longstaff was moving fluidly now, finding inspiration in the simplest strokes. He saw Gattuso's eyes dilate with fear.

Longstaff swayed to one side as Gattuso's blade whistled past. He went on the attack, favouring his adversary's stronger side. The giant seemed unnerved as he tried to anticipate the moment when Longstaff would feint and reverse, and his concentration wavered as their two blades came together. Longstaff flicked his wrist and the *katzbalger* leapt over the great-sword, cutting a bloody line across Gattuso's forearm.

The sword began to slip from Gattuso's fingers. Desperately, he tried to pass it to his left hand, but the point of Longstaff's blade lay at his throat. The crowd fell into silence.

"On your knees."

Gattuso's sword fell to the stone floor with a crash. Longstaff drew a bead of blood with the point of the *katzbalger*. As Gattuso closed his eyes in submission, he looked across at Il Medeghino.

The *condottiero* climbed slowly to his feet and walked to the edge of the platform. His voice was soft.

"Let him live."

Longstaff tightened his grip on the sword and wondered if the old bastard would have done the same for him.

"Don't make me ask twice, Matthew."

Longstaff stepped back. Two hundred fighting men stared at him, hate in their eyes. Il Medeghino climbed down from his platform. He walked round the circle of men, before coming to a stop in front of Gattuso.

"My God, but you motherless sons of bastards have a stretch of work ahead of you." He prodded his champion in the chest. Gattuso, twice the old man's size and less than half his age, hung his head. "Have you thanked him?" Il Medeghino spat. "Have you thanked Signor Longstaff for sparing your life?"

Gattuso stiffened, the bloody arm hanging uselessly at his side.

"Do it," commanded Il Medeghino.

Gattuso raised his head. "Thank you," he muttered.

Il Medeghino held out his hand for the *katzbalger*. Longstaff hesitated. The crowd was growing restless; they'd wanted his blood.

"Give it to me."

"As you wish."

Il Medeghino stared at the blade a moment, and then raised it over his head. The men quietened.

"Which of you can tell me when the fight was won?" Silence. "Step forward if you think you can replicate the Englishman's achievement." Il Medeghino looked at Longstaff. "Not one of them."

He reversed his grip on the sword. Moving with the speed of a snake, he buried the point in Gattuso's throat. The giant's eyes widened in surprise. Blood ran in a waterfall down his jerkin, the sword quivering beneath his chin.

Il Medeghino turned. "I train *condottieri* here. Men who bear my mark are not bound by skill or strength. It is victory or death. Any man who can bear the shame of defeat is in the wrong place. Pack up and go back to your pox-ridden villages, spend your nights snivelling into your mother's tits. You won't be missed."

He was in a fine rage now. Longstaff lowered his head, watching from the corner of his eye as the old man roared at his men, then chased them out of the Great Hall, away from the bloody figure on the flagstones.

Il Medeghino turned to Longstaff. "The thief is yours. I suggest you take him and go."

The hall was empty apart from the old man and his bodyguard. The cage was suspended from the high rafters; the chain looped over and secured to a shoulder-height bracket fixed to the wall.

Longstaff looked at Gottlieb. The bodyguard stood his ground, arms folded across his chest. Longstaff sighed as he uncoiled the heavy loops of chain, set his feet and took the weight. Still weary from the fight, his shoulders burned as he slowly lowered the cage, hand over hand. Il Medeghino frowned – Longstaff cursed; the old bastard had always said his better nature would get him killed. He released his hold and the cage hit the flagstones with a deafening crash. Durant groaned in pain, slumped against the bars. His clothes were torn, filthy with dried blood. Longstaff's expression of satisfaction was not wholly unfeigned.

Gottlieb spat on the flagstones before producing a key and opening the cage door. He dragged Durant out by the hair.

"Put a gag in his mouth," said Longstaff, "bind his hands."

Gottlieb bared his teeth, scars puckering in anger.

"Do it," snapped Il Medeghino.

"As well as you bound me," added Longstaff. He didn't think Durant was stupid enough to show pleasure at his sudden change in fortune, but was in no mood to take risks.

"Your book," Il Medeghino placed the volume in Longstaff's hands. It was big – three lengths of a man's hand by two – Longstaff tucked it under his arm before turning back to Durant.

The Frenchman stood with his head bowed, dark hair obscuring the narrow face. Longstaff pushed him through the doors of the Great Hall. Il Medeghino accompanied them across the courtyard, past the fighting men. Gottlieb unlocked the door in the outer gate, took his master's arm and helped him over the step.

Sparrow was waiting for them on the narrow track. She bared her teeth at Longstaff, furious at having been left outside so long. Il Medeghino smiled. "Good-looking animal. Surprised she puts up with you."

"So is she, most of the time."

Il Medeghino put a hand on his shoulder.

"God has been kind to let me see you one last time. I loved you like a son, you know," he paused. "I am sick, Matthew."

Longstaff didn't know where to look. "How bad is it?"

"You have eyes in your head. The doctors say weeks – months, if I'm lucky. Not enough time to make up for a lifetime of sin. The priests are desperate to forgive me, but I was never scared of life, and I'm damned if I will run from death," he exhaled. "I don't blame you for leaving after Marciano. I know you didn't come back because you wanted to see me, but I'm grateful anyway. Not many fathers are so fortunate."

Longstaff locked his jaw against a sudden swell of sadness, whether for the old *condottiero* or his own lost innocence, he wasn't sure.

"Go," said Il Medeghino. "I need my rest."

Longstaff turned on his heel. He didn't want the old man to see the pity in his eyes. He drew his sword, pressing the point into the small of Durant's back. They marched in single file along the narrow ridge, the hem of Longstaff's coat kicking up dust behind.

When they dropped down from the ridge and were no longer visible from the high walls of the fortress, Durant turned and mutely begged to be released from his gag. Longstaff knocked him off his feet. "Take me to the horses."

The Frenchman stumbled through a forest of stunted pines to a wide clearing. Charcoal burners had stayed here once – Longstaff could see the remains of tall, triangular kilns. Beyond them, the two horses were hobbled in the shade of an oak tree.

Durant's horse snorted with pleasure when he saw his master. Martlesham reserved his welcome for Sparrow.

The Frenchman had left his oversize pack in one of the kilns. He dragged it out with bound hands, poking around among the contents until he found a scalpel. He did not seek permission to cut the ropes and pull the gag out of his mouth. He turned to Longstaff and spread his hands. "I made a mistake," he said. "I admit it. You have every right… "

Longstaff did not let him finish. He swung his fist in a flat arc, knocked Durant down, then emptied his pack onto the ground.

"Mine," he shouted, waving the book he'd taken from Ivan the Terrible. "Where's the palimpsest?"

Durant probed his jaw with a fingertip. "Safe."

Longstaff kicked his chest. The Frenchman caught his boot in both hands, twisted the ankle over on itself, throwing Longstaff to the spongy floor.

"You still need me," he said nervously. "I thought I was dead. Why didn't you tell me you and the *condottiero* were friends?"

"Friends?" Longstaff climbed slowly to his feet, murder in his eyes.

Durant raised his scalpel. Longstaff stalked him across the clearing. Durant threw the sharp blade onto the forest floor, ripping his shirt open.

"Kill me, then. You've earned the right, though only a damn Englishman would kill a man hours after saving his life."

He looked ridiculous, leaves in his hair, puffed up with wounded pride, pink from so many hours above the roasting fire. Longstaff couldn't help but smile.

"Only a Frenchman would drug a man and leave him for dead on a mountaintop."

Durant looked down, muttering, "and only an Englishman would accept a drink from a Frenchman after he's been stupid enough to share a piece of information he should have kept to himself!"

"You're blaming me?" Longstaff threw back his head and roared with laughter.

Durant raised his hands in protest. Then he began to laugh. "God, that hurts," he lifted a hand to his chest.

"Can you ride?"

"Give me a moment," Durant dropped to his knees and began to search his scattered possessions. Longstaff peered over the Frenchman's shoulder. He saw a Coat of Seven Colours, phials with liquids in various, unnatural hues, herbs bound with ribbon, powders in thin leather bags and pastes in tiny glass jars.

Durant saw Longstaff's incredulity. "Powdered pearls," he nudged a leather bag with his boot, and pointed at the phials and jars. "Ground hellebore, roasted bean straw, arnica cream, charas." He opened his shirt, applying a translucent salve to the bruises on his chest. Longstaff inspected his own injuries; a lump the size of an egg on the back of his head, a shallow cut on his cheek and a more serious wound above his hip, which oozed blood whenever he moved.

"Let me have a look," said Durant. "The least I can do."

Longstaff lay on his side and allowed Durant to clean his wound. The Frenchman sewed the edges together in a tidy line, then stood back to admire his handiwork. "Nine stitches and another small scar for your collection."

Longstaff shrugged. He looked at the Coat of Seven Colours. "Does it work?"

"Keep me safe from plague, you mean?" Durant smiled. "I don't believe in magic, Matthew. It's a uniform." He pointed at a dozen pink lozenges, wrapped in fine cheesecloth. "Do you know what these are?"

Longstaff shook his head.

"You will certainly have heard of the man who made them: Michel de Nostradamus?"

"Of course," said Longstaff, looking more closely "are these..."

"His famous rose pills?" finished Durant. He placed one in the palm of Longstaff's hand. "An ounce of sawdust from a fresh, green Cypress tree; six ounces of Iris of Florence; three ounces of cloves; three drams of tiger lily; six of lignaloes. The ingredients are ground into a powder, then mixed with the petals of three hundred roses, but mind they must be picked before dawn," Durant seemed to quote from memory. "Shape the paste into lozenges no bigger than a thumbnail, dry thoroughly and store in a sealed place. In case of plague, keep one on the tongue at all times."

"Do they work?" asked Longstaff eagerly.

Durant raised both eyebrows.

CHAPTER 17

Never in his wildest dreams had Mathern Schoff imagined that Spina would treat him as a messenger from God. The lawyer had ridden post to Bruges. Tired and dirty, he'd gone straight to the Dominican Monastery there and demanded to see the Abbot. He mentioned the name of his secret master, and the whole machinery of the Order was placed at his disposal. Schoff had travelled through Catholic France by coach – an arduous journey over ill-made roads – then wasted two days in Marseille, pacing back and forth in a monk's cell while the brothers arranged his passage to Florence.

He was tired and hungry when he finally arrived at the huge Dominican monastery of Santa Maria Novella. A monk received him at the gates.

"Where is Gregorio Spina. Is he here or in Rome?"

The monk grinned. Simple minded, realised Schoff, biting back a curse. More unnecessary delay. How far behind were the two book-thieves? A second monk appeared, older than the first, with the first flecks of grey at his temples. "What can we do for you?"

"I have information for the Master of the Sacred Palace. It's vital I reach him as soon as possible."

The man sent the fool away with a gentle pat on the shoulder, then turned and gestured for Schoff to follow. The stone corridors of the monastery were silent. The monk opened a heavy oak door and ushered the lawyer into an austere antechamber. "Wait."

"Is Spina here?"

The question fell on deaf ears. The monk closed the door and disappeared. Distantly, Schoff could hear the brothers eating in the refectory and his stomach growled enviously. An hour passed before the same man returned to lead him through cloisters and up winding stairs. They were climbing one of the towers; the stairwell narrowed and still they pressed on, finally stopping in front of a low door. The monk knocked before turning the handle and motioning for Schoff to enter.

A circular chamber, lit by narrow windows at each point of the compass. A writing table beneath one, piled high with books and scrolls. A dark lectern dominated the centre of the room; bearing a single, slim volume, bound in gold-tooled leather. Two cat-tail whips hung from a hook on the wall, above a shallow basin of water. And there Gregorio Spina stood, drying his hands with a piece of cloth.

For a moment, Schoff just stared; the strong features and spotless robe were exactly as he remembered. The Master's eyes shone with a brilliant light.

"Only one thing could have prompted your journey here."

Schoff's weariness fell away. "The Devil's Library," he whispered urgently. "Two men approach. Gaetan Durant and Matthew Longstaff. They have a palimpsest; the Frenchman is convinced it reveals the location of the library." A torrent of words tumbled from the lawyer. "I told them where to find Giacomo Vescosi. I couldn't send them directly to you; they would have been suspicious. Durant refused to give me the palimpsest. It was the best I could do in the circumstances. He insisted he wouldn't part with it, except to put it in the hands of the Otiosi leader."

Gregorio Spina turned to the north-facing window and placed his palms on the ledge. Schoff studied the robed back, desperate for any sign of approval. He hardly saw the green hills beyond until Spina began describing them. He spoke softly, talking of the rich black earth, scattered with the remains of a fallen empire.

"I grew up near here. All children have their favourite hiding places; mine was an ancient maze in the grounds of my family home." He paused. "This land has been a battleground for so long that farmers raise their crops in blood. My father refused to take sides. He said they were all as bad as each other. A noble stand, lost on the mercenaries who came one night, cut off his lips and ears, and watched him bleed to death. They found my older brother hiding in the chimney place. In return for his life, my pregnant mother offered to lie with them willingly," Spina's voice thickened. "She kept them entertained until help arrived and my father's murderers were burned on green wood. Mother lit the pyre, cursed their souls to damnation and took a vow of silence. She entered a convent as soon as my brother reached his majority. I have never seen her since," he shook his head. "Strange to think we've finally reached the end of history."

Spina turned. Schoff searched his face. "Durant and Longstaff will be here soon. I did everything I could to slow them – we have time – but you have to put a watch on Vescosi."

"We've been watching the Vescosis for more than a hundred years," Spina smiled, revealing small, even teeth. "You've done well, Mathern Schoff of Lübeck."

Schoff dropped to his knees with relief. "Don't send me back. My place is here now, with you."

Spina shook his head. "You grew to manhood among heretics. Men who follow me must know without understanding and understand without being told."

It felt like drowning. "Let me try," begged Schoff. "I would rather die in the attempt than return to Lübeck." He remembered Spina's words from their first meeting in Rome and quoted them desperately. "Among the filth, like a diamond at the centre of the Devil's black heart, God has placed a treasure, a weapon to defeat the Antichrist and pitch his hordes back into Hell."

Colour rose in Schoff's cheeks. He staggered beneath the force of Spina's stare, felt it penetrate his soul. The Master of the Sacred Palace stood at the lectern and reverently placed his hands on the book there.

"The only copy in existence, written in secret by St. Benedict of Nursia. When he died, he left it to Pope Vigilius. Three years later, in 546, with the hordes of the barbarian king Totila at the gates of Rome, the book was smuggled away to Constantinople for safe-keeping. It lay forgotten for centuries, gathering dust, until it was discovered by a young scholar named Gemistus Plethon."

Spina opened the cover, fingertips resting on a page of finest uterine vellum. "Do I have your oath, Schoff?"

"You have my life."

"Only your soul has value here," Spina appeared to consider. "God chose you to carry tidings of the Library, just as he chose St. Benedict, a young man born into a family of pagans and stargazers, obsessed with the movements of the planets. Church historians claim he spent three years living as a hermit in the Simbruini Mountains." Spina shook his head. "Benedict spent those years being initiated into his family's secret faith. The men who taught him prayed to an ancient book written in a language only the high priests could understand. No one expected that a humble novice would be able to decipher the text but, with God's help, Benedict succeeded, learning to see through this world of illusion to the seeds of things beyond; *conscious, indivisible, infinite in number and eternal.* He could see them, taste them. In time, he learned to rearrange them, altering reality at will. Benedict grew terrified; the book was a way back to paradise, a way to destroy this world of illusion and bring about the Day of Judgement."

Spina closed the book with a snap. "That night, Benedict had a dream. The time was not yet right. There was still hope. Jesus commanded him to give up everything – wealth, family, position – and devote his life to caring for the faithful."

"And the book... ?"

Spina nodded. "Still in the Devil's Library, where Christ told him to leave it, against the day of Mankind's greatest need. Gemistus Plethon and Cosimo de Medici spent decades searching, without success. It's waiting for us, Schoff." Spina laid his palms on the slim volume. "More power than you can dream of, enough to lead the faithful into the Last Days and scour God's enemies from this earth!"

*

The sun was different this far south: a huge globe, which lounged on the horizon, bathing the green hills in warmth. Longstaff and Durant entered Tuscany down a narrow path, following a stream across a wooded valley and making camp beside a wide pool.

"Matthew?"

Longstaff stared at the cooking fire. They were nearing the end of their journey; if all went well he would be en route for England in a matter of days. He looked at Durant. "What?"

"May I see Il Medeghino's book?"

As Longstaff removed it from his saddle-bag, he caught a glimpse of the small volume he'd recovered from Moscow. Together with Durant's palimpsest, it was everything the lawyer had asked for: three texts that would secure his passage home.

"Here."

Durant ran his fingers lightly over the ivory plate. The fine vellum pages had swelled over the years and it took him a moment to open the metal clasps. "Thank you." He settled by the fire and began to read.

Longstaff gutted two fish he'd caught that afternoon and set them to cook.

Durant stretched; the joints snapping in his long, narrow back. "It seems to be a family journal," he reached for his portion of food. "Successive generations have noted births and deaths. It's a fine book, of course… "

"But?"

"I fail to see how it has a bearing on the location of the lost works of Epicurus."

"You don't know everything, Durant."

"You're right. I must be missing something," the Frenchman tapped his bottom lip. "We'll find out soon enough. What will you do then?"

Longstaff spat in the fire. "I was nine when King Henry's men ripped me from my home. There's a small parlour at Martlesham where my father used to sit in the evenings. Sometimes I can see myself there, beside the fire with a glass of wine in one hand," he frowned. "And sometimes I can't."

Durant nodded. "My father said the future was a plant grown in the soil of the past."

Longstaff tried to compose an image of the parlour, a wife beside him and children asleep upstairs. He remembered Marie, the girl he'd loved in Lübeck. There had been others since then. Agnes – so proud of her fine hands – who had loved him for his strength; Beatrice, who'd loved his wealth and growing fame; and the dancer, Gerda, who had loved him for what he might become.

Sometimes the connection had lasted a year or more, but he'd always kept a distance. Afraid to love, afraid to compromise his dream. "And you?"

Durant closed the heavy book.

"My father was cursed with ambition; he spent a fortune educating me, hoping I'd become a soldier and raise the family into the ranks of the nobility. I would have done as he wanted, if I hadn't fallen in love. Jeanne and I married in secret. My father was furious, but he'd a weakness for beautiful women. We set up home with him and my mother on the estate. I was a happy man, Matthew, until plague took them one by one in '49, sparing me and our young daughter."

He shrugged. "I was young and arrogant. I thought that if I devoted myself to medicine I might be able to prevent similar tragedies from striking others," Durant's eyes were lost in shadow. "My daughter never settled in Montpellier. She was angry. She never stopped being the most important thing in my life, and yet somehow I lost sight of her. Whole weeks went by without a word passing between us."

"What happened?"

"I came home one day and she was gone. Nothing missing, no note, no sign of a struggle. None of her friends could tell me anything and I've been searching ever since. I thought, with all their connections, the Otiosi might be able to help… "

He spoke with terrible weariness. Had he given up?

"She was already beautiful, even at twelve," Durant sighed. "She'd be eighteen now."

Longstaff felt relieved that he and the Frenchman were not friends, with all the obligations that carried. He thought of the neat line of stitches in his side.

"Do you never think of returning to medicine?"

"Like myself better as a freebooter," Durant forced a laugh. "Do you still have the pill I gave you?"

Longstaff nodded. It was safely tucked in his jerkin. Durant smiled.

"I know the recipe because I used to help Michel make them. I studied beneath him in Montpellier," he looked at Longstaff across the dying fire. "Do you want to know what really works against the plague, Matthew? Drink running water, rather than water from a well. Remain out of doors as much as possible and avoid being bled, if you value your life."

"I've never heard the like."

"No," said Durant, "but it was by these simple measures that Nostradamus rescued Bordeaux from plague. He sat for his Doctorate not long afterward; the university wouldn't award him his cap until he renounced unorthodox techniques. I think it was that compromise, made so many years ago, which lies at the root of his ridiculous career as a fortune teller."

Longstaff spat fishbones into the fire. "It seems we were both unfortunate in our mentors."

A dozen miles from Florence, they fell in with a group of penitents. Durant hailed them cheerfully and the men and women waved back, still scourging themselves with lengths of knotted rope.

"Heading for Rome?" asked Durant pleasantly.

"For our sins," cried one, and the others laughed. They were professionals, Longstaff realized, paid to undertake this journey by wealthy individuals whose busy lives forced them to practise piety by proxy. He thought of the haggard penitent in Gernsheim, and remembered something Durant had told him on the riverboat: southerners are supple, able to hold a range of contradictory opinions, as a civilized man should.

The Frenchman stood in his stirrups. "Look there."

Longstaff followed the line of his arm, seeing the walls of Florence in the distance, Brunelleschi's shining dome and the tower of the Signoria, rising like a finger from the rooftops.

The penitents did not enter through the gates of Florence; their meagre fees insufficient for a night in the Medici capital. They peeled off to the left, following a well-worn track around the walls of the city, while Longstaff and Durant rode through the Porta San Gallo. The guards – in dark hose, red and yellow striped doublets and stout leather jerkins – watched the two horsemen, but made no move to delay them, preferring to remain in the shade of the customs house, lounging against their long pikes. The newsmongers were more energetic, pressing for tidings of the north. Durant threw out a few morsels – some true, others the product of his imagination – in return for directions to the Piazza della Signoria.

They rode down Via della Stufa, the long street hazy with incense and the clamour of bells, finally emerging in front of the cathedral. Longstaff paused to stare, half blinded by the glare of white marble.

Durant clicked his fingers. "We haven't come for the sights."

The Piazza della Signoria was crowded, hundreds of people going about their business beneath a towering statue of David. Longstaff and Durant dismounted, walking the horses past merchants in silk lucco and wide-eyed beauties reclining on litters, past stocks where thieves stared at their feet. Longstaff touched the wooden stock of his musket, glancing back at the women who were reputed to spot their eyes with drops made from the belladonna plant, to enlarge the pupils at the cost of their sight.

In a side street, Durant rapped knuckles against a wooden gate, tall and wide enough to admit carriage and horses. They had to wait for several minutes before a face appeared. Durant gave their names and the gate swung open.

The servant was tall, with thin hair bound into a tail. He led the horses to a water trough, before turning, hunched forward over clasped hands. "Please, follow me."

He showed Longstaff and Durant up a flight of stairs, into a large reception room. "Please, wait here. The master will be with you soon."

A beautiful writing desk and two wide couches stood beneath the windows. Fragments of marble – busts and torsos, feet and hands – topped a dozen plinths. A collection of ancient glassware gathered dust on the wide sideboard.

Longstaff dropped his saddle-bag on a couch. At the window, he moved the silk curtain aside and looked down at the horses. Sparrow turned and padded out of the reception room. A moment later, she reappeared in the courtyard, nudging her way between the two horses, making space for herself at the trough.

"Do you think he plans to keep us waiting long?" asked Durant.

The Frenchman looked nervous, thought Longstaff, and tired, his doublet torn and filthy.

"The place seems almost deserted."

The door swung open and a man strode into the reception room, wearing a dark robe and skull cap. Black hair brushed the tops of his ears.

"Gentlemen. You've made better time than I dared hope." He opened his palms in welcome. "I trust your journey was pleasant. Or, if not pleasant, then at least pleasantly uneventful." He laughed at his joke, but the eyes were flat and hard. "My name is Giacomo Vescosi. You have something for me, I believe?"

Durant removed Il Medeghino's book from Longstaff's bag. "I took the liberty of reading it. Your factotum in Lübeck said it would help make sense of Lucretius' letter. I assume you've heard from him already?"

"A letter came from Lübeck several days ago. I have been waiting for you."

"Il Medeghino's book," persisted Durant. "I don't see how it brings us nearer to our goal?"

"First things first, signore. Do you have the palimpsest?"

Durant removed it from his doublet. Standing at his shoulder, Longstaff read the opening words. *Dear Tycho, Your mother and I are both well....* The document was brilliantly white, without a single bump or imperfection.

Durant strode to the window and held it up in the sunlight. A shadow text appeared behind the first. The

Italian took it from him, the wide cuffs of his robe falling away from strong wrists. He pinched the corners of the thick vellum between his fingertips.

"Has no one offered you something to drink?" He indicated a tall decanter on the sideboard. "Help yourselves."

Longstaff splashed wine into a glass, taking a long drink. Durant refused to leave his host's side.

"Otiosi protocols are strict. What prompted you to travel here in person?"

The Frenchman indicated the text, quoting from memory, "*the shining sun does never look upon them, but the moon shows them the way, and we, by Jupiter's leave and damning Ptolemy's eyes, journey with them into Hell.*"

The Italian nodded. "Out of character for Lucretius, I agree. Though hardly a code in the normal sense of the word."

He stepped away from the window and the faint letters disappeared from view. "You've done well, both of you," he placed the palimpsest on the writing desk and rang a bell. The servant reappeared, carrying two heavy purses.

"Signor Longstaff, you have braved the horrors of Russia and achieved everything my colleague in Lübeck asked of you."

Longstaff held his breath, waiting to hear the words for which he'd risked his life in Moscow and faced his past in the shape of Il Medeghino. He looked at his host, who seemed to read his thoughts.

"Present yourself to Sir Nicholas Bacon in London – he'll see that your family estate is returned to you," he pointed at the purse. "Our collaboration is at an end. The money rewards your faithful service."

Longstaff's hands shook as he accepted the purse. "Thank you, signore. It's been an honour."

"And now, if you gentlemen would excuse me... "

"I don't want your money," interrupted Durant. "I would like to help, if I can."

The Italian made a chopping motion. "You have compromised the safety of my home by coming here, signore. Our connection is at an end," he nodded at the servant. "Clement will see you out."

Durant raised a hand, as if about to argue. Giacomo Vescosi's face was hard, his dark eyes flat and dismissive. The Frenchman straightened his collar. "My daughter? Has there been any news?"

"Nothing. I've done the best I could."

"Of course." Durant marched woodenly after the servant, his face set.

Longstaff took the reins of both horses in the courtyard and joined his travelling companion in the quiet street. "I'm sorry. Wait a few days. I'm sure he'll change his mind."

"I am happy for you," Durant wouldn't make eye contact. "The letter is safe. If Vescosi finds the Devil's Library, he'll see that Epicurus's works are printed, and distributed."

"I know how much you were looking forward to meeting him."

Durant shook his head. "I have done my part. I've never been a man for seeing things through to the bitter end. I suppose this is goodbye."

"What will you do?"

Durant used the toe of his boot to up-end a small stone. "You'll go home, of course. Perhaps I'll do the same. It has been a long time since I visited Bordeaux. Maybe I'll just keep looking."

"For your daughter?"

The Frenchman forced a smile. "Perhaps I'll visit you in Suffolk. I never was in England."

"I would like that," said Longstaff.

Durant embraced him. "I won't forget what you've done for me."

Longstaff tried to read his expression, but could only see the outline of his narrow face. He led Martlesham away, down the cobbled street. Sparrow looked back and barked, expecting Durant to follow.

Longstaff stepped into a doorway and examined the purse Vescosi had given him. Enough gold and silver to start a new life in England. Finally, his true life. Sparrow looked at him reproachfully and Longstaff rubbed her thick muzzle. "You and I are going to treat ourselves to the finest inn in Florence."

CHAPTER 18

Longstaff awoke feeling rested and ate a leisurely breakfast, before making his way to the bathhouse where a plump young man looked him up and down.

"Full service?"

Longstaff shrugged off his clothes. "Have the trousers and jerkin brushed and smoked. Burn the rest and send for a tailor."

"Shoulders like yours, you must be a soldier?"

Longstaff pictured the fields around the house at Martlesham.

"I'm a farmer now."

The attendant led him to the steam room. Longstaff paused beside a basin of clean water to splash his face and hair. It only took a moment, but the small gesture felt like a second baptism. He lay down on a block of warm stone. The attendant slapped him with a damp towel and Longstaff felt the tension of the last weeks ebb away.

His new clothes would not be ready for several hours. He borrowed a suit of local clothes – a wide, sleeveless *lucco* and sturdy leather sandals – tucked a soft cap into his belt and stepped into the yard. Sparrow was there, dozing in the sunshine. Longstaff fetched her a bowl of water before striding out in the Piazza dei Peruzzi.

He wandered the streets at random, admiring the exotic flowers in the Boboli Gardens and the trick seats, which sprayed water on unwary visitors. When Durant had said that even life and death were perfumed here, he'd described the city well, but Longstaff didn't spend long thinking about his travelling companion. He'd grown to like the Frenchman, but for weeks they'd spent nearly every waking hour together and Longstaff was enjoying the simpler pleasures of his own company.

He passed the vast building site of the 'Uffizi', and the tapping of a hundred stonemasons' hammers. The whole city was covered in dust, as the labourers raised offices for the city's celebrated merchant family.

Cosimo I, Duke of Tuscany, bore the same name as his illustrious forebear, and directed equally large sums of money to favoured artists and architects, but the similarity ended there. The original Cosimo had claimed no title, ruling the city through force of personality, encouraging novelty in music, painting and literature, commissioning radical new works from Fra Angelico and Donatello, founding a Platonic Academy and slowly turning Florence into Europe's most enlightened city.

The present Duke was a zealous supporter of the Inquisition, a book burner obsessed with discipline and order.

Crossing the Ponte Vecchio, Longstaff walked through the new market, the stalls piled with leeks, onion and garlic, thieves and bankrupts tied to a stone pillar at the centre. Longstaff paused, no longer thief or soldier, but a man of means and estate.

He joined a group of shopkeepers and signori, and listened as the *banditori* read the day's proclamations. Men traded information here and he asked for news of England. A fleshy, middle-aged man stepped forward.

"Peace and prosperity," he said. "The people have put the trials of Mary's reign behind them, taken Elizabeth to their hearts."

Longstaff closed his fist around a coin. "More, if you expect to get paid."

"Your Queen is well advised by Lord Cecil. She is still young. People expect her to make a marriage."

"What of Lord Cecil's brother-in-law?"

The newsmonger didn't hesitate. "Sir Nicholas Bacon has been confirmed Lord Chancellor. With such noble men to advise their queen, the English need have no worries."

Longstaff grinned; he'd never been so close to recovering his family estate. Seized by an urge to tempt fate as he recrossed the Ponte Vecchio, he walked into a jeweller's shop and commissioned a signet ring, describing his father's coat of arms in minute detail. The goldsmith, a fine old man, with a mane of glossy white hair, opened his ledger.

The book.

Ivan's book was still in his saddle-bag. Longstaff ran from the shop, sprinting back to the inn, hardly pausing to wonder why Vescosi hadn't asked for it. A stupid oversight; the sort of carelessness that might put his whole future at risk. His saddle-bags were still on the floor of his room. Longstaff sighed with relief when he saw the slim volume. He pushed it down the neck of his *lucco* and hurried out again.

He knocked at Vescosi's door. "Come on," he muttered in the quiet street.

The door remained closed. It didn't make sense. Even if Vescosi was out, a house this size would never be left empty. Where were the servants?

Longstaff's weapons were back at the inn, except for a long stabbing knife taped to the inside of his wrist. He

pushed the blade through a crack in the heavy gate. The tip
of the knife just reached the latch and he slipped inside.

Deserted. The front door stood wide open. Longstaff
entered the reception room. The wine glass he'd used the
previous day stood unwashed on the sideboard.

He crept up the stairs and walked silently along a silk-
lined gallery. Above his head, a painter's brush had divided
the ceiling into regular squares. Straight lines and perfect
angles which the artist had made no attempt to soften with
curlicues or floral motifs. Each square showed a man at
work. A farmer peered at a sorry-looking sheaf of wheat;
a smiling vintner with flushed cheeks, hem of his smock
stained with grape-juice; jeweller, eyes obscured by thick
lenses, standing with hands clasped behind his back in an
attitude of assumed innocence.

Longstaff put his ear against a heavy wooden door.
Nothing. He tried the handle, knife gripped in his free hand.
The door swung open on silent hinges.

The huge room had been ransacked. Vitrines lay on their
sides, the floor littered with broken glass, upturned plants
and ruined treasures. Dozens of tiny white labels lay among
the debris like confetti. Bookshelves – twice as tall as a man –
stood bowed and empty. What in God's name had happened
here? A punishment? What crime could have invited such
wanton destruction?

Wooden crates stood together in the centre of the room.
Longstaff prized one open, left his knife buried in the lid as
he ran his fingertips across the leather spines of books. The
light was too weak to make out the titles. He pulled the case
towards a ray of sunlight.

He was bent double when the man attacked. Longstaff
fell away from a flashing blade. The assailant landed on top

of him, drove the air from his lungs. Longstaff caught a wrist in one hand; knife's point a fingerswidth from his throat, edging closer. Vescosi's servant, teeth bared, eyes points of hatred.

Longstaff couldn't turn his head. His fingers clawed at the debris on the floor. Soil. A white label. A shard from one of the smashed vitrines. The edge cut his palm as Longstaff stabbed upwards, slit the servant's throat below the ear. Blood sprayed across the room.

Someone screamed. Longstaff shook himself free; a ragged child cowered in the doorway.

"Are there more?" he yelled in Italian.

"I saw you yesterday. I followed you," the boy's voice was shrill with panic. "How was I supposed to know you weren't one of the men who took her away? She never told me what you looked like."

She? "Come here, boy, where I can see you."

He approached on unsteady legs. Eight years old, Longstaff guessed, gap-toothed and grey with exhaustion.

"Someone set you to watch for me?"

"I thought you were one of them. Until…" he gestured at the dead man, keeping his eyes averted.

Longstaff searched the corpse for clues. Nothing in Clement's purse beyond a few pennies. Nothing in the boots or concealed in the folds of his woollen *lucco*. Longstaff stripped the corpse. No papers taped to his body or hidden in the crack of his arse, but the chest had been branded with a dog's head. Longstaff shuddered as he stared at the pointed muzzle, the two rows of jagged teeth. The constellation of the dog was an omen of plague.

He turned to the boy. "You work for Vescosi?"

"My mother did, before men came and took him away."

A dread weight settled on Longstaff's chest. He and Durant had given the Lucretius palimpsest to Vescosi only yesterday.

"When?"

"Days ago. And they took Aurélie. I was in the kitchens. She grabbed me, told me to hide and come back later when the house was quiet. Keep a watch for you and the Frenchman. The men came then. I couldn't see – she'd pushed me into a cupboard – but I heard her fight. When they left, I followed," he added with a trace of pride. "I know where they took her."

Longstaff closed his eyes. *Who was Aurélie and how in God's name did she know who he was?* He wasn't used to dealing with children. One thing at a time.

"Where can I wash?"

The boy's name was Marco. He led the way to the kitchens, loitering in a corner while Longstaff splashed cold water in his face.

"Is the blood gone?"

Nervously, Marco gestured at his neck. Longstaff scrubbed harder. His hands were shaking. That bastard upstairs had come within an inch of killing him. Longstaff scanned the room – a hatch led down to the cellars below. He ran back upstairs, wrapped the corpse in a tapestry and dropped it over the balustrade. None of this was necessary – he had no intention of ever returning to this house – but he wasn't ready to walk the streets of Florence like an honest citizen.

Marco waited in the courtyard while he disposed of the corpse. Longstaff half expected to find him gone when he finally emerged into the sunshine, but the boy had courage.

"This way, signore."

He plucked at Longstaff's sleeve, leading him through the city streets to a brooding Dominican House.

"She's in there. I followed them, signore. That's where they took Aurélie."

Longstaff had no idea who Aurélie was. Neither daughter, nor mistress, nor maid, it seemed, but Marco was adamant she'd know how to find the leader of the Otiosi.

"What does your master look like?"

He was tall, apparently, with a nose like a hawk and tufts of grey hair sprouting above each ear. Nothing like the man to whom they'd given the Lucretius palimpsest.

"Tell me what you heard."

"I already… "

Longstaff shook his head. "Again. Word for word."

"I couldn't see from inside the cupboard, but I heard her fight. The men were laughing, like they were throwing her back and forth. Someone came in and asked if she was the one who carried Vescosi's letters. He spoke so soft I had to strain to hear him. Then he said she couldn't come; she'd slow them down. He ordered the men to bring her here and tell the monks to keep her safe, in case Vescosi proved difficult." The boy shrugged. "His words."

A water fountain stood in the centre of the small square; a shoemaker's store and a weaver's workshop occupied the ground floor of a large tenement building. The neighbourhood was respectable, but hardly luxurious. The Dominicans still had their fine monastery of Santa Maria Novella near the Porto al Prato, but the Order was no longer popular in the city – not since the wild monk Savonarola had made an enemy of the Medicis. These days, it was Franciscans who held the best posts at court, Franciscans called upon as inquisitors or judges, while the Dominicans were exiled to the poorer districts of the city, venturing out to parish churches during the day, spending nights huddled in this House. Longstaff studied it; a stone building shaped like a child's building block. The windows lay barred; the only entrance a heavy wooden door.

"How on earth do you expect me to get her out of there?"

Marco was gone, without a word, vanished into the streets of Florence. Longstaff cursed, but he wasn't surprised. The boy had seen his master abducted and a man slain in the space of a few short days. He'd done well staying as long as he had.

What now? Longstaff marched into the shoemaker's.

"Boots. Let me see what you have."

The young cobbler hurried forward with samples of his work.

"Of course. What do you have in mind, signore?"

Longstaff pointed at a pair of knee-length riding boots.

"Is that the best leather you have?"

The cobbler bowed. "You have a good eye, signore. Look here," he produced a length of flawless doeskin. "Soft and durable. I've been saving it for the right customer."

Longstaff grunted, shifting the man's measuring stool to give himself the best possible view of the Dominican House.

"What are you waiting for?" he snapped.

He spent two hours haggling with the cobbler, then returned the following day and made a grand show of inspecting his progress. All the while, he studied the Dominican House – he knew Sir Nicholas Bacon wouldn't honour an imposter's promise, and the girl was his only connection to the true Otiosi leader.

Longstaff weighed and discarded a dozen options as he talked with the cobbler, each worse than the last. Short of murder, there was no way to reach her. And he wasn't prepared to start slaughtering priests on the word of an eight-year-old boy.

The shoemaker had done an excellent job in such a short space of time and Longstaff tipped accordingly.

"Your neighbours don't seem the most welcoming of souls." He nodded towards the heavy wooden gate. "A cousin of mine swears they have women in there and stay up half the night drinking and eating."

"Cousins talk," shrugged the young man. "These priests are a miserable bunch, scared witless at the sight of a pretty girl."

"Oh?"

"They claim she's possessed. I hear they're starving her, to weaken the spirit before casting it out tomorrow night."

Longstaff controlled his expression. *Tomorrow night.* That gave him a little over twenty-four hours to find Durant. Irrationally, he blamed the Frenchman, and was damned if he'd go up against priests and demons without him.

*

Gaetan Durant refused to leave the city. He could understand Vescosi's anger – Durant had broken with protocol and put the Otiosi leader in danger – but surely he would calm down in a few days' time, when Durant planned to return and plead to be allowed to continue in the search for the Devil's Library. Lucretius was the key and the Frenchman knew the poet's work inside out. Surely, the Otiosi leader would relent.

In the meantime, he sought distraction from his own company, but the novelty seats in the Boboli gardens only made him angry. He went to see one of the famed Florentine plays and was disgusted. Actors dangled from strings. Heaven spun about the earth on revolving discs. Angels descended on ill-painted wooden clouds. Fraud, deception and artifice.

It was noon. Durant lay on his unmade bed in a dirty tavern on the outskirts of the city, trying to concentrate on Lucretius.

> But mind is more the keeper of the gates,
> Hath more dominion over life than soul.
> For without intellect and mind there is not
> One part of soul can rest within our frame
> Least part of time; companioning, it goes
> With mind into the winds away, and leaves
> The icy members in the cold of death.
> But he whose mind and intellect abide
> Himself abides in life. However much
> The trunk be mangled, with the limbs lopped off,
> The soul withdrawn and taken from the limbs,
> Still lives the trunk and draws the vital air.

He tossed the book aside. One day, claimed Lucretius, man would comprehend the hidden structure of the universe. Too late for Durant – wife dead of plague, daughter God alone knew where. With all the resources at their disposal, the Otiosi had discovered no trace of her. Stupid to have allowed himself to hope. He should have demanded more information. What leads had Vescosi pursued? It would have been useful to know, if only to help him concentrate his own search. Durant stared at the ceiling and accused himself of cowardice. So much time had passed – had he grown afraid of what she might have become? Was his desire to find the Devil's Library a way of distracting himself from the fact he'd given up?

No. He remained convinced – the lost works of Epicurus had the power to remake this world. Durant did not know how. He only knew what he'd read.

Nothing but words on paper, black spiders on bleached bone, but Columbus had carried a copy of Lucretius' poem with him when he discovered the Americas. Copernicus had kept a copy in his observatory in Frombork. Both men adding chapters to the poet's tale of a journey to freedom as Man uncovered the secrets of the universe, learned to protect himself from disease and natural disaster, and his own dark nature.

Durant fell into a restless sleep. He dreamed of his daughter, Laure, smiling in a linen dress with short, bunched sleeves and trailing hem. Her hair loosely tied at the nape of her neck, except where a single lock had escaped to fall across her face.

Tears rolled down Durant's cheeks. In the years since Laure's disappearance, he'd dreamed her death a thousand ways, and played the same role each time: the man who abducted her, seduced her, sold her into prostitution, murdered her. A cruel trick of the mind, which drove him from his bed. Angrily, he pulled on his boots and hurried into the streets of Florence, making for the notorious warren of alleyways behind the old marketplace.

It was mid-afternoon and the streets were quiet; the ground floor shops closed, counters covered with sheets of oiled paper or sealed with wooden shutters, a few sallow-faced whores lingering in the dark doorways. A cow's skull mounted on a wooden pole marked the entrance to a tavern. Inside, a handful of men played cards at a battered table. Durant sat with his back to the wall as the landlady brought him wine. She had painted lips and skin like bark. He caught a glimpse of her withered bosom as she set the bottle down. She saw him look and winked. Durant felt sick. The wine was foul. God's teeth, but when he thought of the wine they'd produced on his old family estate, it was enough to make him weep. Durant remembered the colour; a single flame glimpsed against the curtain of night, the taste of love and comfort. He saw warm stone, cool water welling up from natural springs, and well-trodden paths between neat rows of vines. His home before the plague.

Durant thought of his daughter, and the young whores he saw every day on the streets of Florence. "What a world we've made."

He hadn't meant to speak out loud and the card players looked up. Durant forced a smile. "What are you playing, gentleman?" He patted the full purse hanging from his belt. "Is it similar to Landsknecht?"

CHAPTER 19

Aurélie was unharmed, apart from two fading bruises on the upper arms where Gregorio Spina's men had held her, first to stop her fighting, then to drag her through the streets of Florence.

Spina himself had stayed with Giacomo Vescosi, while his men had brought her to this Dominican House and left her in the charge of Brother Jerome. She'd been terrified; mind bursting with Giacomo's tales of death by burning. Seeing Jerome had done nothing to reassure her – he was a tall man, gaunt with fanaticism, lank hair falling past his bony shoulders – but she'd been treated well at first. The preacher had shut her in a monk's cell. A single, barred window beneath the ceiling let in air and light from the square. From the far corner, Aurélie had been able to glimpse the legs of passers-by and hear the shuffle of footsteps; muffled laughter; the price of a freshly slaughtered chicken. Heaven compared to her present accommodation. Her own fault – after three days of silently hoping for a miracle, she'd screamed so long and loud for help that robed men had come and taken her down to a punishment cell. She shivered in her thin dress, remembering rough hands on her back, forcing her down the steep stairs.

She had no idea how long she'd been alone in the darkness before Jerome came, a burning torch above his head. She'd squinted in the glare, trying to see his face. He'd seemed to fear her scrutiny, thrusting the torch through a ring on the wall and retreating into shadow.

"How long have I been here?"

"Sixteen hours."

A little after dawn. Aurélie could have sworn she'd been here twice as long. She pictured the bright sun rising over the rooftops of Florence.

"Your vile behaviour is the talk of the quarter," continued the preacher, "but I am prepared to forgive." He'd taken a breath. "I've come to hear your confession."

Aurélie had bitten back laughter. She still had no idea what possessed her. "You want me to confess? To what? Causing you embarrassment?"

"I'm offering you a chance to return to your former cell."

"If I promise to be a good little girl. You should be ashamed."

The preacher had recoiled in disgust. "Control yourself."

"Me?" Aurélie's cheeks had burned with the thought of her earlier fear. "Coward," she spat at him, groping blindly for words that would hurt. "I feel nothing but pity for you, do you understand? Duped into peddling the pope's lies."

"Witch!"

Now, Aurélie had laughed in earnest. She remembered the moment with pride, standing with hands on hips in the centre of the dark cell. "Would you like me to tell you about witches?"

Jerome had crossed himself.

"The Devil tempts us to sin, isn't that right? Fall into one of his snares, and he takes possession of your soul? The Pope claims followers of the new confessions will go to Hell, and Lutherans claim he's the Antichrist – that anyone who listens to him is similarly doomed."

"Silence, woman!" yelled Jerome. "What demon has you in his grip?"

An idea had popped, fully formed, into Aurélie's head. She'd slammed an open palm against her thigh and seen him flinch.

"Don't you see?" goading him deliberately now. "Whichever form of worship can produce the most witches must be the most pleasing to God. You're always telling us how cunning the Devil is; he'd hardly waste his time corrupting souls that already belong to him. It's only a game," she'd finished. "Just a way of keeping score."

Jerome had fled without a word, leaving her alone in the darkness. She'd seen him once since, just long enough to call him a fool and a coward. He hadn't even crossed the threshold.

How long had passed since then? Days? She shifted on the damp straw, just this slight movement enough to wake the hunger. It was an animal, quiet when she lay still, ready to claw at her belly whenever she moved. She pressed her tongue against the sweating walls. If they left her much longer she would be too weak to fight.

The door swung open.

A skinny, young acolyte, wreathed in a halo of fire. "You're to follow me."

Aurélie rose slowly to her feet, forearm raised to protect her eyes. "A gentleman would offer his arm."

The boy recoiled, as if threatened by a snake. Aurélie sighed.

"Of course. Lead on."

She followed him up the narrow staircase, through a low door and into blessed sunlight. Jerome waited in the courtyard. He'd donned a threadbare robe for the occasion.

"Did she talk?"

"She wanted to touch me."

The preacher nodded. "God will protect you, my son. Make her sit."

A chair had been placed in the centre of the yard. The acolyte forced her down, then picked up a pair of barber's scissors and began to cut her hair. His hands were shaking; Aurélie concentrated on keeping her head still. She closed her eyes, unwilling to watch the long, golden tresses fall to the ground. This was a victory, she reminded herself – they truly believed that she was possessed.

No one offered her a mirror. When the acolyte stepped back, Aurélie raised a hand, to run it across the shorn hair.

A wooden board lay close.

"Lie down," snapped Jerome.

Aurélie shook her head. She wasn't being deliberately obstructive. She was tired and close to tears. The preacher nodded at the acolyte, who took her beneath the arms and dragged her across the flagstones.

She stared at this boy, at his nervous eyes and spindle-thin limbs – the expression on his face was pathetic, as if he were somehow the injured party.

"Tie her."

The boy reached for her wrist. Aurélie seized his forefinger and bent it back. Pain twisted his face and she felt a sudden glow of satisfaction. She bent the finger further, nearly to the wrist, waiting for the snap of bones. With his free hand, the boy back-handed her across the face. There was blood in her mouth and the terrible taste of fear. *What in God's name had she been thinking?*

CHAPTER 20

Matthew Longstaff had a knife in his boot, two more in his jerkin, and wished he had the *katzbalger*. He didn't like these alleyways; so narrow you could run fingertips along both crumbling walls. He was glad Sparrow was with him, the big dog climbing easily over piles of refuse.

Voices approached. Longstaff slipped into the shadows of a doorway. A group of barefoot children came running round the corner, slowing when they saw the dog. Longstaff pinched his forearm before stepping into the alley, coins in his open palm.

"I'm looking for someone."

He described the way Durant swept his hair back from his forehead; the flat grey eyes, and the black doublet and hose. It was his description of the Frenchman's clothes that snagged the boys' attention. They nodded eagerly, leading him deeper into the warren of derelict streets.

Longstaff stared at the cow's polished skull. A low rumble of noise came from the tavern. He gave Sparrow a rough pat on the shoulder. "Wait for me."

Durant sat at a table with three strangers – local men, by the look of it, wearing coarse woollen smocks and wooden clogs – surrounded by a crowd of heavy-set labourers and rake-thin criminals. There was a lazy smile on the Frenchman's face, eyes half-closed as he cradled a wineskin in his arms. A small pile of coins lay in the centre of the table, larger piles in front of the three locals. Nothing in front of the Frenchman, who stopped caressing the wineskin long enough to remove a thin gold chain from beneath his doublet. It bore a pendant – a heavy cross, set with precious stones. Durant studied it a moment, then tossed it onto the pile of coins in the middle of the table.

Longstaff pushed through the crowd; there wasn't time for this. "We have to leave. Now."

"Matthew!" The Frenchman slurred. "I knew I'd see you again."

"Now, Durant."

"Just one more hand. If I win, I'll come meek as a lamb. If I lose, I fear you'll have to kill my new friends," he grinned. "That chain has sentimental value."

Longstaff yanked him to his feet, expression hard as he faced the crowd. "You have his money. Now let us go."

The first man gave way reluctantly. Longstaff kept moving, shielding Durant with his body. The Frenchman pulled free of his grip, wineskin still held beneath one arm. "I haven't paid for the drink," he turned in the doorway. "Keep the chain, dear lady, with my compliments."

Longstaff pulled him into the alleyway, whistling for Sparrow. They were almost at the corner before the doors of the tavern burst open.

The landlady appeared. "Tin and paste," she yelled. "I'll have you flayed alive."

Durant started laughing. Longstaff forced him into a shambling run. Christ and his Saints stared at them from niches in the walls. Shouts reached them from nearby streets, but their luck held. "This way," hissed Longstaff. "Hurry, or I'll gut you myself."

He didn't let up until they reached a modest square, tenements along three sides, a squat parish church on the fourth. He let go of Durant and looked around with satisfaction.

"You're a miserable bastard," muttered Durant. "No sense of humour."

Longstaff marched him to the fountain in the centre and ducked his head beneath the water.

The Frenchman retched. His breath came in ragged, wine-sodden gasps.

"Get away from me," he slid down the side of the fountain and took a long drink from the wineskin. "Don't look at me like that, Matthew. And do not make me drink alone." He pushed the skin into Longstaff's hands. "Drink with me to my daughter's memory. It's seven years ago tomorrow since I saw her last."

Longstaff drank deeply, dropped the skin and stamped on it, sending a spray of cheap wine across the cobblestones.

"Bastard," said Durant, eyes fogged with drink. "I worked it out, you know. Can't believe it took me so long. King Henry killed your father for promoting Luther's ideas, but when Il Medeghino fought at Marciano, he fought for the Emperor," he sneered at Longstaff. "You fought for the Catholic champion, though your father died for Luther's faith."

Longstaff grabbed Durant by the hair and forced his head under the water. He counted to ten, slowly, before letting him up.

Durant took a great tearing breath. His eyes were red, but steady now. He sat himself down on the fountain wall.

"They lied to us," said Longstaff. "Are you listening? The whole thing was a performance."

Durant groaned. "You've been thinking. Nothing good ever comes of you thinking."

"Your precious letter," continued Longstaff. "Who do you think you gave it to? Not the leader of the Otiosi. I've been looking for you."

Gaetan Durant ran a hand through wet hair, his face puffy with alcohol. "What are you talking about?"

"I went back. The place was deserted. You remember Clement, the servant? He tried to cut my throat! You understand? Rewards and money to see us on our way. An assassin lying in wait if we proved suspicious and returned to the house."

"Matthew. You're not making any sense. Who has the palimpsest?"

"Someone with no intention of rediscovering Epicurus, you can be sure of that."

Or of helping me return to England.

"But who?" insisted Durant.

"That's what we're here to find out." Longstaff raised a finger to his lips.

Eight women holding torches appeared in the corner of the square and walked towards the squat church. They were followed by a Dominican priest in threadbare robe, tall and painfully thin, with an outsize head and large hands.

A crude litter bobbed uncertainly into view. A young woman in a shapeless robe lay on the hard board, struggling against the ropes that held her fast. Possessed, according to the rumours, held captive in the Dominican House these past few days.

"Her name is Aurélie," said Longstaff. "She sent a boy to watch for us."

The procession paused at the entrance to the church. The bound woman raised her head and Longstaff caught a glimpse of fierce blue eyes, pale face backlit by the torches. She was gagged, her white blond hair cut nearly to the scalp.

The litter was followed by thirty men and women, crowding after it up the church steps, but shrinking away whenever they came too near.

Longstaff half dragged the Frenchman with him. "We have work to do."

The lowering church was a poor, tumbledown thing with a pitched wooden ceiling. Longstaff and Durant stood at the rear, looking at the labourers and small traders in rough, homespun smocks; careworn women, fingers thickened by years of toil. Longstaff shrank from the low groans of excitement.

The priest's face could have been carved from stone. His shadow fell across Aurélie, still tied to her wooden board. Raising his arms, he spread long, grey fingers.

"Brothers and sisters, now is the time to stand firm against the injustices of this world, which are Satan's greatest trap. The final battle nears and he knows his time of influence is coming to an end. Imagine the bitterness he feels. Soon, there will be no new souls for him to torment in the fires of Hell," the priest's tone became confidential. The congregation leaned in. "We have been blessed. The Master of the Sacred Palace came to me and laid a holy charge upon my shoulders."

"Kill her," screamed a woman.

"Sister," roared the priest, "The Master of the Sacred Palace put this girl into my care. I tried to protect her from the Lord of Hell. Locked her away in a monk's cell. Brothers and sisters, what proof are stone and iron against the hordes of Satan, which stalk our towns and cities and feed on sin and win soul upon soul for their master? What proof is the kindness of priests against the wiles of Satan?"

He sank to his knees. "She spoke abominations. No daughter of Eve can conceive of such foul blasphemies except that the devil speaks with her tongue." There was a storm of protest from the congregation. "She is possessed," he screamed. "I took away her food and water, cut her hair, hoping to starve the demon out. She subjected me to such vileness I thought my heart might stop.

"We shall drive the demon out. Restore peace to this girl's soul. Together, we shall do God's work."

The priest's long shadow engulfed the young woman completely. He reeled back, as if resisted by unseen, supernatural forces. Two of the litter bearers dipped long strips of cloth in bowls of water and slowly bound the priest's hands. The congregation began a low chant.

The priest stood over the bound woman – his eyes were narrow, jaw set – and struck her across the face.

Aurélie was still for a moment, then bucked against the ropes. Durant took a step forward, but Longstaff put a hand on his arm.

"Wait," he said. "Close your eyes if you must, but use your head. They will tear us limb from limb if we try to get her now. You heard what the priest said. He has to keep her safe."

"Burn her," yelled a man.

"When Jesus went forth into the land," cried the priest, "he met a man possessed by devils. Jesus demanded, what is thy name? And he replied, 'My name is Legion.'"

He set about Aurélie's face and body. She struggled against the ropes, hands clawing as the congregation chanted. Longstaff and Durant stood, stony-faced, at the back of the church.

The priest's closed fist crashed against the side of Aurélie's head, knocking the gag from her mouth.

"Ignorant pig," she screamed. "Superstitious fool."

"Do you hear? The demon rises to the surface! He feels the pain I inflict on the host. He runs from the song of her soul, as she learns what she will be spared in the next life. The horsemen ride and the Devil screams in fury, but we are stronger, brothers and sisters, we are stronger."

"Out," yelled another woman.

He struck the girl again. Blood ran freely from Aurélie's nose and mouth. She raged, calling him a pederast, a disgrace to his maker. Longstaff saw fear on the priest's face. He could not let the demon win. He set his feet and struck Aurélie such a blow her eyes rolled back until the whites were showing. She fell back on the board like an empty suit of clothes.

As the congregation pressed forward, Longstaff took Durant's arm and drew him into the dark recesses of the church.

The priest was on all fours beside Aurélie's unconscious body, panting like a dog, greasy hair hanging nearly to the floor. The litter bearers crowded anxiously around, helping him to his feet, leading him towards the door at the rear of the church. He shook them off, seeming to find new strength.

"God praise you, brothers and sisters," tears streamed down his cheeks. "God is generous. He has seen our struggle. He has answered our prayer and released this poor woman's soul from Hell."

He seized a flaming torch, stamped it out and drew a sooty line round Aurélie's body.

"Her sleep must not be disturbed," he half shouted. His movements were clumsy as he drew a lopsided labyrinth on the floor, to confound the demons. The congregation fell into an uneasy silence. The jagged lines grew and grew, forcing them back against the door. The priest stumbled, the bearers hurried forward to catch him, leading him away.

Longstaff listened to the muttering, but the congregation wouldn't enter the labyrinth. One by one they turned and made their way into the square, leaving candles burning on the high altar.

Longstaff and Durant emerged from shadow into the silent church. Aurélie lay in a heap, the blood dry on her face, a bruise around her left eye.

Longstaff knelt beside her. Even caked in blood and dirt, she was beautiful. Delicate hands emerged from the sleeves of her robe and he could see blue veins beneath the skin. He lifted her in his arms; her breath grew rapid, but she did not wake. The nightwatch were walking the streets of Florence, enforcing the curfew, and it took them over an hour to reach Longstaff's inn on the Piazza del Peruzzi. The Englishman gave the night porter a coin and carried Aurélie up to his room.

Durant removed her robe, pulling a clean shirt over her head and slipping her between the sheets of the wide bed. Together, they cleaned her face. Durant checked the pulse; he peeled back her eyelids, then pressed his ear to her chest and listened to her heart.

"I'll go for my things in the morning, but I think she's going to be fine."

Longstaff sat in one of the two armchairs, pointing Durant to the other. The Frenchman smiled, took out his battered copy of Lucretius and began to read. Within minutes, the book fell onto his lap. His mouth dropped open and he began to snore.

Longstaff sat through the rest of the night and watched the young woman sleep.

CHAPTER 21

Longstaff let his body go limp when he heard Aurélie stir, and dropped his head as if he were sleeping.

She woke cautiously, one eye at a time, wincing when she raised herself onto one elbow. She slipped out from between the warm sheets, padded silently to the window and peered round the edge of the heavy curtain.

The room was luxuriously appointed, with a dressing table in the window. Aurélie sat in front of the looking glass and glanced at her reflection, as if afraid to discover how much damage had been done. Longstaff's shirt was several sizes too big for her, the cuffs falling away from delicate wrists.

Longstaff hadn't intended to spy, only to give her a moment's peace when she woke. He smacked his lips and yawned, stirred and stretched on the chair, giving her plenty of time to slip into the bloodied robe and run fingers over her shorn hair.

Longstaff rubbed his eyes. The girl was sitting on the dressing room stool, looking at him with a wary expression. "Good morning," he said. "How are you feeling?"

She did not reply. He spoke softly. "Are you hungry? There's food and water on the writing table."

"I know who you are," she stared at him. "Marco found you."

"A man tried to cut my throat. Marco told me you'd know why. He wasn't able to tell me more."

Her face grew still.

"I'm sorry. A poor choice of words. Marco's fine, as far as I know. He was terrified and disappeared as soon as he'd shown me where they were holding you." Longstaff walked to the window and threw back the heavy curtains, flooding the room with bright sunlight.

Durant stirred in his chair.

"What is it?"

The Frenchman looked grey in the sunlight, eyes still red and glassy. He rubbed unshaven cheeks, lurched to his feet and walked unsteadily to the writing table. He lifted the water bottle directly to his mouth and took several long swallows, before handing it to Aurélie.

"Drink," he said. "If my head's pounding, I can only imagine how yours must feel."

"At least offer her a glass," Longstaff approached the dressing table, he and Durant getting in each other's way. Longstaff retreated to the bed.

Aurélie took a long drink from the bottle. "Thank you."

Durant dropped to one knee in front of her. "I am a doctor."

"I know. I overheard Spina saying you were on your way," she looked at their blank expressions. "Gregorio Spina. The pope's censor. Master of the Sacred Palace." She shook her head, then lifted her hands to her temples.

"Does it hurt?" asked Longstaff.

"It wasn't difficult to convince the priest I was possessed."

Durant's eyes went wide. "You did what?"

"What else could I do? Night and day, he kept me locked in a monk's cell. I was planning to feign unconsciousness at the climax of the exorcism, then look for a way to escape. I wasn't expecting him to hit me so hard. Where's the palimpsest?"

She saw a look pass between the two men.

"Tell me you still have it."

Longstaff spread his palms. "The man we gave it to told us his name was Giacomo Vescosi."

Aurélie put her head between her hands and groaned. "Then he has them both. Spina has Giacomo and the palimpsest," she pointed at Durant. "Bring me pen and paper, at once."

Durant raised both eyebrows. "You'll live, Aurélie. But you've been through a terrible experience. No need to tax your strength unnecessarily. We can talk about Giacomo when you're feeling stronger."

Longstaff saw anger flow along the high, clear lines of her face.

"I want to write a letter," she snapped, "not climb a mountain."

"Of course," Longstaff rose to his feet. "Gaetan, why don't you fetch your things? I'm sure we need to clean her wounds, so they don't get infected."

Durant gave the young woman an uncertain look.

"I'll get some clothes for her, as well. Make sure she rests."

He closed the door behind him. Longstaff looked at Aurélie.

"We're trying to help."

"Then bring me pen and paper. It may already be too late."

*

Durant hurried across the city, making one short stop at a dressmaker's on the Canto di Nello, another at a street vendor to eat a trencher of tripe smothered in lurid green sauce. The Florentine speciality was disgusting, but effective against a hangover.

It took him less than an hour to reach his inn. He packed quickly, settled his bill and strode back through the busy streets. He wanted a glass of wine, perhaps a bath, but kept remembering how Aurélie had struggled as the priest beat her. He'd come across such mad courage before and knew it always led to trouble. It wouldn't take her long to wrap the Englishman around her finger. Longstaff would say something, in that awkward, gallant manner of his, and she'd laugh, and that would be the end of him.

Durant threw open the door. The girl was at the writing table, dipping a quill into a glass inkwell. She did not look up, her hand tracing a calm line across the surface of the paper.

"She should be in bed," he said.

"I am right here, Signor Durant," she replied without turning. "You can address me directly."

"We talked while you were away," said Longstaff. "She knows where they've taken Giacomo and the palimpsest."

Aurélie described a house on the summit of a hill, built around an old watchtower. It was less than a day's ride from Florence and belonged to Spina's older brother, Onofrio.

"We can't storm the villa," said Longstaff, "and Spina knows what we look like, which rules out trickery. One of us will have to ride out to look at the place."

Durant crossed the room and stood peering over Aurélie's shoulder.

"You're standing in my light," her voice was soft, musical. She leaned to one side, offering him an uninterrupted view of her work. "Please."

Durant picked up the paper. "Who are you writing to?"

"A Strasbourg merchant by the name of Michaelis, who wants a buyer for two dozen muskets."

"What use are guns with only two of us to fire them?"

"Giacomo has always made a point of studying his enemies," Aurélie smiled. "Spina's brother has a weakness for modern weapons. Michaelis sent him letters of introduction a week ago. He might be able to get you in."

Durant stared at Longstaff. The Englishman shrugged. "I can't see any harm in talking to the man."

"It's suicide, Matthew. We've never heard of this Michaelis. Even if he can get us in, how do you propose we find Vescosi and the palimpsest?"

"No need to worry about the palimpsest," said Aurélie. "They're bound to have shown it to Giacomo. He knows more about the Devil's Library than any man alive; that's why they took him in the first place."

Durant rubbed his face. "It isn't our fight. This is Otiosi business."

"The Otiosi?" Aurélie shook her head. "Clerks, not soldiers. Diplomats, courtiers, a few timid priests, sharing a weakness for new ideas and a loathing for the Inquisition. But only in the safety of their own homes. Why do think they need men like you?" She looked at Durant. "I saw you this morning, asleep with a copy of Lucretius. I know what drove you to deliver the palimpsest in person. What do you think will happen if the Library falls into Spina's hands? He'll use it to destroy us, then lock the collected knowledge of centuries away in the Vatican."

"What library?" demanded Longstaff.

The young woman stared at him, eyes wide in disbelief. "What do you think we're looking for? A few old books?"

"The complete works of Epicurus," said Durant.

Furiously, the girl shook her head. "The Devil's Library is more than just Epicurus. Giacomo Vescosi has spent his life searching for it, ever since he learned about St. Benedict. The saint's family were members of an ancient cult dedicated to the accumulation of knowledge," she paused, as if determined Longstaff and Durant should grasp the full importance of her words. "Their church was a library, constantly improved and expanded over the centuries. Works of philosophy and history, ethics, politics, dialectics, economics, poetry, engineering..." She stopped, frustration written in every line of her face.

"Did you at least bring me something to wear?"

In silence, Durant gestured at his pack.

"Gentlemen, if you wouldn't mind..."

Longstaff and Durant stood together in the narrow corridor. The Frenchman shook his head. "Gregorio Spina is not a man I want for an enemy."

"He underestimated Aurélie," said Longstaff, "he shouldn't have left her with that fool of a priest. Just think; she encouraged him to think she was possessed."

"You like her?"

"I like her."

Durant rolled his eyes. "Look at us. Waiting here like a couple of serving boys." He suppressed a sudden image of the girl, wriggling out of the Englishman's shirt, bending over the basin to wash her face and armpits.

"It's folly. It will never work."

"There's no harm in talking to the merchant," Longstaff saw the expression on Durant's face and shrugged. "Vescosi is my last hope of returning home."

"She is going to get us killed."

CHAPTER 22

Mathern Schoff knelt on the hard stone floor, at prayer beneath a painting of the crucified Christ. Since arriving at the Villa Spina, this small chapel had become his home. He shifted slightly and a bolt of pain ran up his thighs, into the small of his back. He tilted his head, breathing carefully. *Pain is a teacher.*

There was a cadaver tomb below the painting, carved from dark stone and bearing a short epigram:

I was once what you are, and what I am you will become.

It was intended to encourage reflections on death, but Schoff saw it as an exhortation to follow in Spina's footsteps. He felt another stab of pain. *I was not; I was; I am not; I do not care.* Epicurus' words ran through his head like a prayer – the ultimate heresy. Believe nothing, except that which you can test through observation and logical deduction. Pleasure and pain are the measure of what is good and evil, the soul dies with the body. Schoff shook his head, amazed he could recite these heresies like a children's rhyme.

The painting of Jesus was larger than life; the shadows cast by the heavy limbs appeared to escape the limits of the golden frame. *The physical world is constructed from our sins. To see beyond, deny the body.*

Schoff hadn't slept in days and hunger clawed at his belly. Spina's words ran through his mind like water. *Construct a building in your mind, furnish it. Build a church. Clothe God in your thoughts, as the masons clothe him in stone.*

Schoff joined his hands in prayer. He imagined they were a knife, cutting through the miasma of sin surrounding him. The denser the steel, the stronger the weapon. With God's help he would pierce this world of illusion and see the truth behind. Epicurus called them 'atoms', from the Greek for indivisible. Lucretius described them as the seeds of things. St. Benedict promised that the Book of Aal, at the heart of the Devil's Library, would give them power over these *seeds of things*, enough to rend the veil of illusion and ignite the final battle between Christ and Lucifer. Schoff tried to imagine the atoms in his hands, tried to see them with his soul.

This was the task Spina had set him – first at the monastery in Florence and now here – and Schoff could feel himself edging towards the clarity his master demanded. He was following St. Paul's dictum – *If you live according to the flesh, you will die. If you put to death the deeds of the body by the spirit, you'll live* – surviving on no more than a single hour of sleep at a time and just two pieces of fruit a day.

He resented every interruption, but mealtimes were an exquisite torture, wedged between Spina's two most trusted lieutenants.

Brother Dini was a slight man with nondescript features. A bookmaker once, Spina credited him with having doubled Dominican revenues in little more than a decade. Brother Chabal was reputedly one of the best swordsmen in Italy. Schoff often saw him on the lawn in front of the villa, sparring with another of Spina's men. Tall and thick shouldered, with skin the colour of mud, the monk appeared to take a perverse delight in mocking Schoff's hunger, filling trenchers of bread with pork, roasted beechnuts, wild apples and pears.

The former lawyer would sit beside him in silence, transfixed by the sheen of grease on the man's mouth, hardly daring to breath, afraid to release his hunger.

Gregorio Spina sat beside his brother, the remaining places taken by members of the household. Onofrio Spina would not allow any more of Spina's men to sit at his table, insisting they ate with the servants in the kitchens.

The two siblings could not have been more different. Onofrio Spina was a braggart. Schoff recognised the type; jealous of his younger brother's accomplishments and ashamed of his own pettiness. How could it be otherwise, when Gregorio Spina treated him so graciously?

The chapel door swung open. Schoff looked round in alarm, conscious he'd allowed his concentration to waver. Spina stood in the doorway. Schoff stared at the dark eyes, the neat features and hands, the large diamond on his forefinger, which glowed in the gloomy interior. "Do you have need of me, Master?"

"Presently," Spina sat on one of the low wooden benches. "You look tired, my son."

Thoughts occurred to Schoff during the long hours he spent at prayer. *Insights, granted by God.* He saved the best of them for Spina, hoping to impress, but his mind betrayed him whenever he came into the master's presence. Tears appeared in his eyes; he blinked them back angrily. What was wrong with him?

"I thought you might be Dini or Chabal," he hated himself for the note of petulance in his voice. "They often interrupt my devotions."

"On my command," Spina nodded. "Solitude is a wonderful teacher, but his lessons must be tempered with the society of brothers."

Schoff hung his head. "Of course."

"Do you doubt, my son?"

He could not meet Spina's eyes.

"Do you doubt our mission?"

"No!"

"Then you doubt yourself."

"I am weak," said Schoff. "I cannot concentrate."

Spina's voice was soft. "God expects so much of us. You have to make yourself strong and fierce, Schoff. Do you remember the painting in our church in Florence – the Triumph of the Church, dogs marching at the head of the procession of saints, martyrs and priests?"

Schoff nodded. He had found the dogs terrifying – close-set eyes, teeth like needles.

"The dogs are us, Mathern. Domini Canes. The Hounds of the Lord," he gestured at Schoff to rise. "Come with me. There's something you need to see."

Schoff forced himself to his feet, knees screaming in protest after so many hours at prayer. He'd lost weight and his robe filled with the light breeze as he followed Gregorio Spina across the lawn, hands folded and head bowed, towards a dense stand of trees.

"Only the battle is real," warned Spina. "Christ needs your strength and the Devil revels in your weakness. Guard against pity, my son, with as much vigilance as you guard against lust or greed."

A man called for them to stop. The administrator, Dini, strode towards them, a sheet of paper above his head.

"A rider from Rome, your Eminence."

Spina's expression darkened as he read the message.

"It's as you feared?" asked Dini.

"The fool. To bring such disgrace on the holy office."

"He's a pragmatist... "

"Then he should have become a banker."

Schoff felt the colour rise in his cheeks. They were discussing his Holiness the Pope.

"Send the rider back," continued Spina. "No message. This is something I will have to attend to personally. Soon." He looked towards the trees. "Are you joining us, Brother Dini?"

The administrator shook his head, "Chabal is already down there."

They walked down cold stone steps. Spina claimed to have no idea of the labyrinth's original purpose. "A pagan shrine to superstition, but perfect for our needs."

Giacomo Vescosi awaited them in the central chamber. Schoff stared at the Otiosi leader, grateful for Spina's warning. The devil had disguised his servant well, hiding his true nature behind round cheeks and wide, red-rimmed eyes.

He'd been defiant at first, pawing the palimpsest for hours as if his surroundings were a matter of complete indifference, demanding a reading glass and candles. Sitting, apparently lost in thought, for a whole day.

"There is something," he'd said eventually, "but my memory is not what it was." He'd written out a list of books. "It's not a code in the usual sense of the word. Lucretius was writing to a friend. I need to immerse myself in their world."

Dini and Chabal accused the humanist of stalling for time, but Spina was patient, sending his hounds to the library at the monastery of Santa Maria Novella. A week had passed since then and the days of fear and darkness had taken their toll on the humanist. He shrank from the damp walls of the chamber, flinching when the dogs barked, watching with wide eyes as Chabal prepared a small brazier. The broad-shouldered monk arranged his tools on a low table. Vescosi tried to hide in his nest of filthy straw.

"Spina, this is madness. I don't know how to find the library."

"You lie! You've known since the moment I showed you the palimpsest." He turned to Schoff. "Don't we perform God's work?"

The Lübeck lawyer nodded in reply. Was this why Spina liked to have him near? Had he become the master's conscience; his cold, northern temperament water to the flame of Spina's ardour?

"Yes, we perform God's work."

The brazier filled the room with heavy smoke. Chabal blew on the coals until they glowed in the half light.

"And have I not been patient with him?" persisted Spina. "Have I not brought everything he asks for, though he wilfully obstructs our holy work?"

Again, Schoff nodded. It was hot in the chamber. His flesh cringed as he looked at Chabal's table. He took a deep breath. The air was rank down here. As a lawyer he'd seen men tortured, criminals still insisting they were innocent after their guilt had been established. Not the most pleasant part of his work, but necessary – punishment could not come before a confession.

Chabal seized Vescosi by the hair, dragged him towards the table as he described the objects there. "Choke pear, knee-splitter, Heretic's Fork. Those are for tomorrow. Too much too soon and you'll grow to like it. I've seen it happen, people beg for more."

So had Schoff. The official examiner in Lübeck had been an imbecile, driving his subjects mad with pain when he should have been helping them see reason.

"Strappado first," Chabal tied the heretic's arms behind his back and passed the rope through an iron ring in the ceiling. Vescosi was shaking his head, eyes closed. Chabal pulled the rope taught, lifting him off the ground. The Otiosi leader screamed, more from fear than pain.

"Tell us, you fool," yelled Schoff, hearing desperation in his own voice. "We'll keep at you until you talk. We have no choice. Spare yourself the pain. Tell us what you know."

"Let me down."

Schoff looked round for permission before cutting the rope. The heretic scurried away from him, rubbing his shoulders, making for the low stone table in the centre of the chamber. He'd made a copy of Lucretius' letter and stabbed it with a forefinger, leaving a dark smudge beside one paragraph. "Read it."

"*And never does the shining sun look upon them,*" said Spina, "*but the moon does show them the way.* And then, a single word: VITRIOL."

Vescosi swallowed. "You can torture me, Spina, but you won't hold back the march of progress."

Spina laughed. "Tell me, Vescosi; what do you believe men will make of this world, if you convince them they can make it perfect?"

Vescosi shook his head, fear and contempt battling for control of his expression. Spina gestured at Chabal, who selected thumbscrews from among his tools.

"Vitriol isn't a word," said Vescosi quickly. "It's an acronym: Visita Interiora Terrae Rectificando Invenies Occultam Lapidem."

He waited for Spina to translate the Latin. "*Visit the interior of the earth to find the secret stone.* What does it mean?"

"The Library is hidden underground. You're looking for a network of caves."

"And the rest?"

Vescosi hesitated.

"I don't want to hurt you," said Spina softly. "I couldn't myself; I value your learning too much. Under different circumstances, I feel we might have been friends. That's why I need Chabal, you see." He paused. "Spare yourself, Giacomo. Once Chabal starts, he won't stop. Not until you've revealed the name of every member of the Otiosi. I'll destroy them all, one by one. Tell me where to find the Library and I will leave them in peace. You have my word."

Vescosi dipped his head, licking dry lips, burrowing among the pile of books on the stone table. "One of the texts I asked for," he said, "by a Roman geographer named Strabo. Read from here."

Spina held the book beneath a candle, his rich voice filling the chamber. "*The people prior to my time made it the setting of the story of Odysseus' journey to the Underworld; and writers tell us there actually was an Oracle of the Dead here; and there is a fountain of drinkable water at this place, but people abstain from it because they regard it as the water of the Styx; and the nearby hot springs are supposed to come from the fiery rivers of Hades. And the people there live in underground houses, which they call 'argillai', and it is through tunnels that they visit one another, back and forth, and also admit strangers to the source of knowledge, which is situated far beneath the earth; and they live on what they get from mining, and from those who consult the source, and those who live about the source have an ancestral custom, that no one should see the sun, but should go outside the caverns only during the night; and it is for this reason the poet speaks of them as follows: And never does the shining sun look upon them."*

"'And never does the shining sun look upon them'," repeated Vescosi, eyes closed. "I can't believe it never occurred to me."

Spina snatched the palimpsest, comparing the two texts. "Where is it?" he yelled.

Vescosi lowered his head. "Sooner or later, you would have solved the riddle without me."

"Where, damn you?"

"At Cumae, on the Bay of Naples. Cicero had a villa nearby. Julius Caesar. Pliny. So did Lucretius' patron. All gone now, buried by Vesuvius; a barren landscape known as the Phlegræn Field, or the 'fields devoured by fire'."

"And?"

Vescosi stared at him. "There's a hill, where the plateau of volcanic rock meets the sea. A mighty temple stood there once. Look for the statue of the goddess Luna."

"The moon does show them the way." Spina smiled. "Come along, Schoff. I need some fresh air," he looked at Chabal. "You know what to do."

"No," yelled Vescosi. "I've told you everything."

"Everything?" Spina turned on his heel. "You're a fool, Vescosi – the scope of your ambition limited to a few scraps of parchment. There is only one book of any worth in the Devil's Library; the rest merely clothe it, as our immortal souls are briefly clothed in flesh and blood."

Vescosi stared at him. "What book?"

"There is no life outside heaven and hell," Spina waved a hand "This is a dream, sent by God to help us find Him."

His dark eyes glittered as he shook his head. "Too many of us find Satan instead, the fallen angel who learned to twist the divine laws and lure us to damnation."

He leaned close to the Otiosi leader. "These are the Last Days, Vescosi. Righteous men will march at Christ's side and sinners will be cast into the flames. The book is the key, and I mean to find it. Whatever the cost."

CHAPTER 23

Aurélie insisted they visit Michaelis at once. Longstaff supported her through the streets of Florence; she was still weak, hiding her bruises in a deep hood. It was noon when they reached the Porta alla Croce. Longstaff ran his eyes across every doorway and widow. He strode into the tavern yard – a pair of merchants discussed the merits of a horse, potboys hurried back and forth – before gesturing for Durant and Aurélie to join him.

"Which way?"

She led them through the taproom, up a flight of stairs to a closed door. Durant raised his hand to knock. Aurélie beat him to it, turning the handle and putting her weight against the plain wood.

The young Strasbourg merchant half rose from behind his desk, reaching for the knife at his belt. Aurélie threw back her hood.

"You?" his mouth fell open. "What in God's name have you done to yourself. Who are these men?"

"Friends," said Durant.

"To myself?" said Aurélie. "This is Gregorio Spina's work. Vescosi has been abducted."

Michaelis grew pale. "God's teeth, girl. He knows who I am."

"He knows a thousand secrets. You can be sure he's in no hurry to reveal yours. Did you write to Onofrio Spina?"

The merchant narrowed his eyes. "Why?"

Shrewd, thought Longstaff. Despite his shock, he was already weighing the implications of her question.

"That's where they are holding Vescosi. You have to help us free him."

Michaelis did not reply at once, but flicked slowly through the papers on his desk. "This came from Onofrio yesterday. *Delighted to discover news of my connoisseurship has spread so far. Regret to inform I have house guests at present. Expect them to leave in the next few days. Will send word as soon as it's convenient to receive. Yours in anticipation, etcetera, etcetera.*" He looked at Aurélie, face a picture of sympathy. Trying to hide his relief, thought Longstaff sourly.

"I'll help in any way I can. For the time being, however, there's nothing we can do but wait."

Aurélie shook her head. "His house guests… "

Durant nodded. "His brother Gregorio, along with God knows how many men."

Longstaff had heard enough. "It's time we were going," he stared at the merchant. "You'll send word as soon as you hear?"

"Of course."

"Wait," said Aurélie.

Longstaff took her arm and ushered her out of the room. "Keep walking," he growled, afraid she might try to press Michaelis into smuggling them into the Villa Spina, keep the owner occupied while they ransacked the place for signs of a missing scholar – more than enough to send the merchant scurrying back to Strasbourg.

"It might be days before he hears from Onofrio. We can't afford to scare him."

In the street, she accused him of cowardice. At least she had the sense to keep her voice down until they reached his rooms. "We can't just leave him there."

"Tell her, Durant."

The Frenchman sighed. "We need more information. It's too soon to start involving strangers."

"Michaelis has been a member of the Otiosi for years."

"We don't know him," Longstaff's voice was flat and hard. He reached under the bed for his sword and musket. "I'll be back in a day or two."

"Where are you going?" she stood with hands on her hips, a fierce challenge in her blue eyes.

"Durant's told you already – we need more information."

Longstaff reined to a halt, the valley ahead an elegant quilt of vineyards, ascending into the gardens of the Villa Spina. There wasn't another building in sight, except in the far distance, where a lone cross peaked between a fold in the hills.

He followed Sparrow across a meadow and left Martlesham hobbled among the trees of a hunting park before continuing on foot. Aurélie had told him what happened here during the Italian War, about the bandits who'd attacked the villa shortly before Spina was born and held the family captive for more than a month. Onofrio was the older brother, a boy of six when it happened, and Longstaff wondered what kind of man would choose to remain in a place with such memories.

The villa had been built around an old medieval watch-tower. Longstaff assessed it with a soldier's eye. If the guards knew their business, an attacking force might reckon on losing two men in five before they reached the walls. A long, uphill slog into crossbow bolts and musket balls; at which point the defenders would retreat to the watchtower. Longstaff would bet every gold coin in his purse that it stood alone in a central courtyard, a killing field. One thing was clear; Vescosi could not be rescued by force of arms.

His focus wavered in the late afternoon. With a start, he realised that he'd been day-dreaming about the young woman. She had kissed him when he left the inn. Just a light, apologetic peck on the cheek, but he could still feel the soft caress of her breath. And her voice; honey and pain.

Concentrate, you fool. He looked up at the villa, detecting guards on the walls. If tomorrow proved as fruitless, he'd have to move closer under cover of night. The prospect hardly filled him with cheer as he walked back through the trees to Martlesham. He mounted, remembering the church spire he'd seen from the brow of the hill, as good a place as any to seek a bed for the night and a decent meal. He'd have preferred to sleep beneath the stars, but the people there might be able to tell him more about Villa Spina.

The village was deserted. No horses or cows in the nearby pastures, no smoke rising from the chimneys. Just a dozen empty homes clustered around a low wooden church, with no indication of why they'd been abandoned. Longstaff slid down from the saddle and made Martlesham fast to a hitching rail in front of the finest house.

A shallow bowl stood on the dining table, filled with brown apples, withered to the size of acorns. Longstaff pulled a chair across the unswept floor and sat beside the fireplace, making a cold supper of the provisions in his saddle-bag. Coarse black bread and stringy beef, washed down with weak beer.

There were years of honest toil in this house, and skill; the sort of competence in a dozen crafts that was slowly dying out. And love in the carvings and needlework, the notches made to record the growth of children. Animals would move in soon; foxes, rats and deathwatch beetles. It wouldn't take them long to destroy the traces of a family life. The elm pipes would freeze when winter came and splinter with the arrival of spring.

The mystery kept Longstaff awake long into the night. He thought of his family home in England. Was Jarrel still there, the man who'd sold his father to King Henry? Or was he long since dead? Was someone looking after the old place, or had it, too, been allowed to fall into ruin?

He climbed the church tower at first light, shading his eyes for a view of Villa Spina. The gates lay open, half obscured beneath a cloud of dust. Longstaff ran down the stairs, jumped on Martlesham and set off across country.

The abandoned village lay south-east of the Villa, while the horsemen rode south at an easy canter. Longstaff galloped hard to intercept them. He left Martlesham in a stand of trees, hurried up a small rise and threw himself down in long grass, listening for the rumble of hoof-beats.

There were fifteen men in total. Most of them were in hard-wearing leather boots, jerkin and coat, and carried short, double-edged swords and long pistols in the manner of light cavalry.

Longstaff's eyes lingered on the horseman at the head of the column – tall, thick shouldered, with long black hair and skin the colour of mud, wearing a great-sword tied slantways across his back. A musket hung from his saddle.

Longstaff blinked in the bright sunshine. He saw two familiar faces. Gregorio Spina, who'd passed himself off as Giacomo Vescosi, mounted on a tall stallion, and beside him, the lawyer from Lübeck. Longstaff shook his head. He hadn't given Mathern Schoff a thought in weeks, but how else could Spina have found out about the palimpsest? Schoff had grown thinner, dark rings beneath his eyes.

The riders were nearly past, a couple of well-laden pack animals bringing up the rear. Aurélie had described Vescosi, and Longstaff looked for a man in his mid-fifties with a high forehead and aristocratic nose, but the Otiosi's leader was nowhere to be seen.

The drum-roll of hoofbeats faded into silence. Longstaff spent the next hour cantering in their wake, until it became clear they were planning to bypass Florence. Was Vescosi dead? From the smile on Spina's face, he could only conclude the philosopher had given up his secrets. Longstaff hesitated, uncertain whether to keep following. Durant and Aurélie were waiting in Florence. Longstaff could see the tower of the Signoria in the distance. He turned aside with a curse, spurring Martlesham towards the city walls.

Longstaff had paid the landlord to turn a blind eye to his comings and goings; the man kept his expression carefully neutral as he swept past.

He hurried up the stairs and opened the door of his room without knocking. Empty. He saw a blanket and pillow on the wide couch. The sheets on the bed didn't look as if they'd been changed in days. He heard voices on the stairs. Still arguing, he thought to himself, just as they had been when he left. He sat in a tall armchair facing the window, knowing they wouldn't be able to see him when they entered. He closed his eyes, and pretended to be asleep.

The door opened. Longstaff heard something tossed casually onto the bed.

"You cannot reason with them," said Aurélie. "No point in trying. Last year, Mateo Columbo demonstrated that blood draws oxygen from the lungs. The proof is irrefutable. And how did the so-called doctors of the Church respond? They talked about the prophesies of St. John, who saw an angel lead the Devil away in chains and condemn him to a thousand's years in exile. They reserve their most terrible punishments for the people doing most to advance the cause of human knowledge, and insist they're serving the will of God."

"I agree," said Durant. "They fit their beliefs to their desires instead of striving for the opposite."

"But they can't stop people discovering the truth," said Aurélie, "Not forever. Our numbers grow, victories accumulate. More people are learning to see as we do."

Durant laughed. Longstaff had never heard such enthusiasm in his voice.

"You remind me of Montpellier. I wanted to shake the professors, force them to see the world as it truly is, rather than as it appears in the pages of ancient books."

"Exactly. Think of Miguel de Servet. Burned at the stake in Geneva, with green wood to prolong the agony. He was one of us, you know. And so are you, my friend. A servant of the truth."

Longstaff yawned loudly, stretching his arms as if he'd just woken. Aurélie appeared at his side. She wore a sober grey dress with a high collar. It was a size too small and he tried not to notice the way her breasts pushed against the fabric. She was beautiful, despite the fading bruises.

"I must have dozed off."

"What have you discovered?"

Longstaff rubbed a hand across his face. "Spina has left the villa. He's riding south with a dozen men at arms."

Durant frowned. "You should have followed them, Matthew. Sent word to us when you were able."

"Is Giacomo with them?" demanded Aurélie.

Longstaff didn't have the courage to tell her Vescosi was probably dead. He didn't need to; she read his thoughts as easily as words on a page.

"They won't have killed him," she said. "Giacomo knows too much. He is too valuable alive."

Longstaff looked at Durant for help.

"We have to be realistic, Aurélie," there was pain in the Frenchman's eyes. "If Giacomo is as valuable as you claim, they'd hardly have left him behind."

Aurélie shook her head. "Why didn't Spina kill me? He could have, but instead he had me locked in a monk's cell. He doesn't kill indiscriminately; that's not how he works. He keeps his enemies alive as long as he thinks he might need them."

Longstaff and Durant exchanged a look. "I hope you're right," said the Frenchman, "but we have to assume Vescosi has told Spina everything he knows."

Aurélie glared at him. "You want to follow Spina." It was an accusation, not a question.

"A company that size is bound to attract attention. If we leave now, there's a chance we can pick up the trail."

"I'm not a fool. I know they'll have tortured him, but it won't do any good. You can't understand because you haven't met him. Spina doesn't know what he's looking for. He's desperate, and Giacomo's mind has more twists than a labyrinth."

"You're saying he's sent them on a wild goose chase?"

She shook her head. "I'm saying he'll have withheld something vital. He knows more about the Devil's Library than any man alive."

"And if you're wrong? What if Spina has killed him?

"Then none of us will find the library. Deciphering the palimpsest is only the start."

Longstaff glanced at Durant, but couldn't read the Frenchman's expression. "How did you get on here?"

"I've been keeping an eye on the Strasbourg merchant. He tried to leave yesterday, terrified Vescosi will reveal his name before he's back in protestant lands. I persuaded him to reconsider."

"We'll hear from him today," interjected Aurélie. "Tomorrow at the latest."

Longstaff looked at her.

"Onofrio's bound to send for the muskets, now his guests have gone."

"What do you think, Matthew?" asked Durant.

Longstaff stared at the ceiling. "Giacomo Vescosi is a man of flesh and blood; I'm still not convinced this library is anything more than a myth."

Durant shook his head. "Michaelis may have served the Otiosi in the past, but he wants no part of this."

"We don't need him anymore," said Aurélie. "No one left at Villa Spina knows what you two look like."

CHAPTER 24

Aurélie was proved right three hours later, when Michaelis knocked at the door of their room clutching a message from Onofrio Spina – *Houseguests having finally departed, I await your arrival with pleasure.*

The Strasbourg merchant looked tired, the collar of his shirt damp with sweat. He stood for the duration of the visit, keeping a wary distance from Durant and not attempting to disguise his relief when told he was free to leave Florence.

"I've modified the crate according to your specifications and stripped the bills of lading," Michaelis looked at his hands. "I wish you didn't have to use my name."

"Keep yourself in the public eye until you leave," Aurélie pressed his arm. "You've been of great service."

The guns were in a warehouse on the banks of the river Arno. They couldn't collect them at once; they needed some kind of cart, and horses for Aurélie and Vescosi. Longstaff chaffed at the delay, pacing back and forth while Durant took charge of the negotiations.

"You drive a hard bargain, signore, but I find I can live with it," Durant snapped his fingers. "Pay the man."

Longstaff bit back a curse. He counted coins into the dealer's hands as Aurélie mounted a white mare. The cart was a makeshift affair – two wheels and two planks of wood. He gave it a kick before hitching it to the second horse.

Aurélie took the lead. She seemed to know every street in the city, taking them unerringly to a warehouse by the river.

The supervisor was expecting them – Michaelis had been as good as his word. Aurélie signed for the plain wooden box while Longstaff and Durant hauled it onto the cart. Longstaff cracked the lid to make certain of the contents. The image stayed with him as they rode north. He reached out a hand, resting it for a moment on the unmarked box. It was all the protection they had: twenty-four wheel-lock muskets, made in Suhl to the latest designs, and three dozen bags of powder and shot.

That night, they camped on a hilltop six miles from the Villa Spina, and shared a cold supper of bread and ham. Aurélie was quiet. Longstaff had tried to persuade her to stay at an inn, but she was determined to wait for them here. It was a clear night – cold when the sun dipped below the horizon – and she began to shiver. Sparrow lay down beside her. The young woman smiled as she warmed her hands in the dog's fur.

Longstaff made himself comfortable beneath his long coat, wondering what Aurélie saw when she looked at him. A soldier? It was just a word to her. He raised a hand to his padded jerkin, feeling for the campaign medals sewn into the lining. For the first time in years, he thought of Metz. He'd been twenty-five; thought he'd seen it all when his regiment joined up with the Holy Roman Emperor's army – one hundred and twenty thousand men in total. They'd expected to take the city in days, but the French had expelled the civilians and razed the suburbs, building high ramparts from the rubble. The weather turned and sickness swept the camp, killing sixty thousand in a month. The ground had frozen hard as iron; they'd left the corpses stacked in piles when the Emperor finally conceded defeat.

Longstaff buttoned his coat to the chin, counting the stars until he fell asleep.

They ate breakfast together in the pre-dawn light.

"Bring him back safely," said Aurélie. She was trying to hide it, but Longstaff could see how much she hated being left. She stood on the hilltop, watching as they eased the cart done the slope, back onto the road.

No one at the villa knew their faces – Gregorio Spina had left and his servant, Clement, lay dead in Florence – but it still paid to be cautious. Durant wore new boots, an embroidered shirt and pale grey doublet.

"Remember," he said, as they approached the Villa Spina down an avenue of cypress trees. "I am the Strasbourg merchant Signor Michaelis. You are Mattias Lammermeier, German mercenary and military expert. A man of few words."

Longstaff shifted in his saddle.

"Sure you're ready for this? Less than a week ago you were drunk and dribbling in the stews of Florence."

Durant smiled. "We have to finesse our hosts, not bludgeon them to death. Your usual approach to problem solving will get both of us killed."

"Usual approach?"

"Standing about, waving your sword."

They were less than a hundred yards from the gates. Two massive plinths supported statues of unknown men, both with one arm raised, stone fingers gripping the ends of an iron ribbon into which the Spina coat of arms had been woven.

Longstaff assessed the guards. Like the villa itself, he thought. The costumes might be decorative, but their eyes were hard beneath the slouch berets, the hilts of the short swords worn with use.

Durant dipped his head.

"Michaelis of Strasbourg and my associate Herr Lammermeier. Here to see Signor Spina."

The senior man held out his hand for their weapons.

"You are expected. Your personal arms will be returned when you leave."

Longstaff gave up his musket and *katzbalger*, Durant his slim rapier, but the guards did not insist on a more thorough search. Longstaff watched for signs of a trap, ready to spur his horse and cut a bloody path to the gates.

They dismounted in the stable yard. Longstaff counted eighteen stalls, at least six lying empty. A man glided down the villa steps and strode across the lawn, in his mid-fifties, clean-shaven and paunchy, dark hair falling to his collar in loose curls. He wore a simple linen shirt, breeches and a thin gold chain around his neck.

"Signor Onofrio Spina," announced the senior guard.

Durant bowed. "It's an honour to meet you, Signor Spina. I am Michaelis of Strasbourg. This is Mattias Lammermeier, and his dog."

"A fine-looking animal," declared Onofrio Spina, taking Longstaff's *katzbalger* from the guard and swinging it through a few lazy strokes. "Seen plenty of action, I judge." He looked at the musket. "You use a matchlock weapon, Lammermeier?"

"You know how soldiers are," interjected Durant. "Sentimental to a fault."

He removed a crowbar from his pack and pried open the wooden box, stepping back as if dazzled. The Frenchman was a natural salesman, determined to extract the best possible price. He seized a musket, letting sunlight play along the virgin barrel before pressing it into his host's hands.

"Note the craftsmanship."

Onofrio raised the stock, sighting along the barrel, taking aim at one of his men and miming fire and recoil. He held out a hand to Longstaff.

"Powder and shot."

"Of course," said Durant easily, "I'm sure you'd like to test the weapon's accuracy as well as its power. Might I suggest your men construct a target on the lawn?"

Onofrio gestured to waiting guard. "See to it. And bring wine. Our guests must be tired after their journey."

The wide lawn was dotted with statues. To their number, Onofrio's men added a makeshift scarecrow. Servants appeared from inside the villa, carrying glasses and a bottle of dark red wine. Onofrio poured for his visitors.

Longstaff gauged the distance between the table and the scarecrow. "Perhaps we might move a little closer, Signor Spina?"

Onofrio barked, "If your machine's as good as you claim, we should be able to hit the target from here."

"Load the musket, Lammermeier," Durant smiled at their host, gesturing at the various statues. "You have a beautiful collection."

Longstaff was finished in seconds. There was no need to light a match – the wheel-flint lock would ignite the powder. He waited as Durant examined a marble statue of a boy falling backwards.

"You have a good eye, Signor Michaelis," said Onofrio. "There's a story attached to that statue."

Durant smiled. "I would love to hear about it later."

Onofrio accepted the musket from Longstaff without looking at him. Sighting along the barrel, he fired and missed the target by several yards. He turned to Durant.

"Hardly the weapon you led me to expect, Michaelis."

Longstaff stepped forward.

"Signor Spina, forgive me, but perhaps you're not accustomed to such power. Maybe you are overcompensating for the distance?"

He took the musket from his host and reloaded, aiming and firing in one smooth movement. There was a moment's delay, before a clump of straw flew up from the distant scarecrow.

"Even at this range, it's unnecessary to aim more than an inch above the head," continued Longstaff. "This is a precision instrument. The trigger is sensitive. Keep your hands soft, fire on the outward breath."

Longstaff watched him closely. Onofrio stood upright, setting one foot far in front of the other – a hunter rather than a soldier – but he kept his cheek tight against the stock, placed his left hand at the very end of the forestock and controlled his breathing well.

Not bad, thought Longstaff approvingly, unaware of the man approaching from behind until he cleared his throat. Onofrio jerked the trigger, missing the target by inches. He turned, face dark with anger. "Dini, you idiot, don't you know enough not to sneak up on a man when he's shooting?"

Longstaff looked down, determined not to make eye contact with Durant. Aurélie had mentioned a Brother Dini, Gregorio Spina's right-hand man, responsible for managing the finances of the sprawling Dominican Order. He was dressed in a dark robe of excellent quality, hair neatly smoothed to one side, the bland features oddly monochrome.

"Forgive me, signore, but I thought you'd finished," he turned to Durant. "My name is Bartolomeo Dini. I am a guest here."

Onofrio looked as if he might explode. He handed the musket to Longstaff. "Reload."

"Of course, signore."

Even with the interruption, Onofrio's second shot had been better than the first. "The breeze is deceptive today," murmured Longstaff. "Blowing more strongly from right to left than I had thought."

Onofrio snatched the musket and put the stock to his shoulder, closed one eye and pulled the trigger. Straw danced above the scarecrow's right shoulder.

"Just above the heart!" he shouted.

"Congratulations," said Durant smoothly. "But it is impossible to appreciate the true revolutionary potential of this musket until you've seen it deployed in numbers. With your permission, I would like to distribute a dozen among your men..."

"Is that really necessary?" interrupted Dini. "I don't know what Signor Spina has told you, but he has no need for so many guns, and no intention of paying your inflated prices even for one."

"My brother must hate me. Of all the men in his retinue, why in God's name did he have to leave you?" Onofrio turned to Durant. "My men are already proficient with firearms." He paused, as if seeking the solution to a particularly vexing problem. "I have a suggestion, signore. I'll give your man six of my most useless servants. He can have them for three hours, then we'll gather again, find out if your muskets are as good as you claim. What do you say?"

"I accept," Durant smiled broadly.

CHAPTER 25

While Spina led Durant on a tour of the grounds, Longstaff trained the motley crew of servants until they were ready to drop. He'd have worked them harder still, but worried they would blow each other to bits.

"Stand up straight," he snapped. "You're not servants any more. You're soldiers, brothers, who think as one and act as one."

He had them assemble a series of targets and drilled them for two hours, taking pleasure in the familiar commands. Spina and Durant disappeared into the house when he issued ammunition, continuing their conversation away from the noise of gunfire and smell of powder.

Longstaff let the men rest for five minutes, approaching the youngest, a stable lad of twelve.

"It won't bite," he pointed at the musket. "Don't leave it in the grass. Pick it up, get used to the weight of it." The boy obeyed, his face a mask of anxiety.

"Where do you sleep? With the horses?"

The lad shook his head. "We have a room in the house."

"Imagine the musket is your pillow. Rest your cheek against the stock, keep your hands soft," he raised his voice. "All of you, back on your feet."

Durant strolled across the lawn. "The three hours are nearly up, Herr Lammermeier. Time for you and your charges to show us what you can do."

Four of Onofrio's men appeared, carrying the remaining muskets between them.

"A salesman's work is never done," laughed Durant, opening the crate and arranging the gleaming weapons neatly on their wooden saddles.

Onofrio arrived with more of his guards, all armed to the teeth. Durant engaged him in easy conversation. Longstaff admired the Frenchman's nerve; he didn't think he could have spent so many hours in Onofrio's company without giving himself away. He walked over to inspect his men. Not used to being the centre of attention, they were clearly uncomfortable in their unmatched clothes.

"I'm proud of what you have accomplished in such a short space of time. Ready?"

They nodded with varying degrees of uncertainty. "Yes, sir," said one.

Longstaff took a step back, winked at them.

"Attention," he roared.

Each man drew himself up to his full height, musket-stock cupped in the right hand, long barrel against the shoulder.

"Forward march."

They wouldn't have passed muster in Il Medeghino's army, but it was not a complete disaster. They wheeled left and right on command, presenting arms to their audience and arranging themselves into two short rows of three, one behind the other, at a distance of thirty paces from the targets.

Onofrio seemed to be enjoying himself.

"Impressive," he said as Longstaff approached. "Didn't think they had it in them."

Longstaff bowed. "Drilling infantry is nothing new. It keeps men fit and disciplined. In a typical army, however, with officers in direct command of a thousand men, it serves no tactical purpose," he paused. Dini strode towards them across the lawn. Onofrio waved at Longstaff to continue.

"With officers in command of so many men," said Longstaff, nodding courteously to the newcomer, "it's no surprise that soldiers behave like cattle on the battlefield."

"You would do it differently?"

Longstaff nodded. "Create smaller units, promote men from within the ranks to lead, allowing them to react quickly and efficiently, even in the heat of battle."

"Very good, Lammermeier," said Durant. "Thank you."

Longstaff waved over one of the servant soldiers.

"Every army in Europe issues its men with a variation on the firelock. Not a bad weapon, but poor in comparison to this. Look here. A rotating, geared wheel, powered by a cocked spring. The spark, which ignites the powder in the flash-pan, is generated mechanically. The advantages are threefold; the weapon is more reliable, easier to handle and aim, and has a significantly better rate of fire. Allow me to demonstrate."

Longstaff took his leave with a short bow, turned on his heel and marched to his men. Half a dozen pale faces. "Stand up straight," he spoke softly but firmly, making eye contact with each of them in turn. "Just like we practised. Show these bastards what you're made of." He raised his voice. "On my command, commence volley fire. Fire!"

The first rank fired and dropped to their knees, where they immediately began to reload. The second rank fired and followed suit. There was a long pause – too long – before the first were on their feet again, firing again. Bits of straw flew off the targets.

The second rank fired again. *Better.* The first rank dropped to their knees. Longstaff said a silent prayer that he wasn't about to get someone killed. The second rank fired, then walked through the gaps between their comrades, before dropping to their knees and reloading. Slowly, maintaining the same rate of fire, they began to advance on the straw figures, reducing them to chaff.

Longstaff gave the command to cease fire. Taking a deep breath, he walked over to Onofrio, Durant and Dini.

"That from six poorly trained men," said Durant. "Imagine six hundred disciplined soldiers."

Onofrio's eyes were shining. "Imagine six thousand!"

Dini turned to Longstaff. "Tell me, if these rifles are so much better, why are they so rarely used?"

"Cost," answered Longstaff briskly. "Wheel-lock muskets are twice as expensive to produce as firelock weapons." He nodded at the six servants. Onofrio's men were already disarming them, sending them back to their duties in the kitchens and stables. "Currently, regiments are formed as needed, usually from peasants pressed into service, then dismissed. Promotes a mercenary mindset and limits the time officers have with their men. Without commissioning men from within the ranks and dividing regiments into smaller units, it is difficult to make the advantages of this weapon count.

"But it is the future," he continued. "Soon, a new Charlemagne will emerge, with the wealth and vision to build a professional army. And he'll have Europe at his mercy."

Onofrio looked at the muskets, each one a shining work of art, lying in neat rows on the snug saddles.

"We will talk in the morning, Michaelis. Tonight, you and your associate may dine with me as guests."

A servant led Longstaff up a wide, antler-lined staircase, showing him into a bedroom on the second floor. The walls were covered with dozens of stuffed birds and Sparrow dropped to his haunches, eyeing them warily. Longstaff shrugged off his jerkin and shirt, looking at the large bowl on the dressing table. He was about to plunge his face in the water when he heard a knock at the door. Durant came in, looking pleased with himself.

"Are you ready to go down for dinner, Herr Lammermeier?"

The Frenchman closed the door behind him and lowered his voice.

"I've been at work while you were playing soldiers. Onofrio is just as Aurélie described. A braggart with delusions of grandeur and guards he doesn't need. I posed as an art lover and he took me on a tour of the grounds. There's a grotto in the trees, here long before the house was built according to Onofrio. He would have told me more, but we were interrupted. A man appeared; our host fell silent at once. A poet would no doubt say a shadow crossed his face."

"What man?"

"The very question I asked. A guard, said Onofrio, but he wasn't dressed like the rest of them – leather boots, jerkin, cavalryman's coat. Short sword and pistol."

Longstaff rubbed his face. "What do you make of Dini?"

"Nasty little man. But if Spina's left him here, there's a good chance that Giacomo's still alive."

Longstaff looked at Durant, remembering the inn on the Old Salt Road and the Frenchman saying he lacked imagination. They didn't have that luxury now. "We have to kill him, Gaetan. Otherwise he'll go straight to Gregorio Spina."

Durant removed a small phial from the inside pocket of his doublet. "Leave Dini to me."

Longstaff stared at the greenish liquid. "You really think we can carry this off?"

"Aurélie does. Pains me to say it, but she's cleverer than I am."

Dinner was served on the villa's south-facing terrace, bordered on the far side by a low wall and roofed with vines. The company was still on their feet when Longstaff joined them, Onofrio holding court wearing a scarlet doublet.

"The true hunter moves to a rhythm few can hear, in secret harmony with his prey."

Longstaff saw a fleeting look of contempt on Dini's face.

Onofrio turned to him. "Lammermeier, good of you to join us. Dini you know, of course. And this is my wife, Dorothea."

She was barely sixteen and blushed as Longstaff bowed to her. She had plucked her hairline to frame a pretty face, but the bloom of youth was already fading.

Onofrio gestured at a slim young man with dark hair and startling green eyes.

"My wife's music teacher – a wedding gift from her husband," Onofrio clearly regretted his generosity. "Dorothea's two companions." A pair of plain young women lowered their eyes. "And my dear friend Maria." Onofrio pressed the hand of a woman in her late thirties. She was handsome, after a fashion, with a strong jaw and dark eyes.

"We are an odd number for dinner, but it cannot be helped, Signor Dini," Onofrio laughed, before placing himself at the head of the long table, Maria to his left, Durant in place of honour at his right. He sat his wife at the far end of the table, with Dini and the music teacher for company. Candles cast a soft light.

Servants appeared with a first course of crayfish and fledgling birds. Longstaff had been seated beside Maria, Sparrow curled against his legs.

Onofrio told the servant to pile Durant's plate with thick slices of venison.

"Farmed meat makes a man weak. You'd know, if you'd ever looked a cow in the eye."

Maria turned to Longstaff. "I understand you're the expert on guns, Herr Lammermeier." Her dark eyes were extravagantly made up.

Longstaff smiled. Onofrio was a bastard for parading his mistress, but he knew the wisest course was to pretend he found her charming.

"I hope you weren't disturbed by our short demonstration?"

"Not at all. Like Signor Spina, I find military matters fascinating." Longstaff suspected her smile was as insincere as his own. Durant came to his rescue, leaning across the table.

"Signor Lammermeier fought at Marciano."

"A hero," drawled Maria.

Durant looked at Onofrio. "Eight thousand men died in the battle. If Il Medeghino's men had been properly armed, he might have saved half."

Longstaff bit his tongue.

"Half the princes in Christendom are still furious with Columbus for putting them to the trouble of changing their maps," Onofrio snorted with laughter. "Playing their games with horse and lance, judging modern weaponry as dishonourable. There's nothing honourable in defeat, eh, Michaelis?"

"Nothing at all."

"Signor," the music teacher leaned towards Longstaff. "I have discovered a quite extraordinary talent in Dorothea."

"Good," Longstaff smiled at the girl. He couldn't read her expression and wished he had Durant's way with words.

"Suhl's a Lutheran city, is it not?" Dini's voice was high and nasal. "You can't imagine how frustrating it is, trading with your countrymen. They're all obsessed with the end of the world. It will happen one day, of course, but if a nation is to prosper, businessmen must plan for its indefinite continuation, don't you think?"

"Of course," began Longstaff. Dini's eyes betrayed a dangerous intelligence. Did he suspect something? This time, when Longstaff raised his glass to his lips, he did not pretend to drink.

"Martin Luther brought much pain to the people who loved him most. Dress simply, he said and put tailors and jewellers out of work. Eat meat during lent, he said and destroyed the fishing industry on your northern coast. Paternosters ruined by his thoughtlessness, candlemakers, traders in incense."

"I apologise, Lammermeier," Onofrio's face was red.

Dini was unruffled. "I'm a practical man, Signor Spina. I cannot understand why you've invited these two gentlemen to stay. What can you possibly want with two dozen guns? You don't even need the guards you have."

"These muskets would make Signor Spina's men the best equipped in the country," interrupted Durant sharply.

"Hear that?" Onofrio leant forward on his knuckles. "The best in the country, Dini. There's not many can make the same claim."

"Only one, generally speaking," replied Dini.

Durant helped himself to more meat. "It is time you put me out of my misery, Signor Spina. You promised me the story of your statue."

"Really," interjected Dini. "Again?"

There was hatred in Onofrio's eyes.

"Ignore him," Maria rested a manicured hand on his forearm. Onofrio composed himself and turned to Durant.

"I take it you've heard of Michelangelo?"

"Who in Europe hasn't?"

"Just so, an international celebrity, but his approach to sculpture wasn't always widely admired. He was often overlooked as a young man and decided to discover a classical precedent for his unique style, rather than wait for fashion."

Durant snapped his fingers. "Laocoön. The sculpture in your garden is a copy of the younger son."

Onofrio shook his head. "Not a copy, Signor Michaelis. A study."

Durant burst out laughing. "You're not suggesting Laocoön was sculpted by Michelangelo? Pliny describes it almost exactly in one of his books."

"Quite so," agreed Onofrio. "'A work to be preferred to all the art of painting and sculpture have produced.' Odd, don't you think, that we should have found one of the few classical masterpieces for which we have a detailed description, half buried in a field near Rome?" He shook his head, smiling. "My grandfather and Michelangelo were friends. He was there on the night they buried Laocoön on old Felice's land. As thanks for his help, the artist gave my grandfather a study he'd made for the sculpture."

Durant's eyes went wide.

Onofrio laughed. "And it's not for sale."

The candles guttered; the shadows grew longer. Longstaff assumed a lopsided smile and excused himself. He walked away from the terrace, crossed the lawn to the trees on the far side, assessing the disposition of Onofrio's guards as he unlaced his trousers. A single man made regular circuits of the house. Longstaff was more interested in the stables, where their muskets had been stored for the night. As far as he could see, the low wooden building lay unguarded. He stared up at the watchtower. There was no one in sight, no musket barrel poking over the edge, but it was impossible to be sure.

The servants were clearing plates when he stepped into the candlelight to resume his place.

"Come, come, Dorothea," Maria was saying, "the house talks of how diligently you practise. Your teacher often boasts of your talent."

The music teacher nodded drunkenly.

Onofrio's young wife sat in her blue gown, pale cheeks flushed, a rash of embarrassment blooming above her bodice.

Onofrio stood. "Maria is right. You spend so many hours practising, my dear. I'd like to hear you sing."

She lowered her eyes. "Of course. I'd be happy to sing for you."

"Now," continued Onofrio.

She looked at him in confusion. "In front of strangers… "

"We're all friends here. One song, Dorothea. I insist."

The company followed their host, carrying drinks to the music room. Durant stayed at the table a moment longer, straightening his doublet, chair legs scraping on the flagstones as he rose, tripping Dini.

"Signor, I'm so sorry. Let me help you."

The houseguest pushed him away, brushing spots from his robe. Durant retrieved his glass from the flagstones. "It's not broken. Are you sure you're all right? Here, let me get you another. How fortunate you're wearing black."

Longstaff stood in a corner of the music room, beside a low table covered with sheets of printed music. The elegant markings meant nothing to him. Nor did the names: Giovanni Pierluigi da Palestrina, Claude le Jeune, Josquin des Prez.

He caught Durant's eye. The Frenchman nodded once as the music teacher addressed the room.

"Dorothea and I have been working on a madrigal by the great Orlande de Lassus, whose music speaks to people about their own lives."

Dorothea took a reluctant step forward, caught between the conflicting demands of convention and her husband's command. It was a calculated insult, demanding that she perform in front of guests, and still she managed to offer him a shy smile. Longstaff was surprised by how much he wanted her voice to be the equal of the teacher's boasts. She started badly, striking several false notes, but then the teacher joined his voice to hers and seemed to catch her. She closed her eyes, giving herself to the melody.

Longstaff glanced at Dini, sitting in an armchair and sipping his wine.

Dorothea had a sweet voice. As the final notes faded into silence, the music teacher looked around the room in triumph.

"Very nice, I suppose," said Maria, "though a little mannered for my taste."

Longstaff got to his feet, out of patience with this spiteful charade. "It has been a wonderful evening, Signor

Spina. Michaelis and I cannot thank you enough for treating us so generously, but it is late and we were up early this morning. Might we be permitted to retire?"

CHAPTER 26

Four hours before dawn, Longstaff stood at the dark, second floor window and counted under his breath. He wore black, cheeks and forehead dark with soot from the fireplace, three knives hidden in his clothes. Sparrow watched, reproachfully.

Onofrio's guard appeared and Longstaff stopped counting. Forty-eight. The guard crossed the lawn and disappeared around the building. Climbing out onto the thin ledge, Longstaff said a silent prayer and stepped backwards into the empty night.

His fingers found the window ledge below. Years swinging a double-handed war-sword had made his arms and shoulders strong. Longstaff dropped the remaining ten feet and crouched in shadow, as the guard made his weary circuit of the villa.

He sprinted to the trees on the far side of the lawn. Branches swayed in the night breeze, an owl saluted the three-quarter moon. *Come on, Gaetan.* The Frenchman emerged beside him.

"The grotto is this way."

"And the guard?"

Dini's man stood in moonlight, musket propped yards away against the grotto wall. Longstaff rose like a snake, one arm round the man's throat to stop him crying out. He lifted him off the ground, ignoring the boot heels drumming at his shins. The man clawed at his hands, but Longstaff was implacable, choking him until the body went limp. He changed grip, sensing he would pay a high price for this life, then snapped the man's neck.

He opened the dead man's shirt and traced the moonlit brand – pointed muzzle, two rows of long, jagged teeth – the same symbol he'd seen on the dead servant's chest in Florence.

From a distance, the grotto looked made from melted wax, but the stone was cold and hard to the touch. Longstaff dragged the guard's body inside, leaving it in darkness. The passage narrowed, his shoulders brushed the walls as he groped his way forward. He lit a hooded lamp, revealing a heavy wooden door. Durant dropped to his knees and removed a scalpel and tweezers from a cloth roll.

Tumblers clicked in the silence. Longstaff removed the lamp's hood. Steps led down into darkness. At the bottom, three identical passageways led from an empty chamber.

"A maze?"

"God knows. The Romans had strange beliefs."

Torches were mounted above each of the doors. Longstaff took two, lit them from the lamp and handed one to Durant.

"Always turn left if you want to beat a maze."

"Lead on, Matthew. It can't be that big. As long as we avoid walking up and down the same passages, we should be fine."

They walked in the wavering circles of light cast by the torches. Five times, Longstaff turned left, before they came to one of Durant's soot crosses. The Frenchman added a second mark to the first and turned right.

Claws struck the stone floor behind them. Longstaff turned, stabbing with the dagger. He was beneath the creature, arms raised to protect his face, caught in its death throes. He kicked free and grabbed the torch. A dog lay at his feet, black and white with a broad head like a hammer.

Durant spat a curse. "Let's find Vescosi and get out of here."

The centre of the maze. Longstaff peered through an iron portcullis and saw a second gate on the far side. He heard movement, coming from a nest of filthy straw in a corner of the chamber.

"We're friends," he called. "Here to get you out."

Durant picked the lock. "Can you walk?"

Wide, fearful eyes peered back at them, long limbs curled up tight, tufts of grey hair behind each ear.

"Who are you?"

"Your book finders."

Vescosi moved like a wounded animal. He was tall, with narrow shoulders; one arm hung uselessly at his side. There were burns on his chest and four of his fingernails had been torn away. He blinked in the torchlight, staring at them in turn.

"Matthew Longstaff and Gaetan Durant? I fear one of you will have to support me."

Barking filled the chamber. Another dog threw itself at the second, locked portcullis.

"Time to go," said Durant.

Longstaff hauled Vescosi over one shoulder and ran for the open gate.

"How many are there?"

"Four."

Vescosi groaned in pain as they sped down the narrow passageways. Longstaff clutched his dagger, hand aching for the *katzbalger* under lock and key in the villa.

"Take him, Gaetan," he dropped Vescosi and turned. Three shapes hurtled out of the darkness, paws slapped the hard stone. The leader leapt. Longstaff stabbed with the knife and struck the animal a fatal blow though the eye.

The passage was narrow, the remaining pair could only attack singly and he kept them at bay with torch and dagger, walking backwards past Durant's crosses, waiting for the dogs to recover their courage. They attacked as he reached the entrance chamber. Longstaff took the first through the throat, blinded the second with the torch, before stamping savagely on the wide head.

Durant was on the stairs, Vescosi across one shoulder. Longstaff hurried past, found the dead guard's corpse and threw it down with the dogs. Durant closed the door and started working the lock.

The Otiosi leader slumped to the floor, face ashen in the torchlight. Longstaff put a hand on his arm.

"We must keep moving."

They extinguished the torches, waiting as long as they dared for their eyes to become accustomed to the darkness. Longstaff crept to the entrance and listened to the night, scanning the silhouettes of trees and bushes. Minutes passed before he felt safe to move.

They ran between the trees, supporting Vescosi between them. He was clearly in pain, holding the injured arm to his chest and breathing hard. They lay flat at the edge of the lawn and watched the guard amble among the statues, peacock feather flat against the slouch beret.

"We don't have long," whispered Longstaff, outlining their route to the stables. Vescosi nodded.

"Now," hissed Durant.

Longstaff prayed the young servant had been right when he said the stables lay empty at night. Leaving Durant and Vescosi, he slipped round the side of the building. Horses stirred, but no sign of guards. He opened the stall where their crate had been left. Durant appeared, half carrying Vescosi inside. Longstaff closed the stable door.

The Otiosi leader shivered in the clean straw.

"Aurélie found you?"

"She's waiting nearby."

The two men worked quickly, prizing open the lid, putting the muskets aside. Durant removed the false bottom, revealing a tiny space beneath.

"It's an hour before dawn, signore. Onofrio Spina will insist on giving us breakfast, but with luck we can leave in four hours."

Vescosi stared at the crate. "There's no other way?"

Longstaff spoke harshly. "Kill the guards and ride away?"

"Very well," Vescosi lay down in the crate. Longstaff wedged a horse-blanket above his head. "Stay awake. Keep silent."

Durant turned Vescosi's head to one side.

"Four hours and you'll be free of this place. Good luck, signore," they replaced the rough wooden planks, flush against the side of his face, then the muskets.

"Can you get back to your room?" asked Longstaff.

Teeth flashed in the darkness.

"See you at breakfast, Herr Lammermeier."

CHAPTER 27

Longstaff slept for an hour, Sparrow curled against him on the wide bed. He woke at dawn, washed in cold water and removed his clothes from beneath the mattress, brushing them to erase traces of the previous night. Standing in the window, he listened for sounds of movement in the house, watching as the early morning sun burned away the clouds. Onofrio and Durant emerged on the lawn, strolling among the statues. The Frenchman looked fresh in pale grey doublet, gesturing purposefully at the ruined targets. Onofrio threw back his head and laughed.

Longstaff walked to the terrace. Dorothea and her two companions were sitting at one end of the table. The music teacher was nearby, picking at a plate of bread and cheese. His curls had lost their bounce and there were dark rings beneath his eyes.

Longstaff nodded to them. He was helping himself to food when Onofrio and Durant appeared.

"If you ever reconsider, Signor Spina, I hope you'll think of me first."

Onofrio clapped him on the back.

"Do you hunt, Michaelis? We should ride to the park after breakfast."

"Alas, signore, business calls. My associate and I are expected in Genoa."

Longstaff stood. "I helped myself. I hope you don't mind?"

"Not at all. Maria never rises before midday and Dini sent down word that he's indisposed."

"Nothing serious, I trust?"

Onofrio laughed. "God is rarely so kind," he turned to Durant. "A ten-point stag, Michaelis. Sure I can't tempt you?"

"Save him for me, signore. I hope to hear from you again," he smiled. "Three muskets won't change the world."

"Look around you, Michaelis. The world is fine as it is."

Longstaff followed the sweep of Onofrio's arm across the quilt of fields and vineyards, down to the hunting park in the valley. It was beautiful in the morning light, but he felt no need to linger. "It's time we were on our way, Michaelis."

Onofrio accompanied them across the lawn. Longstaff glanced at the watchtower, half expecting to hear the crack of musket fire. The stables were crowded with Onofrio's men, four of them carrying the crate into the yard. A single cough or groan and they were doomed. Durant removed the lid, taking out three muskets and presenting his host with as many bags of powder and shot.

"Gratis, signore. A token of my esteem."

"It's been a pleasure, Michaelis," Onofrio took Durant's rapier from a waiting guard, handing it to the Frenchman and kissing him on both cheeks.

He flipped Longstaff's *katzbalger* in the air, catching it by the blade, offering it hilt first, then shook his head over the match-lock musket.

"It's a poor salesman who won't use his own product."

"So Michaelis keeps telling me," Longstaff pulled himself up onto Martlesham's broad back, holding his breath as the crate was loaded on their makeshift cart. "Farewell, signore."

The cart rumbled into motion. Remembering Vescosi's injuries, Longstaff winced each time they struck a pothole. Sparrow ran alongside, barking at the crate, but Onofrio's men waved them on through the tall gates.

Giacomo Vescosi began whimpering long before they cleared the brow of the nearest hill. They threw the muskets aside, yanking away the false bottom. Vescosi covered his eyes with one arm and blinked in the sunlight. He was sweating, cheeks stained with tears.

"Do what you can, Gaetan, but hurry," Longstaff looked back – still no sign of alarm at the villa. He kicked the crate to pieces, throwing the guns into a nearby copse of trees.

Durant smiled. "Michaelis would have a fit if he knew."

"To Hell with Michaelis. Can Vescosi ride?"

The Otiosi leader had passed out. Longstaff mounted Martlesham.

"Pass him up, Gaetan."

They galloped down the road, Durant leading the third horse. Longstaff rode with his knees, using his arms to keep Vescosi in the saddle.

Durant looked back when they left the road, making for the hill where they'd left Aurélie.

"What do you make of that?"

Longstaff saw a thin column of dust on the horizon.

"It's a public road. Might be anything."

"Or it might be Onofrio's men."

They urged tired horses up the slope. Aurélie was waiting. She led them further into the copse, pointing to a bed of leaves. Vescosi stirred as Longstaff laid him down. Aurélie passed Durant his medical kit.

"Do something."

Longstaff ran back through the trees, lying flat in the long grass, staring down at the road. Three young noblemen rode past with a servant; too well dressed to be out hunting, they were probably on their way to Florence. Longstaff grinned. He and the Frenchman had dovetailed seamlessly, each man playing to his strengths, knowing the other would compensate for weakness.

Durant joined him an hour later, opening a water-skin and washing his hands and face.

"Any sign of Onofrio's men?"

Longstaff shook his head. "How is Vescosi?"

The Frenchman stretched.

"I've treated the burns, re-set his shoulder and given him something for the pain. The missing fingernails are painful, but hardly life-threatening."

"Can we move him?"

"He needs rest, Matthew. It will be dark in a couple of hours. We can't go any further today."

"Tomorrow may be too late."

"Can't be helped. He's awake. Says Spina is looking in the wrong place," Durant made himself comfortable in the grass. "He wants to talk to you."

Vescosi was thin and balding, with a soft belly and sloping shoulders. He was covered in bandages, eyes more red than brown in the pale face.

"How are you feeling, signore?"

The Otiosi leader managed a weak smile.

"Wiser. Older."

Longstaff glanced at Aurélie, sitting with her hand on Vescosi's forehead.

"I've seen men tortured," he said. "Even the strongest reveal their secrets."

"You're right, Longstaff. I soon as Spina showed me the palimpsest, I realised where the Library must lie, and when he threatened me with torture, I told him. Fortunately, he didn't press me on *how* to find it. If he had, I'd have sent him after you."

Longstaff looked at Aurélie. Had the old man lost his wits?

"Me, signore?"

"Ivan's book," continued Vescosi. "You do still have it?"

Longstaff scratched his jaw.

"It's in Florence; in the strongbox at my inn. No one seemed to want it."

Vescosi began to laugh. "I hope you didn't think I'd sent you all the way to Moscow for nothing."

CHAPTER 28

Two miles north-east of Rome, thirteen men stood in a fringe of trees, waiting patiently for their master to return. Gregorio Spina had ridden ahead, taking only his enforcer, Chabal, for protection. Mathern Schoff was one of the men left behind, still in his lawyer's robes. The others were dressed alike in boots, jerkins and long cavalrymen's coats. Some were former soldiers. Others had been priests or Dominican monks. Some were highborn, destined for the Church, schooled in the scientific and martial arts and reluctant to waste their lives ministering to the poor.

They were brothers now, each man wearing the dog-head brand with fierce pride. Spina had found them, educated them and freed them from the common laws of man. The Hounds of the Lord were predestined for Heaven, chosen by God to combat heresy and usher in the next great age of Grace.

They stared at Rome, free of the sprawling shacks and lean-tos that grew like boils from most city walls. Here, the poor found space enough for their hovels among the ruined temples and palaces.

Spina and Chabal rode through the *Porta Pia*, dismounting in clouds of stone dust as labourers swarmed above, rebuilding the old Aurelian walls. The two men led their horses away from the deafening ring of hammers, Chabal a step ahead of his master, making for the Via Nomentana.

The traffic grew thick as they neared the centre. Lords and Churchmen in carriages, traders on carts or bent double beneath their wares, forced into two narrow lines on either side of a wide trench. More dust and hammers, sweating men at work on the old Roman aqueducts.

Gregorio Spina curbed his impatience and shuffled past the obstruction. A rubble-strewn gap in the buildings allowed him a glimpse of the Angelus, where Mathern Schoff had appeared with tidings of the Devil's Library.

Had he been motivated by a desire to glorify God, the Pope's efforts to restore this ancient city would have been admirable, but Pius IV built so people would remember him and dampened the fires of the Inquisition so they would love him. Now, according to Spina's spies, he was about to offer concessions to a clutch of rebellious bishops, desperate to prevent them making common cause with Luther's heretics. Fury swelled in Spina's chest. The greatest prize in Christendom lay waiting in the south, but conscience forced him to delay his journey to speak out against this unholy course.

They reached the headquarters of the Dominican Order in Rome, rode past the church's austere façade and entered the adjacent monastery. They were recognized immediately. A novice hurried forward to take their horses.

The prior of Santa Maria sopra Minerva approached, mouthing the ritual greeting. Spina cut him off.

"This isn't an official visit. I need fresh clothes, appropriate for an audience with his Holiness. Send a boy; let the Apostolic Palace know I'm coming."

Spina had served his novitiate here. He strode towards the vestry. His journey towards the Devil's Library had begun in these corridors. He remembered the hours of prayer and study, constant hunger and the jealousy of his peers.

He changed out of his riding clothes, adjusted a freshly laundered robe and smoothed his dark hair around the tonsure. The prior would be waiting, readying a carriage and horses in the courtyard, but Spina had no patience for the trappings of rank. He beckoned Chabal through a hidden door and approached the church along a short passageway, to emerge opposite Michelangelo's statue of the risen Christ, body unmarked by flagellation or crucifixion. The cross, and the whip he held, turned into instruments of triumph through the miracle of the resurrection.

Beckoning for Chabal to follow, Spina walked silently across the polished marble, into the rutted streets of Rome.

They took the most direct route, ignoring the broad boulevards, cutting down towards the Tiber through narrow, broken alleys. Spina heard movement behind the empty windows, footsteps on the flat roofs above. Chabal loosened the broadsword in its scabbard, eyes moving left and right beneath his heavy brow, as if hoping a group of robbers would attack. Spina smiled; none would be so foolish.

The boy had delivered his message. Blue and orange-clad halberdiers lowered their weapons respectfully as Spina strode towards the arched gate. In the atrium, he replaced his riding boots with soft-soled shoes. Chabal did the same, unbuckling his sword and leaving it with the guards.

The Master of the Sacred Palace strode past clerks and secretaries, nodding to acquaintances without pausing, up three flights of stairs to the Papal apartments, leading Chabal through the Hall of Constantine and the Room of Heliodorus, where the Pope's secretary met them.

"Your Eminence," he bowed. "We've missed you recently."

The young man ushered them into his office, pointing to a hard bench. "His Holiness begs your patience," he said, sitting and bending over his work. "He is at prayer and loath to interrupt his devotions."

Pius IV kept Spina waiting for nearly an hour; a typical politician's trick. A bell rang behind the secretary's desk. "His Holiness will see you now."

"Stay here, Chabal."

Pius stood with his back to the door, staring through a narrow window at the pilgrims flocking in St. Peter's Square. He was in his mid-sixties, the body still strong, filling the cassock with power.

He turned as Spina approached, fixing his subordinate with pale eyes.

"Your Holiness," whispered Spina, black hair grazing the Pope's pectoral cross as he bent to kiss the Ring of the Fisherman.

"So you've reappeared at last. Where have you been?" Pius didn't wait for an answer. "I knew the Booksellers' Guild would be furious, I knew the returns would be slender, but I never dreamed it would cost so much. Look!"

He snatched a piece of paper from his desk and flung it at Spina.

"Patience, your Holiness. The booksellers will soon grow weary of protesting, while we build a comprehensive picture of our enemies."

"Weavers and tailors? A merchant purchasing schoolbooks for his children? These men are not our enemies."

Spina smiled. Pius had given the same excuse for curbing the power of the Inquisition, winning favour with the people and diverting funds to his precious building projects.

"Your Holiness, many of these booksellers work with illegal printing presses. They use passwords, distributing banned works to trusted customers. In the last month alone, we've seized new editions of Lucretius, Zeigler, Cornarius, the works of Mateo Colombo… "

"Don't bring him up again, Spina. I warn you."

"It was a mistake to spare him, your Holiness."

"Should I execute a man for believing the evidence of his own eyes?"

"Of course. When it contradicts God's word," Spina shook his head in frustration. "Halt this programme and you blind us to the Devil's actions." He saw the Pope's lips twist in distaste. "The Last Days approach… "

Pius raised his voice. "Let me remind you, it's a sin to speculate on the End of the World."

"On the date, your Holiness. Not the fact." *And not a sin to bring it about; the further this world was allowed to fall into depravity, the more souls would be lost to the pits of Hell.* Spina drew himself up to his full height. "I hear you're planning to countenance interpretations of Scripture other than your own?"

Pius narrowed his eyes, brows meeting above his long nose.

"I won't ask where from."

"Are the rumours true?"

"Of course not. I'm simply offering to accept advice. In return for unequivocal condemnation of Luther's doctrine."

Spina inclined his head. It had been a mistake to come.

"Compromise is unbecoming in God's anointed."

The Pope lost his temper. He listed Spina's faults in exhaustive detail. The Master of the Sacred Palace remained silent, thinking of Raphael's glorious paintings in the Room of Heliodorus: the tax collector flogged by angels in the Temple of Jerusalem; blood leaking from the sacrament to wash away men's doubts; Peter and Paul, swords drawn, framed against a sunlit sky. God always intervened when His Church was threatened.

The artist had understood – the Lord rewarded faith, not intrigue, and guided the true defenders of His Church towards salvation – whereas Pius was a talented man undone by worldliness, unable to exalt faith above reason, uncomfortable at the mere mention of Satan. Let the Pope make his tawdry deals. Hadn't God put Benedict's book into Spina's hands? Sent Mathern Schoff to Spina with news of the Devil's Library? Chosen Spina to discover the Book of Aal and undo Satan's work? Scour God's enemies from this world and lead the faithful into battle at Christ's side.

"I hardly expect you to understand," concluded Pius. "A member of a monastic order, withdrawn from the world… "

"Of course, your Holiness," interrupted Spina.

The Pope frowned, sensing defiance: "I mean it. I won't stand for meddling."

"Of course, your Holiness."

Spina collected Chabal from the secretary's office. He paused in the Room of Heliodorus and stared up at the stars, fixed by Raphael's art to the vaulted ceiling.

"Because thou art lukewarm," he whispered, thinking of Pius, "neither hot nor cold, I will spew thee out of my mouth, who have fallen prey to Satan's wiles."

The true stars were fixed to an immobile sphere, beyond which Heaven lay. The Earth was an unmoving object at the centre of the universe, orbited in perfectly circular paths by the four celestial bodies – the Moon, Venus, Mars and Saturn.

Everything above the Moon was formed of ether. This world below of air, fire, earth and water. Four elements, corresponding to the four seasons, the four ages of man, the four humours and the four planets. Somewhere, deep beneath the Earth's crust, lost souls twisted in Hellfire.

Spina closed his eyes, marvelling at the perfection of God's design, pitying men like Columbus and Copernicus for claiming their discoveries as victories of reason over revelation. Satan's dupes, led astray by Lucretian heresy.

These were the Last Days and the Father of Lies had slipped his chains, conjuring new continents across the seas, holding a mirror to the heavens while his servants stalked the fields and cities, to sow doubt and reap the souls which fell.

But it was not too late. The Book of Aal would show him how. Reach in among the seeds of things, undo the Devil's lies and usher in the next great age of Godliness. Spina rested a hand on Chabal's forearm. The Lord had placed a heavy burden on his shoulders.

CHAPTER 29

Longstaff closed the door of his room and walked downstairs to the dining room. It was barely dawn, but the landlord – a fat, wet-lipped man in his forties – was already up, serving a group of prosperous merchants. Longstaff waved him over.

"Good morning, Schiuma."

The man eyed him warily; the Englishman paid well but he was an awkward guest who kept odd hours, inviting guests to stay and disappearing for days at a time.

"Are you breakfasting with us, signore?"

"I'll take a slice of bread with me. I'm leaving."

"Permanently? We shall miss you, signore," Schiuma led him to a cramped office, sitting at a desk to make out the bill. Longstaff counted coins from his purse. "And my things?"

Schiuma opened the strongbox. Longstaff saw clothing, weapons, rolls of paper, musical instruments and several heavy moneybags. The landlord passed up his own possessions, wrapped in a length of canvas – a new pair of boots and Ivan's book.

Martlesham was with Durant, Aurélie and Vescosi at an inn beyond the Porto al Prato and Longstaff had a long walk ahead, following the river east to west. It took him twenty minutes to reach the Piazza della Signoria. At the Fountain of Neptune, he scanned the crowds before striding across the square towards Giacomo Vescosi's street. He slowed as he passed the house; as on the previous evening it appeared deserted. He picked up the pace and reached the enormous Piazza Santa Maria Novella shortly before nine o'clock.

No sign of his companions. A monk passed, in white habit and black *cappa*, and Longstaff lowered his eyes. They'd been stupid to meet here, a stone's throw from the largest Dominican monastery in Florence.

Workmen were erecting two giant standards at either end of the square – Cosimo wanted coach racing here – and Longstaff mingled with the crowds of onlookers until he caught sight of Durant, mounted on the chestnut. Aurélie rode beside him, side-saddle on the palfrey in her grey dress. Laughing, the Frenchman reached over to touch her forearm. The performance of man and wife so convincing that Longstaff's fist clenched when he saw the fading bruise along her cheek.

The Otiosi leader walked ahead, dressed in a dark robe and holding the bridle of Aurélie's horse; the faithful retainer accompanying his lord and lady into the city.

Longstaff fell into step beside them.

"Do you have it?" asked Vescosi.

Longstaff nodded.

"And the house?"

"Empty."

"Is it being watched?"

"Not as far as I could tell, but I'm just one man, signore. I still say this is folly."

"On the contrary, Longstaff, they'd never believe we'd be so..."

"Stupid?"

"Spina and his men are in the Bay of Naples," replied Vescosi. "We'll never have a better opportunity."

They walked on in silence, Longstaff in front of the riders, Vescosi dropping behind. The old man was recovering well from his injuries.

Durant provided cover as Longstaff pushed a blade through a crack in the heavy gate. He flicked open the latch and ushered the others inside. The empty house still hadn't been discovered by thieves and everything was as he'd seen it last. A layer of scrum covered the surface of the water trough. Longstaff kicked it over, filling it from the pump so the horses could drink. He crouched beside Sparrow. "Stay here, girl. Warn us if someone comes."

Durant and Vescosi were already inside, climbing to the scriptorium. Longstaff followed with Aurélie.

"Botticelli," she said, seeing him look up.

"Who?"

"The painter, Sandro Botticelli. This house has been in Giacomo's family for generations. It was his grandfather's brother who started the library. Niccolò had a mania for collecting. Not just books, but statues, medals, cameos, tableware. People thought he was mad, placing value on ancient stones, but the collection was famous by the time he died. People still talked about it when Giacomo was a boy," she pointed at the ceiling. "The stonemason has Niccolò's face."

Longstaff looked at a man covered in dust, who met his gaze with eyes steady as a spirit-level.

Vescosi stood amidst the wreckage of his life's work — shattered vitrines and torn books, ruined alembics and crucibles, exotic plants ground underfoot and spotted with dried blood. It reminded Longstaff of the corpse mouldering in the cellars below.

"Bastards," the Otiosi leader dropped to his knees beside the worktable, high spots of colour in his cheeks. He held up a small glass disc, squinting at it in the dim light.

"Weeks of hard work went into this. Remember, Aurélie? All that grinding and polishing."

He lifted a wooden box onto the worktable, keeping the injured left arm tight against his chest, placed the disc into a small hole at one end. Before Longstaff could stop him, he crossed to the window and pulled open the heavy drapes.

Somehow, the box trapped sunlight and threw it in concentrated form onto the empty bookshelves, reproducing the tall tower of the Palazzo Signoria and every one of the crenellated battlements, but rotated through one hundred and eighty degrees.

Vescosi laughed, seeing the expression on Durant's face.

"It's a wonder we've discovered so little about our world over the centuries. The earth is a treasure chest, signore. The keys are patience and an open mind. Create a hypothesis, think of all the different ways it can be tested and set to work. What could be simpler?"

"We don't have time for this," Longstaff stood in the window, scanning the Piazza della Signoria for signs of danger.

"Durant," Vescosi pointed at the heavy worktable. "Tip it over."

The Frenchman set his feet and heaved. The box slipped from the scarred surface and the image of the Palazzo disappeared from view. The table fell with a crash. Vescosi pushed Durant aside, drew a knife from his robe and pressed the tip into a hairline crack. Longstaff saw panels on the underside. Vescosi removed a dozen thin pages from the hidden compartment, cross-written in tiny handwriting.

"Lists of Otiosi members and safe-houses, sympathizers, donors, printers and distributers. Spina neglected to press for this information; he's obsessed with finding the Library. And rightly so – it poses a far greater threat than our small organisation," he smiled at Aurélie. "We do what we can to keep the flame of curiosity alive, but we're no match for the Church, with its vast resources and willingness to crush dissent with torture and execution. If Spina finds the Library, he will make certain those volumes never see the light of day. The accumulated knowledge of centuries will disappear into the Vatican cellars. Instead of setting Man free, they'll be used to keep us in chains. With such an advantage, the Pope's theologians will find it child's play to conceal the truth, ensuring our achievements continue to emerge deformed, still-born victims of their perverted concern for our souls."

"We should leave," interrupted Longstaff from the window. The piazza looked peaceful, the door of the scriptorium was open – and the door of the reception room, where the windows were filled only with silk. They would hear Sparrow bark if anyone came in by the gate, but it was madness to linger.

"You're coming with us, Signor Longstaff?" asked Vescosi.

"What?"

"I'm sure Aurélie has spoken of Mateo Columbo, who demonstrated that blood draws oxygen from the lungs? Did she mention why the Church threatened the anatomist with torture and condemned his discoveries to the *Indices Librorum Prohibitorum*? They fear his work shows that Christ was still alive when Longinus pierced his side with a spear."

There was a long silence in the scriptorium.

"You see what's at stake, signore. I'm not a fool. I have no plans to storm the Vatican, waving a copy of *De Re Anatomica* above my head. The Pope would nod his head and the common people tear me limb from limb. But the accumulated knowledge of the ancients? A cleansing tide, my friend, powerful enough to dowse the flames of Hell."

Vescosi smiled, producing a letter from his robe.

"You've earned your reward a hundred times over. The volumes in the Devil's Library offer freedom. Ride with us in the same spirit or return to England and claim your birthright with our blessing."

Longstaff took the letter, turning it over in his fingers. *Home*. Walk away, ride for Genoa. He'd be in Dover within the month. He had faced Ivan the Terrible and Il Medeghino, survived murderous attacks, posed as a dealer in muskets, all in order to reach this moment. Why then, did Vescosi's offer feel like a punch in the gut?

Aurélie measured him with bright blue eyes. He looked at Durant.

"You know what it means to me, Gaetan. I vowed I'd never set foot on English soil unless I could do so under my own name. This might be my last chance."

Durant sighed. "We can't stop now, my friend."

Longstaff stared at him – the word carried heavy obligations. He closed his eyes, thinking of the boyar he had killed in Livonia. The dead guard at the Villa Spina. The assassin he'd killed in this very room. He'd always known there would be a price for so much blood.

CHAPTER 30

Mathern Schoff grew stronger on the journey south. He was no longer a blur, loose aggregate of features and characteristics. The lawyer was all angles and sinew now, a coherent whole formed in pursuit of a single goal, predestined for heaven, exempt from the common laws of man.

He slept with the Hounds of the Lord beneath the stars and rode with them by day. They changed horses daily – no one dared deny the Master of the Sacred Palace – and kept up a fierce pace from dawn to dusk.

Schoff hardly ate or slept; the pleasures and demands of the body were nothing to him now. He barely saw the people they passed on the road, poor souls with no clue of what was at stake. Long hours in the saddle took no toll on his energy; his skin felt translucent, the spirit shining through, a pulsing globe, illuminating the blasted landscape.

Not far from Naples, the Phlegræn Field was a barren plateau running straight into the sea. A place where fire burst from the rocks and clouds of sulphurous gas hung over the fissures. It required no imagination to understand why the ancient men of Cumae had called this place the entrance to the underworld.

They reached the ruined temple an hour before sunset. It was just as Vescosi had described; a cone-shaped hill in an otherwise flat landscape. On the summit, a temple consecrated to Jupiter, god of the skies.

They picked their way through the rubble. The roof had collapsed, but a dozen marble columns still stood. Jupiter sat on his throne, one hand stretched out before him. Once, the great, stone fingers must have held his lightening bolt, but the precious metal had long since disappeared. He faced an avenue of ruined statuary, all that remained of the lesser residents of Olympus. The Hounds of the Lord spread out, searching for the goddess Luna.

"The moon shows them the way," muttered Schoff to himself, standing apart, staring out to sea. He could see the flat summit of Vesuvius and, far across the bay, a faint smudge that must be Sorrento. To his right, a tangled forest of stunted trees bordered the plateau. Schoff looked down at the fishing boats pulled up on the black beach below. It was strange to think that life continued in this hellish landscape. He heard a shout behind him. Chabal and several men raised the statue of the moon-goddess onto a plinth. She was robed, face hidden beneath a thick layer of moss, and held a scroll in her left hand. "The scroll stands for knowledge," snapped Spina. "Follow where it leads."

The statues faced each other. Schoff followed the line of Luna's hand, down towards the sea, and saw cooking fires in the village below.

The Hounds of the Lord ignored the ancient steps, riding round the conical hill in a wide circle, out of the sulphurous mist in a single wave. They fired their pistols together, a clap of thunder in the still night. Chabal drew his war-sword. Others reversed their pistols, to use the long straight butts as clubs. The villagers scattered before them. Only one man died. He was old, too slow to avoid the charging horses. The sound of the impact played in Schoff's head. The sound of a butcher hacking meat.

He saw a neat vegetable garden; healthy leaves offering shade to roots and tubers. A bell rang wildly, men and women screamed. The hounds snapped and snarled at the villagers, herding them onto a patch of open land in front of their church, a wooden stockade facing out to sea. Spina ordered his men to build a bonfire.

The villagers sat on the ground with hands on heads. A group of mothers in long skirts tried to protect a dozen crying children. The hounds had been careful; they weren't here to kill.

The air was heavy with the stink of sweat and fear. Spina addressed the villagers; Schoff marvelled at his self-control. These people looked well-enough fed, for this bleak plateau, but there was something insubstantial about them.

"We need guides," Spina's voice was loud. "To lead us through the caves and tunnels. We're looking for a library or temple. Take us to it and you'll be rewarded."

Schoff looked at the children, eyes wide with terror, and thought of his own childhood in Lübeck. He'd often played on the docks, listened as the old tars told their stories of leviathans, strange lights in the sky, storms that should have torn their ships to shreds. He remembered the tale of the St. Gabriel, a ghost-ship that haunted Africa's Atlantic coast. A three-masted carrack whose sails hung in tatters, oak hull streaked with filth, encrusted with barnacles and which sailed more swiftly than a Portuguese ship-of-the-line. He shuddered and turned his back on the surly, unresponsive villagers.

Chabal appeared in the doorway of the wooden church.

"Found their storeroom. Cured meat, flour, wine, salt and spoiled vegetables. Scraps of tin and pewter hammered flat and stacked against the far wall," he shrugged.

Spina smiled at him. "There are riches here, my friend. More than you can imagine. And secrets more dangerous than your sword," he turned to the villagers. "Which of you is the headman?"

No one replied. Chabal moved through the crowd like a wolf, seized a man by the shoulder and threw him forwards into the glare of the bonfire.

"You and I are going to be friends," Spina smiled. "We are going to do God's work."

The headman wore a colourless smock and worn leather sandals. He pointed at the old man, lying crumpled on the ground.

"You dare to speak of friendship?"

Schoff could not bear to look at him. He looked at the women, standing with heads carefully lowered. All but one. She was young, with short dark hair, beautiful by the light of the fire. She stared at Spina with such proud hatred that Mathern Schoff took several steps towards her.

"No." There was panic in the headman's voice. As he moved to intercept the lawyer, the point of Chabal's sword touched his throat.

The hounds fashioned a rope collar and dropped it around the headman's neck. The young woman was separated from the others and forced to her knees. Chabal sauntered to the bonfire, heated his dagger in the flames, held the glowing point a hairsbreadth from the girl's eye.

"No," begged the headman. One of the hounds twisted the rope, choking him.

Chabal smiled. "You can protect her from wild animals. Build a shelter to protect her from the elements. But you can't protect her from us. This lesson you have to learn."

The woman did not make a sound. Her lips were pressed into a hard line. She stared past the knife, never taking her eyes from Spina. Schoff could feel her fear, the effort she was making to harden it, make it into a weapon.

"Notice how she refuses to beg for mercy," Spina's voice was soft. "Her courage is quite magnificent, in its way."

The headman struggled silently against the rope collar as Chabal drew the point of the knife across the woman's cheek. She bit her lip to keep from crying out and Schoff smelt burning flesh.

Spina gestured at the weeping headman.

"We have made our point."

Schoff needed to be close to Spina. He watched while the hounds pitched tents, listened as the Master of the Sacred Palace gave his orders.

"Place the headman in chains and secure him in front of the church. Separate the men from the women."

"They live in the caves," Chabal pointed to a large fissure in the rock. "There's a long tunnel runs parallel to the rock face, about five yards deep. Several side chambers – one big enough to house the women and children."

"Put the men in the church for now," said Spina. "We'll talk to them again in the morning."

Chabal kicked the old man's corpse. "And him?"

"We don't want unexpected visitors. Rig him as a scarecrow."

A groan escaped the man they'd taken for dead. Chabal looked at Spina, who shrugged.

"You have your orders."

Schoff moved round the tent, lighting candles and pouring wine.

"You understand, don't you?" Spina placed his hands on a table taken from the caves. "It was the only way to ensure their cooperation."

Schoff nodded, not trusting himself to speak.

Spina forced a smile. "They will understand soon enough."

"They will. Then they will thank you."

"They may not know the exact location of the Library, but they know how to find it." Spina looked at Schoff. "Do you still doubt?"

He shook his head. "There is power here. I can feel it."

Spina drank. "They're more fortunate than they know. At least their suffering has meaning."

Schoff remembered the look on the young woman's face.

"We should pray," he opened Spina's travelling chest and reached for two short cat-tail whips.

The Master of the Sacred Palace shook his head.

"Not this evening, Mathern. Not here. Bring the case and my writing implements."

Schoff retrieved quill and paper from his chest, and the rosewood box containing St. Benedict's secret writings. Spina unlocked the case with a key he wore around his neck. He opened the book reverently, lips moving as he committed the words to memory. He dipped the quill in ink and formed the strange glyphs with quick, decisive strokes. Part memoir, part dictionary, this was the key to deciphering the Book of Aal – the volume which had shown St. Benedict how to reach among the seeds of things and bend them to his will. It was close now, waiting for them in the Devil's Library, but useless unless Spina mastered the ancient script.

Schoff stood in silence for several minutes, watching in admiration. What more could he do to help? They were so close. Soon, they would have the means to make war on the Devil himself.

Schoff shivered, the cool evening air raised goosebumps on his arms. Was he ready? Would he stand or run when the hordes poured forth from Hell. He looked longingly at the cat-tail whips. Spina spoke of a way to emptiness – a way to understanding. He had starved himself; denied the flesh, but had he mastered it? Schoff stepped out of the tent, moving silently, so as not to disturb his master.

Spina's men were nailing planks across the doors and windows of the wooden church, laughing at the headman. Schoff hurried past, head down, making for the entrance to the tunnel. The air was sluggish inside, smoke from the torches eddying against the low ceiling. He entered a womb-like cavern. Many of the women reached out to him, while the children shrank away. Schoff pressed on into the far corner of the cave, where the young woman lay on a pile of dirty straw, holding a scrap of damp cloth against the scarred cheek. Schoff's breath grew fast as he leant forward to whisper in the darkness, fingers reaching out to trace the line of her jaw. "I am predestined for heaven, exempt from the common laws of man."

CHAPTER 31

They rode south, covering twenty miles on the first day before camping beside a stream. Longstaff tried to give Vescosi the book he'd taken from Ivan the Terrible – the small volume, written on middling parchment and neatly bound in red leather. The Otiosi leader looked up from his place by the fire and traced the words on the title page. *On the Planets, their Characteristics and the Orbits they describe around the Sun.*

"Give it to Aurélie," he said. "Her Greek is the equal of mine, and her eyes are better."

He strolled away. Aurélie sat nearby, curled against Sparrow. Longstaff put the book in her hands, watching as she turned to the opening page. A small wrinkle appeared between her eyes as she focused on the text. "*When we observe the movements of the stars and planets,*" she translated fluently, "*we see the higher, inward purpose of the Gods.*" She smiled at him.

"Thank you."

Longstaff took pains to ensure they did not exhaust themselves, limiting the number of hours they spent in the saddle each day, knowing they would need their strength when they reached the Phlegræn Field. The further they went the more they encountered the ruins of the past, looming out of the landscape like the remains of a race of giants. A cracked face as big as a house, the cheeks still smooth. A huge stone arm, rising in mock salute from the muddy shallows of a pond, a titan disappearing into soft, swallowing earth.

Vescosi grew talkative, as if inspired by the ruins. Durant stayed close, never missing an opportunity to ask him questions. Longstaff tried to follow their conversation, which leapt with dizzying speed from articles of faith, to the science of patterns and the very laws of nature.

He cantered up alongside Aurélie. She no longer sat side-saddle, having discarded her dress in favour of hose and a tunic which fell to her knees. She rode well, with a straight back and light hands. As they passed an old oak, standing alone at the side of the road, Longstaff broke off a stick and threw it for Sparrow to fetch. The dog stared at him with an expression of such wounded dignity that Aurélie burst out laughing.

"She's a cross. Gets her strength from her father and her intelligence from her mother."

"She is beautiful."

"She is," he agreed, looking at Aurélie's wrists, poking from the tunic's sleeves, delicate as a bird's. He glanced at the musket strapped to the palfrey's saddle, picturing it in the crook of her arm.

"Do you know how to shoot that thing?"

She shook her head. "I was hoping you might teach me."

That evening, while Durant and Giacomo saw to the horses and built a fire, he led her through the trees to a wide meadow. Putting a hand on her forearm, he brought her to a gentle stop.

"Look there," he whispered. "Do you see the rabbits?"

He raised his musket, took aim and touched the firing pan. Thirty paces away, a plump doe collapsed among the wildflower. Sparrow ran forwards to collect their supper.

"You've a wheel-lock gun," said Longstaff, "so the firing mechanism is automatic. No need to worry about matches and tinderboxes." He smiled. "Let me see you load it."

He showed her how to stand and gave her a cloth pad he'd made to dampen the recoil. She fired a dozen balls, growing accustomed to the weapon.

"Another," she said.

"How's your shoulder?"

"Fine."

"It will hurt like hell in the morning."

She insisted, and he gave her powder and shot.

"Fire on the outward breath, the trigger an extension of your finger, the barrel of your eye."

She raised a finger to her lips. "Listen."

Longstaff heard the call of an owl in the distance, the faint tapping of a woodpecker. Aurélie pointed at the branches of a nearby tree. In the gathering gloom, he saw the silhouette of a small bird.

"You've known Vescosi a long time?"

"All my life."

"Man of his word?"

She stared at him. "Why do you ask?"

Longstaff couldn't put it into words – a vague suspicion that something was being kept from him.

"I'm here on my own account now," he shrugged, thinking of the letter for Sir Nicholas in his jerkin.

She poured powder and ball into the musket-barrel, tamping it down, then a few more grains in the pan.

"Are you a Lutheran, Matthew?"

Longstaff frowned, the monk's name forever associated with his father.

"People say you can measure a boy by his heroes," continued Aurélie, "a man by his reasons for giving them up.

Giacomo's hero was Martin Luther. Not a popular choice in Florence, but he's always been different. Even as a child, he wanted to be responsible for his own life. Most men are secretly terrified – my father was – giving his conscience into the hands of priests, dreams to Fate and staking his fortune on the roll of a dice. Giacomo thought Luther pointed to a better way; faith, not obedience. Courage instead of fear.

"He wasn't the only one. People believed in Luther's message. Not princes or priests, but people – farmers and peasants, small tradesmen, servants. The best of them banded together, drafting a document called The Twelve Articles of the Black Forest, demanding the abolition of serfdom and death tolls, the right to elect and depose their own clergymen. They wanted to see the 'great tithe' used for public purposes."

Aurélie held the musket at her waist, eyes on the meadow. A brace of rabbits hopped into view.

"They were trying to make the world a better place. And the Lords gathered their armies and slaughtered them by the thousand. Giacomo gave up his hero because Luther supported the nobles, turning his back on the men he'd inspired to action. Do you understand? For Giacomo, tragedy is a good man who would have been great if only he'd had the courage of his convictions."

She took a deep breath before raising the musket to her shoulder, barrel tracing a steady line. She was smiling when she pulled the trigger. Sparrow bounded forward to collect her prize.

"I brought plenty of powder and shot," she said. "We can have another lesson tomorrow, but now I think we should get back. The others will be waiting for their supper and I have a book to read."

The road was in good condition, the trees cut well back on either side. They overtook merchants, a party of pilgrims, a noblewoman escorted by four men-at-arms. Slowing to exchange greetings but rarely stopping, they covered the ground at a steady, mile-eating canter and spent the third night at a crowded inn. The yard was full of merchants banding their wagons together and hiring mercenaries; signs the road would soon grow less hospitable.

Sure enough, the first caravan they passed the following morning was twice the length of any they'd yet seen, swordsmen riding in front and behind. The forest grew wilder, creeping closer as the day wore on. They cut through the trees an hour before sunset and made camp beside a stream.

"No lesson this evening," said Longstaff.

Aurélie fetched her musket. "Teach me how to strip and oil it."

She was inclined to rush. Longstaff shook his head.

"Cut corners now and it will let you down when you need it most."

She pulled a face, before rising to her feet and stretching. "How many more days to Naples?"

"Three, according to the innkeeper."

"I want to bathe," she said. "I won't go far."

Longstaff watched as she followed the stream into a stand of trees. He stared at the fire, imagining the soft shrug of clothes falling on grass. The water would be freezing. Would she go in slowly, one inch at a time? He heard a distant splash, a muffled shriek followed by a peal of laughter. And then silence. He pictured her in the shallow water, the current tugging at her hair.

The road was quiet the next day. A courier in the morning, another long chain of wagons around noon. Another lonely campsite that night. Aurélie shook Longstaff awake soon after dawn.

"Smoke in the distance."

He sat up, rubbing tired eyes. "A village. Nothing to worry about."

"I know what it is. They may have food. I'm sick of rabbit."

"It won't be what you're used to."

She grinned. "You get your things. I'll tell Giacomo where we're going."

*

Durant woke with a start. Vescosi sat a few feet away, cross-legged beside the remains of their fire, regarding him with steady eyes. Durant looked round – no obvious signs of danger, but something told him to be on guard.

"Where are the others?"

"Gone to find food," Vescosi shifted. "I've been waiting for the chance to speak with you alone."

Laure! Durant placed both palms flat on the ground, bracing himself for news of his daughter's death.

"Tell me."

"Five months ago, I received a letter from an official in a small French town. Among other tasks, he is responsible for recording the births, deaths and marriages in his district." Vescosi paused. "A woman was married not long ago. Unusually, she signed the register in her own hand – Laure Barthes, née Durant."

"It's a common name," Durant's voice broke on the final word. He lowered his eyes in embarrassment.

"There were several discrepancies, though the date of birth she gave is the same as your daughter's. She gave her hometown as Arles, for example. In the past we've raised your hopes in vain and I wanted to be sure. I asked my contact to investigate further. He maintains that her accent is pure Bordeaux, and describes a woman with black hair and pale skin."

Durant rose to his feet. "Why in God's name are you only telling me this now?"

"You are still interested, then? You never asked for news of her."

Durant flinched.

"I understand," said Vescosi. "You've been searching for so long." He leaned forward. "She gave her true name and age. Is it possible that she finally wants to be found?"

"Where has she been?"

"My correspondent had instructions to observe her from a distance."

"But he heard her speak."

"Overheard her. He wrote that she looks older than her years, with a careworn expression and marks of illness around the eyes."

Durant felt sick. *He hadn't asked. Had he hoped to find freedom from the hope and guilt which had kept him roaming the continent for all these years?*

"Where is she?"

Vescosi looked down at his open palms. "I'll tell you when we find the Devil's Library."

The Frenchman stared in disbelief.

"I've spent my whole life searching for the Library. If it

is your daughter, a short delay will hardly make a difference. Not after so many years."

"I might be killed."

"And? I thought you were a devotee of Lucretius, for whom the soul dies when the body dies."

Vescosi might look like an absent-minded scholar, but there was clearly a core of steel at his centre. Durant shouldn't have been surprised – this man had spent his life waging secret war against the might of the Roman Church. He pictured his hands around the old man's neck, and knew immediately that he couldn't do it. "You gave Longstaff a choice."

"Not really. There was never a danger he'd leave. He's looking for a home, and believes he's found one in you, and possibly in Aurélie. He'd never forgive himself for sailing north while the two of you rode into danger. Nor could you, I suspect, though you're the kind of man who might discover that too late. Well?"

Wearily, Durant shook his head.

"The books in the Devil's Library were written by men," said Vescosi. "Help me return them to their rightful owners, then go to your daughter knowing that you've made a difference."

*

Longstaff and Aurélie walked through a forest of beech trees towards the sound of washing bats. A broad-shouldered woman, sleeves rolled to the elbows, kneading linens against a wooden board. Two more beating shirts and shifts at a trestle table, while water boiled in a nearby kettle.

Longstaff cleared his throat. The women started in terror. They would have run, but for Aurélie's intervention.

"We're travellers," she said, "passing through. We want to buy food?"

"We'd be grateful for anything you can spare," Longstaff put a few coins on the trestle table. "We'll wait over here."

He lay down beside the stream as the youngest woman took his money and disappeared into the trees. Aurélie walked to the table.

"I can take her place."

"No need."

"Let her if she wants," said the broad-shouldered woman. "What would you rather, see her sit idly?"

Aurélie picked up the bat, slapped the wet shirt on the table. The woman stared in disbelief. Watching from the riverbank through half-closed eyes, Longstaff grinned.

Three silent peasants arrived with bread and cheese, armed with spades and pitchforks.

"Thank you," Longstaff rose to his feet. The men didn't speak, setting the provisions on the table and stepping back.

Longstaff dipped his head. "Say goodbye, Aurélie. It's time to go."

They walked away, not looking round until they were deep in the forest. Aurélie started laughing.

"What?"

"Nothing," she put her arm through his.

"Never used a washing bat before?"

She shook her head. "Too busy reading."

"And," Longstaff couldn't resist asking – she hadn't said a word about it – "what does Aristarchus' book say?"

"I assumed you knew," she looked at him. "You don't read Greek?"

He spread his hands. "Just a humble soldier."

"Who speaks Italian, German, and English."

"I lived in all three places, but I was never a scholar."

"What were you, Matthew?"

He sighed. "A child, a merchant's ward, a soldier, a freebooter."

"More lives than I've known, however good my Greek. I'm glad you decided to come with us."

CHAPTER 32

They left the road behind. Rolling meadows gave way to a broken shepherds' trail and Longstaff spurred ahead of Aurélie's horse, leading along the cliff-face until they came to a steep valley. They climbed throughout the afternoon, following the path of a stream, sinking to their knees at the top and drinking the cold water.

"Naples!" Vescosi pointed to a grey smudge on the horizon. "We have a friend in the city, if necessary." He tapped Aurélie on the shoulder. "You remember, the young man who showed such an interest in our experiments with lenses?"

She nodded. "Giambattista della Porta."

Durant stretched, joints cracking along his back. He hadn't said a word in hours, riding at the rear of the party with his head bowed.

"I've heard the food is wonderful," he said. "They have a dish; slices of aubergine fried and baked with tomato, mozzarella and basil."

Longstaff laughed – this was more like the Durant he'd come to know.

"Continue south and we'd come to the ruins of Herculaneum," continued Vescosi, "where Memmius had his summer house. Where Lucretius once entertained his patron with tales of the Devil's Library, only a few years before the town was buried in larva. But our destination lies west, across the Phlegræn Field."

They looked towards the lowering sun. The meadows grew dry and dusty before disappearing into a barren plateau of black rock. "We'll camp here," continued Vescosi. "We could all do with a decent meal and a good night's sleep."

Durant gathered wood for a fire, Aurélie saw to the horses and Longstaff watched Vescosi pace restlessly beside the stream.

"What aren't you telling us, signore?"

The Otiosi leader looked at him, stretching his injured shoulder.

"It doesn't make sense," persisted Longstaff. "Why is Spina so desperate to find these books?"

"I told you. The scrolls will give the Church a huge advantage over anyone challenging their authority."

Longstaff shook his head impatiently. "Spina's no fool. Safer to kill me and Durant, burn the palimpsest and forget the whole thing."

"Perhaps he intends to destroy the Library."

"A lot of trouble to destroy something no one's heard of in a thousand years."

Vescosi stared towards the Phlegræn Field, glowing red in the setting sun. He sighed, then gestured for Aurélie and Durant to draw near.

"My great-uncle knew more than Cosimo de Medici realised, and Spina told me more. All those volumes, the accumulated knowledge of centuries; he couldn't care less. He's after a single volume, and there's nothing he won't do to get it," Vescosi looked at Aurélie. "*I entered my innermost soul and beheld truth. The seeds are God; immutable, indivisible, infinite in number, eternal.*"

"Lucretius?" she asked.

He shook his head. "St. Benedict. His family were members of the cult who built and maintained the Library. They believed they were descended from the first men, who had left paradise of their own free will, in search of the knowledge that would allow them to return as equals. According to the legend, their God, Aal, gave them a book at the gates of paradise, showing them how to return if they ever succeeded. They preserved this book across the centuries, recopying it when necessary. Only two men in every generation knew how to read it and Benedict was one," Vescosi sighed. "You've all read Lucretius. You know his theory of 'atoms'. Benedict claimed he could see them, manipulate them at will. He did not work miracles through prayer, but through the conscious application of techniques described in the Book of Aal."

Aurélie stared at him, clearly hurt he hadn't confided in her sooner.

"And?" Durant raised his head. "Does the book exist?"

"How should I know?" Vescosi stared at his palms. "Perhaps. Plato described the material world as a precipitate of our mental processes. It's not real, in other words, except in as far as we perceive it. And if it's only an illusion, it can be altered. Think of the miracle of transubstantiation – bread and wine turned into the body and blood of Christ through a process the Church describes in very similar terms. Every culture has tales of levitation, healing by touch. They can't all be invention."

"Lucretius also described the seeds of things as immutable," offered Durant quietly, "infinite in number and eternal. *I believe there is a pattern*, he wrote, *which can be understood by man.*"

"That's the question," Vescosi smiled at the Frenchman. "What might be possible if we learn to read God's pattern? St. Benedict was a gentle man, devoting his life to curing the sick and lame, but Gregorio Spina is cast from a different mould. He believes the Book of Aal will show him how to destroy this world and usher in the Last Days, as foretold by St. John. The final battle between Christ and Satan; sinnners will be sent to Hell, the righteous to heaven, and no more need for this poor world of ours." He pulled at the tufts of hair behind his ears. "*I will call for a sword, saith the Lord God, and set every man against his brother. I will plead with pestilence and with blood and rain upon his bands, an overflowing rain of hailstones, fire and brimstone.*"

He sat beside the fire, removing the Otiosi papers from his robe. "No sense in taking them further. We'll hide them here," he stared at each of them in turn. "If anything happens to me, Sir Nicholas Bacon is well placed to carry on my work."

CHAPTER 33

They broke camp at dawn, riding west. The green meadows grew dry and dusty as the morning wore on, before disappearing into the 'fields devoured by fire', a hellish landscape of craters, pools of boiling mud, fountains of steam rising from holes in the hard crust. The stench of sulphur filled their mouths like dust, as Longstaff led them into a winding split in the rock. It was even hotter here, the going harder – the horses had to navigate countless small landslides – but hidden from prying eyes.

Vescosi broke the silence. "Centuries ago, people came here to consult the Sibyl in the caves beneath Jupiter's temple. She 'sang the fates and wrote her prophesies on oak leaves'. She lived for a thousand years, poor woman – a poisoned gift if ever there was one, unaccompanied by youth – and was already a withered crone when she offered nine books of prophesy to the king of Rome. Twice, Tarquin refused. Twice the Sibyl burned three books, doubling her price each time. Tarquin bought the last three. He learned how to win the favour of the Gods and grew his small city into the greatest Empire the world has ever known.

"A library of books," he added in a faraway voice. "Magical books which enable men to speak with the gods. The Church adopted the Sibyl as a prophet, claiming she foretold the coming of Christ. Michaelangelo painted her in the Sistine Chapel, sitting beside an open book. I can't believe I didn't think of it sooner." He began to quote.

Longstaff didn't recognize the verses. Later, Durant told him they were by the Roman poet Virgil.

Aeneas
Makes for the hilltop, where aloft sits throned
Jupiter, and a cavern vast, the far
Lone haunt of the dread Sibyl, into whom
The Delian bard his mighty mind and soul
Breathes, and unlocks the future
The Mighty face of the Euboean rock
Scooped into a cavern, whither lead
A hundred wide ways, and a hundred gates;
Aye, and from which as many voices rush,
The answers of the Sibyl.

Sparrow dropped to her belly, a low growl at the back of her throat. Longstaff caught the stench of rotting meat. He raised a hand for silence and dropped the other to the hilt of his sword. They dismounted, crept silently forwards, climbed up the deep trench and peered over the lip of rock.

A single, petrified tree stood on the blasted plateau, a man hanging by his wrists from a low branch. There was still flesh on the bones. Scavengers – wolves and wild dogs most likely – had made a bloody mess of his legs and a Heretic's Fork had been fastened round his neck. A thin collar held the long, double-ended fork in place, the tines at one end fixed in what had once been his jaw, the tines at the other embedded in his chest.

Longstaff couldn't imagine what crime would merit such a terrible death. Durant spat in disgust. "Spina is using human scarecrows," he sounded furious. "Whatever he's doing here, he doesn't want to be disturbed."

"Look at the stain on the rock," said Longstaff. "Poor bastard bled to death here. They left him with cuts on his legs and feet — hanged him high enough to keep the torso out of reach of scavengers."

"Any sign of who he might have been?"

Longstaff stared at a few wisps of white hair, still clinging to the man's shrivelled scalp.

"Someone old."

Vescosi pointed past the corpse, at a tall conical hill rising from the flat landscape like a crookback's hunch.

"I suspect Spina and his men are on the far side. If I'm right, they're looking in the wrong place. We need to visit the Temple of Jupiter on top of that hill."

Longstaff looked up; four hours to sunset. He could see a line of trees less than three miles away, bunched together where the plateau of volcanic rock came to an end.

"Follow me." They retraced their steps along the trench until it opened into a wide basin.

"What do you propose, signore?" asked Vescosi.

"We stay here until nightfall," Longstaff looked at Durant. "When it's dark, take them into the trees north of the hill."

"And you?"

"Wait for my signal, Gaetan. I'll let you know if it's safe to approach."

They watered the horses and made themselves comfortable on their sleeping blankets. They were all restless, feeling the weight of the savage landscape.

Longstaff's head hurt. He felt sealed away from the world, as if this shallow basin of rock were a womb. He looked around. Durant's tired eyes were hidden in shadow. Aurélie's cheeks were smudged with tears.

"What is it?" he demanded.

"This place," said Vescosi, shaking his head clear. "The Roman geographer Strabo. He claimed it was the gases here which allowed the Sibyl to slip between worlds." He took a blanket from his horse and tore it into strips, dipping them in water. "Quickly, cover your faces."

Matthew Longstaff wasn't a superstitious man, but this landscape made him uneasy. He loped towards the hill, moving quickly, putting Aurélie and Vescosi out of his mind. They had Durant and Sparrow to look after them and plenty of food and water; more than enough for the next twenty-four hours and he'd be back before then – assuming he didn't fall into Spina's clutches. He blackened his face and hands and covered his dirty blond hair with a woollen skull-cap, before easing himself out of the trench. He lay in the shadows, staring at the steps cut into the side of the hill, as he scanned for guards and picked out a path in the dying light.

The place seemed deserted. Longstaff waited for the moon to disappear behind clouds before approaching. He listened for the tell-tale sounds of men; shoe-leather against stone, urine splashing against the earth, muttered curses, the scrape of whetstone against steel. He heard nothing; even the birds were silent. There was only the sound of the ocean, a distant roar on the edge of hearing.

He climbed the steps, taking more than an hour to reach the ancient temple at the summit. Here he crouched in the darkness and waited until his heart calmed, the sweat drying on his back. Still no signs of life.

Longstaff prowled among the rubble. He had the Gods for company, but the long centuries had turned them all to stone. He barely glanced at Jupiter on his throne, or Luna on her plinth. The temple roof had collapsed, but a dozen marble columns still stood; he used them for cover as he made his way to the hill's seaward side, seeing the glow of fire below and a smudge of light on the far side of the bay – Sorrento, he guessed. He was more interested in the village at the foot of the hill.

Another set of steps led towards the sea. Longstaff was halfway down before he came across the guard, dozing at a bend. He waited for a break in the clouds, needing the extra light to cut away from the staircase, across the face of the hill, angling down to a point above the small fishing village. He felt his way through the darkness, toes testing for loose stones, trying to keep at least one hand on the ground. He did not look down – didn't want the fire's glare to steal what little vision he had – and did not stop until he was almost on top of the village. He found a shallow ledge and lay flat on his back, to let his aching limbs relax against the cold stone. Rolling onto one forearm, he stared down the cliff of twisted stone. He was directly above a wooden stockade, a fire burning in the wide-open space beyond, close enough to hear the low murmur of guards sharing a joke. He couldn't see them. Even when his eyes adjusted to the firelight he could only make out the shape of a man, chains cruelly fixed to stop him lowering his head.

The first pale fingers of dawn stretched across the sky. Longstaff saw a rough wooden cross mounted on the stockade. Spina's men had put aside their riding clothes and strapped swords around their monk's robes. Two of them aimed muskets at the building, as a third unlocked the heavy door. Half a dozen men shuffled into the light and made directly for a water-barrel. It was hard for Longstaff to tell them apart; all wore filthy smocks and identical expressions of weary resignation. They stood in line, with bowed shoulders, as ropes were fastened like leashes round their necks. More men in robes appeared, took hold of the ropes and led the captives towards the cliff-face. Longstaff ducked out of sight, listening as they entered the cave below, exchanging greetings with a group moving in the opposite direction. He raised his head and saw two more of Spina's men herd a flock of women towards the black beach and make them fast to a row of wooden stakes. More men were released from the church, watered, and led to their fishing boats. They did not look at the women as they passed. One by one the men cast off, dropping anchor close to shore and setting their fishing lines.

Longstaff listened more than he looked, only raising his head at intervals for another glimpse of this hell on earth. He saw Mathern Schoff, studying papers at a trestle table, and the big, muddy-faced monk entering a tent pitched between church and beach. Longstaff lay flat on his back; getting the rhythm of the camp, the taste of it sour in his mouth – bitter flavour of exhaustion, captors and captives going through the motions. Longstaff was surprised. From everything he knew about Gregorio Spina, he had expected more.

It was mid-morning before the dozing guard of the previous night came strolling down the steps. He drank from the water barrel, exchanging a few words with his two-man relief.

"Anything?"

"Nothing but stone and sky and boredom. Which of you has the temple today?"

"I do."

"Wave to civilization for me, will you?"

The three men laughed. "For all the good it will do. There's fish if you're hungry."

Which of you has the temple? Longstaff shook his head in wonder, imagining Il Medeghino's reaction.

"Call yourselves the Hounds of the Lord? A one-armed whore could take this place in the time it takes you sons of bastards to say your prayers." Was it incompetence or complacency? Both probably. Spina was Master of the Sacred Palace in Rome, accountable only to God and the Pope.

Lunchtime. Fish cooking in the open. Longstaff's stomach began to growl. He ate a piece of black bread and drank from his water-skin. The Lübeck lawyer sat comfortably in the shade of the squat church; spitting distance from the chained villager, who lay in the sun like cured leather. It was getting hot on the narrow ledge, as well. Longstaff soaked the strip of cloth Giacomo had given him and covered his head. With the village quiet, he fell into a half doze.

The fishermen returned to land three hours before sunset and dumped their catch on the beach. Black-robed men came to escort them to the church, only releasing the women once the door was safely locked. More monks appeared from the caves beneath, piling lengths of knotted rope on Schoff's table. They were mapping the tunnels, realized Longstaff. The lawyer unrolled his papers and questioned the men closely before making additions to the tangled confusion of lines.

Another monk appeared. Longstaff tried to count them; he'd seen fifteen ride south from the Villa Spina. He looked for as many different faces here, but it was hard to tell them apart. They were all dressed in identical robes and the heat had made him tired. The newcomer pushed a woman ahead of him, looking for the big, muddy-faced monk.

"She wants to see Spina."

Longstaff saw him look towards the tent. Schoff raised his voice.

"She can talk to me, Chabal, if she has something worth saying."

The woman walked woodenly towards the water barrel. Longstaff saw a fresh scar on one side of her face. She approached the man in chains, who lapped eagerly at her cupped hands. She stared down at his matted hair.

"Why are you doing this to us?"

"You know why," called Schoff.

Longstaff saw the effort she made to control her expression before turning to face him.

"The man you killed. Give us his body at least, so that we can lay him to rest."

Mathern Schoff shrugged. "What good will it do you? You need a priest to conduct a funeral."

"He was our priest."

"Then you should be pleased for him," said the lawyer, stepping nearer. She flinched, spitting on the ground between them.

"He serves the Church in death, as he did in life, providing for our privacy," Schoff's voice grew dark. "Providing food for scavengers. Where he'll remain until you give us what we want."

She stared at him. "You've already taken everything we have."

"Not everything," smiled Chabal.

The headman stirred. "Leora, enough. Go back to the cave. Now."

At dusk, two robed men came down the hill and one went back up, which confirmed Longstaff's suspicion that Spina posted a guard in the temple during the day, but left the place empty at night. He waited until it was dark before leaving. The monks ate together at a long table beneath him. The glare of their torches would render him invisible, their conversation cover any noise he made. There was still no sign of Spina, but Longstaff had seen enough.

It was a hard climb, his limbs sluggish from the long day spent lying motionless. He left the single guard far to his left and took his time, making sure of every step, reaching the deserted temple shortly before midnight.

He paused to catch his breath. He didn't think it would be difficult to signal the others. Durant would have remained as close to the hill as possible. Longstaff looked north, where the plateau of rock disappeared into a thick tangle of trees... and froze.

Something moved. A bird? A breath of wind? He crouched behind a broken plinth. The moon emerged from clouds, throwing the temple into ghostly relief. Longstaff remained absolutely still. Only his eyes moved, searching the silhouettes of scrub and statue for anything out of the ordinary. Long minutes passed before he was certain. Someone was there.

The moon slipped behind cloud. He crept through the ruins, spotting a grey figure standing beside the statue of Jupiter, musket held in the crook of one arm. Longstaff rose like a knife through shadow, one arm around the gunman's throat to stop him crying out, one crushing the musket against his chest.

"Aurélie?" he hissed in disbelief. "What in God's name? Where are the others?"

"Safe."

He could feel her heart, beating fit to burst, body rigid in his arms. He stepped away.

"Fool," he hissed. "You might have got us all killed."

"There's no one here. I was worried you wouldn't find us."

Longstaff curbed his anger. No harm had been done. He pulled Aurélie into the shadows behind Jupiter's throne.

"You're shivering," he said, surprised. It was a warm night and he was sweating from the long climb.

She stared up at the ruined arch. "Only the initiated were allowed to pass this threshold."

She had a beautiful voice. Longstaff traced the line of her short hair, unable to read her expression in the darkness.

"Has something happened?"

She smiled at him. "It feels as if we're chasing a dream. A pair of adventurers, a woman, an old man recovering from torture."

"The men below are chasing a nightmare. We're dead if they find us here," he looked at the distant trees, where Durant and Giacomo must be waiting. They'd need thirty minutes to cross the plateau, another hour to climb the hill.

"Sit with me a moment," said Aurélie. "I know I should be more careful. Giacomo's always telling stories about the terrible things that happen to women like me."

She shook her head. Longstaff guessed she'd been here some time, growing pensive among the statues.

"He loves you like a daughter."

"Is it possible to love something you don't understand?" she took Longstaff's rough, callused hand in hers. "Giacomo peers into my head. He tries to hide it, but he thinks I'm unnatural." She stared at him. "You are a rare man, Matthew.

You don't care what I believe. You look into my heart and you still like me."

Her hand was cold, but he resisted the temptation to take her in his arms. She reached up and touched his face.

"You're blushing. Only humans can, did you know? It's awareness of our own existence that lights the fire – when we're nervous or ashamed, taken by surprise or flattered. And when we're aroused," she dipped her head. "There," she said, "now I'm blushing, too." Without looking up, she ran her fingertips along the line of Longstaff's jaw.

"Aurélie..."

"Don't talk."

CHAPTER 34

She was falling asleep against him – his clothes for a mattress, hers for a blanket. *Madness*. Longstaff shook her awake. He shouldn't have let it happen, not until they were far away from here.

He disentangled himself, climbing onto Jupiter's throne and looking at the distant trees. Aurélie sat up, makeshift covers falling to one side.

"That's where they are?" he pointed. "You're sure?"

"I'm sure, Matthew. They're waiting for your signal."

Longstaff looked up at the clear, night sky – two hours until dawn – still time, if they hurried.

They gathered twigs and dusty weeds from the temple floor, before climbing a short way down the hill. Satisfied no trace of the signal-fire's glow would be seen from the village, Longstaff took out his tinderbox and lit the small bundle.

"If they delay, we'll send them back. Try again tomorrow."

The flames died quickly. Aurélie held Longstaff's hand in the darkness, sitting beside the charred sticks. It wasn't long before they heard movement below – Durant and Giacomo, climbing up to meet them.

Assuming Spina's man kept to the same routine, Longstaff reckoned they had an hour. He glanced at Aurélie, hands on hips, staring up at the statue of the moon goddess Luna. Her pale skin had turned golden on the journey south and he smiled, thinking of Onofrio Spina's young wife – it was impossible to imagine Aurélie plucking her hairline or wrapping herself in so many yards of velvet she could barely move.

The goddess looked melancholy in the dawn light, but her pose was dynamic, left foot forward, right arm raised aloft.

"The scroll represents hidden knowledge," said Aurélie. "*The moon shows them the way*, according to the palimpsest. Luna is the moon, therefore the scroll should point us to the Library."

"Down to the village," said Longstaff. "Where Spina's looking."

"Without success. What are we missing?"

Vescosi was sitting on a low wall, catching his breath after the long climb. He reached into his robe, producing Aristarchus' slim volume: *On the Planets, their characteristics and the Orbits they describe around the Sun.*

"I took the liberty of retrieving it from your pack, Aurélie."

He looked at Durant. "The key passage in Lucretius' letter; have I remembered it correctly? *The shining sun does never look upon them, but the moon shows them the way, and we, by Jupiter's leave and damning Ptolemy's eyes, journey with them into Hell.*"

Durant nodded.

"Ptolemy believed the sun revolves around the earth, just like the Roman Church. Aristarchus believed the opposite."

"Like Copernicus," said Durant.

"Correct," Vescosi gave the book to Aurélie. "Look for his description of the moon's characteristics."

She flicked through the pages. "*The moon shields us from our worst instincts and urges us to reflect before we act. Her sadness comes from being so little heeded.*" Aurélie looked at the statue. "The scroll," she said. "It's in the wrong hand!"

"Bravo," applauded Vescosi. "Now tell me, when is a left hand a right hand?"

"When we see it in a mirror."

"*And urges us to reflect before we act,*" repeated Vescosi, nodding.

"We need a mirror."

"We don't have one," said Durant. "And it wouldn't do us any good; not unless we know where to hold it."

Longstaff approached the statue. Luna's right arm was turned away from her body at waist height. He ran fingertips along the rough stone. He was a soldier and the word 'shield' echoed in his mind. *The moon shields us from our worst instincts.* He found two shallow ridges on the forearm, one above the wrist, one below the elbow. He moved away from the statue, walking with his eyes trained on the ground.

"She wore a shield," he said. "A round shield, I imagine. Isn't that an image of the moon? But I can't see it anywhere."

Giacomo clapped his hands. "Of course. But we don't need to find the actual shield. Any flat object will do."

Longstaff strode to the top of the stone stairway, listening for the guard's approach. They still had time, but it paid to be cautious.

"Hurry. And keep your voices down."

It took them forever. They tried and discarded a dozen flat stones, cloaks, even Aristarchus' book, before Vescosi pronounced himself satisfied with a sword. Durant held it tight against Luna's right arm as the Otiosi leader used a stick to extend the line of the scroll. They were completely caught up in the work, oblivious to the danger.

"There," said Vescosi, pointing to a patch of earth a few yards from his feet. "Not literally, of course. The position of the scroll and set of Luna's arm indicate a straight line, but without the shield we can't be sure of the angle. Aurélie, fetch the cloth roll from my bag."

"There isn't time," said Longstaff.

Vescosi ignored him, lying flat on the ground with one eye closed, peering north towards the distant trees.

Aurélie came running back. "So you were right. Spina is looking in the wrong place."

"Fitting, don't you think?" Vescosi smiled. "A prince of the Church defeated by a heliocentric view of the universe." He unrolled the cloth, selecting a compass from the collection of instruments, each held in place with a slip of ribbon. "We have the line," he announced at last. "No way of knowing if the entrance is fifty yards or fifty miles from here, but if we keep to this heading, we'll meet it eventually." He rose to his feet, beating the dust out of his robe. "Now we can leave."

Longstaff shook his head. "We've missed our chance to cross the plateau before the lookout arrives." He herded them across the temple courtyard, pushing them towards the tall columns on either side of Jupiter. "Hide, all of you. Not a word."

He left them in the shadows, returning alone to lie in wait.

The guard was whistling a tune, eyes on the sky. He was armed – a short, double-edged sword swung from a wide belt – but walked with his left hand on the hilt.

Longstaff let him pass before he stepped out from behind the statue, to wrap an arm around his throat and choke him until the body went limp. He shifted his grip, about to break the man's neck when the others emerged from hiding – Vescosi lost in thought, Durant tapping fingertips against his teeth. Neither approached. Aurélie gave him a sad smile before she closed her eyes. Shaking his head, Longstaff dropped the unconscious guard – there had been too much killing, too much of it weighed on his conscience alone.

Durant drew near, seeming to read his mind. "I shouldn't leave you to shoulder so much of the burden."

"You haven't been yourself, the last few days."

"Just tired. I'm with you now."

Longstaff smiled. "See if you can find a rope."

"Safer to kill him."

"He won't be missed before evening. We'll be far away by then."

CHAPTER 35

The sun – and the threat of discovery – lay heavy on their backs as they cantered across the plateau. Longstaff breathed a sigh of relief when they reached the forest of stunted trees running along the northern edge. He took the lead, with Durant bringing up the rear, trees growing closer until the small party was forced to dismount and walk the horses. The birds stopped singing. The track petered out and they continued in single file, picking their way through the undergrowth. Vescosi tapped Longstaff on the arm.

"Do you think you could help me climb one of these trees?" he nodded at a gnarled trunk, damp with moss and lichen. "I can't see the sun. I need to confirm our heading."

Longstaff looked past the philosopher. The undergrowth seemed to blur ahead of them.

"What in God's name..." He drew his sword to hack a path through briars and brambles, startling a family of crows. Seven flew past with a great beating of wings. Longstaff bit back a curse. A thin and twisting coil of smoke hung in the air ahead. He cut his way closer and found himself staring into the jagged mouth of a cave. Longstaff muttered a curse; it was like looking directly into the Devil's black throat.

"No need to go climbing trees."

Vescosi was still at his shoulder. "*By Jupiter's leave and damning Ptolemy's eyes,*" he murmured, "*journey with them into Hell.*"

They left the horses in a nearby clearing. Durant emptied his pack, searching through the contents until he found a jar of lamp oil. Longstaff split several long sticks and collected bundles of moss. Durant soaked them in the oil and bound them to the sticks. He found candles, gave Longstaff a handful and tucked the rest in his doublet. He stared at his possessions lying on the hard earth – bone saw, phlebotomy cups, herbs, powders, phials – then threw the empty bag over his shoulder.

"Ready!" he said.

"What's the bag for?"

"One of us has to think ahead," Durant smiled. "How many books can you push down the front of your jerkin?"

Longstaff looked at the Frenchman's slim sword. "I've never seen you use that thing."

"Pray you never have to."

Vescosi stood among the tumble of roots and stones, peering into the opening. Fumes danced in the sluggish air. "Time to cover our mouths again."

"Wait here," lighting his torch, Longstaff took a deep breath and squeezed between the narrow jaws. The air was warm inside, damp walls and a rough stone floor, a perfectly rectangular opening on the far side, taller than him and barely as wide. The cave was natural, but men had been here, fashioning it according to their needs.

"Come in," he shouted.

One by one they came, a reluctant Sparrow last of all. Aurélie walked directly to the dark opening.

"Durant," called Vescosi, "bring my bag." He lay in the dust, compass in hand. "Assuming it holds to this orientation, the passageway runs east to west."

"We could be in Naples by nightfall, with rooms in a fine inn and all the food and drink we can stomach," said Longstaff.

No one listened. Aurélie started down the passage and the rest followed. Sparrow dropped to her belly, shaking her broad head from side to side.

Aurélie led, musket slung across her back. Longstaff was caught in two minds. He wanted to push past the others and take over the lead, but someone had to protect their rear. His companions only had eyes for what lay ahead.

The tunnel seemed endless. Rectangular niches had been cut into the walls at shoulder height, the floor of each smooth with ancient wax. Longstaff walked with a hand on Sparrow's head – to comfort the animal, he told himself. Vescosi kept making them stop. He could hear the Otiosi leader counting his steps, lying down each time he reached a hundred, asking Aurélie for his cloth roll.

Vescosi rose to his feet and uncovered his mouth. "We're descending. The gradient is slight, but absolutely consistent."

"Do you feel it?" said Aurélie. A cool breeze rising from the depths to meet them. She walked faster. "Stop," said Durant.

She'd missed it. A second passage leading away from the first. Longstaff saw an uneven floor, walls smooth and free of niches. Beyond that, all was darkness.

"What now?"

Durant hunkered down, running his hands across the stone. "Pivots. There must have been a door here once."

The four of them stood close together, torches above their heads.

"We should keep to the main passage," said Aurélie.

Vescosi shook his head. "Think of the niches – they're set too close together for the simple purpose of providing light. This main tunnel must have served a ritual purpose. If Durant is right about the pivots, the second would have been hidden. A secret passage, in other words, known only to initiates."

"We have to split up," said Durant.

"No," said Longstaff. "We stay together."

"Signor Durant is right," said Vescosi. "We don't have time to waste walking up and down every tunnel we find."

Longstaff looked at Aurélie. Her expression made it clear she agreed with Vescosi and Durant.

"Fine," he said. "Aurélie and I will continue along the main passage. You and Gaetan take the other. Count your steps. Turn back when you reach five hundred."

The temperature continued to rise as Longstaff and Aurélie pushed on into the darkness. The air was foul with sulphur.

"Listen," said Aurélie. "Do you hear?"

"Water."

They hurried forward, almost tumbling down a long flight of steps. Longstaff grabbed Aurélie by the arm, pulled her to safety and held her close.

"Careful."

Side by side, they walked down the steps. "God's teeth," spat Longstaff.

"The River Styx!" said Aurélie. "Remember Strabo? Remember Virgil? The Romans believed this was the entrance to the Underworld. Of course there has to be a river." She laughed, before shaking her head in wonder. "How in God's name did they discover it was here? The stairway meets it perfectly." She raised her torch. Steam rose from the black water. Longstaff saw steps rising on the far side.

"We should turn back," he said. "Tell the others what we've found."

She knelt on the lowest dry step and pushed up one sleeve.

"Wait," said Longstaff.

"Hot, but not scalding," she grinned up at him. "Time to get our feet wet."

Aurélie went first, using Longstaff's sword to probe the way ahead. Longstaff followed close behind, their two hands wrapped around one torch. The water was hot but not unpleasant, the current fast but not dangerous, and the riverbed mercifully free of debris. Ten careful steps. The water never rose above waist height.

Longstaff looked back at Sparrow, staring at them from the far side.

"Come on."

She shook her head, started climbing backwards up the staircase.

"Wait here," muttered Longstaff. He waded across the river, crouched to scratch Sparrow between the ears. He tried leading her to the water's edge, but she ducked her head, setting up a low warning growl at the back of her throat.

"For the love of God, I haven't carried you since you were a pup," Longstaff heaved her onto his shoulders and rejoined Aurélie.

Eyes sparkling in the torchlight, she handed him his sword.

"Time to find out what's at the top."

Longstaff insisted on taking the lead. They passed through a high stone doorway and saw two orbs of light in the distance, two torches burning merrily in a huge, circular chamber. Durant and Vescosi.

The walls were smooth and bare, the floor a chaos of scattered tesserae, broken statues and human bones. A battle had raged in this chamber, long ago in the distant past. The mosaic was so badly damaged it was impossible to make out the original design. A round table lay on its side in the centre of the room, next to an eight-sided pit.

"You took your time," Durant upended a piece of marble with his boot. "Nothing here but lies and trickery."

"What's happened?"

Vescosi looked at Aurélie. "The second passage was a short cut to this chamber. This whole place is an elaborate hoax, set up to make people believe they were visiting the Underworld. Did you cross water on your way here?"

"Yes."

Vescosi nodded. "Corrupt priests preying on rich fools, leading them through drifts of vapour, down dark and menacing tunnels to an underground river. There must have been a landing stage originally, a small boat to ferry them across," he gestured around at the ruined chamber. "Got up to look like the Palace of Hades. Visitors would have been tired, dizzy from the fumes, perhaps drugged.

"Look there," he beckoned them towards the pit in the centre of the room. Longstaff peered down. Eight feet deep, he judged, the floor covered in a thick layer of... what? It looked like leaves.

"Snake-skins," said Vescosi. "The table would have been moved aside and the visitor pushed into a pit of harmless snakes, experiencing for himself the days when Earth was covered in a plague of serpents." He shook his head. "Maybe there were books here once. Who knows? I'm sorry, Aurélie, but there's nothing sacred about this place, nothing but sleight of hand and mummery."

"No," said Aurélie, "you're wrong." She brandished Aristarchus' book.

Durant sighed. "None of us wants to admit defeat, but we've been over every inch of this room."

"Think," said Aurélie. "Jupiter is a planet, not a God. The moon is a planet, not a Goddess."

"Actually…" began Vescosi. She cut him off. "According to Aristarchus' conception of the universe, the moon is a planet. We began our journey on Earth. We travelled to the moon. What comes next?"

"Mercury."

"And the God, Mercury; what is he famous for?"

"Trickery," a light came on in Giacomo eyes. "And what is this chamber, if not a trick?"

Aurélie dropped her musket and jumped into the pit.

"We've looked," said Durant. "Nothing but dried snake-skins."

"Matthew," she called, "I need a damp cloth."

He handed one down to her.

"Hold the torch so I can see." She scrubbed at the panels. "Eight sides," she muttered, "like a baptismal font. Eight is the number of re-birth."

Four of the sides were plain, each of the others carried a simple sign.

"A lightning bolt," said Longstaff, looking down, "a sun, a pair of crossed spears, a heart."

"The sun is often used to represent knowledge," offered Durant.

"The lightning bolt is Jupiter's symbol," said Vescosi. "Remember Lucretius' letter: *the moon shows them the way, and we, by Jupiter's leave, journey with them into Hell.*

Aurélie shook her head. "Aristarchus describes human history as a journey through the universe. Mercury stands for trickery. It stands for the confusion felt by primitive man, assaulted by a million new sensations, unable to pick the true from the false, the real from the ephemeral. The centuries rolled by and men and women developed self-awareness, beginning to exercise judgement. That's when they were seduced by Venus/Lucifer."

"What?" Durant shook his head. "Venus and Lucifer have nothing to do with each other."

"Not any more," Vescosi was grinning, "but they might have in the past. Think of Isaiah. *How thou art fallen from Heaven, O Lucifer, son of the morning.* And the morning star is Venus, of course."

Aurélie nodded. "According to Aristarchus, Lucifer and Venus are male and female representations of temptation. The book describes a time in our history when we became wise enough to find our true path. As soon as we did, however, we found reasons to go astray."

"That would explain the snakes," said Durant.

"And this pit," added Aurélie with a smile. "A cavity or a shaft, depending on your point of view."

"Then we have to break through the wall marked with a heart," said Durant.

"Pass me a stone."

He handed her a marble head, face too badly damaged to identify the god.

"Are you sure?" asked Vescosi. "The men who built this place might have laid traps."

"Maybe we should think this through," said Longstaff.

There was a wild look in Aurélie's eye. She turned like a discus thrower, away from the heart, and smashed the heavy marble head into the crossed spears on the opposite panel.

The thin sheet of stone exploded and the breath of Satan filled the chamber. Heat blasted into Longstaff's face, mind filling with the stench of blood, iron and charred corpses. Through gritted teeth, he forced his eyes open.

"Aurélie," he shouted. He could see her curled in a corner of the pit, whipped by the snake-skins, which rose on the winds of hell, turning madly in the air above him. Noise like the wail of war-horns. Close now, nearly upon them. Longstaff threw up an arm to protect his face, but the danger was already receding, rushing past them into the tunnels, falling back into the depths from which it had risen.

There was absolute silence in the chamber.

"Aurélie?" whispered Longstaff.

"I'm all right," she was struggling to stand, eyebrows burned away, cheeks the colour of a bruised peach. She began to cough.

"What in God's name… " began Durant.

Vescosi wrinkled his nose. "Some form of gas, air trapped in these tunnels for aeons. There must be a second entrance; it's the only possible explanation."

CHAPTER 36

One by one, they passed through the shattered panel, huddling at the top of a steep flight of steps, breathing through their mouths to lessen the stench of sulphur. The roof was low. Durant, the tallest member of their party, was forced to stoop.

"The pit represented Venus/Lucifer," explained Aurélie. "If I'd broken through the panel marked with a heart, we'd probably have ended up walking in circles."

"Or worse," muttered Longstaff.

"The nearest planet to Earth is the moon," said Vescosi, "then comes Mercury, then Venus, then Mars."

"Exactly. The God of War, represented by crossed spears."

Aurélie continued talking as she led them down the stairs. "Aristarchus claims mankind was created for a hidden purpose, which we creep towards across the centuries. In the beginning we were no more aware than animals, but in time developed consciousness. At which point we promptly fell prey to the temptations of Venus/Lucifer. To free ourselves from pleasure…"

She paused at the bottom of the staircase. "Assuming we'd want to; Aristarchus does because he thinks we have a secret destiny. I don't know whether he intends his book to be understood literally or as metaphor?"

"The cult of Aal did not originate in Rome," said Vescosi. "I spent years tracing its slow passage west, finding evidence the Library was located on the island of Samos in the third century before Christ. Aristarchus grew up there; his observations on the nature of the universe are so extraordinary, I thought there must be a connection."

Despite the stench and heat, Aurélie laughed. She was wild, Longstaff realized; courageous in a way he could scarcely fathom.

"To escape the false consolations of pleasure and achieve our true purpose, we need self-discipline – the quality most closely associated with Mars. Aristarchus goes on to say we'll be judged at some future point, when Jupiter will decide if we've learned enough to be allowed into the presence of his father, Saturn, who guards the tree of knowledge at the centre of the universe."

They heard the sound of running water, growing louder as they made their way along a narrow tunnel. The left-hand wall disappeared and they saw vapour rising from an underground stream the width of a spear, running in a man-made channel only inches below their feet. Durant turned to Longstaff.

"It smells like a sickroom," he said. "The smell of death, like a fever."

The stream grew angrier as they followed its path, almost boiling in places. The heat was crushing, the air like sand in Longstaff's throat. His trousers were already bone-dry. He ripped off his shirtsleeves and threw them to one side. Vescosi hitched up his robe. Aurélie removed her jerkin and tunic and stripped down to thin shirt and hose. Durant discarded his doublet, but stubbornly refused to give up his bag.

The walls had a different quality here, the stone no longer smooth, but gnarled and twisted.

"They look like petrified tree roots," said the Frenchman, "but surely we're too deep underground."

Longstaff had seen too many battlefields. In the red glow of the torches, he thought the whorls and ridges looked more like viscera than vegetation.

The stream grew wider and calmer. It became a river and the wall on the far side slowly disappeared from view. The temperature dropped. The roof soared up into inky blackness and the smudges of light cast by their torches failed within yards for want of anything to illuminate.

But there was something in the distance, a bridge of white stone, leading to a black island in the centre of the sluggish river. The design was simple; three wide steps up to a flat walkway, supported on seven thick columns. Longstaff overtook Aurélie, the stones reassuringly solid beneath his feet, throwing up such a glare he was forced to shield his eyes. He held the torch out in front of him. The bridge wasn't long, but seemed to disappear into a void. He reached the keystone — three times the size of the others — and saw words carved deep in the surface. He brushed away the dust. Vescosi stood behind him. "The letters are Greek," haltingly, he translated the ancient warning.

For him that stealeth from this Library, let the book change into a serpent in his hand and bite him. Let him be struck with palsy and all his members blasted. Let bookworms gnaw his entrails in token of the Worm that dieth not, and when at last he goeth to his final punishment, let the flames of Hell consume him forever.

"I don't believe it," Vescosi's eyes were glazed. He hurried to the end of the bridge and disappeared.

"Giacomo," shouted Aurélie.

"Come here, child," there was a catch in his voice. "By the grace of God and his saints, come and see what we've found."

"Wait," snapped Longstaff. "Stay behind me."

The single wall of darkness split in two, formed a wide corridor and curled away in the distance. Longstaff stood for a moment, trying to understand what he was seeing. It was impossibly beautiful after the horrors of the journey.

Vescosi sat with his back to them, cross-legged on the floor, slowly shaking his head.

"I have candles here," Longstaff could hear the awe in Durant's voice. "Let's put the torches out before we go any further."

The island was the Library. What had looked like black walls from the outside were the backs of bookshelves, made from a hardwood Longstaff did not recognize, half petrified with age and rising up to the height of three men.

Durant distributed candles. Longstaff collected the torches, carried them across the bridge and extinguished them carefully. When he returned he saw two lights bobbing away down the corridor, but Vescosi was still on the floor, tears on his cheeks, candle held between his palms as if praying. Longstaff helped him up.

"I never really thought… "

The shelves were divided into thousands of pigeonholes, a golden plaque beneath each one, giving the author's name and title of the work. Longstaff raised the candle; some scrolls were as thin as reeds, others as thick as his forearm, all were neatly rolled on wooden pins.

"Areobindus," read Vescosi. "Damian, Bassus, Vittigis, Indaro, Chrysippus, Malthanes." He clutched Longstaff's forearm. "I've never heard of any of them. Look here," pointing to another plaque. "I don't even know what language this is."

Longstaff pulled him gently away.

"I'm trying to understand," Vescosi shook his head. "We think St. Benedict visited this place at the beginning of the sixth century after Christ, and those were violent years. The early Christians were ruthless; the evidence of slaughter we saw in the first chamber... " He turned to Longstaff. "Did the priests of Aal take their secret to the grave? Did they die defending this Library? Did the Christians even know it existed?"

Longstaff led him further along the curling corridor, trying to catch the others. "It's like walking into the centre of a shell."

Vescosi stopped. "You're right. The Golden Spiral."

"What?"

"A pattern of numbers; 1, 1, 2, 3, 5, 8, 13 and so on. Each number is the sum of the previous two, do you see? If you use them to create squares, then draw circular arcs to connect the opposite corners of each square, you create the Golden Spiral. It appears everywhere in nature, in the branching of trees, the shape of leaves on a stem, the uncurling of a fern. A man named Fibonacci discovered the principle in the thirteenth century. But, of course, he didn't discover it," Vescosi stared at Longstaff. "We don't learn," he said, "we re-learn. What a world we live in, signore."

He went back to the shelves. "First, we have to make sense of their cataloguing system," he was speaking to himself, attention fixed on the scrolls. Longstaff left him there.

Aurélie stood before a wall of books. Actual books, displayed face up on sloping shelves, leather bindings set with inch-long metal studs to keep them elevated. Longstaff had been acquiring books long enough to know the codex had been invented by early Christians, while Romans, Jews and Greeks persisted with scrolls.

"What have you found?" he asked.

"The Gospel of Thomas," she pointed. "The Gospel of the Egyptians, The Gospel of Truth, The Second Treatise of the Great Seth. Origen mentions some of them." She stared at the rows and rows of books. "They don't exist," she said, shaking her head. "These books have not existed for over a thousand years. Do you know what we've done, Matthew? The world will never be the same again."

Longstaff took her hand. It was the first time he'd seen her look scared.

"Quickly," shouted Durant. "I've reached the centre."

The centre of the shell.

A circular room with a lead statue of Saturn in the middle, surrounded by six massive candelabra. Durant placed a candle in each, hardly breathing as light crept across the chamber.

The God was old and ugly, leering from the top of a slender pedestal, tall scythe gripped in one gnarled hand. And there, propped on Saturn's right hand – held low, palm facing the entrance – was the book Spina was so desperate to find.

Vescosi appeared at the entrance. He hardly glanced at the sacred book of Aal, but walked instead around the hardwood cases, reading the names on the golden plaques.

"Epicurus!" He moved along the shelf. "There must be fifty scrolls by him alone."

"There are works here dating back seven and eight centuries before Christ," said Durant.

"I still can't understand the cataloguing system," continued Vescosi, pulling at a tuft of hair. "We don't know which of these volumes they truly valued." His voice dropped an octave. "Can they ever have imagined, in the days of the Roman Empire, what a treasure this would become?"

Durant opened his bag. "We have to decide what to take."

"Take?" Vescosi stared at him.

"You're not planning to read them here?"

"It might be dangerous to move them. We should wait, raise money from the Otiosi. Buy this land and catalogue the collection properly, methodically."

Durant shook his head. "With Spina and the entire Roman Church arrayed against you?"

Aurélie stood before the statue of Saturn and stared at the Book of Aal, modestly bound in brown leather, protected from contact with the god's hand by untarnished silver bosses. She reached out and touched the flat spine.

"We can't just leave," she opened the volume and turned the pages, running fingertips across the strange glyphs. "The parchment has hardly swelled at all."

She looked at Vescosi, who rested a hand on one of the tall bookcases. "That river is full of sulphur. These shelves seem to have petrified with the passing of the years." He shrugged helplessly. "Who knows what secrets were lost with the men who built this library."

He cross to stand beside Aurélie, staring at the sacred book. "It must be the copy St. Benedict made. The high priests guarded access to the ancient script, producing a copy every century and destroying the previous incarnation. It took him three years, copying and studying until understanding finally dawned."

"Can you read it?" asked Aurélie.

"Not a word," Vescosi closed the book. "But Spina may be able to; he has St. Benedict's key."

They each chose ten scrolls from the shelves. Longstaff picked at random. He didn't recognize any of the names, didn't know whether they were works of poetry or politics or history. He was finished first, remaining with the bag while the others brought him their selections. Durant chose six of the thickest scrolls by Epicurus and four previously unknown works by Lucretius. Aurélie's quick eyes found lost texts by Pythagorus and Aristotle.

"And the forbidden Gospels," she grinned, running back along the corridor.

Vescosi selected works by Euripides, Sophocles and Menander, greatest playwrights of the ancient world.

Longstaff smiled at him, quoting, *"To preserve the last remaining scraps of the past.* The Otiosi will need a new task, signore."

Vescosi stared at the Book of Aal. "What should we do – take it with us or destroy it now?"

"Your decision," Longstaff gestured at Durant's bag, already dreading the journey back to the surface. "I'm just the pack animal."

Aurélie screamed.

Longstaff whipped his sword free and ran into the corridor. Figures appeared, walking in pools of torchlight: the muddy-faced monk, wearing leather trousers and jerkin; Spina, carrying a plain, rosewood box; and Mathern Schoff, his knife pressed against Aurélie's throat. The Lübeck lawyer held her tight, forearm crushed against her throat. She was clearly in pain, biting her lip to keep from screaming.

Longstaff gave way before them. Durant appeared beside him, rapier in one hand. Sparrow crouched on the right, teeth bared.

The big monk drew a broadsword from the scabbard on his back. Heavy-lidded eyes glinted with pleasure.

"I know who you are, Matthew Longstaff. I've been hoping our paths would cross."

"No need for that, Chabal. We're all men of the world here," Spina looked composed, robe unmarked by sweat or exertion. "Did you really think I wouldn't post a guard in the temple?" He shook his head. "A rider arrived two days ago to say you'd been seen in Florence. What were you doing there, I wonder?"

He turned dark eyes on Longstaff. "The messenger also brought word of Dini's fate. A heavy blow for the Dominican Order and a great personal loss for Chabal; he and Dini were close. You owe us a debt, gentlemen, and it's time to pay."

Longstaff looked at Aurélie. "Let her go."

Schoff twisted the knife against her flesh.

"Drop your weapon, or the whore dies."

Longstaff looked for doubt or pity in Schoff's face. Finding nothing but madness, he dropped the *katzbalger*, Durant's blade following his onto the stone floor. Chabal threw him a length of rope.

"Tie the dog to the statue."

Slowly, Longstaff looped the rope round Sparrow's neck and led her to the pedestal. Vescosi emerged from the far side, holding a candle and the Book of Aal.

Chabal gave Longstaff no chance to react, backhanding him across the face and seizing Sparrow's rope, making her fast.

Spina stood at ease. "I have six men on the bridge, Giacomo. There's no way off the island."

Vescosi opened the book, candle-flame inches from the pages.

"Let her go."

Spina ambled round the statue. "That book will show us the way to paradise."

"Bedtime stories, Gregorio. If there ever was a magic book, it was Lucretius, appearing after so many centuries and opening our eyes to the true glory of God's creation."

"Devil's magic," said Spina. "But every poison has its antidote." He pointed at the lead statue. "He was known as Aal once, Lord of knowledge. The Romans named him Saturn..."

"And the Church renamed him Satan," yelled Aurélie.

Spina merely smiled. "Precisely. For who else but Satan tempted Man to leave the Garden of Eden? Perfect, don't you think, that the Dark Lord himself should provide us with the means of his destruction. Now do you begin to see the true glory of God's design?"

Aurélie closed her eyes. "He's mad."

Schoff cut her, a single bead of blood tracing a path along the collarbone. Longstaff clenched his fists, staring across at the *katzbalger*. Chabal laughed, blocking his path, leaning easily against the broadsword.

Spina withdrew a slim volume from the rosewood box, bound in red, gold-tooled leather.

"It was in Niccolò Vescosi's possession for twenty years. It shaped his life, as it has yours, Giacomo." Spina opened the book, reading from a page of finest uterine vellum. "*The priests teach that Aal sent his people out of Paradise, telling them to return by the path of knowledge. Over time, his followers descended into foolishness, hoarding texts and wasting their lives in empty ritual.*

"*There is a myth preserved among the Romans that Aal's Age ended when the last immortals departed Earth. In truth, these angels did not leave, but only stepped behind a veil of illusion. The Book of Aal teaches us to see them; the seeds of things beyond – immortal, immutable, indivisible, infinite in number. The seeds are God."*

Spina smiled at the Otiosi leader. "Do you think it was chance that led Gemistus Plethon to seek out Cosimo de Medici in Florence?" he replaced St. Benedict's book and set the case on the floor. "The Last Days approach, Giacomo. God arms us for the coming Battle."

Vescosi raised the candle. A page of the sacred book began to brown, a coil of smoke rising from the surface.

"The coming Battle? You're a coward, Gregorio, terrified of a future you don't understand."

Spina shrugged. "I haven't come here to argue. Kill her, Mathern."

"Wait!" Vescosi stared at Aurélie, body sagging with defeat. He dropped the book, stepping away.

"A wise decision." Carefully, Spina wrapped the Book of Aal before secreting it in his robe. Schoff threw Aurélie at Durant, covering both with a pistol.

"We passed your scarecrow, Gregorio," said Vescosi softly. "Is that your idea of paradise?"

"That old man? His death served a purpose greater than anything he achieved in life. God will reward his sacrifice."

Vescosi laughed.

"What?" demanded Spina, eyes narrowing.

"The idea that a man like you could work miracles."

"A man like me?" Spina smiled. He drew a dagger from his sleeve. With one swift move he buried it in Giacomo's belly. "And how would you describe a man like me?"

Vescosi collapsed to the ground, blood pumping from the wound.

Durant reacted first, smiling at Schoff as he kicked the
katzbalger. Longstaff rolled, intercepted the blade and rose
into a fighting stance.

"Nobody move," shouted Spina. Durant shielded Aurélie
with his body, to stop her from running to Vescosi's side.
Schoff had one shot in his pistol. The Master of the Sacred
Palace looked at Chabal.

"Your way," he snapped. "Make it quick."

"With pleasure."

Longstaff attacked – cut right and left – slashed at
Chabal's knees, pivoted on the defensive stroke and struck
hard at the broad chest.

Chabal parried easily. "I expected more of you, Longstaff."

He drove at the Englishman, to land heavy blows without
extending himself. Longstaff tried to counter. He parried,
swayed left, feinted right – Chabal kept forcing him back,
their blades blurred in the candlelight.

Longstaff set a trap: deliberately repeating himself every
sixteen strokes, then twelve, then eight. His aim, to draw the
enemy blade into a straight thrust. He rose on the balls of
his feet, ready to slip inside and strike at the face.

Chabal disengaged and inclined his head in appreciation.
"Better."

He beckoned the Englishman forwards, arrogantly
repeating the pattern, inviting him to spring his own trap.

Sparrow snarled, straining at the short rope.

Longstaff couldn't beat Chabal's defence. He chopped
from left to right. Chabal danced away, smiling. Again, the
same diagonal slash.

Sparrow lunged. The statue rocked. The dog sank teeth
into Chabal's boot, forcing him to glance down; Longstaff
closed, already roaring in triumph.

Spina darted forward, knife held low in one hand, stabbing him in the thigh.

Longstaff limped backwards, stumbling as his heels struck Vescosi's body. Chabal kicked Sparrow – a savage blow to the ribs – and raised his sword to finish her off.

Longstaff lunged, forcing Chabal to re-engage. The broadsword whipped towards him and met the *katzbalger* – but the monk was stronger, better.

Think, Matthew.

Durant? Still covered by Schoff's pistol. Longstaff tried to work his way towards the Frenchman. Spina appeared at Chabal's side, dark eyes shining with pleasure.

Longstaff cut at Chabal, conscious that his strength was fading. The big monk turned his blade.

"Still think you can win?" Chabal shook his head. "It's over."

Longstaff looked past him, eyes locking on Sparrow's. Muscles bunched in the dog's broad chest. She leapt, the rope snapped taut – statue slipped from the pedestal. Spina's mouth fell open as Chabal seized his shoulder and shoved him clear of the god, too late to avoid the scythe. The lead point tore a hole in Spina's stomach and pinned him to the floor.

Chabal stared in horror. Longstaff thrust, took him between the ribs, kicked him to the ground, reversed his sword and opened the bastard's throat. He sank to his knees and put weary arms around Sparrow's neck.

Mathern Schoff screamed and stumbled away from Durant. His pistol wavered as he looked at Spina. The Master of the Sacred Palace raised an unsteady hand from his belly, brows gathering in confusion at the sight of so much blood.

Schoff fled.

Aurélie cradled Vescosi's head, stroking the high brow. "Live, damn you."

The Otiosi leader stared at the thousands of scrolls, ghost of a smile tugging at his bloodless lips.

"I cannot imagine the world they'll make," his eyes came to rest on Longstaff. "Look after her."

The face darkened, body arching in pain. Durant pressed a forearm across his chest, holding him down, applying pressure to the wound. "Tell me," he yelled. "Don't die on me, you bastard."

"Calais."

The body went limp. The head fell sideways in Aurélie's lap. The Frenchman hung his head. Without looking, he reached out and closed Vescosi's eyes.

Spina still lived, pinned to the library floor, muttering through blood and mucus.

"My body is weak, my spirit is strong," slick palms on either side of the scythe. "My spirit is strong, this wound only a precipitate of my thoughts. A pure mind sees what it chooses to see. A pure soul can remake the world."

Durant hurried to his side, hooked fingers beneath the statue and heaved. The Master of the Sacred Palace screamed as the scythe shifted back and forth, fresh blood pumping from the wound in his belly. The Frenchman collapsed against Saturn's back, shaking his head.

"Too heavy," he said. "I can't shift it."

"God brought me here," sobbed Spina. "I mastered the ancient language. Where are my men? Tell them to look for the Book of Aal."

Longstaff spat. "Damn it, Gaetan. There are six men on the bridge."

They were dead, if Schoff caught them in the central chamber. Running hands along the bookshelves, they hurried down the black corridor until they heard the tramp of feet. Aurélie raised the musket as a man ran into view, fired and struck him in the chest. He sat down hard, staring at the burning torch while his companions took cover. His fingers opened, the torch rolled across the stone floor, stopping a sword-length from the precious scrolls.

"Back," shouted Longstaff.

They crouched low, waiting in the silent corridor.

"Where are they?" whispered Durant.

Longstaff took Aurélie's musket, edging towards the light.

"Mathern Schoff?" he called.

"I want the Book of Aal."

Longstaff remembered seeing Spina put it in his robe. He heard Durant running behind him, back towards the centre.

"You can have it. When we're safely away from here."

Schoff laughed. "Now. If you want to live."

Durant appeared at Longstaff's side. The two men exchanged a glance in the smoky light, before the Frenchman threw the Book of Aal. It landed beside the torch, sliced nearly in half by Saturn's scythe, pages wet and heavy with Spina's blood.

"Come and get it, Schoff."

The Lübeck lawyer screamed in anger. Another of Spina's men stumbled into the torchlight. Longstaff shot him in the head.

"Not until we're out of here."

"Look around you," shouted Aurélie. "The Book of Aal is ruined, but it brought us here. Think of the knowledge, Mathern. The difference it will make."

"I was not; I was; I am not; I do not care," Schoff's voice was strangled. "You want to spread this filth? Teach men the soul dies when the body dies, have them grub around in the earth like insects when their eyes should be on God?" They heard him laugh. "These works belong in Hell." They heard the sound of breaking glass, caught the faint scent of lamp oil. Flames appeared in the corridor, darting greedily from scroll to scroll. Trailing torches down the shelves, Spina's men ran for the bridge.

CHAPTER 37

Death by burning, flesh black as coal at the centre of a bonfire. Longstaff had seen men burned at the stake, struggling at the top of tall pyres, hair moving in the waves of heat, choking to death on thick coils of smoke. He caught the scent of burning paper – burning hair, the sickly sweet smell of cooking flesh. The flames came dancing down the corridor, blocking any chance of escape. Aurélie ran towards them, determined to sacrifice herself if it would save the books. Longstaff put her over his shoulder and sprinted to the centre of the shell.

They were all going to die, unless he could think of a way to get them out of here.

The bookshelves were the height of three men, three yards wide. Longstaff tracked bloody footprints through the chamber, gathered speed and barrelled into the shelf. Nothing. He climbed, pigeonhole to pigeonhole, threw himself over the top and turned in the air, hooked fingertips against the lip. He didn't think it would move. He heard a crack, rocked forwards, heaved back again. Slowly, the section began to topple. Longstaff hauled himself up, a second before it crashed against the far side of the corridor. And now they fell like dominoes. Smash after booming smash echoed across the cavern's high roof, as they forced a paper lined path to the island's edge.

"Run," he yelled above the snapping flames. Durant grabbed Aurélie, half carrying her up the fallen bookshelf.

Smoke writhed across the chamber. Flames curled around the entrance, poking into pigeonholes. Longstaff heard Spina scream, even above the sound of tortured timber.

Durant pushed Aurélie into his arms.

"Go."

The Frenchman turned back. He clambered down the shelf, fell on the bag of scrolls and books.

Longstaff ran, Aurélie beside him, leaping from shelf to shelf. He heard the scrape of wood on stone as the smooth outer wall of the library slipped into water. *Please God, let it float.* The sluggish current was taking hold as they leapt aboard. Longstaff turned.

"Gaetan!" *Where was he?* There, bent double beneath the heavy bag. Already, a clear yard of water had opened up between the island and the gently bobbing shelf. Durant threw the bag. Longstaff leaned forward and hauled it aboard. Durant jumped, landing with his legs in the water and scrambling onto the makeshift raft.

Longstaff looked past him, at another shadow in the darkness – Sparrow. He half caught her, half fell beneath her on the wildly rocking raft. Durant laughed.

"A fitting end for the Lord's hound," he said. "Killed by a dog."

The underground river flowed smoothly round a bend in the tunnel and the Library disappeared. They heard the fire's snap, shelves collapsing – a sound like the end of the world – and then silence. In his jerkin, Longstaff found his tinderbox and one of Durant's candles. He looked at Aurélie by the light of the weak flame, saw the hurt and fury on her face.

"We have Durant's bag," he said. "There must be two hundred scrolls in this section of shelf. More than people have found in a century scouring monasteries and castles."

The river gathered speed. Longstaff felt a change in the air, heard a whisper in the distance. He did not look at Durant or Aurélie, did not want them to see the fear in his eyes. The air began to press. Longstaff swallowed to unblock his ears. A rising wind blew out his candle, leaving them in darkness.

"The bag," shouted Durant. "Hold onto the bag."

Longstaff closed his fist around a clutch of thick laces. He reached for Aurélie. There was a crash, an eruption. Water whipped his face – cold water; a second river ran through these tunnels, an angry river that hurtled into them with the force of a storm.

The wide shelf rose on its side, Longstaff felt himself slipping. He had Aurélie by the waist, pressed her to him as they tumbled under. The bag was above, his world an unfathomable tangle of limbs and water. The weight was terrible, as if planets had been hung from his ankles, a vast pressure building in his chest, choking him.

He fought to raise Aurélie, heard her vomit a non-stop stream of water and curses. The bag was low in the water, Durant sprawled across the top. Longstaff heard Sparrow whine in pain as he fought the current, rolled onto his back, feet striking jagged rocks. The darkness was total. He could hear the shelf ahead of them, crashing through the tunnel, slowing then speeding away. The water's roar grew louder. Longstaff's head sank, pulled under by the heavy, waterlogged jerkin. As he raised his arms, pushing Aurélie clear, he thought of the campaign medals hidden in the lining. Fallen comrades marched before him. He saw the parlour at Martlesham, Aurélie beside him in front of the fire. Saw his own blue eyes in his father's face. *It's no disgrace, dying for your faith.*

The world flattened. Aurélie became a sketch, a dozen strokes in charcoal. Longstaff heard the soft murmur of

an infinite number of voices, growing louder. The roar on
the far side of silence. He smiled, about to breathe the
water when the tunnel narrowed, catching the bookcase
in its teeth.

Durant grabbed his jerkin as the bag crashed into the
shelf. They struggled upright, felt their way along the side of
the bookcase, pulling the bag between them. But the water
was rising, already up to Longstaff's waist, slamming against
the obstruction. He heard timber screaming, buckling.

"Hurry," he pushed Aurélie against the smooth side
of the tunnel. Her fingers found a ledge. Longstaff made
a thief's ladder with his hands, heaving, hauling himself
alongside, the wound in his thigh burning in protest, arms
and shoulders shaking with exhaustion. He hoisted Sparrow
and the soaking bag, with Durant pushing from below.
The Frenchman scrambled up as the river redoubled its
furious assault on the bookcase. They heard it splinter in the
darkness. And then it was through, borne away on the black
torrent of foam.

The ledge had not been carved by nature. Longstaff's
fingers ran through grooves that could only have been made
by men. How long had it been here, running beside them in
the darkness?

"Do we go back," yelled Durant, "or press on?"

Longstaff had no desire to return through the maze of
dark tunnels and broken corpses. He helped Aurélie to her
feet before lifting the water-logged bag onto his shoulders.

"Stay with Gaetan. Don't let go of him."

They walked in darkness, feeling their way. The roar
of the river grew even louder — there were rapids here,
perhaps a waterfall — and then began to fade as the path
swung away. Longstaff could hear Durant and Aurélie

ahead of him. He did not know how long they walked, just kept putting one foot in front of the other, one hand pressed to his thigh, fingers caked in drying blood, pain reduced to a dull ache. He remembered Vescosi's words – *There must be a second entrance.* Slim hope to hold against the night, the deathly silence, broken only by the exhausted shuffle of their feet, Sparrow's low panting, the wet straps chafing at his shoulder.

He saw the shadow of movement. The darkness had been absolute for so long he thought his mind must be playing tricks on him. There. A smudge of grey against the black; the hint of a silhouette. Sparrow loped ahead of them, towards the light at the end of the tunnel. She chased her tail in the gloomy beam, barking madly, startling a colony of bats. Durant pushed past, clawing through briar and bracken, scattering leaves and sticks, forcing his way towards green grass and blue sky.

Longstaff staggered into sunlight, dropped Durant's sodden bag and looked round. An hour past dawn on a cloudless day. They'd emerged on the side of a steep hill. Safe, for the moment. They'd survived death by burning and drowning, escaped God's warriors and the tunnels below. No one was following – Schoff and the rest of Spina's men must believe them dead. A valley lay below, a river running towards the sea.

Aurélie sank to her knees, stared at the bag, breathing hard as she pulled at the straps and raked through the ruined contents. Sodden clumps of parchment fell away from wooden rollers, ink leached from the pages of forbidden Gospels. Longstaff lifted one of the scrolls. It fell to pieces in his hands.

"Something must have survived."

Tears rolled down Aurélie's cheeks. "All gone," she bit her lip. "Giacomo died for nothing."

Her look warned Longstaff to stay away. He continued searching through the bag. A scrap came away in his hand. He laid it on a flat stone, hoping the sun's warmth might reverse the passage of time. A gust of wind flipped it into the air.

Durant shivered and turned away. Longstaff stared at his narrow back, sharp shoulder blades visible through the shirt. This wasn't the time to ask what Vescosi's final word had meant: *Calais*. Aurélie seemed to have forgotten it entirely.

"Giacomo died to save our lives."

Aurélie began to cry as she remembered the man who'd shown her how to think. She accused herself of failing him. What if she hadn't let Schoff capture her? What if she hadn't smashed the panel bearing Mars' crossed spears? Longstaff did not follow her lead. He knew there were accusations he could level at himself – Spina had been right; there'd been too many coincidences, too many occasions when luck had favoured them – but that could wait for another time.

Gently, he gathered Aurélie in his arms. They were lucky to be alive. She seemed so small against his chest. Her protector was dead, home destroyed and her dream reduced to ashes in the caves below. He stroked her hair, and slowly gave way to exhaustion.

CHAPTER 38

They slept, protected from the sun's rays by overhanging leaves. It was mid-afternoon when Longstaff stirred, woken by the sound of crying. He lay on his back, listening as a note of anger wove itself into Aurélie's sobs, grew louder, burst in a brief thunderclap of rage.

He rolled onto one elbow. She sat with her head in her hands. Durant was nearby, watching with a helpless expression on his face. *What do we do now?*

Longstaff pressed Aurélie's hand, remembering a man chained to the ground, others leashed together like dogs, women bound to stakes. Spina had travelled south with fourteen men. He and three others were dead in the Devil's Library, which left ten. Too many under normal circumstances, but Mathern Schoff thought they were dead.

"We came to find a library," he said. "To put an end to Spina and his men. It's time to finish what we started."

He looked at Durant. The Frenchman nodded.

They climbed out of the valley, took a bearing at the summit and tracked back to the clearing where they'd left the horses. Longstaff's big grey with the cast in one eye, Durant's high-stepping animal, Aurélie's palfrey and Vescosi's sway-backed chestnut. They were thirsty, angry at having been left so long, but still there; Schoff hadn't found them, probably hadn't thought to look.

Longstaff signalled quiet, creeping through the trees. This time, no twisting coil of smoke appeared to lead him to the cave; Spina's Hounds had stopped the narrow mouth with rocks.

There was no sign of Aurélie when Longstaff returned to the clearing. Durant was looking at the heap of medical equipment. He glanced at Longstaff's thigh, told him to sit and lower his trousers. He cleaned the wound with iodine and sewed the edges together.

"How many this time?"

"Ten."

Longstaff nodded, shrugging out of the jerkin; there was no sign of Sir Nicholas Bacon's letter, stripped away in the tunnels below. He took the needle and thread, repairing the tear in his trousers while Durant removed the scrolls from his pack. They were ruined – dried in lumps the size of Longstaff's fist, flaking like an old man's scalp.

Aurélie appeared, wearing fresh hose and tunic. Her face was pale, cheeks red from scrubbing at the tears, eyes hard and flat when she saw Durant.

"No," she snapped. "We're not leaving them."

The Frenchman didn't argue. He'd cast his doublet aside before reaching the Devil's Library. He shrugged into the plague coat, bright strips of colour strange in the gloomy clearing. Longstaff made space in his saddle-bag for a dozen herbs bound with ribbon, powders in thin leather bags, pastes in tiny glass jars. Durant found room for his bone-saw and phlebotomy cups in Vescosi's pack.

They led the horses to a stream, knelt beside them and drank their fill of the brackish water. The trees were thinner here, undergrowth sparse as it gave way to the bleak plateau. Longstaff produced soldier's rations; a cheerless supper staring up at the conical hill, waiting for night to fall. Durant reversed his coat of seven colours. Aurélie stripped and oiled her musket, while her teacher ran a whetstone down the *katzbalger's* sharp edge.

They rode in moonlight, leaving the horses at the base of the hill, climbing in single file, creeping through Jupiter's deserted temple. Longstaff saw a length of chain among the rubble, wrapped it round his shoulders before starting down the stairs.

The sentry was stationed halfway between temple and village. Longstaff crawled near, dropped the chain around his neck, put a knee in the small of his back and crushed the windpipe.

"Nine," he whispered in the darkness.

He led them away from the steps, across the face of the hill, angling down to a point above the small fishing village. He'd been this way before; less than three days ago, though it felt like weeks. Durant and Aurélie followed him to the same shallow ledge. Carefully, the three of them peered down.

Six men in monk's robes, working by the light of a bonfire. Two standing beside a table, picking over bits of worked silver, golden rings, copper broaches, melting them down in small crucibles. The remaining four piled driftwood and sticks of furniture against the church's wooden sides.

"What are they doing?" whispered Aurélie.

Longstaff and Durant exchanged a look. "Getting ready to dispose of the evidence. They won't want word of this reaching Rome."

Longstaff heard the low intake of breath as she caught his meaning.

"But… "

Durant put a hand on her shoulder.

"That's why we're here."

"The men are locked inside," Longstaff pointed at a shadowy figure, chained to the hard earth. "Most of them, anyway. And the women and children are in the caves." He gave Aurélie his matchlock musket and tinderbox. "First yours, then mine, then yours again. Fast as you can, Aurélie."

He rose with the first light of dawn, spinning the chain around his head.

"Be careful," Aurélie placed the musket-stock against her cheek, closing one eye.

They scrambled down the cliff of twisted stone. One of Spina's men turned to stare, wood falling from his hands, mouth open in slack-jawed disbelief. Longstaff released the chain, humming through the still air, wrapping round the monk's neck.

Two men ran at Durant. He heard the crack of musket fire, saw one of them drop. The second crouched, looking round in terror. Longstaff kicked him in the head. The remaining pair were running for the caves. Aurélie fired again, winging one; he tripped on the hem of his robe and fell heavily.

As Longstaff disappeared into the dark tunnel, Durant looked at the men lying in the village square. There were times he despaired of life, rarely more than now as he cut their throats.

Seizing a torch, Longstaff ran through sluggish air, black smoke eddying against the low ceiling. Someone tried to block his way. The face was familiar; two days ago Longstaff had spared this man's life in the ruined Temple of Jupiter. He parried a feeble stroke and cut him down without mercy.

"Three."

He pressed on, entering a womb-like cavern. Two dozen women and children cowering against the far wall. Schoff stood in front of them, flanked by two men in monk's robes. He was smiling, gesturing at a water-barrel, inviting the women to drink.

Longstaff thought of the wood piled against the church. He shook his head as the full horror of Schoff's plan dawned on him. Fire for the men, poison for the women – the loyal lieutenant, determined to remove all traces of the master's failure.

"Bastard," he spat.

Schoff spun, eyes widening. "I watched the Library burn. You're dead."

"Sorry to disappoint."

Face contorting in rage, Schoff screamed at his two men: "Kill him!"

Longstaff charged, not giving them time to separate. He threw his torch at the nearest, who flinched, sword-arm rising to protect his face. Longstaff rolled and took him in the belly.

"Two," he stepped back, loosening his shoulders, waiting for Schoff's last man.

The monk attacked bravely, swinging his sword in a whistling arc. Longstaff let him come, body and blade in perfect harmony, slipping inside a wild slash and burying the *katzbalger* in soft flesh. He stood back, watching as the man's chin dropped to his chest, hands lifted to the stomach. The knees gave way and he collapsed slowly to the ground.

"One," said Longstaff.

Schoff stood beside the barrel. "I am a man of God."

Longstaff sheathed his sword. "I'm not going to touch you," he gestured. "Drink."

A woman, with a scar down one cheek, stepped away from the crowd. Her face was calm as she claimed the dead monk's sword, then turned on Schoff.

"No," said Longstaff. "Let him die by his own hand."

She ran fingertips along the sharp edge before placing the point against Schoff's chalk-white throat. "Choose," she whispered.

"I am Elect, predestined for heaven. Spill one drop of my blood and you'll spend eternity in Hell," he kicked the barrel over. The woman set her feet, hands cupping the hilt, jaw clenched as she pushed the weapon home.

*

Durant knelt beside the wooden church, sword discarded for a scalpel, probing the lock.

He nearly had it when a tide of women flooded round, desperate for their menfolk, rushing at the building. The men roared in reply, demanding freedom, hammering at the stout walls with their fists.

Durant forced himself to take a deep breath, closed his ears to the shouts and rotated his wrist with painstaking care. The lock sprang open.

Men came streaming out, taking wives and sisters in their arms, lifting wide-eyed children on their shoulders.

Durant stepped away, ignored, mind's eye conjuring images of these people as they might have been; charred flesh, lungs black with smoke. Two unsmiling men were staring at him and he closed his coat, hiding the bright strips of colour.

Longstaff appeared from the caves. Aurélie ran to join him.

"Are you hurt?"

Durant snorted. The Englishman was filthy – blood leaking from his thigh where the stitches had come apart

— but the blue eyes were as steady as ever. Durant felt a sudden, irrational surge of rage. Guilty conscience, he told himself, lifting fingertips to his chest.

A woman knelt beside the man in chains, holding a cup of water to his chapped lips and supporting his head. Durant approached, working the padlock, heard the satisfying click and fall of tumblers. The woman turned when he smiled at her, hiding the scar on her cheek, and pulled the long chains through eyelets on the man's iron collar.

*

Longstaff stood beside Aurélie at the edge of the square, watching a middle-aged man place hands either side of his wife's face and stare into her eyes, smiling at what he found. Others were less fortunate, seeing humiliation in the eyes of wives, parents and children. They turned away in shame, eyes falling on the bodies of the dead monks.

Durant drew near. "We should leave."

The woman with the scarred cheek straightened, mouth twisting as she caught the scent. She gestured with hands still smeared in Schoff's blood.

"Take the children to the beach."

Mothers caught her meaning first, herding their families towards the water. Then fathers, laughing with the children, trying to make a game of it, until only a handful of men remained. They worked in silence, stripping the dead, stamping on the heads and genitals, gutting them with fish knives. Aurélie buried her head in Longstaff's chest.

It wasn't blind fury; the men chose their victims, remembering instances of cruelty from the days of captivity. Longstaff shuddered, imagining such an end must mark the life that came before, a shadow to make mother's shiver, playmates run away and hide.

The woman approached, standing so she blocked their view.

"We're sorry for your suffering," said Durant.

"There are six missing."

"All dead," said Longstaff. "No one is going to come looking for them."

She stared at him. "We owe you nothing."

Aurélie attempted to explain, about Gregorio Spina and the Devil's Library. She lapsed into silence beneath the woman's contemptuous stare.

"We're leaving," said Durant. "There is no debt."

CHAPTER 39

Night was falling when they reached their campsite of four days earlier, turning tired horses at the brow of the hill and looking back across the Phlegræn Field, red in the setting sun. Longstaff dismounted, unsaddled Martlesham and led him towards the stream. Sparrow loped into the trees. Aurélie followed, pausing to wash her face and hands in the cold water.

Longstaff took care of the horses, removing the packs and rubbing them down. Durant collected the saddles and threw them in a rough circle beside the stream. He looked through their bags, assembling the last of the food – sour apples and a loaf of hard, black bread.

"We need supplies."

Longstaff nodded. Should they take the narrow shepherd's path in the morning, or turn south for Naples?

Aurélie returned with an armload of wood. They built a fire, leaning on the saddles, sharing the dry bread.

"They do wonderful things with roe venison in Grenoble," said Durant. He looked exhausted. "In Bordeaux, there's a place cooks bream in butter sauce with nuts and seeds."

Sparrow appeared, dropping a rabbit at Longstaff's feet.

There wasn't much flesh on the animal but it gave them something to do, skinning, gutting, spitting, watching it cook on the low flames. Longstaff divided the meat into four meagre portions.

"And?" he asked, looking at Durant.

The Frenchman forced a wan smile. "I've tasted worse, though never in Bordeaux or Grenoble."

Aurélie rose to her feet and dragged Durant's heavy pack to the fire. The scrolls had dried in thick clumps, breaking apart in her fingers like rotting wood. The forbidden Gospels had fared better – a careful abbot might want the parchment for his novices – but the ink had washed away. She went through the bag, piece by piece, before finally raising a hand in defeat. Papers scattered on the breeze.

"I don't know what I was hoping."

She turned to Longstaff, not meeting his eyes. "I have nothing, Matthew. Giacomo was my home, the only person who ever cared about me."

Longstaff raised her chin. "You have courage and intelligence – more than anyone I've met. And you have me."

She touched his face. "But your dream. Returning to England, regaining your family home," she walked away from the fire, digging at the base of a withered oak to recover Vescosi's Otiosi papers from their hiding place. "He always said the Devil's Library was a dream. This was his true work. He told us to take them to England. Sir Nicholas is a man of honour, he'll keep the terms of your agreement."

Durant sighed, shaking his head in the firelight.

"That's not all you have to offer him," he held a thin scroll, dry and perfectly preserved. "*On Freedom and Conscience*, according to the plaque. It's by Epicurus, probably the very copy Lucretius donated all those years ago." He saw the look on Aurélie's face. "Old habits die hard – I hid it in my shirt before Spina arrived. I imagine Sir Nicholas will understand its value."

"You're willing to let us have it?" asked Longstaff.

Durant smiled at him. "Vescosi told me about Saturn as we rode south, the God of Melancholy who devoured his children in a fit of anger. The Book of Aal was Spina's dream. A dream for men who want to be gods," he raised the scroll. "I'm more interested in what it means to be human. You're welcome to it, Matthew, but please, let me read it first."

Longstaff put a hand on his shoulder. "You can read it on the way to London, Gaetan. The forests round Martlesham are full of deer." He smiled. "We'll stock the ponds with bream."

"As long as we travel via Calais."

Aurélie stopped leafing through the papers. "Giacomo's last word. What did he mean?"

The Frenchman didn't reply. He seemed to be struggling for words.

"Your daughter?" whispered Longstaff.

"A woman called Laure Barthes. It might be nothing."

"Vescosi knew where she was, and wouldn't tell you?" Aurélie sounded shocked. "I'm sorry."

Durant shook his head. "He told me with his dying breath. I hardly understand it myself, but I'm grateful he waited so long."

They threw the scrolls on the fire, adding wood to build a great blaze in memory of Giacomo Vescosi. In a low voice, Aurélie described the man who'd raised her, smiling as she remembered the way he used to pace in his scriptorium, weighing arguments in his open palms.

Joints snapped in Durant's back as he sat cross-legged on the ground, and carefully unrolled Epicurus' text. Aurélie crouched at his side, leaning forward to trace the words. *On Freedom and Conscience*. Longstaff glimpsed her delicate wrist, blue veins beneath the skin, saw the familiar wrinkle appear between her blue eyes as she began to read.

What a creature is Man. Incomparable in reason, infinite in faculties. What need has he of angels, who can move and feel as angels do? What need of God, who has it within himself to penetrate the deepest mysteries? How perfect he is, the beauty of the world; how short-lived and fearful, the terror of his fellows. Man is dust, made of the four elements of earth, air, fire and water, and animated by the fifth, the quintessence...

Longstaff watched the ashes rise; last scraps of the Devil's Library, winking into darkness.

If you have enjoyed this book, the author would very much appreciate it if you could leave a review on Amazon or the store from which you bought the book.

Also by
Crux Publishing

The Finish
by Angela Elliott

It is 1769 and these are violent times. London's Covent Garden has long been a centre of hedonistic pleasure. Kitty Ives, an alluring whore, takes a man to her bed and wakes to find him dead. Scared she will end up on the gallows, Kitty decides to uncover the identity of the murderer.

The Finish is the first terrifying and mysterious episode in the Venus Squared series, comprising *The Finish*, *The Surety*, *The Debt*, and *The Trade*.

Bogman
by R.I. Olufsen

When a mummified foot, a pile of bones and a split skull are discovered in a Danish bog, is it a case for the police or archaeologists? It becomes a case for Chief Inspector Tobias Lange when it is confirmed the remains are those of a young male, early twenties, beaten to death with a blunt instrument about two decades earlier.

Tobias finds himself on the trail of eco-warriors, Sami protesters safeguarding reindeer rights in Lapland and a disaffected young woman estranged from her family. Then another incomplete set of human bones turns up, and then another. When the trail takes a turn into a murky world of sex trafficking and illegal immigrants, Tobias starts to fear for his eco-warrior daughter Agnes....

10305729R00193

Printed in Germany
by Amazon Distribution
GmbH, Leipzig